PRAISE FOR Counterfeit Lover

*"Love takes a wild and original ride. **Counterfeit Lover**
gives an exciting new face to romantic thrillers."*

—Mikel J. Wilson, bestselling author
of the Mourning Dove Mysteries

*"**Counterfeit Lover**'s unpredictable twists and turns
will keep you turning the page . . . you'll never be able to
guess what comes next. Farmer has managed to weave
a unique and wholly original love story!"*

—Robert Tate Miller, screenwriter
and bestselling author

*"The Golden Age of Hollywood crashes into
today's hi-tech movie industry. Can true love survive?"*

—Holly Kammier, bestselling
author of Lost Girl

*"'If they're telling the truth, I'll be rich and famous.
If they're lying . . .' And so begins Darrin Clark's immersion
into Hollywood. **Counterfeit Lover** from author J. C. Farmer
is the opening salvo into a world of iconic political
and Hollywood luminaries, past and present,
a new world beyond anything one can imagine."*

—Laura Taylor, 6-Time
ROMANTIC TIMES Award Winner

COUNTERFEIT LOVER

#1 IN THE AMERICAN FAIRYTALE SERIES

J. C. FARMER

FROM THE TINY ACORN . . .
GROWS THE MIGHTY OAK

*"For everyone who gives love,
rather than hoping to find it."*

Contents

A sneak peek at **Book 2** of the **American Fairytale series:**

As Good As It Gets

"You want me to put my head in *that*?"

The strange machine boasted robotic arms, needles and lasers, and it resembled a torture device designed by Dr. Seuss. I stared at the man who thought I'd be crazy enough to stick my head in it.

"It'll make you rich and famous," Dutch Hollander said. "Don't be a wimp. You've been a chicken your entire life."

The insult hurt, especially coming from one of the most powerful people in Hollywood. Sure, I was a failure in many ways, but he'd picked the quality I hated most about myself. *Cowardice.*

Dutch and I were alone in a plain-looking white trailer at a studio in Burbank. The trailer was empty except for the bizarre contraption. I pretended to examine its hydraulic arms, wishing I could ask Janie for advice. She had an audition today, and I wondered how it was going.

"This is the chance of a lifetime, Darrin," the studio chief prodded. "Just stick your damn head in the machine."

I wanted to leave. For two years, I'd been desperate for anyone in Hollywood to notice me. *Anyone.* Now I had the full attention of the president of Digital Impact, which recently became the world's biggest movie studio.

This was my second audition. The previous week, I'd read a few lines from various scripts in Dutch's lavish office. I'd been so intimidated, I could barely function. Today, Dutch had escorted me to a sound stage filled with rows of identical white eight-wheeled trailers. We stood inside one of the trailers, discussing the strange machine it contained.

Prescott "Dutch" Hollander looked exactly as he did on TV. He was about fifty, portly, with a bulbous nose and a resemblance to W.C. Fields. A billionaire thanks to a streak of blockbuster movies starting in 2020, he wore an elegant pin-striped suit with suspenders and gripped a cigar in his right hand.

I was the complete opposite: twenty-one, thin, cheaply dressed and penniless.

"When we researched you for this part, I was shocked that any man could be so gutless," Dutch said, goading me. "Your life reveals a relentless pursuit of cowardliness."

"Perhaps I have dreams besides being famous."

"Shit," he snickered. "We know you don't give a crap about being a movie star. You don't care about acting. All you want to do is impress that girl, what's-her-name..." Dutch flipped open the neatly-organized file he held. "Janie Norman. You moved to LA to be near her and became an actor to impress her. Yet, you haven't gotten a single part, and you're too scared to try to ask her out. She must be *really* impressed."

Fuck you. "You don't know anything about me." He knew *everything* about me. I longed to look inside the red file the studio had gathered on me, which was even thicker now than at my first audition.

The trailer door swung open and another man entered. With his blond ponytail, shabby sideburns, and peace symbol tattoo, he looked like a forty-year-old hippie. I wondered if he'd owned his faded Van Halen t-shirt for years, or if he'd bought it at a high-end store on Melrose.

"This is Teddy Millner, our Director of Technology," Dutch said, patting Teddy on the back.

First names only, I reminded myself. "Nice to meet you, Teddy." I shook his hand.

"So, I finally get to meet Darrin Clark. Dutch says you're perfect for this part, and that you've signed all our non-disclosure agreements. I'm really looking forward to working with you."

It seemed impossible that this hippie programmer, beloved by nerds and engineers, was the focus of the entertainment industry's wrath. Teddy had taken the core power of Hollywood away from movie stars and put it into the hands of geeks. Movie executives and A-list actors remained rattled by this realignment of importance.

Teddy's animation technology was so advanced, even experts admitted they couldn't distinguish human actors from computer simulations. "Live action" blockbusters could be filmed without actors. Digital Impact continuously produced billion-dollar blockbusters without the need to hire a single actor. Every other studio was in peril of bankruptcy, unable to keep up with the technological advances, and even the most famous stars feared for their careers.

Why, I wondered, would Dutch and Teddy spend time with a nobody like me? Seven years ago, after climbing the ranks of Disney and Warner Bros., Dutch shocked the world by teaming with Teddy and founding a new movie studio. Dutch had risked everything, but now he was the undisputed king of Hollywood. If he really wanted an actor, he could snap his fingers and movie stars would line up.

Get the fuck out of here. My brain continued to scream warning alarms. I felt like a lab mouse about to be fed to their mechanical beast.

"Darrin is frightened by this machine, and life in general," Dutch said. "His existence centers around a girl named Janie Norman, whom he's loved since they were kids in North Dakota. He got into theater—high school plays and community stuff—just to be near her. He's a chicken-shit loser and never even asked her out."

"She's older. I couldn't date her in school." *I'm pathetic. I sound wimpy, even to myself.*

"He pretends he wants to be an actor to spend time with a girl he's scared of."

"Very chivalrous," Teddy said.

"Loverboy works at Chevron, operating the cash register, and Janie works at Starbucks. For two years, they've auditioned for parts without a crumb of success. And Darrin still hasn't made any attempt to date her."

"How do you know all this?" I demanded.

Dutch grinned. "We know everything."

I longed to punch his snarky face. "Once I have a good job, I'll ask her out." *I sounded so lame, I hated myself.*

"Do it today. I'm offering to make you a movie star in a block-buster film. You have a million-dollar contract. Be a man and stick your head in the machine. You can have Janie, or a supermodel if you prefer."

"Don't bully him, Dutch." Teddy put his hand on my shoulder. "It's wise to be cautious, Darrin. However, this machine has been used many times. It's completely safe."

"If it's safe, why do you need me? Tons of famous actors will take any job Digital Impact offers."

"I trust my gut. You're perfect for the part," Dutch said. "I love your background. Tell Teddy how you learned to do voice impressions."

I looked down at my feet, self-conscious. *How had the studio found that out?*

"C'mon, Darrin. It's endearing. Just tell Teddy," Dutch prodded.

"In North Dakota, we had a farm. Gosh, I used to plow ten hours a day. I spent the time on our tractor imitating actors from my favorite movies."

"Darrin's very talented," Dutch said. "He just doesn't have the balls to be successful."

"Maybe you didn't explain the machine well enough, Dutch." Teddy turned toward the metal contraption, which reminded me of a glass-bubble salon hair dryer from the 1960s. "The robotic arms control lasers and X-rays that assess your skin texture, facial features and skull structure. This data is fed into the computer, which triggers the injection arms. It's like a robotic artist painting your face with pro-collagen protein."

"Forget the techno-babble. It's basically a lip injection of collagen, but over your entire face," Dutch said.

"Sit down," Teddy encouraged. "We won't force you to do anything. But we're offering everything."

His sanguine voice gave me hope. The money and fame they

promised might give me a shot with Janie. I sat and reclined until the mechanized appendages hovered over my head. Tiny sockets spun miniature needles that seemed eager to attack.

I started to panic. My heart thundered in my chest. Sweat coated my body. I sat upright. "Sorry, I can't do this."

"Breathe deeply," Teddy said. "If you decide to proceed, you'll be given anesthesia."

Dutch puffed his cigar.

"Try to relax," Teddy continued. "The needles are too tiny to hurt even if you were conscious. A computer moves them from cell to cell across the skin. The whole process takes under two hours . . . ."

Teddy droned on while I thought about Janie.

I've been a fool, pretending Janie could love a loser like me . . . but if I was a movie star . . .

I imagined Janie's smile if I had a car to drive her to auditions, instead of accompanying her on the bus. *We could go to nice restaurants. I'd buy her the clothes she deserved. This is my one chance.*

"Give me the anesthesia," I interrupted. "Quick, before I change my mind."

Teddy slid the needle into my arm.

Dutch smiled.

I didn't care if they watched. I pulled out my phone and sent perhaps my final text ever to Janie.

Dutch may be trying to kill me. Seriously.

The drowsiness hit quickly. *If they're telling the truth, I'll be rich and famous—I'll take Janie to the Oscars . . .*

If they're lying . . .

Trading Places

———◦———

Larry Coates jumped back as his Auto-Omelet2000 squirted eggy fluid onto his pajamas. The wiry, spectacled billionaire grabbed a screwdriver, and started to fiddle with the contraption.

Jenny, his bristly-haired brunette wife of 40 years, laughed. "How much did you spend on that piece of crap? $15,000?"

"So, it has some glitches. I'm convinced 3-D food printing is the future," Larry said.

"Cooking isn't supposed to be automated. It's an art," Jenny said, tucking bread slices into the toaster.

Larry used the screwdriver to pry open the lid of the omelet printer. He looked quizzically at dozens of computer chips.

Jenny pulled the screwdriver out of his hand. "Honey, you don't have to buy every gadget invented. And you certainly don't have to fix them."

"But, I could make it work . . . ."

"Larry, we're full-time philanthropists now." The Coates Foundation donated over $10 billion per year, mainly to alleviate poverty and eradicate diseases.

Larry wrapped his arms around her waist. "You're right." He kissed her. "I have an idea I want to discuss with my brilliant and beautiful wife."

"What's that?" Her eyes brightened, mirroring his excitement.

"What if there was a charity equivalent to Bitcoin?"

Jenny's eyebrows shot up. "Hmm . . . it would be efficient, trackable and convenient. That's genius, honey. It would benefit retailers while ensuring charity—"

Jenny suddenly screamed, looking past him. Her coffee mug shattered on the elegant kitchen floor.

Larry turned, only to be paralyzed with shock. Three people had entered the room. One looked *exactly* like him.

He fought to breathe. The man was a perfect clone.

The second person looked identical to his wife. If they stood side-by-side, Larry wouldn't know which one he'd married.

The third person was a middle-aged man. Average appearance and no distinguishing features. His face looked so generic, Larry couldn't even guess his race.

Something about the extreme plainness of the man's face made him hard to look at. But he was pointing a handgun at Larry, so he had the billionaire's full attention.

"Hello. I'm Joe Plain," the man said. "That was terror number one."

"We've been cloned," gasped Larry.

"No, they're not clones," Joe Plain said. "Sit down, and I'll explain."

The replicas reached into Larry's and Jenny's pockets and took their phones.

"How did you get in?" Larry demanded. "This house has the world's most advanced security."

"I'm Larry Coates," the identical Larry scoffed. "Why would my own security stop me?"

"I'll explain everything," Joe said. "But first I need you to drink something." He handed Larry a small vial of liquid.

"What's this?" Larry asked, his fists clenching.

Joe Plain aimed his gun at Larry's real wife. "It will relax you, not kill you. However, I'll kill your wife if you don't drink it in ten seconds. I don't want to, but I will."

Larry stared at the milky white liquid. Every instinct told him not to drink it. Yet the man's merciless eyes revealed a dark soul who wouldn't bluff. Larry gulped down the bitter liquid.

He waited for a reaction but felt fine.

Joe Plain gave an identical vial of liquid to his wife and aimed his gun at Larry. "Your turn."

She drank.

Soon, Larry felt lightheaded. He panicked as each breath required more effort.

Joe casually lowered the gun.

"What's happening?" Larry pleaded.

"I lied. That was a lethal dose of poison."

Larry and Jenny glared at each other in panic. Their eyes bulged.

"That's terror number two," Joe noted. "I'm a connoisseur of fear."

Larry wobbled on his feet. "Why kill us?"

Joe smiled. "I haven't killed you. I've just replaced you. Larry and Jenny Coates will live on. You're part of a magnificent plan. Your money and power will help me create the future."

Both Larry and Jenny clutched the counter, struggling not to collapse. "What about our philanthropy? We're saving millions of lives around the world. Our work is critical."

A wide grin filled Joe's generic face. "Your money will be used for something very different. You'll be even more famous than you are already. You are going to cause some of the worst catastrophes in history."

Larry's gut filled with rage. He watched his wife's eyes flare in horror.

"That's terror number three," Joe continued. "There are always three terrors. First, when you realize you're not unique; second, when you learn you're going to die; and finally, when you discover your legacy will be abhorrent evil."

As Joe spoke, Jenny lost her grip on the counter and collapsed to the floor. Larry took a step toward her, his knees buckled.

Joe wrote something on a notepad. "I'm studying a science I call 'fearology.' This is important research."

"You're a psychopaaa . . ." Larry succumbed to the drug and slipped into darkness.

Joe Plain checked their pulses. "Dead. Put their bodies in the bags."

He watched the new Coates zip the old Coates into two black body bags.

"I'll send men to dispose of the corpses in ten minutes," Joe said.

Before he left, Joe patted new Larry on the back. "Congratulations. You're now the richest person in the world."

"Thank you. You won't regret this," Larry said. "I'll do everything you instruct."

"Of course, you will. Otherwise, you'll be replaced."

Joe Plain reached into his breast pocket and checked his list, another grin spreading across his vapid face as he read the next name.

Almost Famous

I awoke slowly, feeling disoriented and drowsy. I kept my eyes closed. *Where am I? Didn't Janie and I both have auditions today?*

The skin on my whole face tingled. *The machine.* I remembered where I was. *The trailer.*

Shit. What have they done to me? What did I agree to have done to myself?

The overhead lights were too bright as I cautiously opened my eyes. I was reclined on the leather chair, exactly as I'd fallen asleep. The manifold apertures of the machine were still over my head but raised several feet above me. A clock showed over two hours had passed.

A large mirror covered one entire wall of the trailer. I stood and searched for my reflection—

Impossible.

My heart pounded like gong.

A ghost.

I collapsed backwards onto the chair. The anesthesia must have serious side effects. I was hallucinating . . . I'd seen the ghost of James Dean.

Searching the room, I checked to be certain no one else was here. Breathing slowly in and out, I calmed myself and stood again to look in the mirror.

James Dean's ghost stared back at me. His mouth opened wide as I shrieked. His arms raised as I lifted mine in terror.

I touched my ear. James Dean did the same and jolted back in shock.

I took a deep breath, examining his nose, cheeks and eyebrows, which were now my features. My face appeared totally new. My skin texture had smoothed; a birthmark was missing; a scar under my eye was gone; my plump cheeks, freckled nose, and thin unsymmetrical lips now looked graceful and refined. I wasn't inspecting a mask or makeup of an impersonator. I had *James Dean's face.* He had been one of the actors whose voices I'd imitated during my first audition with Dutch.

I felt nauseous. I wasn't here. I wasn't in the room. James Dean was here—*I'm not.*

"Bring me back." I screamed, scanning the empty room for help. "I want my face back!"

The trailer door burst open. Two people rushed in. First Teddy Millner entered, followed closely by a long-haired brunette, the studio executive who'd been present at my first audition.

Jacqueline Dumont's svelte figure showcased her matching crimson Armani pants and blazer. Even in my state of panic, I couldn't help noticing how sexy she was for someone twice my age.

"You're hyperventilating. Try to calm down." Jacqueline helped me back to the chair. "Drink some water," she said, offering me a glass.

"I don't want water. I want *my face back.*"

"It's a reversible process," Teddy assured. "You'll be yourself again soon. In a few short hours, you'll be home, looking like your normal self."

I can change back. Thank God! I must have been daydreaming about Janie when Dutch had mentioned that fact.

I forced my breathing to be rhythmic, slow and deep. If the studio hid this, what else were they hiding? They were using me and desperate actors like me for their unparalleled success.

"Digital Impact doesn't have advanced animation. It's lying to the world. The studio uses a machine that changes faces."

"Yes, that's the big secret," Teddy said. "We film everything with live people."

In the mirror, a fascinated James Dean listened.

So, *this* was how they had made blockbuster movies about people like Elvis, Eleanor Roosevelt and Martin Luther King, Jr.

"Other studios are chasing us in the wrong direction, trying to copy our fake digital animation," Teddy added.

"Which is why we protect our secret so carefully," Jacqueline said. "That's why you had to sign so many non-disclosure agreements. Dutch warned you that there was no turning back once you agreed. Now you know why."

I looked at the machine with awe. "It's amazing."

"It's basically a three-dimensional Xerox machine for faces," Teddy said. "It's like high-tech facial collagen, controlled by microprocessors."

James Dean nodded approval in the mirror. I was so incredibly handsome.

"Besides the organic tissue injected in each cell, the needles also add a proteolytic enzyme that functions as an anti-inflammatory," Teddy continued.

"Our expert hair stylist fashioned your hair while you were asleep," Jacqueline said. "That's why the process took so long today."

In the mirror, James Dean stroked his fingers through his . . . my . . . hair.

"I can't be seen in public like this."

"After filming today, we'll change you back, and you'll go home as yourself," Teddy said. "Advances in anesthesia have made it completely safe."

"We're filming *today*?"

"Yes. The movie's been in production for a while."

"You can't mention your part or the transform-machines to anyone. Ever. Even your closest friends," Jacqueline cautioned. "You can only tell people that you've been cast in a yet undisclosed movie."

How could I impress Janie if my role was secret and I looked like someone else?

"Dutch promised I'd be a famous movie star."

Teddy pointed at the mirror. "You are."

Hmmm. "Will I even be in the credits?"

"Not as an actor," Teddy said. "But you'll receive a million dollars. That should help you win your girl."

I examined my new face, tracing my strikingly handsome features with a fingertip. My old face was round and boyish. Now I was attractive enough to make women swoon. I felt virile and daring. If Janie could see me now, she'd fall in love with me.

"What movie are we making?" I asked, imitating James Dean's voice.

"Come and see."

Jacqueline and Teddy escorted me across the immense sound stage past numerous trailers identical to the one we'd exited. As we walked, I strutted, trying different postures and gaits, each one feeling more confident than the one before. No one could tell it was me. Talk about liberating.

I'll be the boldest, baddest James Dean ever.

One wall of the sound studio was lined with trailers parked side-by-side. We arrived at a trailer with his name—*my* name—on the door.

Teddy punched in a security a code and the door unbolted.

"This door will lock and unlock according to your filming schedule," Teddy said.

We entered the spacious trailer, which looked like an apartment. There was a living room, bedroom, bathroom, and kitchen with fifties décor but modern appliances.

"Look in the closet. We'll wait for you," Jacqueline said.

I stepped into a huge walk-in closet neatly organized into about sixty outfits. A note was attached to the mirror: "James, please wear outfit #27 today."

My hand skimmed over fastidiously maintained fabric. What would Janie think of this . . . she loved vintage clothing. We could barely afford second-hand thrift store sales.

Each ensemble included a photograph. I located outfit #27 and studied the accompanying photo labeled: "*March 7, 1955, Dinner in Beverly Hills with Natalie Wood.*" The garments in the photo were identical to the ones on the hangers: khaki slacks, a loose hanging white t-shirt under a collared tan shirt, an unbuttoned black trench coat, and black shoes.

I put on the ensemble on, noticing the worn knees and soft texture. They'd clearly been worn before. Could they possibly be the actual clothes from the photo?

For a minute, I stared at the mirror, practicing poses and facial expressions. It felt supernatural, as if my soul had been placed in another body.

If only Janie could see me.

My mind drifted back to North Dakota and Grafton Elementary School, to the first time we spoke. I was in second grade. Long dark hair, big blue eyes prettier than mountain lakes. I didn't know her name yet, just that she was older than me and that it was like floating on a cloud whenever I saw her. Often, Janie looked sad—I found out later she'd lost both her parents. When she would occasionally smile, the whole world became warm and sunny, even in the middle of winter.

She terrified me, she was so lovely. On the day we met, I was heading to the gym with my basketball, and I realized our paths were going to intersect at the door. I looked in panic for an escape route. I wished I was invisible.

"Hi." She did a little curtsy.

"Hi."

Her eyes danced with joy. "Today, I'm leaving Grafton."

My heart sank. "You're moving?"

She giggled. "Not really. Rehearsal starts today for the school play. When you act, you get to wear fancy costumes and travel all over the world and you don't need a dime."

She turned and skipped toward the auditorium.

My friend Brian snatched my basketball away. "Too slow, Darrin." He tried to spin the ball on his index finger.

Janie glanced back at me and waved.

"Keep it," I told Brian, heading toward the auditorium. "I'm joining the play."

A loud knock pulled me out of my memory. James Dean smirked at me in the mirror.

"Hurry up. You're needed soon," Teddy shouted through the closet door.

"Wow, you're perfect," Jacqueline exclaimed when I emerged in my new threads.

She and Teddy showed me a stack of binders on a desk.

"Your filming schedule is in the master binder, along with your character study schedule," Jacqueline explained.

"There's a binder about every aspect of James' life, and videos to watch," Teddy said. "You're going to be thoroughly tested, so memorize everything according to the schedule."

"All of this is about James Dean?"

"Don't worry about that now. It's time to start your new life," Jacqueline said.

They led me to a door at the opposite end of the trailer from where we'd entered. Teddy put his hand on the doorknob. "I wish we could come with you, James, but we're forbidden."

"But you're executives."

"You'll see. It's very strict," Jacqueline said. "I'd do anything to be able to walk out with you."

"It's going to blow your mind," Teddy said.

Jacqueline fixed my collar. "Forget anything you've ever seen before."

My heart beat wildly with curiosity and fear. "Do I look okay?"

"Not that voice!" Teddy cried.

Shit. I'd used Darrin's voice. "Do I look okay?" I repeated in James Dean's voice.

"You're glorious." Jacqueline kissed me on the cheek and pushed me through the door.

A Blast from the Past

I was in the 1950s.

If I looked carefully, I could faintly discern the sky-colored walls of a humongous sound stage, but they were blended expertly into the landscape. Vintage shops surrounded a Main Street: a malt shop, beauty salon, gas station, classic diner and white gazebo in a well-manicured park. On the wide, clean streets, the chrome of classic 50's cars—a Ford Fairlane, Chevy Impala, Thunderbird, and others I couldn't identify—glistened in nostalgic splendor.

Oh, my God. I kept walking.

On a park bench, Elvis Presley sat talking with Albert Einstein. Nearby, President Eisenhower entertained a young Katharine Hepburn. Leaning against a barbershop pole, Jimmy Stewart flirted with Natalie Wood. Elizabeth Taylor, Shirley Temple and Audrey Hepburn giggled together at a soda fountain. Next to the park gazebo, Joe DiMaggio and Jackie Robinson played catch. Walt Disney, Roy Rogers, Louis Armstrong and Buddy Holly were playing cards at an outdoor café. Dozens of other American legends were present, each appearing absolutely authentic and natural.

The sensory overload was overwhelming. I was dazed with emotions until . . .

A vision appeared, and she made every other crazy thing I'd seen today pale in comparison. Smiling ethereally, as if she defined beauty with each gesture, Marilyn Monroe got out of a cherry-red Nash Rambler convertible. She laughed breezily at something Humphrey Bogart said. My chest tightened and suddenly, the only thing that mattered was being near her.

This was a feeling that normally occurred around Janie, and no one else. Yet, I simply couldn't pull my gaze away from Marilyn.

Guilt stabbed me.

Janie and I had never even kissed, yet in my heart, I knew we were soul mates. My destiny. I was fiercely loyal to her. Until this moment, I'd been certain I couldn't love anyone else.

"Great news, everyone. James Dean has joined us," a loud voice proclaimed. Orson Welles stood with sanguine authority on atop a ladder near the diner, his voice electronically magnified.

Everyone turned toward me. They clapped. It was a whimsical feeling—Elvis, Einstein, Eisenhower, and so many other legends applauding *me*.

Marilyn smiled, and I felt myself blush.

"We film in ten minutes. Scene 16. Inside the diner."

Orson climbed down the ladder and hastened toward me, hugging me enthusiastically. He was a big man, tall and hefty and emanating zestful energy. "You look great, James. The epitome of youthful defiance."

"Thank you. I'm still getting used to looking like him."

"No. No. You don't *look* like James Dean," Orson admonished. "You *are* James Dean."

I thought Orson intended to slap me. Instead, he grabbed my arm and led me away from the other actors. "You don't look like anyone but yourself, James. Didn't you listen when they explained that? You're James Dean. You have no other identity. While you're in character, there's no hint of any other identity."

"I'm sorry."

"We have a very friendly set," Orson said. "Everything is casual, except our Golden Rule: 'If you have the face, you're the person.' This is strictly enforced."

Orson turned and walked toward the diner.

Fine. If the studio wants James Dean, I'll give them the James-Fuckingest-Dean ever. I'll be the coolest, cockiest, damn-I'm-top-shit, most-confident bastard he's ever seen.

Grace Kelly, Natalie Wood, and Audrey Hepburn had moved to a bench by the gazebo and were chatting gaily. I was dreadfully shy with girls. Darrin would turn the other way. But I wasn't Darrin. Not today.

I strutted straight toward the women, feeling invincible. Swagger oozed out of me. They couldn't see my real face. They didn't know who I was. Why should I be afraid?

"You ladies look lovely today. I thought I'd better come over to keep other men from bothering you."

The three women laughed, and I felt emboldened.

"You look as dapper as ever," Natalie said, acting like we were old friends. Her eyes twinkled, and she looked adorable. "Have you met Grace and Audrey?"

Grace gave me a hug. The former—or was it future?—Princess of Monaco was wearing a long blue evening dress, her lustrous hair in a classic bun.

"James and I know each other," Grace said. "The last time we talked was at a fundraiser with Rock Hudson."

"We haven't met yet, James," Audrey said, offering her hand. "I'm a huge fan. I love *Rebel Without a Cause*. I'm jealous Natalie got to costar with you."

Whoa. These women were experts at their characters. I really needed to study the binders and videos.

I lifted Audrey's hand and kissed the back of it. "Well, now we're costars." I indicated around us. "We're lucky to be famous in the 1950s."

"Oh, there are other sets, James—your career was just too short," Grace said. "Orson won't let you see any set besides that of the fifties."

"Our movie covers the forties to the present," Audrey added.

Natalie nodded. "The sets of the sixties and seventies are amazing. I wish you could see them."

"Dying young sucks," I said. I wondered why actors were prohibited to even see other sets.

Someone tapped me on the shoulder. "We're waiting for you, kid." It was Humphrey Bogart, in a trench coat and fedora hat, smoking a cigarette. "Follow me."

"Until later, ladies." I winked and followed Bogie toward the diner.

Bogie was gruff and standoffish, so I didn't attempt small talk. He had been selected as cinema's "greatest male star" by the American Film Institute, and perhaps this had made his head swell.

When we walked past Marlon Brando and Ronald Reagan, I gave them the peace sign. Well, in the '50s, I guess the "V" would stand for victory. Either way, I had no inhibitions. However, I was jealous they could film in different decades. Everyone seemed healthy and in their prime, and I wondered how well the machines changed ages, and if they could modify skin on places besides the face.

Inside the diner, Orson directed us to our positions. Elvis and Bogie sat on barstools at the counter while I had a booth to myself. Marilyn Monroe was the barmaid. The diner's walls were amber with jade green drapes, and vinyl records were displayed in glass frames.

The film crew astonished me. Alfred Hitchcock was behind the camera; Cecil B. DeMille was the gaffer; John Huston operated the boom. Why would they modify the *crew's* faces? The studio was taking authenticity to the limit. It seemed excessive, but with an unlimited budget, I supposed you could do anything.

"You only have a couple of sentences today, James. They're all on this page." Orson handed me a piece of paper. "Don't worry, you talk plenty in other scenes."

"What's the name of our movie?"

"*American Fairytale*," Orson said. "It will be the biggest blockbuster in history. From now on, your lines will be brought to your trailer days ahead so you can memorize them."

For twenty minutes, I did nothing but nurse my drink in the background as they filmed. Elvis and Bogie chatted with a flirtatious Marilyn, while I projected a mien of anguish and rebelliousness. My heart fluttered being so close to such loveliness; Marilyn possessed an impossible combination of sensuality and innocence. I could barely wait for my turn to speak with her.

I only had ten words, so I had to be extra suave. Marilyn sauntered across the room to my booth. Her movements were captivating, yet surprisingly familiar.

"Hey, handsome, are you here to rescue me?" Marilyn asked.

I looked into Marilyn's eyes and instantly knew her identity. They'd changed her. Her skin and face and hair were completely transformed. But I knew.

I stuttered, couldn't get out my line.

"CUT!" Orson yelled.

Marilyn, Elvis, Bogart, and Orson glared at me, perplexed by my failure to form words.

"Don't worry. You're just nervous," Marilyn said. But I'd know those eyes anywhere.

Janie.

Orson said, "Let's try again."

"Relax, James," Marilyn/Janie giggled. She returned behind the bar to begin the scene again.

Did she recognize me?

We shot the scene again, and I executed my lines perfectly. Orson complimented me, and we proceeded to the next scene.

My mind was spinning. Janie gave no indication she knew I was Darrin. *How can she not recognize me? Am I that good an actor? Or is* she?

The guilt I felt dissolved. I wasn't betraying my soul mate. I could be in love with two women without any shame—they were both Janie, after all.

I had spent my life dreaming about becoming the man Janie could love. Maybe, now I had.

It reminded me of the playacting Janie and I used to do in my barn. When we were kids, she would come over almost every day, and we'd pretend we were stars on Broadway and the farm animals were the audience. Janie would radiate with joy for hours, and I'd behold a side of her the rest of the world never saw. Once again, I felt I was the only person who really knew her.

During a break, I approached Bogie. "In the movie, what's my relationship with Marilyn?"

"You're madly in love with her," Bogie said. "Marilyn is just your friend, but you're obsessed with her."

I paused, contemplating this. "Do I have competition?"

"Oh, yes. Lots of competition. However, one man is far superior to the rest."

"Who's that?" I asked.

Bogie smiled. "Me."

The arrogant prick. Bogie spoke of Janie casually, as if he was worthy of her.

Bogie patted my shoulder. "A little rivalry is always fun."

What a dickhead. I hoped our script included a scene in which I'd get to punch him.

We continued filming, and I experienced a novel sensation. For the first time in my life, I desired to be the focus of attention. I liked myself. I wanted everyone to see how handsome and talented I was.

It was astonishingly easy. I watched myself in mirrors when I could.

While looking identical to James Dean, everything I did was praiseworthy.

I waited for a signal from Janie. Did she know I was Darrin? It crushed me to think she didn't recognize me. As best friends, we'd shared our secrets since childhood.

"Did I spill something on my outfit, James? You keep staring at me," Janie laughed, during a ten-minute break. She winked and flitted away toward Audrey Hepburn. I loved being James Dean.

Maybe it's better if she doesn't know. I'm finally in a position to romance her.

I was no longer just a friend. As James Dean, I could win her. My heart raced, and I wondered if the script had a kissing scene. As long as we had these faces, I decided to think of us as James Dean and Marilyn Monroe. A new chance, unlimited possibilities.

Everything felt perfect, except Humphrey Bogart was an epic asshole. He played "You Belong to Me" on the jukebox and swept Marilyn into his arms more intimately than the script required. She didn't protest enough as they danced, even as Bogie's hands slid further and further down her hips.

"Great expressions, James," Orson cried at the end of the scene. "Brilliant acting. I could see envy smoldering on your face."

"Thanks," I muttered. I wasn't acting. I was manipulated. *They've given me the face and forced the emotions.*

No wonder they hadn't given me time to prepare—my whole life had been a rehearsal.

After three hours, Orson announced we were done and could return to our trailers.

Bogie slapped me on the back. "Keep up the good work, kid."

I headed toward Marilyn. She must have figured out my real identity by now.

"Fabulous job today, James," a jovial voice said, stopping me.

I turned to see Elvis. The King of Rock and Roll looked vibrant and in his prime, exuding a supernatural charisma as if crowds of fanatical fans adored his every movement. He smiled cheerfully like we were best buddies.

Elvis moved in close and whispered. "It looked like you were about to talk to Marilyn. I want to warn you."

"About what?"

"In case the studio cast someone you know. They're devious like that. Most of us have relationships with people in different parts. It's tempting to reveal our identities to them, but Dutch always finds out—I've seen several actors fired for doing that. The other person gets fired, too."

I sensed Elvis' sincere concern. "I don't want to break any rules."

"These sets are paradise, but don't be mistaken," Elvis whispered. "The studio will replace us without a thought. They've invested millions in us and expect absolute loyalty."

I glanced around, wondering if we were being watched.

"Dutch and the other bigwigs aren't bad," Elvis said. "But nothing escapes their notice."

"Do you think—"

"Here comes Orson. I'll see you tomorrow." Elvis hurried toward his trailer.

"You were fantastic, James," Orson praised. "When you return to your trailer, your back door will be locked. Because we have more actors than transform-machines, everything is scheduled so no one accidentally runs into someone else when they have their other identity."

"Why would it matter?"

"Because each distraction makes this world less real. Just follow the master schedule in your first binder. It outlines times for studying your character, times for memorizing your lines, times for filming, and times for being transformed."

When Orson walked away, I went to my trailer. As he said, the back door was bolted shut. The clock showed 7:12 p.m., while another clock-like device displayed my transformation time to be 7:25 p.m. This gave me 13 minutes.

I entered my closet and changed from outfit #27 to my modern clothes. Then I browsed through the materials on the desk. I counted fifteen binders about James Dean, each labeled with a facet of Dean's life: "Parents' Background," "Ages 0-8," "Friends," "Teachers," "Hobbies," "Romantic Partners," among others, including corresponding videos I logged onto from a private account. The detail was astounding. My master schedule showed exactly what I was supposed to study and do each day. Tomorrow, September 25th, I was expected to arrive at 8:04 a.m. and study binder #1 until filming started at 9:36 a.m.

Janie would have as many outfits as I did, as meticulous a schedule, and as much to study.

At precisely 7:25 p.m., I heard the bolts on my backdoor unfasten. I opened the door, and Teddy escorted me to one of the transformation trailers. I sat in the reclining chair under the machine, and Teddy gave me a needle of anesthetics.

Visions of Janie danced in my head as I slowly drifted unconscious . . . .

I awoke at 9:07 p.m. The mirror revealed my normal, unattractive features. Even my hair was styled the same as usual, although I'd had a haircut.

"You couldn't even let me keep James Dean's hairstyle?"

"Sorry," Teddy said. "You can't show any hints of James Dean."

Ten minutes later, I sat on a bus from Burbank to North Hollywood, where I shared an apartment with Janie and two young musicians. I gazed at the people beyond the bus window, feeling oddly superior.

I share the world's greatest secret.

Luckily, we were only actors. I imagined the technology in the hands of criminals or terrorists or dictators. A single one of the machines would make anyone unstoppable.

The Terminator

"Give me some privacy," Opal Wallace instructed her entourage when they reached the Presidential Suite of the Waldorf Astoria.

"Okay, but you have lunch with the governor at noon. At 3 p.m., you're having tea with the British ambassador, and at five you're interviewing Senator—"

Opal shut the door on her assistants and breathed in the tranquil atmosphere of the Presidential Suite. The key was to keep things in perspective. As long as she was home by 7:30 p.m. to tuck her kids into bed, it would be a successful day.

It was hard work being America's most beloved media personality, with a popular talk show and her own television network. She had to glow with humor and warmth while on TV, yet be a stern businesswoman behind the scenes.

Opal had started life as the daughter of a poor Texan cotton farmer, relying on her tenacity and talent to create a fifteen-billion-dollar media conglomerate. Ofttimes, she missed the simpler life. For now, she needed a warm shower and to prepare her questions for the governor.

"Congratulations. Today, you're being reborn."

Opal jumped. She'd assumed the suite was empty, but two impossible faces stared at her.

She tried to scream, but the sounds refused to form.

"Be quiet, or I'll shoot you."

A man aimed a gun at her, his face more petrifying than his weapon. It was a vacant face. Not ugly. Not attractive. Chilling as there was nothing unique about it. It had every normal feature, but was so generic it appeared inhuman.

The other person looked identical to her. A perfect twin. She was dressed in different clothing, but otherwise a flawless replica of Opal.

"Who are you?" Opal gasped, hyperventilating.

"I'm Joe Plain. This is your replacement, the *new* Opal Wallace."

"How . . . how is this possible?"

Joe Plain held out a glass of a milky liquid. "Drink this. It will calm you. It's harmless, but you need to be calm when I explain."

"Hell, no!"

"Then I will shoot you." Joe pointed at the device attached to the barrel of his pistol. "This is a silencer. No one will hear anything."

Opal glanced between the glass and the gun.

"I'm not a patient man. I'll give you five seconds," Joe said. "Five. Four. Three . . ."

The man was insane. Opal gulped down the liquid.

"Okay. I drank it. What the hell is going on?"

The insane man held a stopwatch and a notepad. "I lied. That's poison. In about fifty-two seconds, you'll be dead. I'm timing it to optimize my system."

"What?" She reached for her phone, but her twin grabbed her wrist. She felt too weak to resist.

"Why didn't you just shoot me?"

Joe Plain examined her and jotted something on his notepad. "My plan for the world requires a deep understanding of fear. These replacements provide valuable learning opportunities on my journey as a fear guru."

"Please. Is there an antidote? Save me, and I'll do anything you say."

Joe wrote again in his notepad. "The new Opal Wallace is more trustworthy. She knows the consequences of disobeying me."

"I have children. Have mercy," Opal pleaded.

Joe noted the degree of desperation on her face and terror in her eyes. "Your kids will be better off the way new Opal will raise them. It will prepare them for the new world I'm creating."

The original Opal struggled to say something, but was too feeble. Her knees wobbled; finally, she lost consciousness.

Joe checked the stopwatch and noted the time. He checked her pulse. "She's dead. I'll send some men up here with a crate to take away the body."

"Yes, sire," new Opal Wallace said.

"Enjoy your media empire." Joe stepped into the Waldorf-Astoria elevator.

New Opal nodded obediently. "Yes, sir. I'll follow your instructions."

No one gave Joe's ultra-plain face a second glance as he walked down Park Avenue. Joe had personally designed his face by scanning the 3-D images of 500 different people into a transform-machine and blending an average of them. He created the perfect generic face. He could walk through any crowd and be instantly forgotten. In effect, he rendered himself invisible.

Joe checked his watch. It had taken twenty-five minutes to make $15 billion and gain control of a media empire. Joe frowned. His time was too valuable to continue at this pace.

His objective required him to control hundreds of powerful people. As much fun as these replacements were, he needed a more efficient method.

A League of Their Own

"Acting is all about honesty.
If you can fake that, you've got it made."
—George Burns

"I'm out," Elvis ceded, laying his cards on the table.

"Me, too," Marilyn said.

"I raise $10," I said.

Bogie grinned. Ten dollars was a lot to my character and Bogie knew it. He was a rich nightclub owner. I was an unemployed vagabond. "I'll match and raise $2000," the asshole said.

I looked at my poker hand: three kings, an ace and a six. "I'll write an IOU."

"No offense, kid, but an IOU from you ain't worth much."

Bogie surveyed Marilyn up and down. "I'll tell you what. I know Marilyn asked you to go to the Academy Awards. I'll consider that invitation worth two grand."

I glanced at the four of us in a mirror. From every angle we resembled a nostalgic poster—four Hollywood legends playing poker.

"You can't bet a date," I said.

"You can bet anything—life's a gamble," Bogie scoffed.

I checked my cards and feigned anguish, although the script already determined who'd win. I tilted my head, imitating the real James Dean. Orson grinned from his position near the camera.

In the movie, I was a penniless romantic, desperate to prove my love to Marilyn. Humphrey Bogart was a cavalier playboy who flew Marilyn to exotic clubs around the world. I had to endure Bogie and Marilyn filming passionate love scenes. Even worse, I expected James Dean to die in the 1950s while Bogie and Marilyn would continue into the '60s.

Every character played themselves in the movie, yet their lives turned out differently than in reality. So, I didn't know *when* I'd die. The script changed incessantly. In my four weeks of filming, I'd already seen a dozen major changes.

In 1973, George Lucas had filmed *American Graffiti* chronologically from the first scene to the last, so each actor's psyche advanced concurrently with the plot. Orson had doubled down, never letting us know where the script was heading. In some versions, I married Marilyn and we lived happily-ever-after. Usually, I died a tragic death.

"The cards aren't going to play themselves," Bogie grumbled. "Are you going to accept my deal?"

I wished next time Bogie transformed, the machine would sew his mouth shut.

"Don't do it unless you're sure," Elvis advised.

Marilyn smiled sympathetically. I'd fallen deeply in love with her. We flirted, and I verbalized my adoration. It was the antipode of our relationship when our faces weren't altered. I'd found a moral loophole that let me love two distinct women.

"Fine. I call." I placed my cards on the table. "Three kings."

"Nice try, kid," Bogie smirked. "Full house." He showed three fours and two jacks.

"Damn. I hate cards," I grabbed my jacket and stormed out of the scene.

Once off-camera, I stood beside Orson and watched.

Marilyn flirtatiously wagged her finger at Bogie. "That wasn't very nice."

Bogie pulled Marilyn onto his lap. "I've never claimed to be nice." His hands moved around her hips. "Quite the opposite."

My jaw tightened and my fists clenched. Rage threatened to overtake me. I knew what came next—a love scene between Marilyn and Bogie.

"This game is obviously over," Elvis said. He walked off-camera beside me.

Bogie and Marilyn's faces were inches apart. "How would you like to sing in my joints? You've got real talent," Bogie said.

"Me? Really?" Marilyn swooned.

They leaned into each other and started kissing.

I was burning up. I couldn't help myself. I stepped toward Bogie.

Elvis grabbed my arm and pulled me back. "Follow me. We're not filming for a while."

"Where?"

"Albert's trailer. He's studying with John."

We crossed the sound stage and entered Einstein's trailer. He and John Wayne were reclined on a couch beside piles of binders about their characters. Study groups like these were popular, as we quizzed each other about the stupid trivia we were forced to memorize.

"Glad you're joining us. I still have some of your binders," Albert said.

"Fuck studying. Fuck the movie. Fuck Bogie."

"James is a bit upset," Elvis explained. "Marilyn and Bogie are doing a love scene. Do you have any beer?"

John tilted back his cowboy hat. "I reckon I'll have one, also."

"Me, too," Albert added. I had a strong desire to comb the physicist's unruly locks and see how he would look.

Elvis went to Albert's refrigerator and returned with four Budweisers.

Albert opened one of my James Dean binders. "Let's review your part in *Sailor Beware*."

It was a musical *I'd* done with Dean Martin and Jerry Lewis in 1952. Albert was trying to distract me, so I regurgitated the script.

During the month we'd been filming, I'd forged strong friendships. It felt as if we'd gone through boot camp together. Yet, I didn't know anything real about them. I knew James Dean's life inside-out, but I didn't know any other actor's real name. Elvis had become my best male friend ever, and I could sit next to him on a bus and not recognize him.

Talking about our past lives was a terminal infraction—certain to get an actor fired—yet the studio seemed to allow us to study our characters together in our trailers. We weren't certain if the studio conducted covert surveillance, but we assumed so, even in our trailers.

"I hate Bogie, but I'm more pissed off at Orson," I said. "Marilyn is kissing Bogie right now. On the 1960's set, she's been filming romantic scenes with President Kennedy. And in some of the scripts, she falls in love with Joe DiMaggio."

"They're probably jealous of you, too," Albert said. "The scripts usually make the audience cheer for you."

"I'll kick Orson in his nuts, if you want," John offered.

Elvis laughed loudly. Albert grinned.

I loved these guys. They understood me. And none of them were rivals for Marilyn.

I turned to Elvis. "Have you read next week's script? We're filming in Las Vegas."

"Yep," Elvis said. "And it seems completely possible we could die."

"Why are they risking your lives like that?" John asked.

"Because none of us will use stuntmen," Albert replied. "Steve McQueen punched Orson once, when Orson tried to replace him with a stunt man. That's how they got Steve to jump off a building on a motorcycle."

I shuddered to think of a stunt man being transformed with my face. I'd fight anyone before relinquishing James Dean's identity.

"Stunts must be a problem for the studio," Elvis said. "They want to meld to our characters, but stuntmen hinder that."

"Actually, stunts are easy for the studio," Albert said. "We're expendable. They can let us risk our lives, and, if we die, replace us with another actor."

"We're disposable puppets," I grumbled. "They pull the strings, make us do anything they want, and discard us without concern."

"Yes, well . . ." Einstein hesitated a moment. "Personally, I believe there's something more going on. I think they're testing us."

"What the hell does that mean?" asked John.

"The studio is molding us, forming us. They want to test what they're creating," Albert said.

"Test . . . *what*?" I asked.

Albert shrugged. "Perhaps the stunts are to test our commitment."

"Or our bravery," Elvis speculated.

"But why?" I asked.

Albert looked at me. "It involves more than just a movie, I suspect."

"Yes. Something secret and dangerous," Elvis added.

The thought sent chills up my back. Keeping Janie safe was more important than dating her. Both were essential.

"Albert, if you loved a woman who was being pursued by a lot of rich, handsome men, what would you do?"

"Find what makes you different," Albert said. "And then make this attribute crucial to her."

How was I different? I'd risk everything for Janie. I didn't care about my career, wealth, the movie, or even my life. None of the other suitors would sacrifice these things.

Albert looked at me almost apologetically. "I don't want to seem paranoid, but have you considered that you're the age you die?"

24 years young. "Yes. Why?"

"Just be careful. I can't help but notice that the scripts have killed you in many different ways," Albert said. "The Vegas stunt seems designed to see how much danger you'll face to prove your love for Marilyn."

Viva Las Vegas

"Gambling. Booze. Skirts," Bogie reminisced. "The Strip had the best of everything."

"Music. That's what Vegas means to me," Elvis said. "I'd play two concerts each night and then sing gospel with my friends 'til the sun rose."

Seated in the back of a cushy limo, I'd let Marilyn, Elvis, and Bogie do most of the talking on our four-hour trip. Dusk formed beyond the windows, and a vivid rubicund glow illuminated the Nevada desert. Each of us had a warm buzz, as we tried to resist thinking about our looming stunts.

Marilyn looked angelic in a lacy white bridal gown, complete with gloves and veil; Elvis wore the shimmering golden holographic pantsuit from his 1957 tour; Bogie donned a vintage white tuxedo; I wore outfit #49, the jeans, unbuttoned shirt, black vest and cowboy hat I'd worn in *Giant*.

"Look. Vegas!" Marilyn cheered.

Our four faces pressed against the limo's windows as we approached the Neon City. There was something impossible about being who we were, *where* we were. We headed straight down the Strip, past the Mandalay Bay, Luxor, New York-New York, MGM Grand, Bellagio and other colossal casinos which hadn't been dreamed of in the 1950s.

"Shit," Elvis said as the Stratosphere tower grew on the horizon. The 1,149-foot tower, officially named "The Strat," resembled a giant with its head in the clouds.

"I'm officially terrified," Marilyn declared. "Maybe we should've used stunt men."

Elvis, Bogie and I glared at her.

"I'm kidding. I'd die before seeing another Marilyn."

"Vegas is full of Marilyn impersonators," Bogie noted.

"That's flattering," Marilyn said, "But they don't have my face."

"If the studio lets anyone die, it will be me," Bogie said. "I've already filmed my legacy scenes. Dutch loves those things."

The legacy scenes were Dutch's pet. They consisted of acting in front of a green screen so computers could compare our motions with our original counterparts. Supposedly, they'd help us perfect our respective characters.

"You don't die in any of the scripts, Bogie," I said. "It's always me."

Marilyn looked at me with a concerned expression, and I saw a hint of Janie-ness. No one else would notice. Even when we weren't filming, she was a flawless Marilyn.

Our limo stopped at the rear entrance of the Stratosphere, where a sign proclaimed: "The tallest building west of the Mississippi since 1996."

It was strange to be in a modern building, instead of the 1950s set, but apparently this scene was part of a dream sequence which Orson said fit perfectly in his next version of the script.

Wearing masquerade masks—colorful feathered masks which covered our entire faces—we exited our limo and strutted toward the casino. We held party horns to our lips, tooting avidly, and impersonated impersonators until we reached the elevator.

Stepping onto the open-air rooftop produced a sensation like standing on an airplane wing in flight. I felt dizzy and tried not to look down. Orson was busy directing the final preparation of lights, cameras, and props. Marilyn held a bouquet of roses as a long white train of embroidered lace fabric was attached to her wedding gown.

According to the script, Marilyn had agreed to marry Bogie on New Year's Eve. I'd gotten drunk, passed out and wasn't sure if this was real or a nightmare.

"Places," Orson yelled. "Timing is everything. We only have one chance to get this right."

Elvis held a Bible while standing beneath a simple white lattice arch at the edge of the roof. Bogie was at his side.

My eyes remained glued on Marilyn as she sashayed to a red carpet.

Assistants straightened her long white gown. In a billion years, molecules could never have arranged themselves into a lovelier sight. However, Marilyn wore the wedding gown for the wrong man.

"James, are you listening?"

I ripped my gaze away from Marilyn.

"Remember, there's no reason to be scared. If you fall, just pull the ripcord," Orson said, patting the parachute on my back, which was camouflaged to look like my shirt. "My original script had you BASE jumping off the roof, but our lawyers said that would be illegal." He winked at me. "However, I'm sure you'll find a way to make the scene exciting."

As I moved downstairs to my position on the balcony of a lower deck, I wondered what Orson meant. Did he want me to purposely fall?

Cameras were arranged to film me on the lower deck, and there was a monitor for me to watch the unfolding activity on the roof, where Orson provided Marilyn with last minute encouragement.

"It's your wedding, Marilyn," Orson said. "Look blissful, not frightened."

Marilyn forced a jittery smile.

"Action!" Orson yelled.

Pachelbel's Canon played. Marilyn proceeded solemnly toward Elvis and Bogie, towing her white gown behind her.

She finally stopped beneath the white arch. Elvis looked gravely upon the couple. "Marriage is the most sacred of all human states. Are you both ready for this lifelong commitment?"

"Yes," Bogart said.

"Yes," Marilyn agreed.

I cringed.

A light blue helicopter flew overhead with paparazzi leaning out the window.

Elvis frowned at the paparazzi. "Place your hands together," he instructed.

Marilyn and Bogart peered into each other's eyes as they held hands. Elvis faced Bogie.

"Do you, Humphrey DeForest Bogart, take this woman, Norma Jean

Baker, to be your lawfully wedded bride, to honor and love, as long as you both shall live?"

"I do," Bogart responded.

A rope ladder dropped from the helicopter, and a man with a camera climbed down the ladder onto the Stratosphere's steel antenna. As security guards looked up at him, he began to snap photos. The paparazzo and security were all actors, but they seemed very real.

Elvis turned to Marilyn.

"Do you, Norma Jean Baker, take this man, Humphrey DeForest Bogart, to be your lawfully wedded husband, to honor and love, as long as you both shall live?"

Marilyn hesitated. I watched transfixed. The pause was a crushing weight . . .

The helicopter hovered on the far side of the building from me. I sprinted towards it.

There was a short, hidden platform on my deck, protruding about four feet out from the balcony, and I was supposed to jump from it. The ground menaced 1000 feet below. As I ran onto the deck, I could see the rope ladder dangling from the helicopter. The hard-to-see end of the ladder was about equal with the balcony.

A cacophony of questions flooded my head. Would I reach the rope ladder? Could I hold on? Would the parachute work? Did Orson want me to fall?

The rope ladder dangled about ten feet away from the building, but it looked more like twenty. How impressed would Janie be by this stunt? Was it worth dying?

I knew the faster I ran, the further I could jump. My brain sent conflicting messages to speed up and to slow down. I imagined my arms and legs thrashing in the air if I missed the ladder.

What if I couldn't find the ripcord as I plummeted toward the ground?

I'm James Dean. I'm brave. I smiled as a jolt of exhilaration brazened my heart. My feet hit the platform, and I jumped.

Soaring through space, time melded into dark blue sky; a serene moment of weightlessness, then the pitiless tug of gravity.

My right hand reached for a ladder rung. I gripped it for life, hanging awkwardly by one arm until my left hand also found a rung. My feet searched the air for rungs to stand on, but the ladder swung wildly in every direction. After a few seconds of twisting, hanging hell, my hands were tired and sweaty; every time my foot nearly pressed onto the ladder, it swiveled out of reach.

I'm going to fall. I peered downward at my two feet, fumbling uncontrollably around the swinging ladder. The Las Vegas pavement below was speckled by cars, which looked like tiny dots of paint.

Finally, by moving my feet in unison along the rope, my feet found rungs. However, this didn't provide the stability I'd expected. With nothing to leverage against, my legs swung forward until my feet were above my head. At the same time the helicopter jolted upward.

I'm going to die at 24 . . . again.

I struggled to pull my legs down without my feet slipping off the rungs. The difficulty increased as the helicopter accelerated and curved around the tower. Somehow, I got my feet beneath me with my body upright, just as the flying machine ascended rapidly, yanking me with it.

Suddenly, the wedding arch was below me.

"Don't marry him!" I shouted. "I love you, Marilyn!" I yelled instinctively, unconcerned about matching my scripted lines.

Marilyn looked up. "James? You're crazy."

The paparazzi madly snapped pictures. The helicopter pilot had positioned me in the most dramatic spot possible.

"We're soulmates, Marilyn!" I shouted.

"Too late!" Bogie bellowed.

"I love you, Marilyn. Marry me."

Marilyn looked horrified. Orson had given her two alternative sets of lines, in case she was too frightened to follow the preferred script.

"Just say 'I do'," Bogie demanded. "We're only two words from matrimony."

"Listen to your heart, Marilyn," I implored.

Marilyn looked at me beseechingly, as I dangled a few feet above her.

Bogie forced Marilyn to look in his eyes. "Say 'I do'."

Marilyn pushed Bogie away. "I want to wake up."

"It's James' nightmare," Bogie said. "You have to marry me."

"Bogie is right," Elvis said. "You can't make choices in someone else's dream."

Marilyn grinned. "We're making choices by discussing this."

Bogart grabbed her shoulders: "Say 'I do'."

"I don't!" Marilyn held out her hand.

I grabbed it.

We clutched each other's hands and were lifted into the air. Her white gown undulated in the wind, her wedding train billowing and fluttering.

An explosion suddenly shook the tower. The rope ladder reverberated, my legs slipped off the ladder. The sky blazed in showers of flaming lights and thundering noise, a fortune worth of fireworks the studio had spent to emulate New Year's Eve.

I grasped Marilyn as explosions erupted. The sky burst into a dazzling tapestry of pyrotechnics. My feet found the ladder, and I thanked the heavens I hadn't fallen.

"If she's going, I am, too." Bogart lunged at the rope ladder links beneath Marilyn's feet.

Bogie reached as far as he could, but the ladder moved too quickly. He missed. Bogie's face etched in fear as he had stepped off the tower. Hanging in space, he appeared destined to fall.

Elvis grabbed the back of his tuxedo coat. For a moment, I wondered if they'd both fall, but Elvis pulled them to safety.

The helicopter flew vertically. I clutched Marilyn in a mix of fear and ecstasy—dangling 1,200 feet above Las Vegas as fireworks blazoned on every side.

The helicopter soared down the Strip past neon casino lights, and my heart beat faster than ever. This fear had nothing to do with falling. I'd never held Janie so close before.

Our chests pressed together, her face next to mine. It was warm and wonderful, yet dazzling, like an electric shock overloading my senses. At the end of the Strip, we circled back toward the roof of the Stratosphere and I wished the feeling would never end.

According to the script, when we returned to the tower I would give Marilyn a quick kiss. This was scarier than jumping off the tower. Too soon, we hovered above the Stratosphere roof. I pulled my head back to separate our bodies, and literally saw fireworks reflecting in Marilyn's eyes. I held my breath. How long should I make the "quick" kiss?

Hell, I almost died. I may never get to kiss her again. I pressed my lips against hers, and the world went silent. I closed my eyes, and there were no fireworks, just heaven. I'd dreamed about this forever, but the moment far exceeded the dream.

It might have been a long kiss or brief kiss, my brain couldn't tell. When I opened my eyes, I was surprised to see Marilyn's face instead of Janie's.

Orson euphorically waved his arms. "Cut. Cut. That was wonderful."

The helicopter lowered our feet to the rooftop. Elvis and Bogie greeted us, popping champagne. We hugged each other—I even hugged Bogie. I soaked up pure elation: the stunt, the kiss, and my identity.

Marilyn kissed my cheek. "You're amazing."

I *loved* being James Dean.

Clueless

Sherlock Holmes would be absinthe green with jealousy.

Detective Winkler intended to solve the crime-of-the-century before the rest of the LAPD even knew a crime had been committed. Sherlock Holmes had never faced anyone as clever or menacing as the generic-faced man, whose villainy spanned the gamut and involved the nation's most powerful people. Yet, single-handedly, Detective Winkler had verified the generic-faced man's misdeeds and untangled the web of celebrities recruited to be part of his crime ring.

Trevor Winkler, Detective III in the Robbery Homicide Division, was eidetic—meaning he possessed the one-in-a-billion trait of remembering everything he saw with perfect memory. Most eidetikers became mathematicians, scientists, or chess grandmasters. However, Trevor had decided to use his gift to put bad people in prison. The work entertained him, and he had achieved astronomical success.

At age twenty-seven, Trevor had already solved twice as many homicides as any detective in the history of the LA Detective Bureau. He never worked with a partner, because quite frankly, they slowed him down. The chief of detectives had learned to stay out of his way. Trevor intended to join the FBI at age thirty and the CIA at age thirty-five. By forty, he would either be attorney general or director of the NSA—he hadn't determined his preference yet.

The key to nonpareil crime solving wasn't investigating leads—any detective could do that—it was perceiving abstruse leads. This required spotting anomalies in vast data among broad fields. Combining his photographic memory with modern technology, Trevor discerned incongruities in nearly-imperceptible patterns.

The generic-faced man hadn't made a mistake. Trevor had been viewing surveillance video of a celebrity suspected of tax fraud, and the plain-looking man merely stood in the background. He was so ordinary-looking, he would have been forgotten by anyone without eidetic memory. However, Trevor recalled seeing him three weeks previous in a surveillance video of a musician involved with drugs.

Trevor had checked the generic-looking man with the face-recognition software of the National Crime Information Center. Surprisingly, he was not in any database.

For the past thirty-six hours, Trevor had reviewed video, searching for the plain man, looking for patterns. He'd discovered the generic man in six separate locations, always with powerful people. Unraveling the malfeasance revealed a massive criminal conspiracy, involving billions of dollars, dozens of the world's largest companies, and many of America's most beloved public figures. The generic man was at the center.

Trevor was finally sure he'd picked the right career path. Sometimes his job felt like a game as he stopped a serial killer or drug ring. He was eliminating evil, yet he'd wondered if he would have benefited society more as a scientist. That concern was over. Ending the generic-faced man's rampage of crime and corruption would, quite literally, save the world.

While Trevor stared at his computer, he heard the door to his office open. Only the police chief would enter without knocking, and Trevor wondered why the chief was in the building so late at night.

"Holy fuck!" Trevor cried.

The generic-faced man stood in the doorway of Trevor's office.

Before Trevor could scream, the man aimed a revolver at him.

"Hi, I'm Joe Plain."

He was followed into the room by another man—a doppelgänger of Trevor, identical in every way.

"Double fuck," Trevor said.

Trevor's mind parsed through everything he knew about Joe Plain and added the ability to replicate people. "You're going to kill me, and replace me."

"Correct." Joe Plain's face formed an inhuman smile.

Trevor knew his coworkers had gone home and there was no help for him on the floor.

He pointed at his replica. "Keep me alive, instead of him. I'll be far more useful. I've got a photographic memory. I know everything."

"Have you heard of fearology?"

"No. Which means it doesn't exist."

"And, yet, I have mastered it." Joe pointed the gun at Trevor's stomach as he held up a vial of liquid. "Drink this, and your death will be painless."

"Wait, you don't understand. I'm eidetic. I can help you with anything."

"If you were smart, you'd realize I don't *need* anything."

Trevor's brain calculated the possibility of survival of different scenarios. No luck. Whatever he did, he would die. However, Trevor discovered his curiosity was even greater than his fear.

"How did you replicate me? You can't have cloned my DNA. Clones age too slowly." Trevor approached his replacement and carefully examined the face and neck. "Every freckle matches mine. There are no scars. It can't be surgery." He felt the cheek of his identical twin, who indignantly drew back. "It's not makeup or a mask."

He turned to Joe Plain. "I've never failed to solve a mystery. Tell me how you replicated me, and I'll drink the poison."

Joe held out the vial. "Drink it first, and I promise to tell you. You've got ten seconds, before I shoot you."

Trevor glanced around his office, where he'd used brilliance and technology to defeat so many criminals. He sniffed the poison, and tried to identify any chemicals. Cyanide? Mixed with cyclosarin? He drank it in one gulp. The concoction was slightly salty—he guessed the toxic mix included sodium fluoroacetate.

"You'll be dead in less than a minute."

"Okay, tell me how this is possible," Trevor said.

"You're an interesting case. Very little fear of death, but great fear of the unknown."

Trevor weakened with each passing moment. He had ten or twenty seconds left of consciousness. "Tell me quickly, I must know."

Joe laughed. "I don't waste time on dead people."

Trevor realized with horror that he'd never understand this. Joe Plain clearly enjoyed his suffering. Trevor tried to calculate how many people Joe was going to kill before he stopped, but there were too many unknown variables. Joe's ultimate goal was an indecipherable puzzle.

Before he collapsed, Trevor considered the effort he'd put into investigating Joe Plain, and made one final calculation.

The chance anyone else could stop this evil bastard: zero.

52

Fatal Attraction

"Hearts will never be practical
until they are made unbreakable."
—The Wizard of Oz

Janie fell into my arms , and my heart stuttered. Pure ecstasy. No cameras, no script and, best of all, she had her real face. Years of daydreaming hadn't prepared me for the marvel of having Janie's face inches from mine.

My ankles wobbled, unused to skates. I summoned every ounce of strength to keep us from falling on the ice. Cautiously, I lifted her to a vertical position.

"Even the three-year-olds are better than us." Janie laughed as tiny kids zoomed past.

Other couples skated confidently, holding hands. Teenagers skated backwards, showing off. In the center of the rink, daring little girls in ballerina outfits did heroic spins.

Ice skating at the Hotel del Coronado was a Hallmarkesque annual tradition, combining a classic winter activity with the quintessential Californian hotel.

We were beside the ocean in 77-degree weather, surrounded by lofty palm trees and the hotel's iconic red turrets, while beneath our feet was a temporary outdoor skating rink. The hotel had unveiled the nation's first electrical Christmas tree in 1904, and then introduced beachfront, holiday season skating in 2004. The cost of keeping ice frozen under a blazing sun didn't seem to be an issue.

I kept an arm wrapped tightly around her, partially so we didn't fall, but mainly for the feeling of holding her body. Janie wore jean shorts and a white blouse. Her long dark hair glistened down her back, and she smelled like jasmine, but by far her most enticing feature to me was her natural face. Her crooked nose and sparse eyebrows weren't glamourous, but that face was all I'd dreamed of and adored for almost two decades.

"I can't believe we're at the beach," Janie said as a bikini-clad woman ice skated past, wearing sunglasses and a Santa hat. "Sunbathing and skating seem like un-combinable pleasures. It's like mixing Christmas with the Fourth of July."

Today was Thanksgiving, and I'd brought Janie here for strategic reasons. Marilyn Monroe had filmed *Some Like It Hot* at the hotel in 1959. After skating, Janie and I would enjoy our turkey meal in the palatial Crown Room, the most elegant of venues. My hope was the seduction I was working as James Dean would carry over to our real lives.

The Hotel del Coronado was the ideal spot to see if I could break through the steel partition separating our identities. After filming for eight weeks, we'd still never discussed our roles in the movie. Today, I hoped that would change, or at the least I'd confirm she knew I played the part of James Dean.

"A lot of movies have been filmed here." I dared to gently rest my hand on the small of her back as we took a few timid steps forward on the ice.

Janie didn't reply. She gazed at the ocean where kite surfers skimmed over the water.

I pretended to slip, and reached for her hand. She didn't pull away—maybe because we were both holding each other for balance. I tried to stay calm, not reacting to the wonderfulness of the moment.

When I was twelve and she was fourteen, we'd held hands as we bowed after a school performance of *Guys and Dolls*. That was the only other time we'd had significant physical contact when we weren't Marilyn and James.

"Who's your favorite actress from the fifties?" I asked. It felt gratuitously naughty to dance around the edge of our draconian contract.

Janie grinned at me. "Grace Kelly. I've always admired how classy she was."

Was Janie flirting? I felt potent. I was holding the hand of the most beautiful woman in the world. Even lovelier to me than when she transformed. Could I push further? Could I ask if she knew?

A family skated by us, a mother and father holding hands with a toddler in the middle. I wondered if Janie and I both had the same thought.

"Do you miss your uncle?" Janie asked.

"Every day, but especially on holidays." Janie and I were both orphans, but my uncle had provided me a loving home, something she never had. "I feel guilty having Thanksgiving without him."

Janie looked solemn. "You've never told me about the fire."

"I wanted to spare you."

"We're best friends. You can tell me anything."

My mind drifted to the smells and sounds of that dreadful night. "I'd finished my chores and had climbed to my loft in the barn. I was supposed to be doing homework, but was just daydreaming."

Janie nodded encouragingly. "Daydreaming about what?"

"You."

Janie stared at her skates. We were still taking small steps on the ice, holding hands.

"What were you doing when the fire started?"

"I'd logged into our high school drama department's website, and was watching our performance of *The Music Man* from your senior year."

"I was Amaryllis, such a small part. I really wanted to be Marion the Librarian."

"It was a special time for me, our last school play together. You lit up the stage like a Broadway star. I had my headphones on, and I didn't hear the beams on the roof break . . . ."

My voice weakened as I relived the tragedy. Janie squeezed my hand.

"I was focused on your performance when something hot landed on my back. I looked up from the computer, and discovered I was engulfed in flames."

Janie's eyes widened. "The barn loft was on fire?"

"The entire barn. I yanked off my headset, and the noise was awful. Beams were collapsing. Flames covered the stairs down from the loft. I had a crazy thought that dozens of fire-breathing dragons were attacking me and I was going to be burned alive.

"The barn was falling apart above and below. Smoke was everywhere. I tried to get to the stairs, but the heat was too strong. The hay blazed like a sea of yellow flames. Fire crisscrossed the walls and the wooden planks of the loft were incinerating.

"I resigned myself to die, and wondered if it was my fault. I'd kept the barn clean and was careful with flammable liquids. Maybe a rodent had chewed through a wire.

"Then I saw a stream of white foam shoot through the yellow blaze by the stairs. Uncle Stanley appeared with a fire extinguisher and fought his way to me. When he reached me, he handed me the fire extinguisher.

"'Grab this. My arms are tired,' he said.

"It didn't make sense. His arms were never tired. He worked all day carrying farm equipment. But I grabbed the extinguisher and headed down the stairs. The foam created a tiny haven from the flames."

"It's a miracle you survived," Janie said.

"I got outside with only minor burns. I was gulping fresh air when I turned around and saw my uncle. He was rolling on the ground covered head-to-toe in flames."

"Oh, Darrin." Janie turned to gaze at me empathetically. Her eyes were big with compassion and affection . . . maybe even love?

She turned too fast and lost her balance, her skating skills inadequate for quick movements. I put a foot forward, looping my arm around her and somehow preventing her from falling. She was in my arms in a giant dip, as if we'd just finished the tango. Our faces were almost touching.

I saw confusion in her eyes. A look I'd never seen before. If we were ever going to kiss, this was the moment. There might never be a better chance.

I boldly pressed my lips to hers. For a moment, I felt the softness of the most perfect tender skin.

"Darrin!" She shoved me away. I tried to catch her, but I failed, and she landed on her butt.

My heart shattered. She'd rather fall on ice than kiss me.

"We're not like that . . . ." Janie sputtered.

I put out a hand to help her, but I didn't look at her. I turned away.

Don't cry. I willed myself to forbid a single tear.

I pulled her up, and Janie put her hand on my arm. "I love you . . . but as a friend."

"It was just a weird moment. I didn't mean to."

"I need you, Darrin." She hugged me. "You're my only family and my best friend. I can't mess this up. There's so much going on in my life now, I couldn't survive without you."

It finally occurred to me—she doesn't know I am James Dean.

"I'm not just saying this," Janie said. "I promise, we'll always be there for each other, and spend every holiday together. I just don't have more to offer."

I wiped my wet cheeks on my shirt sleeve. My heart started to recover as I felt the warmth of a new form of confidence.

As Darrin, I was inadequate. I was better off without him. However, as James Dean, I would win her affections. James Dean was sexy, clever and successful, and maybe already making inroads into her heart.

The Way We Were

The Ferrari Berlinetta purred and skidded simultaneously as I turned from Santa Monica Boulevard onto Wilshire Boulevard.

"Perhaps you should slow down," the saleswoman suggested. She was a stiletto-wearing blonde with Cartier sunglasses and a purple stripe in her hair, about thirty, who had flirted with me at first. Now, she clutched at the edge of her seat.

"The V12 engine has five pounds of horsepower for every pound of car. Why not use them?" I asked.

Being James Dean had made me a car enthusiast. I was ecstatic, speeding around Beverly Hills in the high-performance race car. Most incredible of all, I could afford it.

I accelerated and the startled saleswoman shut her eyes and clinched her teeth. How did she expect I'd test drive a Ferrari racing car? I craved this car. James Dean deserved it.

But damn, I'd have to be Darrin whenever I drove it.

Janie had bought a Nissan. A fucking *used* Nissan. And she hadn't improved her wardrobe either. Our contracts demanded that we didn't give any indication of our other identity, yet I couldn't understand why she didn't let herself splurge a little.

I tried to see things from her perspective. While my life-passion was Janie, her life-long aspiration was to be an actress. I relished the thrill; she feared upsetting the studio.

The Ferrari made me feel like James Dean, even without his face. Down to the depths of my soul, I wanted this Ferrari.

However, buying the car wasn't strategic. I needed to maintain her friendship with Darrin, while making her fall in love with me as James. Purchasing an extravagant car as Darrin would do the opposite of impressing her.

You want restraint, Janie? I'll show you God-damn restraint.

I returned the car to the Ferrari dealership, where the saleswoman quickly directed her charms at another customer. I took a bus to a used car lot in Burbank, bought a Taurus and paid in cash.

Each day since Thanksgiving, I'd grown to despise my Darrin identity more. Luckily, I hardly spent any time as Darrin. My waking hours were almost all as James—glorious time spent flirting with Marilyn, filming, and studying. I dreaded leaving the studio each day, since it meant changing back into my loathsome original self.

Today was my second day off in over two months—the first since Thanksgiving—and I was stuck all day with my Darrin face. Yet, it provided me with a chance to see my uncle. I felt terribly guilty about not visiting him for so long.

I drove my used Taurus onto I-5 and headed north toward Bakersfield, where Uncle Stanley lived. My only living relative, he had watched me pine for Janie for years. I'd trusted him with countless secrets about my life, and he'd never let me down.

Some people assume farmers aren't very wise, yet my uncle was the wisest man I knew. Wisdom, I'd learned, only required humility and a lot of time spent thinking.

A fool is someone who doesn't put love first. Wisdom from Uncle Stanley.

However, was my new plan insane? If I seduced Marilyn into loving James Dean, how would I convert that love back to Darrin?

The 90-mile drive passed quickly. I used the time to review James Dean's life. It astounded me how much he had changed society before dying at age 24. Before James, adolescence had been treated as a problem to be outgrown. After James, youthful defiance was considered heroic. James Dean's legacy to fashion was nothing less than jeans, t-shirt and bold hair. His legacy to the American psyche was brazen brashness.

Cultural experts credited James with forging America's attitude more than any other historic figure. He preceded rock and roll. Elvis, Jim Morrison and Bob Dylan all named him as a role model. After James, no one wanted to grow up. He was essentially the founder of American pop culture.

Did Janie feel as much pressure portraying Marilyn, America's immortal sex symbol?

A balmy Southern California morning displayed out the window as I drove past scenic fields where laborers harvested strawberries and other crops. The farm work reminded me of the sacrifices my uncle had made for me. He'd raised me as if I was his own son; my real parents had died when I was two. After the barn fire and his resulting injuries, my uncle had sold the farm and moved to Berggren House, a private facility ten miles west of Bakersfield. This had given me the freedom to move to Los Angeles.

Soon, I turned onto an unmarked road and the white walls of Berggren House came into view. Centuries ago, Berggren House had been a Spanish mission. It maintained its proud Moorish architecture, with bleached walls and a graceful chapel surrounded by the stone pilasters of a two-story arcade. The mission had been bought in 1984 by a Swedish doctor named Gustav Berggren, who'd renovated it into a long-term home for burn victims.

No signs identified the facility. People moved to Berggren House because they wanted isolation. I knocked on the large wood door and was rewarded with an exuberant greeting by a tall, thickly-bearded man.

"Hello, Darrin. Your uncle said you might visit us today."

"Hi, Leo," I said, shaking the tall man's hand.

Leo was the friendliest person I'd ever met, yet I had trouble looking him in his deep hazel eyes. Like all the residents at Berggren House, his face was severely scarred and discolored. Plastic surgery had reconstructed his ears, nose and lips, but it couldn't hide all the burn damage.

Leo escorted me into the central courtyard of the mission. As austere as the building's exterior, the interior was warm and inviting. The highest structure was the chapel, which merged into two stories of Roman arches forming a rectangular perimeter.

There were benches and fountains, but the quadrangle's key feature was a stage in its center. As usual, most of the residents were seated near this stage. There were forty residents, and I knew almost all of them. Visitors were rare, and they always treated me very special.

Leo pointed toward a bench where my uncle and his friend Annabelle sat. They jumped up to greet me.

Uncle Stanley hugged me and then scolded, "Stop sending money, Darrin. I have no use for it here."

"Then buy Annabelle something online."

She grinned widely, her affection for my uncle apparent.

Uncle Stanley wore jeans and a maroon t-shirt. My gut still recoiled whenever I saw the streaks of scar tissue on his face. In my memory, his face was perfect, like before the burns. Annabelle wore a lovely sundress and heavily-applied makeup. She always adorned her hair with a large blue bow—blue was my uncle's favorite color.

"Stanley brags about you constantly. His nephew, the movie star!" Annabel's green eyes sparkled when she smiled, but splotchy burns moved her face in odd ways. I forced myself to make eye contact, although my heart trembled with sorrow. "He says you've been very mysterious. Can you tell us what the movie's about?"

"Sorry. Not yet. The studio made us sign a strict contract."

A beautiful vocal harmony came from the stage, and I turned to watch four people singing "Wouldn't It Be Nice." The Beach Boys would've been proud.

"That's Desert Roar. They're still the champions," my uncle said.

"But a new group called Heaven's Harmony may dethrone them," Annabelle said. "Their lead singer just arrived and is amazing."

Singing competitions were the main form of entertainment at Berggren House. The residents were zealous about them. Desert Roar had reigned for months, a position held in great esteem.

I'd never heard my uncle sing a single note before he came to this place, but within a month of his arrival at Berggren House he was singing daily in a quartet.

"So, Darrin, have you asked out Janie yet?" Annabelle asked.

"I'm working on it."

"A man takes a big risk by moving too slow." Annabelle looked at my uncle, but he didn't seem to notice. "Well, I'll leave you two alone. I'm sure you have things to discuss." She again smiled her warm yet heartbreaking smile and made her way toward the stage.

"What's wrong, Darrin?"

My uncle could always read me. "The studio is brainwashing us."

"Brainwashing?"

"They've forced me so deep into my character, my real life feels like a lie."

"Maybe this is normal for the star of a big production."

I shook my head. "It's crazy excessive. I'm only supposed to eat the food my character liked, do the activities he did, and listen to the music he liked. And there's military-tight secrecy."

"I bet tons of actors would give anything for an opportunity like yours."

"They don't know what we endure. Our contracts are absurd. The studio controls every aspect of our lives. We think they spy on us. They'll fire us if we talk about real life. They've made some actors get hypnotized for certain scenes. They'll do anything to make us more like our characters."

"Maybe that's why their movies are so successful. I suggest you put up with whatever crap they throw at you, as long as it's safe and legal."

"The problem isn't that I dislike it. I enjoy it too much. I'm addicted. I don't think I *could* stop."

I wanted to tell my uncle everything, including the existence of the face-changing machines. Any secret was completely safe with him. However, integrity had a flip side. My uncle would be disappointed in me if I broke my word to the studio.

Heaven's Harmony was performing "Electric Love" and it sounded like BØRNS was live on stage. They were really impressive.

"What's the difference between acting and lying?" I asked.

My uncle reflected for a moment. "I supposed it's where your ego is, whether you're trying to entertain people or deceive them."

"What if you're trying to make them love you?"

He raised his eyebrow, knowing I meant Janie. "Love isn't a single performance, it's a promise about the future. You have to live up to the expectations you're creating."

"I want to."

"You've never faltered there. You've always given Janie your full attention."

"So, deception is okay, if your intentions are true?"

My uncle surprised me with his answer. "True love deserves every risk to be taken, and every sacrifice to be offered. Otherwise, you're denying her the chance to know the full depth of your love."

We listened to Heaven's Harmony as I contemplated this.

What more could I possibly do to make Janie love me?

I could steal a transform-machine.

I could become whoever she wanted, even if it wasn't James Dean.

"Whatever you're scheming, remember the truth will come out," my uncle said.

That was my dilemma. Whether I won her heart as James Dean or someone else, I either had to convert that love back to Darrin or find a way to live another identity.

Annabelle hurried over. "You're needed on stage, Stanley. The Four Musketeers are next."

That was my uncle's group. Boy, I hoped they'd improved.

They hadn't. They hacked their way through "By the Light of the Silvery Moon" like they were chopping wood with a rolling pin.

"I love watching your uncle sing," Annabelle said dotingly.

"Do you think love is like being struck by lightning? Or does it bloom slowly like a flower?"

Her green eyes sparked. "Neither. Love is like nuclear power. There's unlimited useful energy, but it's highly dangerous. It must be carefully controlled."

I laughed.

Annabelle pensively studied me. "Your uncle says he's too old for romance." A tear navigated down her misshapen face. "I'm not sure if it's because of his blemishes or mine."

I looked away, embarrassed. I resolved to ask Teddy Millner what the machines could do for burn victims.

It was a relief when Uncle Stanley's quartet stopped singing and he returned to us.

Annabelle hugged him. "That was wonderful."

My uncle shrugged. "We're doing our best."

"I've got to leave. We're filming early tomorrow," I said.

My uncle and Annabelle escorted me toward the large wooden door. While we walked, Annabelle asked, "When did you first know you loved Janie?"

"Janie never invited me to meet her foster parents, but every day she came over to play in our barn. She invented background stories for the animals. One of our goats was a World War II hero. My horse was a knight who rescued fair maidens—"

"Our largest pig won three Super Bowls," my uncle interrupted.

"By the time we were teenagers, she'd developed a history for every animal. Sometimes we'd act out their stories, either by improvising, or Janie would write a script."

"That's so sweet . . . she created a world with you," Annabelle said.

"The heroes in Janie's stories were always lonely, but never gave up hope. Love always triumphed. One day, I realized her compassion was even stronger than her imagination. Somehow, right then, I knew I'd love her forever."

We reached the door, and I said goodbye to my uncle and Annabelle. I was about to leave, but Leo stopped me. "Wait, Darrin. We have something for you."

I looked back, wondering what gift they could have. In unison, the residents of Berggren House burst into harmony. They sang "Good-night, Ladies" with altered lyrics:

"Good-night, Darrin . . . Good-night, Darrin . . . Good-night, Darrin, we hope you'll be back soon . . . ."

I stood under the great Moorish architecture being serenaded. The unrestrained affection of these disfigured souls was too great, and tears formed at my eyes. I waved and exited before they noticed I was crying.

In my rearview mirror, the Darrin face I hated so much looked back at me. An average-looking face, which caused me such misery. No burns, no scars, just not handsome. I flipped the mirror away, and dreamed of being James Dean again.

All the way home, the chorus of "Good-night, Darrin" rang in my ears.

Dance Fever

Jimmy Stevenson was severely depressed and couldn't stop dancing. It was an awkward combination.

He couldn't let his neighbors see, but as soon as he entered his apartment, his feet began tapping the ground and shuffling back and forth. He danced as he went into the kitchen and heated a plate of baked ham and beans, Gene Kelly's favorite meal. He carried the food to the living room and watched *Singin' in the Rain* on his TV. He ate with a plastic fork and knife, because he'd purged his home of anything with a reflective surface.

Jimmy's feet never stopped tapping the entire meal. He kept dancing as he washed the dishes and frolicked to the bathroom. No mirrors, of course. Any reminder of his original face thrust him deeper into depression.

He tapped his feet as he peed, trying to distract himself. His transformation time wasn't until the next morning at 8:47 a.m. Nights were the hardest, although mixing Nytol and Prozac seemed to help.

Since childhood, Jimmy had devoted his life to becoming a famous dancer. Until recently, his career had been a failure. He'd earned money teaching ballet to young girls, supplementing his income by providing dance lessons to adult couples who stepped on each other's toes.

The transform-machines changed everything. The studio invited him to audition. Soon, he had Gene Kelly's face and was gliding across studio sets with Debbie Reynolds and Judy Garland.

Within a week, he was hopelessly addicted. Life as Gene Kelly brought more bliss than he'd ever imagined, while also exposing the wretchedness of his former life. Depression hit when he realized that, sooner or later, the movie would finish. The studio wouldn't need Gene Kelly. Once they finished filming, his life would lose its meaning.

He had three options. When the movie completed, he could become a Gene Kelly impostor, wearing a mask and doing street performances. Or, on the last day of filming he could try to escape the studio and live on the lam with Gene Kelly's identity. Or, suicide.

As Jimmy washed his hands in his mirrorless bathroom, the doorbell rang. He went to the door and looked through the peephole: Opal Wallace.

Jimmy stepped back. Was he hallucinating? He checked again. The media mogul stood waiting at his door.

Jimmy opened the door and saw that Opal wasn't alone. The billionaire stood beside an ordinary-looking man clad in a black suit. Something looked abnormal about the man's face—yet it seemed 100% normal in every way.

"Hello Mr. Miller, I'm Opal Wallace, and this is my friend Joe Plain. We have a business opportunity for you. May we come in?"

"Of course." Jimmy refrained from dancing as they entered his small apartment.

Opal glanced around the modest home. "Dutch Hollander told me that you're playing Gene Kelly in a movie."

Jimmy was thrilled that she knew. He almost corrected her, to clarify that he wasn't "playing" Gene Kelly, but actually *was* Gene Kelly. However, he couldn't explain this.

"Why would Dutch tell you?" Jimmy asked.

"Because we're filming a commercial. Dutch offered to have Gene Kelly dance in our commercial, which will jointly promote the movie," Opal said.

Jimmy's foot tapped excitedly. This was an extra chance to be Gene.

"The commercial is for a new beverage," Joe said, handing Jimmy a vial of milky liquid.

Joe turned to Opal. "Take a video of Mr. Miller as he tastes it for the first time."

Opal raised her smartphone and aimed it at Jimmy. "Go ahead. Try it."

Jimmy took the cap off the vial and swallowed the liquid.

"It's tasty. A little salty, but I like it."

Opal kept videotaping him, as if she expected more to occur. Joe held a stopwatch.

"It's delicious. It will be a great commercial . . . hey, I'm feeling a little strange . . . what's in this . . . I think I'm going to fall . . . ."

Jimmy looked at Joe and saw pure evil behind his plain facial features.

Joe smiled, and Jimmy knew he'd been poisoned.

His confusion turned to panic. He'd never be Gene Kelly again. They'd bury him as Jimmy Stevenson. He stumbled around the room, trying to be graceful and not fall, a dance of death.

Joe was thrilled by the agony on Jimmy's face. The drama would make an extraordinary video. When Jimmy finally hit the ground, his feet jolted around a bit, kicking in several directions. At last, his feet stopped moving.

Joe signaled for Opal to stop recording. He felt Jimmy's pulse.

"He's dead. Give me your phone."

Joe groaned with pleasure as he watched the video Opal had made. The torment and fear were palpable. He looked forward to using it in the future.

He sent an untraceable email that would land in Dutch's inbox, boasting about what he'd done to Gene Kelly. Joe wished he could see the fat studio chief's facial expression as he watched another actor in his movie meet his demise.

You Only Live Twice

"I knew I belonged to the public and to the world, not
because I was talented or even beautiful, but because
I had never belonged to anything or anyone else."
—Marilyn Monroe

"I think I was murdered."

I grabbed Marilyn around the waist and kissed her neck. "If you're dead, how could you feel this?"

"James, stop it." Marilyn pushed me away. "I'm serious. I've been studying the evidence."

It was Christmas Eve. We were in her trailer, studying our character binders.

"I've read every police report and biography," Marilyn said. "My body was covered in bruises. No drugs were found in my mouth or on my body. My autopsy was halted before it was completed. Someone high in government ordered it stopped for unknown reasons."

Her jaw clenched as she irately ruminated on these facts. I didn't interrupt.

"There were no drinking glasses found near my bed. How could I have swallowed all those pills with no water?" Marilyn scowled. "There was no indication of suicide, but lots of evidence of a cover-up. My body was moved before doctors could examine it. My diary was stolen. The official reports were altered to change the time of my death from 10 p.m. to 4 a.m."

"I'm sorry. Your death has always been surrounded by speculation and theories. I don't know if we'll ever know the truth . . . ."

Marilyn shook her head. "I dated powerful men who'd do anything to prevent scandal or blackmail—one of them killed me. Maybe because I got pregnant. What I always wanted most in life was to be a mother, but my lovers and the studios always made sure it never happened."

I felt sorry for Marilyn. At the same time, I was furious at Janie, because she'd made plans tonight without me.

It seemed contradictory, but her identities were so distinct, my emotions treated them separately. Marilyn was flirtatious, open and straightforward. On the other hand, Janie claimed our friendship was precious to her, and we'd spend holidays together. Yet tonight she planned to leave me alone on Christmas Eve. She wouldn't even tell me whom she was spending it with. I kept brooding over all of the handsome actors and executives at the studio, wondering which one she was dating.

"I was destined to be unhappy," Marilyn lamented. "I always dated men who couldn't offer what I want."

"What do you want?"

"A family. A stable marriage. Children."

"What about love?"

She shook her head in disdain. "Men promise love. They never deliver."

"I will." I moved quickly and kissed her on the lips.

"Are you crazy, James?" Marilyn shoved me in the chest. She pointed around the ceiling. "They're watching us, or at least listening."

"I'll take that risk." I moved toward her, placing my hands on her waist and trying to get a kiss.

She squirmed away. "You're like every guy. I thought you were romantic. Most men at least take me to dinner before trying to kiss me."

"Dinner? We can't leave the set."

"A girl deserves to be courted," Marilyn said.

"See me tonight as Janie." There, I said it.

Marilyn slapped me. Hard. The sound of her smack echoed off the wall. "I don't know any Janie! Get out of my trailer!"

I rubbed my cheek. "After your transformation, meet me at the water tower."

Marilyn slapped me again, even harder. "I don't know what you mean. Get out." She shoved me out the door and slammed it shut.

I shouted through her trailer door. "The water tower. Tonight. I'll wait for you."

I was so frustrated, I didn't care if we were being spied on.

After waiting two hours, I officially declared myself the world's biggest idiot. I knew I was pathetic, yet I decided to wait a little longer.

She's not coming. She doesn't care . . . She might not even know I'm James Dean . . .

Yet, if she's dating another actor in our movie . . . she must know his real identity.

Unrequited love was like starving, an unceasing ache in my stomach I'd had for years, which all the food in the world could never heal. It tormented my thoughts day and night. "What more can I do?" I cried, kicking the curb near the water tower.

My humiliation had an audience. Tonight was the studio's annual Holiday Party and the line to enter was next to the water tower. VIPs in ritzy tuxedos and glittery gowns eyed me disdainfully, treating me like the buffoon I was. In contrast to this apex of glamour, I loitered in jeans, a sweatshirt and my Darrin face.

Worse than the scornful gazes was the fact that I hadn't been invited to the party. I could hear raucous merriment from the studio's backlot streets. Was Janie at the party? Who'd invited her?

I had to find out.

A short fence protected the water tower and I scampered over it when no one was watching. I grabbed the metal handholds leading up to the tank and started to climb. I looked down almost immediately and cursed myself for being so stupid. It would be a pointless, humiliating death if I slipped. My wrists and calves both tingled, reminding me that any wrong move could be fatal.

I'm climbing a ladder, just for a glance at the party, while Janie's on a date at the party. It made me feel worthless.

I stopped caring if I fell or not. Janie wouldn't even be in Hollywood without me. I'd comforted her through her bleakest periods. Every time she'd given up, I'd encouraged her, even against my own best interests.

I recalled Janie at her lowest point, two years earlier, walking out of an office building, her head down like a demoralized POW, mascara running down her cheeks.

"They said I'm too fat," she had sobbed, pressing her face into my chest. Janie had entered the building overflowing with hope, and re-emerged looking like a puppy beaten with a stick.

"What happened?" I demanded, raging with hate at whoever had done this.

"They told me I lacked talent and wasn't thin enough to be an actress."

We were in Chicago, in the parking lot of a crappy brick building, after driving twelve hours so she could interview with a talent agency.

"They don't know shit about talent," I said. "They're not legitimate. Look at this lousy place. Besides, you shouldn't have to pay an agent to interview you."

"That's the worst part. They suck, and I'm beneath their standards." Janie covered her face with her hands and bawled. Not one of her little cries, but a despairing howl. She was so pure and innocent, and I was helpless to stop her pain.

It was the first time either of us had been outside of North Dakota. I'd wanted it to be special. I'd tried to save enough money to get tickets to a performance in Chicago's Theater District, but they were too expensive. Instead, I'd made a reservation at a fancy restaurant.

As her tears soaked my shirt, I cautiously put my arms around her and hugged her. She didn't resist.

I'd supported her dream, even though it would kill mine. I'd helped her contact talent agencies all over Chicago, although I knew if they hired her, I'd lose her forever. In two weeks, I'd graduate from high school, and there wasn't really any option for me, besides staying in Grafton and being a mechanic. The owner of a garage in town had offered me a job, and I didn't want to be a farmhand. My uncle had sold our farm after the fire.

Janie had worked as a waitress since her graduation two years earlier. We did community theatre together in the closest city, Grand Forks, and on weekends I'd help her mail headshots to agents. I prayed each night for her success, and felt guilty whenever I hoped she'd change her mind—and decide my love was better than the fleeting glamour of show biz.

"I'm terrible," Janie sobbed. "I should just give up."

My heart melted.

"A talent agency in Chicago is like a butler for an outhouse," I said.

Janie laughed.

"The real agents are in Los Angeles, in shiny glass offices," I said.

"With tans and Teslas."

"Exactly. That's why, as soon as I graduate, I'm moving to Los Angeles."

"What?" Janie lifted her head off my chest to peer at me. I wasn't sure why I'd said that, but it stopped her from crying.

"I'm obviously not staying in Grafton. To be an actor I have to be in Hollywood," I said.

"You're leaving? You don't even have a headshot."

"I'll get a professional one in LA and start auditioning."

Janie beamed at me with admiration. It was worth trashing my future for the expression on her face.

"What about your uncle?" Janie asked.

"He sold the farm. He doesn't need me."

"But you take care of him."

"My uncle encouraged me to go to LA," I lied. "He wants me to follow my dream."

Hope spread across Janie's face. She wiped off her tears.

"You should come with me, Janie. If we rented an apartment together, it would save money."

On the drive back, Janie was exuberant, planning the details of our drive to California. She wanted to leave the day after I graduated.

After dropping Janie at her apartment, guilt hit me like a sledgehammer. The dread of telling my uncle almost suffocated me. I drove slowly to the small home we had rented and parked in our driveway, waiting to get up enough nerve to tell my uncle I intended to leave.

Through the living room window, I spotted my uncle watching baseball on TV. A lump hit my throat when I saw his deformed, bandana-covered face. I'd never get used to it. How could I abandon him in this condition? He hated going out in public even for groceries.

He clicked off the TV when I stepped inside, eager for my news. "So, how was your trip? Tell me everything."

I shared the details. I felt like a traitor as I reached the part of telling Janie I intended to move to LA. Still, I repeated the conversation candidly.

"That's perfect," my uncle said. "There's a burn facility in California. I was thinking of moving there, but I didn't want to leave you alone."

"Really?"

Uncle Stanley put his hand on mine. "The barn fire will be worthwhile, if it finally gets you to take a chance."

My arm hit a metal bar at the base of the water tank and my daydream abruptly ended. I'd reached the top of the ladder.

I shimmied along the edge of the water tower, settling on a metal ledge. From my perch, I peered over the studio's backlot. Dutch spared no expense with anything he did. To create Impact Studio, he'd purchased three smaller Burbank studios and combined them into this grandiose studio lot. Everything he did had to be the biggest and best, including this party.

Exterior set designers had created a North Pole Village framed by lights strung between Christmas trees. In the center, a dance floor was surrounded by two-story-tall reindeer, snowmen, angels and elves.

From this height, I could only recognize two people. Santa Claus' red suit was unmistakable; Dutch Hollander was near him, so rotund that he made Santa look skinny. The other people looked minuscule, but they were VIPs, as only the most prominent people in show business had been invited.

I spotted a security guard squinting upward. Please look away. I remained motionless until she headed toward the party.

Janie would love this view of the studio, with the backlots lit up and the festivities glowing. I burst with happiness every time I realized her dream had come true. She'd always maintained a pure view of Hollywood, even though many people in our small town considered it superficial or self-righteous.

"Hollywood is the world's storyteller," she used to say. "For two hours, you can be a Pennsylvania miner, a Wall Street powerbroker, or an inner-city teacher. Movies change people."

She was right, of course. Done correctly, entertainment wasn't just about fantasies. It created empathy. The face-transforming machines had even more potential. They could take this voyeurism and make it reality. Anyone could become . . . anyone. Not vicariously, as a movie-watcher, but actually changing—

"DARRIN, COME DOWN IMMEDIATELY!" boomed a voice over a megaphone.

I looked down and saw Dutch. The obese studio chief stood below me with about ten security guards. He looked like a bowling ball in front of bowling pins.

"COME DOWN RIGHT NOW!" Dutch boomed again.

Shit. My short career was probably over.

Star Wars

The limousine stopped at the Getty Center's parking structure next to the tram, which transported visitors to the billion-dollar museum at the top of the hill.

Chief of Police William Bernardo assisted his wife, Sophia, out of the limo. They boarded the tram, poised to enjoy one of the most breathtaking vistas in Southern California, overlooking the San Gabriel Mountains, downtown LA, and the Pacific Ocean.

"I feel giddy," Sophia said, squeezing her husband's hand. "CNN says this is the most exclusive party ever. The media is jealous they're not allowed."

William had finally made it to the top, he realized. He clasped Sophia's hand and looked down upon the city he protected—a gorgeous wife, a distinguished career, and social interaction with the world's most famous people.

Soon the Getty came into sight, an architectural marvel constructed from 1.2 million square feet of clef-cut Italian travertine. A huge banner hung over the entrance:

'Our Cup Overflows' Charity Gala—Hosted by Larry Coates and Opal Wallace

The tram stopped, and the world's richest man was waiting to greet them.

"Welcome to the gala," Larry said.

"Wow, I didn't expect a personal greeting," William said. The LA Police Chief introduced himself and his wife.

"We're glad you're here. It's going to be a unique evening," Larry said.

"I'm as excited as a kid," Sofia said. "It's going to be the best Christmas Eve ever."

Sophia and William stepped inside and scanned the entrance hall.

"Oh, my, we don't belong here. Everyone has won an Oscar or a Grammy," Sophia said.

"Not everyone," William said. "I see two former presidents."

"Well, that makes me feel much better."

The police chief and his wife moved into the museum courtyard, which was jammed shoulder-to-shoulder with partygoers.

"Who do we dare talk to?" Sophia asked. "Everyone is mega-famous."

Suddenly, Opal Wallace stepped in front of them.

"Hey, I recognize you—" Opal proclaimed. "You keep this town safe. I'm very grateful for the work of the LAPD."

Sophia almost knocked her husband down to shake Opal's hand. "I think you're amazing . . . I've seen every episode of your show. I'm Sophia Bernardo, and this is my husband, William."

"Let me get you a drink." Opal gestured to a server, who instantly appeared with a tray of exotic drinks.

The police chief studied the server. Something was wrong. William's trained eyes instinctively constructed a police profile: Average chin. Average cheekbones. Average nose. Average forehead. Race unknown. No distinctive marks.

In four decades of police work, he'd never imagined such a plain-looking person could exist.

Opal took flutes of a milky liquid from the server and handed them to Sophia and William. "These are delicious."

As they sipped their drinks, every celebrity paused their conversation and turned to watch them. It was strange. The most famous people in the world . . . all staring at them.

William had to be hallucinating. Emerging from the crowd and walking toward them were two people identical to him and his wife. He felt lightheaded; his legs wobbled. William looked at his wife and her face was pale.

"Help! We've been drugged," the police chief cried.

He extended his hand for help, but not a single person moved to assist. Everyone watched, but no one interfered.

"We are the entertainment," he perceived.

The perfect duplicates stopped beside them. William glimpsed the horror on his wife's face. Then, she fell. He reached for her, but he faltered.

He plunged downward. *I'll never solve this case* . . . .

His body hit the floor with a thump, and people clapped. Immediately, men in white tuxedos rushed through the crowd, picked up the bodies and carried them away.

Joe Plain turned to the new police chief. "Enjoy the party. You'll get your instructions soon."

"Yes, sir. I'm ready."

Joe turned to new Sophia. "The spouses are in the Sculpture Garden. Go join them."

Once Joe walked away, the famous people started chatting again. A two-time Best Actress winner turned to VMA's Artist of the Year. "That was boring. I didn't even recognize them."

"Me, either. It's more fun to watch celebrities get replaced. I wonder who's next."

Before he finished speaking, a famous comedian arrived. Opal and Joe Plain reached their prey quickly. The comedian saw everyone watching and bowed to the crowd as he drank from his flute. As soon as he collapsed, everyone looked around eagerly to see who'd be next.

Now this is an efficient way to replace people, thought Joe.

Yet, Dutch Hollander's decision to host a party on the same night had complicated things. The celebrities who attended Dutch's party instead of his would need to be dealt with later.

The Good, the Bad, and the Ugly

"**D**ON'T MAKE ME WAIT!" Dutch bellowed.

I didn't have any other options, so I began to climb down the steel rungs of the water tower.

If Dutch fired me, I'd never get to be James Dean again.

I climbed down slowly, realizing this might be my last chance to ever be in the studio. As I descended, I looked at the indistinguishable faces below. In a way, the machines were like adding distance: faces could no longer be relied upon to identify a person. You couldn't tell who was who.

Did this make everyone equal? Was it possible to become an entirely new person?

None of this would impact me any longer, since my involvement with the machines was likely over. I reached the bottom and prepared to face my punishment.

"Follow me, Darrin," Dutch commanded.

I walked beside the studio chief while a retinue of security trailed behind us. We proceeded in silence. Would I be fired?

Dutch led me amongst various sound stages and a backlot street recreating an Old West town.

"Where are we going?" I ventured.

"The Costume Design Center," Dutch said.

When we reached the building, which was basically an 80,000-square-foot climate-controlled closet, Dutch guided me to the tuxedo department. "Take your pick."

"What?"

"Anyone who climbs a tower to see my party deserves an invitation," Dutch said. "But first, you need a tux."

The studio president waited while I hastily picked a tuxedo. I was tempted by a 1950s tux, but that would be pushing it, so instead I chose a modish one.

Dutch turned his back while I changed.

"I've always wanted to climb that tower." He patted his round belly. "I'm worried I'd get stuck."

"I'm sure the special effects people could get you down, sir."

Dutch snorted. "I like you, Darrin."

After I dressed, the studio president helped me with the tuxedo bow tie. I knew it was rare for an actor to get this much time with him.

"Sir, could I ask you a question about the transform-machines?"

"Of course."

"Have you considered how they could help people disfigured by burns?"

His eyes flashed kindness, revealing a compassionate side. "We absolutely have. Teddy Millner is researching that and many other uses."

"Really? Wow." As we returned to the party, I told Dutch about my uncle and the other residents of Berggren House.

"Helping people like your uncle is one of Teddy's priorities," Dutch said. "I'll tell him to keep you informed."

Dutch took long strides as we crossed the studio he'd created. I felt honored to be with him.

"I suppose, in a way, the face-changing machines could make someone an entirely new person," I said.

"People are more than appearance, Darrin."

"I know. But other traits can change, too."

Dutch shrugged. "Skills can be developed, I guess. But character traits are more innate."

He seemed settled about this, so I didn't push further. However, it seemed to me that personality could also change. In fact, traits could be divided into those that could be trained and those that were decided.

Then were all changes possible? Could qualities like patience and kindness be altered at will? That would truly create a new person.

We arrived at the North Pole Village, and Dutch enthusiastically ushered me in. "You're going to love this, Darrin."

He spent the next hour showing me off to his VIP buddies. The presidents of Disney, Fox, Sony, Universal and Warner Bros. all laughed as Dutch embellished my endeavor.

"He risked his life just to look at my party . . ." Dutch bragged. "He was dangling there, 100 feet high, and I was sure he was going to fall, but somehow he regained his balance . . ."

Dutch was boisterous, his charm infectious. I felt like a museum piece being appraised by experts as I shook hands with the world's top movie directors and producers.

Dutch's executive assistant, a shapely blonde woman named Devon, followed us and eyed me with overt distrust.

There were fountains of champagne, towers of sushi, and elves running a dessert factory. It was splendid beyond my imagination—and then it was suddenly a million times better.

I spotted Janie.

She wore a red Mrs. Claus suit, standing between elves and Santa, getting her picture taken with party guests. Our eyes met and her expression was priceless.

As if on cue, Dutch introduced me to Rex Shackleford, Hollywood's most renowned playboy. Rex was VP of Operations at Digital Impact and reported only to Dutch. He was a rakish man with sleek black hair, with the gumption to have brought two dates. I recognized both pretty faces from magazine covers.

"Rex, I want you to meet Darrin Clark," Dutch said. "He's an actor who almost died climbing the studio's water tower, trying to spot people like you."

"Nice to meet you, Darrin." Rex had a gleam in his eye as if he was full of secrets. "These are my friends, Sveltlana and Katalina." His dates kissed my cheeks, one on each side.

"Ladies, would you get us some drinks?" Rex said.

As soon as the women departed, Rex turned to me. "You're the guy playing James Dean."

I looked at Dutch, who nodded. Rex was a studio executive, so I assumed I could talk freely. "Yes," I said.

"I review the dailies with Orson sometimes, while he's deciding what footage to edit into the movie. You're fantastic."

"Thank you."

"Marilyn Monroe is so damn sexy. And she's into you. Have you slept with her yet?"

My mouth opened, but no words came out.

Rex slapped me on the back. "You need to hit that, Darrin. Then tell me about it."

"Sex in character is forbidden by their contract," Dutch said. "Besides, they can't leave the sound stage."

Rex winked at me. "I want to use the machines to change my girlfriends' faces. Imagine the possibilities." Dutch glared at him. "But of course, I never would."

"The machines aren't a sex toy," Dutch said sternly.

Rex elbowed me in the ribs. "Too bad, huh."

Jacqueline Dumont joined us, looking glamorous in a silky strapless candy apple red dress, which perfectly highlighted her slim figure. Dutch, Rex, and I complimented her on her outfit, but Devon didn't seem pleased.

"I think you've done a marvelous job transitioning from farm boy to movie star," Jacqueline said.

"Darrin is interested in how the machines can help people with burn injuries," Dutch said.

Jacqueline's eyes beamed enthusiastically. "It's very promising, Darrin. The studio is working on many non-entertainment uses of the machines. Burned skin is one of the most exciting. Teddy is in charge of that and sent me some promising test results last week. I'll make sure he shows you that report."

"Thank you, that's fantastic," I gushed. "This will change so many lives."

"We want to help people, Darrin. However, secrecy is still our top concern," Rex said.

"Absolutely," Dutch agreed. "Darrin understands that. The machines are going to propel him to the top of Hollywood."

I smiled appreciatively. *The top of Hollywood.* I certainly was meeting powerful people. Yet, I didn't see how far I'd advance in my career, since I couldn't talk about the movie and wouldn't get credit for it.

Live and Let Die

Joe Plain caressed the 25-inch barrel of the M40A5 sniper rifle.

Through the 12x50mm scope, he had a clear view of Rodeo Drive. His perch atop the roof of a clothing store was in the ideal spot, and he scanned the crowded street from the Beverly Wilshire Hotel to Brighton Way.

Joe turned the crosshairs onto the face of Elvis, centering the X on his boyish chin; then he moved the crosshairs to Audrey Hepburn, to Jimmy Stewart, and down the street to dozens of other hapless potential victims.

Of course, this wasn't the real Rodeo Drive, but an elaborate set made for a scene in Dutch Hollander's movie. The imitation Rodeo Drive was identical to the real one, except for a large piece of art, which Joe knew was critical to the scene. In the center of the street, a giant female shopper had been created, an elegant red-haired woman who would have stood 60 feet tall if she'd been standing. However, the colossal redhead shopper was reclined on the ground, leaning on one elbow, poised amidst proportionately-sized bags of retail treasures.

Finally, Joe spotted his target: James Dean.

Joe zoomed the scope's crosshairs onto James' face. What an arrogant ass, Joe thought as he watched his target flirt with Marilyn Monroe. He was tempted to pull the trigger right then. However, this wouldn't create the optimal amount of fear.

Joe could have selected any of the actors in the movie as his target, since it would scare the rest of them. The actors would fulfill a critical role in Joe's plan, and fear would allow them to be controlled. James Dean had been selected for personal reasons.

Joe wasn't normally patient, but he resigned himself to waiting a few minutes and not shooting until James Dean was the center of attention.

Speed

"Keep your speed constant at fifty-two," Orson instructed.

My heart was racing at 100 mph. I had just learned to balance on the machine, and now I had to somehow keep a constant speed.

"The engineers have designed the stunt perfectly. As long as your speed is constant, it's completely safe," Orson continued. He looked a little guilty for making me do something so dangerous.

My hands were sweating, and I thought I might throw up. My mind raced for excuses to avoid the stunt.

"Are you sure you want to do this?" Marilyn asked.

I faked a smile. "Absolutely. It's going to be fun."

Ten minutes later, Orson was filming Marilyn, Bogie and Elvis at an outdoor café on Rodeo Drive. Marilyn wore a chiffon Versace mini cocktail dress and a Tiffany diamond necklace, both holiday gifts from Bogie in an earlier scene.

Although presently off-camera, my heartrate was skyrocketing. Since the Vegas scene, I'd encouraged Orson to give me more dangerous stunts, as this was the most effective way I could think of to impress Marilyn. As soon as Orson devised this death-defying feat, I regretted my prodding.

It was December 26. Yesterday, Janie and I had spent a perfect Christmas together. We'd strolled the beach in Santa Monica and laughed at selfies I'd taken with her in her Elf costume the previous night. I knew she was burning with curiosity about why Dutch had bestowed such close attention on me, but she hadn't asked.

After our beach walk, we'd hiked in Griffith Park. Then, we saw a movie at The Grove. In the darkness of the theater, I'd considered holding Janie's hand, but decided not to risk ruining a perfect day. After all, Darrin was only her platonic friend.

In the glow of these memories, I sat proudly on a red Triumph motor-cycle and observed the scene. The set was active, full of shoppers and café patrons, each one a famous legend. Nearly every actor in our movie was present and in this scene. Only Gene Kelly was absent. The actor playing Gene must be very sick to miss time in character. On one of the roofs, I noticed a man moving, probably a set designer who'd come to watch. If Orson saw him, he'd be lucky not to get fired.

On cue, I drove the motorcycle toward the café. I was on camera now. I'd practiced riding for a few days, and felt almost comfortable when going slow and straight. Every time I twisted the throttle, I had to convince myself not to be afraid. *I'm James Dean. I'm James Dean. I'm James Dean.* James Dean would be thrilled to perform this stunt.

"James!" Marilyn waved. "Over here."

Bogie frowned as I drove the motorcycle to their outdoor table and parked beside it. Bogie gave Elvis a disapproving stare when the King of Rock pulled out a seat for me.

"Bogie bought me a whole new wardrobe," Marilyn said, holding up a half dozen shopping bags.

"We're going to Paris next weekend to open a club," Bogie said. "Then to the Cannes Film Festival."

Marilyn laughed. "He even bought me a tiara."

She held up a graceful, sparkling jewelry piece, and I imagined elegant parties with her on Bogie's arm. As she lifted the tiara into the air, a man on a gold motorcycle snatched it out of her hand and zoomed away.

"Someone stop him!" Bogie yelled.

I jumped onto my motorcycle, and it roared to life. I smiled at Marilyn and shot after the criminal. The robber dodged a few cars and sped down the center of the street. I accelerated in pursuit.

A Maserati pulled onto the street, forcing the robber into the far-left lane. There were too many cars for him to escape if he stayed on the street. He glanced back at me, smiled, and drove onto the median, heading toward the giant statue of a female shopper. The robber sped up and drove his motorcycle up the purse of the artwork as if it was a ramp. He jumped into the air, soaring twenty feet before landing.

I looked at my speedometer: forty-five. Not fast enough. My jump had to be at precisely fifty-two.

The Maserati blocked my way, and I aimed toward the median as I added throttle. Orson promised I'd be fine if I had the right speed.

I checked the speedometer: fifty-four. Too fast. This was crazy. Just balancing was hard enough without keeping a constant speed.

In my peripheral vision, I spotted movement on the roof where I'd seen the man before.

What the fuck? The man was leaning over the roof holding a rifle.

I glanced up and almost crashed when I saw the man's vacant face—he had a vile grin on a strangely plain face.

I skidded to a halt. A bullet buzzed past my ear. Or was it my imagination?

"Cut!" Orson cried.

I pointed to the roof. "Up there. A guy had a gun."

Everyone turned upward, but the man was gone.

"Chicken," Bogie said loudly.

"No, really. A man had a rifle," I declared.

Orson pointed at three studio security guards. "Check the roof and all around the building. Be careful."

Five minutes later, a guard called Orson from the roof. "There's no sign of anyone."

"Look harder," Orson instructed.

"So, what did this alleged gunman look like?" Bogie asked me.

"He was very average-looking. I couldn't tell his race or age."

Bogie rolled his eyes. "Average-looking? That's the best description you have?"

All the actors had gathered around. Bogie was enjoying this. "You know, kid, it would be nicer to us to just admit you're scared, rather than waste our time."

I imagined my fist hitting his nose, followed by a knee to his gut. Instead, I stayed silent, hoping for corroboration of my claim.

The security guards reported to Orson several times, reaffirming there was no sign of any gunman. They couldn't find any bullet or shell casing. As we waited, I felt everyone's eyes on me. The studio had spent millions on the set. The evidence made me look like a coward. Even Marilyn had a questioning look in her eyes.

After an hour, with no hint of the plain-faced man, Orson approached me with a sympathetic expression. "We'll find a stunt man who looks like you from the back. We won't need to transform his face. We'll show the jump from the back."

"No. I can do it."

I was insistent. Finally, Orson consented. We began the scene again, Bogie acting even more condescending than ever. However, I was too afraid to be concerned about Bogie.

Would the gunman or the jump kill me?

Once again, the robber stole the tiara, and I jumped on the Triumph. Soon we were both speeding back toward the artwork of the reclined shopper. The robber successfully executed a jump over the sculpture's purse, and then the Maserati forced me toward the center of the sculpture.

I checked my speed: fifty-three. I throttled back a tiny bit and glanced up at the roof where the man had been. I didn't see him.

Speed check: fifty. I wondered about my odds of survival.

I added some throttle as the motorcycle tires transitioned from street to gown, and drove up the torso and shoulder of the sculpture. My eyes fixed on the spot where the motorcycle would run out of artwork. A split-second later, I was flying.

Palm fronds, store fronts and pedestrians seemed frozen below me. I was suspended in space and it was eerily quiet. Then I descended and landed smoothly on a shopping bag, with an almost imperceptible thump, and drove down the bag onto the ground. Adrenaline rushed through me and I nearly screamed in elation, but I still had to catch the thief.

I merged seamlessly onto the street and dodged several cars before swerving onto the sidewalk, following the thief as had been choreographed. Finally, he crashed into a flower stand. I plucked the tiara from his hand, did a U-turn, and roared back down Rodeo Drive to where Marilyn, Bogie and Elvis watched.

Marilyn beamed. Bogie looked like he'd been cheering for the thief. In the script, I was supposed to toss the jewelry piece to Marilyn without stopping and blast away—but I wasn't in the mood for that.

I screeched to a stop in front of Marilyn, stepped off the motorcycle and looked into her eyes. I slipped the tiara onto her forehead.

Bogie moved forward. "Thank you. Marilyn and I are grate—"

He shut up when I kissed Marilyn on her lips. I held her passionately, prolonging the kiss, my heart racing more than it had during the stunt. When I pulled away, Marilyn stared at me with big doe eyes.

I winked at her, climbed on the motorcycle, and roared down the street.

"Bravo!" Elvis cried.

Clear and Present Danger

———— ~~ ————

A drone stopped by her chest.

"Whoa! What's this?" Marilyn asked as her eyes adjusted to the darkness.

The drone hovered in front of her, and she noticed it was carrying a tray with a glass of wine. She picked up the glass and sipped while examining her surroundings.

Perhaps I'd gotten carried away. Using all the resources of a movie studio, I'd transformed the diner on the set to a romantic venue. Everything I could imagine, I'd done to make the atmosphere unforgettable.

Marilyn examined the streams of lights floating mysteriously around the ceiling, forming patterns of flowers, trees, and constellations. She walked to a table, where cute robotic animals offered her meats, fruits and cheeses.

"This isn't what I was expecting." She accepted chocolate from an adorable talking bunny.

I'd invited Marilyn to dinner and a movie, using a formal printed invitation I'd left in her trailer a week earlier. I'd been preparing for this evening since my visit to my uncle, but the time was unfolding perfectly. It was two days after our passionate Rodeo Drive kiss, which I hoped would spring into even more romance. Marilyn and I were free from 5 p.m. tonight till noon tomorrow while Orson filmed the scene with Einstein, Tesla, and the other scientists. The night was ours to use as passion led.

When I'd asked Orson for permission to use the interior of the sound stage's diner, he'd said he'd need to check with Dutch. The studio president had called me himself, and given his blessing. It had been an awkward conversation, as Dutch found my situation humorous, yet my portly boss had said yes.

It had taken me a few days to cover the furniture and walls with dark green satin sheets. I'd decorated the room with movie props, filling empty space with movie memorabilia. Then I'd placed bouquets of lilies, azaleas, and tulips on every unused surface.

"How did you learn to use all these special effects?" Marilyn asked as a constellation of stars spelled her name.

"Teddy Millner taught me. He's a romantic at heart. He even showed me how to program these drones in coordinated patterns."

"He's by far the nicest studio executive I've ever met, and I've met a lot," Marilyn said.

Teddy had also brought me a binder full of test results of how the transform-machines could help burn victims. It looked like they could fix almost any skin problem. However, as much as I longed to, I couldn't discuss the machines with Marilyn.

"Hey, what's this, you dirty rascal?" Marilyn asked, when she spotted what resembled a semicircular bed. "I thought we were going to watch a movie?"

In the center of the dance floor, I'd created a bed-like object, and surrounded it with three 80-inch curved television screens. The TV's had been programmed to loop through videos of romantic destinations around the world—Victoria Falls, The Taj Mahal, Fiji, The Grand Canyon, etc.—with syrupy music matching each location.

"It's not a bed, it's two sofas and some footrests shoved together. If you recline in the center, it's almost like traveling the world."

Using blankets and pillows, I'd created the coziest niche possible.

Marilyn wagged her finger at me. "Now, you better behave . . . yet it does look incredibly comfy."

She sat on the makeshift bed and scooted across the blankets until she was in the middle. I followed behind until our legs were touching. Her bosom pressed against me through her white sweater as she leaned on me to get into a comfortable position. With sultry, sexy eyes, she gazed at me. Heaven on earth. Everything was as perfect as I'd imagined. Would we even watch the movie?

My mind started to unravel, slipping into the usual daze I experienced whenever I found myself near Janie. I couldn't let this happen. I needed to remain in control.

Be fearless. Be manly. Be James Dean.

I'd spent my life trying to impress Janie as a platonic friend. My new tactic required the opposite behavior. Janie endowed Marilyn's nature completely whenever she had her face, even off camera. My strategy was to target her as Marilyn—an iconic sex goddess who needed to be impressed and entertained—while maintaining a constant undertow of tenderness in order to appeal to the wholesome farmgirl deep inside her.

Marilyn Monroe had never really picked a lover, but had been captured by the most aggressive, confident pursuers. She'd dated rich, powerful Alpha-males, who didn't take no for an answer.

I directed a drone carrying a wine bottle to hover over us, and refilled Marilyn's glass. The next drone brought us crackers and cheese. Marilyn nestled even closer into my chest. I massaged her shoulder with one hand and clicked on the movie.

Fifty First Dates began to play on the center screen. "Wow, it's so high tech. I've never seen anything like this. It feels naughty." Marilyn rested a hand on my leg.

The drone lights on the ceiling formed a heart with Marilyn's initials in the center. Her eyes glinted joyfully. "I can't believe you did all this for me."

I put a hand under her thigh and twisted my body over hers. Marilyn smiled as our lips moved towards each other. My heart quivered in anticipation. This would be our first kiss in private.

"Hey, are you guys in here?" The malt shop door opened, drenching us in light.

Bogie stepped into the room and switched on the lights. My props and drones looked like childish toys in the brightness. "It's lucky I found you, Marilyn," Bogie said. "We need to rehearse for tomorrow's scene. We're dancing a waltz together at a party in Europe."

Marilyn and I jumped apart and sat up.

"Get out, Bogie, or I'll have drones slice off your giant ears," I shouted.

"What's going on in here?" John F. Kennedy stepped inside the diner's entrance and stood beside Bogie. He projected a handsome grin when he spotted Marilyn.

Marilyn slid off my makeshift bed and smiled at JFK. "Hello, Mr. President." He was only a senator in my world, but Marilyn was also filming with him in the 1960s sets.

Bogie and John both kissed Marilyn on her cheek and wrangled for her attention. I seethed with anger, thinking the situation couldn't possibly get any worse.

"So, this is where the party is," another voice said.

Frank Sinatra swaggered into the room. "Interesting digs," Frank said, examining the lights hanging from drones. He went to the table with the robotic animals, taking some cheese from a squirrel and a glass of wine from a raccoon.

"How sweet. It's like being in a Disney cartoon."

I was ready to explode. My date had become a sausage fest of Marilyn's former paramours. My fists clenched as I fought the urge to scream.

Bogie pulled on a string of lights held by a passing drone, and the drone crashed. The other drones bobbed around, not sure what to do. "It's like the kiddie room at a carnival," Bogie said laughing.

The three men looked at the makeshift bed I'd made. "Marilyn is a grown woman," President Kennedy said. "Did you really think this would impress her?"

Be cool. Don't lose control.

I wanted to shout and fight, but if I behaved like an immature little boy, I'd look even worse. *Calm yourself. There will be future chances with Marilyn.*

"I left something in the kitchen." I gritted my teeth and walked into the kitchen. As soon as the door closed behind me, I gripped a counter and tried not to hyperventilate.

We'd been so close to our first romantic kiss in private. I'd waited my entire life for this moment, and it had nearly been perfect. Those conceited assholes had ruined everything. They didn't know Janie like I did. I'd loved her forever, and they were just acting.

I peeked out from the kitchen and saw the three men charming Marilyn. They'd surrounded her like wolves hunting a bunny. They reveled in impressing each other and delighted in the game of seduction with the prize of a chance at passionate sex.

I wished Marilyn would ask them to leave, but she seemed quite happy. My heart felt like the tar used to patch a road which everyone drove over. I headed toward the back exit of the malt shop for an easy escape. It would save a lot of humiliation.

"Somewhere over the Rainbow" was playing, the ukulele Hawaiian version from Fifty First Dates, which I hadn't paused. I listened instead of leaving.

It had to be the world's most therapeutic song . . . breathing calm and slow, I realized my position with Janie was a billion times better now than I could have imagined three months ago. For a decade, I'd failed to date Janie. Now I was so close. The competition had elevated, but so had my status in her life.

I could succeed at my dream. That needed to be my focus, not these assholes.

There were just two hurdles to overcome. First, I needed to make her fall in love with James Dean. Then, I had to transfer that love to an identity I could live outside the studio. It was all possible, with careful planning . . . and a transform-machine.

Retreating out the back of the diner would make me seem weak. I took a deep breath and stepped back into the main dining area. *Be cool. Stay composed.*

Marilyn was slow dancing with Joe DiMaggio—when had he gotten here? Bogie, Frank and JFK stood nearby, drinking and chatting.

All these rivals were exceedingly handsome and confident. They weren't concerned about the competition. I felt hopeless and inadequate.

They are failures! They'd had chances with Marilyn before, and she hadn't stayed with any of them. They'd provided Marilyn with excitement and helped her with her career, but they were jealous, controlling womanizers. Well, DiMaggio wasn't a womanizer, but he was the most jealous of all.

I intended to learn from their mistakes.

Besides, I had a great advantage—they didn't know she was Janie. They were just actors, trying to satisfy their egos and indulge their lust.

I looked at myself in a mirror and saw a terrible hypocrite. I'm James Dean trying to romance Marilyn Monroe... and I'm judging them for being actors?

If my rivals were half as deeply into their characters as I was, their new identities had become second nature. This explained why they were so confident. They had seduced Marilyn in the past and, being certain of their authenticity, were sure they'd succeed again.

Marilyn finished dancing with DiMaggio, and headed towards me. My heart quickened. Maybe she realized my love was the sincerest. I felt light and buoyant as she gave me a dazzling smile.

"You're sweet, James," Marilyn said, kissing me on the cheek. She continued past me to Kennedy, Bogie and Sinatra, followed by DiMaggio. JFK handed her a drink, and her four paramours laughed heartily at something she said.

I was sweet? A peck on the cheek? This was the kiss of romantic death.

Silence of the Lambs

The special look in their eyes made it worthwhile.

Joe Plain entered a warehouse where hundreds of terrified people glared at him with fear and loathing. The putrid smell and despairing faces fit Joe's imagination of a concentration camp, which in a way it was.

The poor souls were memorizing their future identities fervently, hoping they'd be selected. They made a show of holding their identity folders as they stood next to their cot while Joe passed.

Joe felt like a prison commander inspecting a barrack. However, he was actually their judge, executioner, and potential savior. Joe could make them someone great and powerful. Or he could terminate them.

Joe had purchased this warehouse in Glendale to hold future replacements. The industrial warehouse was furnished with rows of military-style bunks, and the captives watched him with trepidation as he strode down the center aisle.

He had met them in different places, but now they all had the same goal—memorize their parts perfectly, and hope Joe Plain blessed them with approval. Some would receive the identities they wanted, others would not. Some had even volunteered, before learning the horror their life would become.

Joe strutted from one end of the warehouse to the other, followed by his four brawny bodyguards. Joe had tested many potential bodyguards and selected the ones who most enjoyed violence. They'd been promised special identities, if they proved worthy.

Absolute control was gratifying, but it wasn't Joe's true love. Joe's passion was fear.

Killing someone actually diminished your power. When you killed someone, you had one less person to control. On the other hand, fear could be sustained and enjoyed. Joe's great talent was converting fear into power. And power into fear. A wonderful cycle.

Joe stopped near the main door of the warehouse floor. It could be seen from nearly all the bunks. "Place the sign there," he instructed.

One of his bodyguards lifted a five-foot-long sign over his head and pressed it against the warehouse wall. Another guard took a hammer and nailed the sign to the wall.

Joe stood back to admire the sign. He'd conceived the message himself:

If I am not back soon, keep waiting.

It was very funny, Joe decided. He proudly surveyed the room, examining the petrified, defeated faces. Memorize and wait. That's all they could do.

"No one gets to have a new identity today," Joe announced. He savored the anguish before he exited the warehouse's main interior, followed by his bodyguards.

"Stay here," Joe told his guards. He climbed the stairs to the office on the second floor. The room had been designed to be the foreman's office, a row of windows overlooking the warehouse main interior. Gazing through the one-way windows, Joe saw his captives chatting with frustration and hopelessness. It calmed him like watching pet mice run around in a glass cage. They were too afraid to be angry with Joe. A mouse didn't get angry at a cobra.

The suitcase Joe had requested was on his desk, brought by an army colonel he had created by replacing the original. Joe opened it and saw a green brick with a small circuit board strapped to it. The C4 bomb was beautiful in its simplicity. Joe couldn't help himself and picked it up and cradled it like a baby.

After James Dean ruined things at the Rodeo Drive set, Joe had been enraged. A minor setback, but his first. Joe had disliked James since their first interaction at the studio. Now, he burned with a desire to make him suffer.

The bomb would fit perfectly in the podium which Dutch would soon be using at the sound stage. As his other identity, Joe could come and go from the studio as he wished, and easily learn Dutch's schedule, so it would be simple to place the bomb. Soon the actor playing James Dean would have to watch people he cared about die.

The person Joe needed—and desired—dead more than anyone else would be eliminated. James and many others would be crushed.

Joe took pride in his ability to act logically and strategically, while harnessing the fury smoldering inside him. Anything that hindered his plan, even in the slightest, would be brutally punished. By New Year's Eve, James Dean would no longer be a concern.

Joe placed the C-4 and its remote detonator back in the suitcase. He pondered the blast radius it would create at the studio. There were people he wanted to harm and those he must not. He was honing his skill at producing the perfect mix of death, fear and grief.

An Affair to Remember

The crowd gave me an excuse to press against Marilyn. Boldly, I put an arm around her waist. I smelled the lemon and neroli in her Chanel No. 5 and pulled her closer.

"Dutch told me to wear my dress from *The Seven Year Itch*," Marilyn said.

I admired her shapely legs, and imagined the dress blowing upward, revealing her thighs as it did in the iconic movie scene. The thought sent an impulse to my groin.

Forty-eight hours had passed since my fiasco of a date. Marilyn had been extra flirtatious since then—with both me and my rivals. I couldn't tell if she was simply enjoying the attention, trying to behave like the original Marilyn, or selecting a romantic partner. Maybe all three.

Almost the entire cast from the 1950s was crowded together, in a festive mood as tomorrow was New Year's Eve. Our attention was focused on a raised platform, which had been built in the sound stage for this occasion. Above the dais on a large screen, a clip was looping from the original *Star Wars*, the scene in which Princess Leia grasps onto Luke Skywalker as he swings on a grappling hook across a chasm on the Death Star.

Dutch, Rex, Teddy and Orson stood on the platform. Marilyn and I were behind the gazebo, pushing forward, trying to get a better view.

"I'm tingling with excitement. They're going to announce something historic," Marilyn said.

Dutch walked to the podium and greeted us with an avuncular smile. "Welcome, everyone. You're all doing fantastic. The movie is going great, and today we begin another important phase of your work.

"Each of you is a legend. But will you be a legend 10,000 years from now? You deserve to be. You're the original icons. Unfortunately, you'll be forgotten by future generations unless you keep up with innovations in media formats.

"For example, one of you is the world's greatest sex symbol," Dutch continued. A photo of Marilyn replaced the *Star Wars* loop on the screen. "Another of you is regularly ranked as the greatest actor in history." Humphrey Bogart's face was shown next to Marilyn's.

A jolt of jealousy hit me.

"What if we could do this?" Dutch asked.

The photos disappeared and the *Star Wars* loop was shown again. However, this time Marilyn and Bogie had replaced Leia and Luke. Marilyn looked artificial and awkward. Somehow, Bogie looked completely real, as if he had been originally cast as Luke Skywalker.

The gasp of awe from his audience made Dutch smile.

Dutch stepped aside, and Rex moved to the podium. "How can Bogie look perfect in a movie he never filmed?" Rex asked. "It's because most of our 1940s' cast, including Bogie, has already filmed their legacy scenes. These scenes only take a few hours, but they're one of the most important parts of your contract."

Marilyn frowned. She hadn't been considered a big enough star in the forties to be included in that cast.

"Today we'll begin filming legacy scenes of our 1950s' cast to ensure your immortality," Rex continued. "When we finish, we'll have a 3-D digital database that can be used in any media format the future imagines. Even holograms, robotic images or virtual reality. Once your legacy scenes are done, we'll be able to place you in any setting, in any costume, doing any action. Teddy Millner is leading this project, and he'll explain how it's done."

Teddy approached the podium, looking nervous. He'd never addressed us as a group before. In contrast to the expensive suits worn by Dutch, Rex, and Orson, Teddy wore a Rolling Stones t-shirt and a pair of faded jeans.

"The legacy scenes are filmed by special cameras in front of a green screen," Teddy said. "Motion sensors will be attached to your body and you'll be given a series of movements to perform."

The video screen showed Bogie in front of the green screen, performing actions like walking, jumping, throwing, punching and kicking.

"Next, you'll recreate famous scenes that your character did. It's your movement and expressions that matters, not the words."

The video screen showed Bogie reenacting a scene from *Casablanca* in front of a green screen.

"You are each 99% identical to your character, and the results are amazing."

The screen split, showing the scene of *Casablanca* on both sides. The left side was labeled "Original", the right side labeled "Created from Legacy Scene."

The reproduction was almost flawless, but I discerned tiny differences between the original and the new Bogie.

"Then you'll get hypnotized and repeat the scenes," Teddy said. "The hypnotism exposes any mental biases which might produce inaccuracies."

The screen showed Bogie in front of the green screen again, repeating the scene. His expression seemed slightly more serious.

"Computers will correlate all of this acting, creating a perfect enactment of your character. Compare Bogie in 1942 with Bogie now."

The split screen view of *Casablanca* was shown again, but now they were identical. Either it was a fraud or the technology was perfect.

"The differences are gone. We will have a 3-D digital rendering that can flawlessly portray you. Then, we can put you anywhere."

A scene from *Titanic* appeared, with two lovers at the bow of the ship. However, Bogie was holding Kate Winslet instead of Leonardo DiCaprio. It should have been shocking, but it wasn't. It looked natural.

"The detail is far more accurate than the human eye can see, even in three dimensions," Teddy added.

I whispered to Marilyn. "This makes us expendable. It doesn't matter if we're injured or fired."

"Or dead," Marilyn whispered back.

Teddy smiled at his audience. "The legacy scenes will never be used without your permission. Dutch and Rex have guaranteed—"

A deafening explosion shook the room. Teddy was thrown backward as the podium exploded into flames. People all around us screamed as we were showered with smoldering wood and debris.

An ominous cracking sound filled the air. I saw terror in Dutch's eyes as the wood beneath his massive body started to fracture. Then the platform collapsed, knocking Dutch, Rex and Orson to the floor.

I grabbed Marilyn and pulled her behind the gazebo, safe from being trampled. I held her tight, trying to think as people scattered around us. A bomb most have been inside the podium. Through the smoke, I saw Jimmy Stewart and Ike Eisenhower holding fire extinguishers, putting out flames on the wreckage of the platform and the sound stage wall.

When Dutch's silhouette appeared through the smoke, I ran to him.

"Are you okay?"

"He's dead." Dutch stood over Teddy's bloody and broken body.

A few feet away, Orson cursed as Grace Kelly wrapped a cloth around his leg. Rex was walking in a circle, looking dazed.

Dutch seemed unharmed physically, so I went to Rex. "Are you okay?"

"Um. I think so." He was clearly in shock, so I inspected him for possible injuries.

"You don't seem hurt. Maybe you should sit down," I suggested.

Alarms screeched and sirens drew nearer to our location. It triggered something in my mind. For months, I'd be trying to plan a way to leave the studio in character. This was an opportunity to escape, maybe my only one. I shook off the thought. I couldn't abandon my friends in an emergency. I looked around to see who I could help.

Aside from Teddy, there didn't seem to be any serious injuries. Everyone hurt was being attended by several people. I didn't see a way to be useful. Dutch, Rex, and many other people clustered around Teddy's body.

I didn't want to be disrespectful of Teddy. What would Teddy tell me to do, if he'd survived? The chaos would only last a few more minutes.

Teddy would want me to take advantage of the situation.

I won't forget you, Teddy. I'll find out who did this. I hope you'd approve of what I'm about to do.

I walked back to where Rex was sitting. "Can I have your car keys?"

"Huh. Why?"

I glanced toward Marilyn. "To have sex."

Rex grinned. He handed me a keychain. "You have to tell me the details."

"Thanks," I said, rushing toward my trailer.

I returned to the gazebo with a duffle bag and grabbed Marilyn's hand. "Follow me."

"Where?" Marilyn asked.

"Out of here."

I led Marilyn to the sound stage wall behind the podium carnage. The wall was badly burnt and with a kick of my foot, the wood split apart. A few more kicks, and there was an opening.

I glanced back to where Teddy's body was encircled by people. "It feels wrong to leave him."

Marilyn clasped my hand. "Teddy would understand. Take me away from here, James."

I squeezed through the opening. Marilyn followed. It was dusk and Mount Lee looked purple in the distance. Sirens were coming from multiple directions.

"Hurry," I said, taking her hand and leading her across the studio lot to Rex's personal parking spot.

"Oh heavens, a Duisenberg?" Marilyn gawked at the 1920s symbol of glamour with its long flowing fenders and luxurious curves.

"A Duisenberg Model A. It used to belong to Rudolph Valentino, according to Rex."

"It's so romantic. I wish I had a fur stole."

The sirens sounded even closer. "Get in." I opened the convertible door. This was infinitely more seductive than my used Taurus.

"We can't. We'll be seen," Marilyn protested.

I reached into my bag and handed Marilyn a masquerade ball mask with long flowery feathers. I put on my mask, which was a lion.

"They're so cute," Marilyn giggled as she put on her mask.

"It's almost New Year's Eve. People will assume we're going to a ball."

The eight cylinders purred when I started them, and I sped toward the studio entrance. The sirens increased until the sound became painful, and then the gate opened for three fire trucks. As the last truck entered, I switched lanes, flashed my pass and shot out the gate before it shut.

"We're free!" Marilyn screamed.

"I've been planning ways to escape for weeks. I've had this bag ready and have been waiting for any chance." My gut ached as I pictured Teddy's bloody body. "I never imagined it would happen because of a murder."

Love Me Tender

For the first time in half a century, Marilyn Monroe and James Dean were alive and free. I would grieve Teddy's death when I returned to earth. At the moment, I was flying too high.

Each time a car passed, Marilyn held her mask in front of her face, giggling blissfully until she took it off again. Somewhere under there was Janie, but she was behaving almost fully like Marilyn. The combination of danger, rebelliousness, freedom and romance was intoxicating. I was only James Dean; I didn't even want to think about the name Darrin.

I glanced at Marilyn as we drove from Sunset Boulevard to Coldwater Canyon. Seas of sparkling lights illuminated The Valley on both sides of the convertible. A part of me hoped she didn't know who I really was.

A truck passed our Duisenberg. Marilyn pulled off her mask, stood up, lifted her hands, and shrieked in rapture. Her platinum hair danced in the moonlight as her legendary dress undulated like a sail in a storm. In the midst of this fame-crazed metropolis, I was—in every significant way—alone with the most famous actress of all time.

I felt guilty for being so exuberant when a friend had just been murdered. Forgive me, Teddy. This opportunity may never happen again.

I turned from Coldwater Canyon onto Mulholland Drive. Marilyn bounced and screamed, her hands raised like she was on a roller coaster. She seemed happier with every swerve and acceleration. I saw a woman who'd struggled as a child, been manipulated as an adult, and now only wished to be unbridled to live her own life.

I drove to my favorite view of The Valley, a secluded opening at the top of Mulholland, and parked between an oak tree and the cliff. Across the Valley, the famous Hollywood Sign shone in white lights. A glimmering horizon twinkled like moonlight on an ocean.

"Well, razz my berries," Marilyn said, standing to admire the view. She bounced into her seat, sitting cross-legged with a zestful gaze. "What's in the bag?"

I reached into the duffle bag and revealed a bottle of wine.

Her face beamed. "Dom Pérignon 1953—my favorite."

"And your favorite music. Sinatra and Fitzgerald."

"Far out, James. You're the most."

Marilyn quickly gulped her first glass of bubbly. I did, too.

She lifted her enticing legs onto my lap. "You're my hero. You freed us from our tyrannical overlords."

I brushed her hair back with my fingers and kissed her neck. "This is historic. We need to make it worthwhile." I placed my other hand on the exposed part of one of her silky legs.

"You're such a bad boy." She laughed and nearly spilled her drink. "Oops." A few drops landed on the upholstery.

"I wonder if this really was Valentino's car?" I pondered.

"Why not? This is the real dress from *The Seven Year Itch*. It's worth more than the car."

My finger gently traced Marilyn's cheeks. No master painter could render colors so skillfully—her creamy skin, ivory teeth, sapphire eyes, auburn eyebrows, lush ruby lips . . .

I opened the bag further, showing her the bread, cheese, meat and fruit I'd prepared.

"Yummy." Her tongue traced her lips seductively. "This will be the most perfect date in history. Literally."

"That's up to us." I put my hands on her face and kissed her.

Our mouths melded, and I tasted the wine on her tongue. She moaned and forced our bodies together.

It was heavenly. I closed my eyes. For years, I'd dreamed of kissing her.

I cupped her breast, and she moaned louder. My tongue and hands explored, and she sighed hungrily, pushing our bodies close. I opened my eyes, surprised to see Marilyn's face where I'd been imagining Janie's.

Well, their body was the same . . .

I pulled the dress off her shoulder. She wasn't wearing a bra, and my mouth went straight to her left nipple. Her marvelous, firm, voluptuous breast was in my mouth. I sucked hard, my hand between her legs.

"Oh, James, yes," Janie cried.

No, not Janie. She was Marilyn. I needed to think of her as Marilyn while she was. That's what she wanted. Besides, it was Marilyn's voice and Marilyn's face. It didn't make sense for Janie to be with James Dean.

My fingers probed further, as my expanding staff pressed against my pants.

"Oh, yes, don't stop," Marilyn moaned.

A car drove by, and she covered her breasts with her hands.

"Wait . . ." Marilyn sighed. "Is there somewhere private we could go?"

I took a deep breath and restrained myself. "Yes. I know the perfect place."

"Drive fast," she said as I started the Duisenberg and pulled onto the road.

We put on our masks, and Marilyn fed me as I drove, first grapes, then blackberries. She kissed my neck as her hand massaged my leg. I badly needed to loosen my belt.

My whole body trembled with each glance at her—an untamable spirit with glistening eyes, flowing moon-lit hair, and unconstrained laughter.

"Where are we going?" she asked when I headed toward Old Pasadena.

I turned onto Raymond Avenue. "I've got a surprise for you."

We drove past several industrial buildings, until I turned into a parking lot full of cars behind a row of enormous connected warehouses. I parked in a dark spot beside a fence.

"Follow me." I grabbed her hand, and together we ran in the moonlight, laughing as we hurried toward the back of one of the massive warehouses.

The first door we checked was unlocked, and we stepped inside.

"Oh my God, James. I've heard about this."

Flower-covered floats, the size of houses, filled the warehouse.

"It's like stepping into a watercolor painting," Marilyn exclaimed.

She spun around, dazzled by the millions of colorful flowers. She smiled at me. "The fragrance . . . this must be how heaven smells."

"These floats will be in the Rose Bowl parade in two days," I said.

In the distance we heard a radio and voices. The row of warehouses was conjoined, revealing floats as far as we could see. Some of the floats had lights directed on them, people still busy attaching flowers.

"Those are volunteers, working on floats that aren't finished yet," I explained. "The work never stops during the final week before the parade."

We walked around several floats, each over 30-feet tall. There were jungle animals, mermaids, and ballerinas—all made out of flowers.

I led Marilyn to a float that looked like our solar system. It had a huge sun in the middle, about forty feet high, and nine planets circling it. "Climb on."

I helped Marilyn onto the float, and we climbed a ladder to the sun. A platform was hidden in the middle of the sun, where float-riders could stand and wave to spectators. Marilyn reached down and threw yellow, orange and red flower petals into the air.

"Marigolds, poppies, and roses," she said with delight.

We took off our masks and embraced each other. As we kissed, even more blood rushed to my groin, making me harder than I thought humanly possible.

"Sit down," she said, and pushed me onto the petals.

Marilyn stood near me and oscillated her body playfully like a stripper. People were working in adjacent warehouses, but I was beyond caring. She fulgurated with feral energy, an instrument of pure joy—half angel, half sex-goddess.

Slowly, very slowly, she pulled her dress over her head, wiggling her hips seductively. Her spectacular near-naked body hovered over me, her breasts so full and perky they took my breath away.

Did she know it was me? Janie was so damn loyal to the contract that she'd never hinted at our real identities. I needed to tell her I was also Darrin. But what if she stopped?

Marilyn knelt beside me. She unloosened my belt and then her hands were in my pants. She grabbed my hardness, and I feared I'd explode right then.

"Let me undress you," I said, stalling. I pulled off her panties and threw them on the petals.

"My turn." Teasingly, bit by bit, she used her mouth to pull down my underwear. "Impressive."

She pushed me onto my back, and lowered herself onto me until she straddled me. The fit was perfect. My entire life seemed made for this moment. I now knew what Janie looked like naked, and I was lodged deep inside her. She arched her back and gyrated; my pleasure soared to places I'd never imagined

Her incredible breasts bounced as we made love. In my mind's eye, I saw Janie's face. This was our first time. It should have been with Janie's face.

I hope she knows it's me. I hope she loves me. I focused on her eyes and settled for Marilyn's face.

Our connection was miraculous, our muscles in perfect sync. Our body—it was as if we had a singular body—pulsated like a well-oiled machine. Her ecstasy multiplied mine. When I looked in her eyes, I felt like I was exploring all the way to her soul.

We tried to be quiet, so the flower-placing volunteers wouldn't hear us. However, whatever happened, I didn't think I could stop.

Marilyn had a puckish smile as I approached the peak of pleasure. Each gyration of her hips sent me to the brink. I doubted I could last much longer, but I didn't want to finish. I planted my feet on the ground, put my hands behind Marilyn's back, and stood, making sure I stayed inside her.

"James?"

"Trust me." I hoped this worked as I intended.

She squeezed around me, and I continued thrusting inside her. Carefully, I lowered her on the petals and continued to pound into her.

In this position, I could kiss her while we made love. I tried to be tender, not kissing too forcefully, but my hips thrust harder and harder.

"James. James!" Marilyn was getting louder. All my thoughts were inside of her. I couldn't withhold much longer.

If we die making this movie, I'll never make love to Janie while she has her real face.

The pleasure became unbearable, and I released inside her.

Marilyn seemed to time her climax to my own.

As we recovered, she snuggled next to me. I tried to memorize her smell and touch. The universe was flawless. I wanted the whole world to feel as magnificently happy as I did.

What did this mean? Were Janie and I dating now? Or just Marilyn and James? For Marilyn, was this just casual sex? We weren't being spied on here, so maybe she'd break her contract, and we could talk about our identities.

After a few minutes of silence, Marilyn spoke softly. "Teddy was the nicest of them. I can't believe he's dead."

I wanted to linger in my bubble of joy, but beneath the surface I, too, felt grief and fear. Lighthearted, post-sex pillow talk isn't possible when your friend was just killed.

"Teddy was the only person at the studio I trusted," I said. "He was trying to use the machines to help my uncle."

"He was so friendly. I can't imagine anyone wanting to hurt him."

She didn't acknowledge knowing Uncle Stanley, although they were close. "Someone put a bomb in the podium. I'm just not sure Teddy was the target."

"Who would do such a thing?"

"Someone who wants to stop the movie."

Marilyn frowned. "Lots of Hollywood bigshots lost jobs and fortunes because of Teddy's animation."

"Whoever put the bomb in the podium knew about our movie and had access to the sound stage. He probably knows about the machines, too. He may even have been with us in the sound stage to detonate it."

"How can you be sure it's a man?" Marilyn asked.

"Because it's probably the same man who had a rifle on the roof of the Rodeo Drive set."

"Oh my gosh, I hadn't thought of that. Now everyone will have to believe you. Do you really think that man was in the audience with us today?"

"I bet he was watching, either with us or on one of the studio's surveillance cameras. I wonder what the studio will tell the police."

Marilyn's eyes got big. "Oh, James, I'm afraid. The drastic security has seemed wrong from the beginning. Now one of our friends is dead."

I hugged her tighter. "The machines are too powerful. Think of the temptation. They make you unstoppable."

"Gosh, do you think a killer has use of a machine?" Marilyn asked.

"Imagine the panic if the public found out a murderer could change faces. No one would trust anyone."

"I understand the intense security, but not the total immersion in our parts. It's far too extreme." I held Marilyn's face in my hands. "The machines are being used for something besides our movie, Marilyn. I feel it in my gut. That's what got Teddy killed."

She took several deep breaths, contemplating this. "The studio is making us do these legacy scenes, so it doesn't matter if we die. Do you think they expect we might die?"

"I don't know. Some actors from the 1940s have already done their legacy scenes, and they have been fine."

We discussed the movie for a few minutes, and I was impressed with how observant she was. I could have concentrated better, if she hadn't started teasing my manhood with her finger.

"I feel happier and safer right now than I have for a long time," Marilyn said. "I know you won't betray me."

"I think—"

Marilyn interrupted me with a kiss. She kissed my lips gently several times. Then she grinned as she lowered herself and kissed my neck. Then my chest. My stomach. This is really happening... I held my breath in anticipation.

She teased my shaft with her lips and tongue, alternating from kissing the sides to sucking it in deep. My rod had to be breaking laws of physics, being so hard and sensitive simultaneously. Somehow, she sensed whenever I was close to coming and prolonged it by softly caressing the periphery with her tongue.

Marilyn glanced at me playfully as she nibbled on the tip. "You can call me by my real name," she mumbled, without taking me out of her mouth.

Now? She picked now to step out of character?

"Really? Your real name!"

"Of course. You know my name isn't really Marilyn." Her lips lingered around my hardness.

Finally, this charade was over. I could hardly believe it. Janie was opening the iron partition between Janie and Marilyn. She was going to break the most severe part of our contracts.

"What's wrong, James? You look so serious." Marilyn pulled her mouth from me. "You know Marilyn Monroe isn't my real name, don't you?" Her eyes sparkled mischievously. "My real name is Norma Jean Baker."

She flaunted a deep, naughty laugh. Then she sucked me deep into her throat. She cupped a hand around my balls, pushed me deep and brought me to total ecstasy.

I almost shouted, "Oh, Janie" as I exploded in her mouth, but I caught myself and said "Oh, Honey."

After my climax, she massaged me with her mouth, extending my pleasure. She truly was a sex goddess. Finally, we snuggled on the petals and I was in paradise, holding my lover tight as nine flower-planets circling around us.

"Marilyn and Norma Jean are completely different," Marilyn confided. "However, they're both part of me. Sometimes I feel like a glamorous sex symbol . . . yet, sometimes I still feel like the scared little girl who grew up in orphanages."

She looked at me earnestly. "No one knows who my father was. My mother was committed to a mental institution. Imagine the horror of growing up in an orphanage while both your parents are still alive."

She was so deeply in her character, I envied her.

"I'm so sorry. People forget how much your childhood shaped you."

Marilyn looked at me apologetically. "I shouldn't have mentioned it. Tonight was perfect." She leaned forward and kissed me on the cheek. "I only want you to call me Marilyn. I feel safe and confident around you, not at all like Norma Jean."

"The truth is, Marilyn, we may not be safe. Someone involved in the studio is a murderer, and we don't know what they want."

"Maybe Dutch was the target," Marilyn said. "He's fired a lot of actors. He's a dictator at the studio, forced us to sign oppressive contracts, and he's probably the one spying on us."

"Rex is worse. He has no scruples at all. He wants to change his girlfriends into celebrities and have sex with them. He makes me uncomfortable, asking my opinion about which celebrities he should pick."

Marilyn gasped. "That's like . . . virtual rape. The studio is being led by a tyrant and a pervert."

"But are they murderers?"

"Don't you mean targets? Dutch, Rex and Orson were also on the platform."

"No, I mean murderers. Maybe whoever placed the bomb knew exactly where it would be safe to stand on the podium."

"Dutch and Rex did step away while Teddy was talking," Marilyn said. "If the studio is committing a crime, it seems at least one of them would have to know about it."

"It could be Dutch or Rex, or someone we haven't met, but the murderer must have a connection with the studio. Dutch is too fat to be the person who shot at me, but anyone could have placed the bomb. I would bet that someone with access to the transform-machines is misusing them and Teddy got in the way somehow."

"But Teddy was making Dutch, Rex, and everyone else connected with the studio filthy rich."

"True. This means the killer's goal is bigger than money."

"What's bigger than billions of dollars?"

"I don't know. Dutch and Rex must have records somewhere. Maybe we could break into their homes or offices . . ." My voice trailed off as I realized how hopeless this was.

"We need a strategy," Marilyn said.

"They control us completely. We're being spied on all the time. There's no one we can trust."

Marilyn thoughtfully studied me. "The key is that they underestimate us—that's how I accomplished most of what I did. Men thought I was a ditzy blonde, but I always came out on top. I even started my own production company and produced The Prince and the Showgirl myself, when the studios said I wasn't worthy to co-star with Sir Laurence Olivier. I learned how to survive."

"You may have been murdered."

"Well . . . yes," Marilyn admitted. "But not this time. We're going to solve this together." She punctuated her assertion with a kiss.

I stared at Marilyn's unparalleled beauty and marveled at the woman behind the face. I loved her boundlessly, just as I loved her other identity, Janie.

A different woman had died in 1962, and I felt heartbroken at the world's loss. This time, I would protect her. Her spirit and charm were too precious to disappear from the earth a second time.

What Lies Beneath

When we'd escaped from the studio, I hadn't considered how we'd return. The night had been monumental, fully worth getting fired, which seemed likely. We'd made love twice more. Even after Marilyn fell asleep in my arms, I stayed awake, listening to her breathing and cherishing her warm naked body as we lay atop the fragrant float. Unfortunately, I finally had to wake her.

"We need to leave. It's almost sunrise."

Marilyn yawned, stretched and gave me a smile. We dressed, and she followed me down the ladder. In the distance, volunteers were still flowering floats. We ran out of the warehouse and climbed into the Duisenberg.

"Um . . . James, these masks aren't going to be good enough in daylight," Marilyn said.

She was right. Our chins and foreheads were exposed. And, how could we explain wearing masks when we reached the studio gates?

"Hand me the tablecloth," I said.

I tore the white cloth into strips and we wrapped our faces in the fabric. On top of this we wore sunglasses. We looked like cool mummies in a Duisenberg as we waved to other early-morning drivers.

The guards at the studio gate approached us cautiously when we stopped.

"We both had minor burns," I said. "Rex let us use his car, because he felt bad for us."

The guards walked around the car. "We were told to expect you," one of the guards said, handing me a note.

The gate raised, as I read the note.

"It says, 'Go straight to J.D.'s trailer'," I said to Marilyn, as we drove onto the studio.

"If we're fired, it's all over for us . . . ." Marilyn despaired.

"Maybe it's Rex. He can be manipulated."

"I just hope it's not Dutch," Marilyn said.

We parked and entered the sound stage with the machines. We unwrapped our faces as we walked past the trailers with the machines and entered my trailer.

Who was playing music so loud? Then I saw him . . . .

The King of Rock stood on my coffee table, strumming his guitar amid a rousing rendition of "Don't Be Cruel."

Elvis kept singing as Marilyn and I watched, confused but impressed. The actor playing Elvis was extremely talented. He finished dramatically, jumping off the table while prolonging the final note.

"I talked to the fat bastard and the skinny pervert. I'm not going to let you get in trouble."

"You convinced Dutch and Rex not to punish us?"

Elvis nodded. His expression became serious and he gestured toward the trailer front door. "Let's step outside."

We followed him out of my trailer, which was probably bugged, and into the center of the sound stage away from any buildings. "Teddy is dead," Elvis said.

"We know."

"Do you know who killed him?" Marilyn asked.

Elvis nodded. "Yes."

I was stunned.

"You do?" Marilyn asked.

The King of Rock appraised us. "There's a lot I want to tell you, I just had to make sure I could trust you." He chuckled. "I doubt our enemy would be so reckless as to risk everything just for a date."

"Enemy?"

He handed us each a business card. "Come to this address, and I'll explain everything."

I examined the card. "M.G." was printed at the top, above a map of northern Malibu with an "X" near the ocean.

"You want us to go there as our other identities?" I asked.

"Yes."

"Are you sure it's safe?" Marilyn asked.

Elvis chuckled. "It's my home. It should be safe."

"Wow. We're going to meet each other," I said.

"Come to my house on January seventh. We're not filming that day," Elvis said. "There are spies among us, so be very careful. Don't mention this to anyone."

Elvis showed us the back of our cards, which had times written on them. Marilyn's was 11:25 a.m.; mine was 11:35 a.m.

"Come separately and be punctual. Make sure you're not followed." Elvis was acting paranoid, or perhaps prudent.

"Are M.G. your initials?" Marilyn asked.

"You'll learn everything at my house," Elvis promised. "Every question you have about the movie, the machines, and the murder will be answered."

A Walk in the Clouds

"At first, dreams seem impossible, then improbable,
and eventually inevitable."
—Christopher Reeve

Malibu, with a coastline of twenty-one miles but a population of only 12,000, lacks a downtown, offering instead a cluster of modish surfing communities and beach shops.

At 11:31 a.m., I reached Malibu Riviera, an exclusive enclave near Point Dume. I'd taken an indirect route and didn't think I'd been followed. Navigating the map on Elvis' card, I proceeded through secluded palm-lined roads teeming with vegetation. Passing opulent estates, I arrived at a wrought iron gate covered with musical notes, which from studying with Elvis, I recognized as identical to the gates of Graceland in Memphis.

Surveillance cameras focused on my vehicle and, at precisely 11:35 a.m., the gate opened on its own.

I drove down a long, curving road lined with towering palm trees. A gigantic stone mansion appeared—in Europe, it would have been called a castle—complete with turrets and chimneys, and high stone walls.

There were no cars in the circular driveway in front of the mansion, but down a short drive I spotted a large gravel parking lot full of what seemed to be beige cars. I turned down the path and realized they were cars covered in identical nylon tarps.

I parked on the gravel and covered my Taurus with a tarp, noting the number "288" imprinted on it, and headed toward the entrance of the building. The mansion was surrounded by a forbidding ten-foot-high stone wall. At night, it would have been terrifying, like approaching a gargantuan haunted mansion. I wondered if Janie was already inside.

When I reached the grand front doors, no one was there, so I lifted the medieval-looking iron knockers and hit it several times against the door. Despite the loud knock, no one answered. I checked the doors and found they were unlocked.

I cautiously entered an ostentatious foyer garnished in carved mahogany and adorned with paintings of exotic landscapes. Victorian portraits hung along a sweeping staircase. I was alone except for the ancient suits of armor guarding the banister.

A burgundy door opened to my left, startling me. Jimmy Stewart emerged. "Hello, Darrin. Right on time."

Jimmy always looked people straight in the eyes, as if he could see into your soul, but was too kind to feel anything but compassion.

"Sorry . . ." I was dreadfully ashamed. I shouldn't be here. As Darrin, I couldn't be with Jimmy Stewart.

Jimmy smiled. "It's fine. Welcome to Malibu Graceland."

I tried to hide my trepidation. "Malibu Graceland? Is that what Elvis calls this place?"

"Elvis will explain everything. Follow me."

Jimmy led me through the doorway from which he'd emerged. We entered a huge room with baronial mirrors, majestic murals and glittering chandeliers. In drastic contrast to these decorations, the room was filled with twelve cabin-like wood structures that looked like they belonged in the woods.

"This used to be the ballroom," Jimmy said. "You'll be using cabin six."

He escorted me to one of the square rustic structures inside the grandiose ballroom. The cabin's interior was empty except for a transform-machine.

"Take a seat."

"What's going on, Mr. Stewart?"

"Call me Jimmy. You'll get answers very soon."

"May I look in the other cabins?" I was sure Janie was in one of them. I wanted to check to see if she was becoming Marilyn.

"Sorry, no. Sit down so we can get started."

"You're going to make me into James Dean, right?"

"Of course."

I was plenty scared, yet I trusted Elvis. Besides, this was too elaborate a plan for them to kill us. I was eager to see what would happen next. I sat, watching Jimmy control the settings of the machine.

"That looks complicated. Is there a manual?" I wondered if I'd be able to transform myself if the occasion arose.

"I never saw a manual. Teddy taught me everything," Jimmy said, his tone shifting sad as he administered the anesthesia . . . .

"Are you awake?"

I heard Jimmy's soothing voice. When I opened my eyes, I saw him grinning at me.

I turned to a mirror and was elated to see James Dean's reflection.

"Put on the outfit. I'll wait outside," Jimmy said.

Hanging on the wall was outfit #35 from *Rebel Without a Cause*: white shirt, red jacket, dark pants. I changed quickly and approved my flawless appearance before exiting the cabin.

Jimmy escorted me across the ballroom to a staircase. "Go through the door at the end."

He left, and I climbed the stairs. Opening the door revealed an octagon parlor with a royal purple floor mosaic and eight white marble columns. Elvis sat on a white sofa, eating a sandwich while reading documents.

Elvis stood. "Welcome, James. You've almost made it. Just one more thing to do."

We sat on the sofa, and the King of Rock handed me a single sheet of paper.

"We call this our Code of Conduct," Elvis explained. "It's short and simple. If you have any reservations, don't sign it—Jimmy will transform you back, and you can leave without repercussions. However, you must sign it to enter Malibu Graceland."

I read the short list:

CODE OF CONDUCT

I.   I will show gratitude for my celebratory status by always behaving with dignity, humility and respect.

II.   I will never expect, request or accept preferential treatment because of my status as a celebrity.

III.   I will not treat others differently based on their degree of fame or lack thereof.

IV.   I will promote entertainment with virtuous messages that motivate people to strive toward their highest standards.

V.   I will use my fame to reduce poverty, promote peace, expose prejudices, and expand freedom among all people. I will work unselfishly to meet these ends.

I, <u>James Dean</u>, hereby agree to these five principles. I will follow them to the best of my ability. I will submit to the rulings of Elvis and his Court in regard to any failings to adhere to these standards.

"What is this, Elvis?"

"It's my hope that Malibu Graceland will stand for more than just pleasure."

"I can't be seen in public. How do these rules affect me?"

"The code may, or may not, ever apply to you," Elvis said. "Yet, it binds us all together. The oath is shared by every person who has ever entered Malibu Graceland, even myself."

"What does it mean, 'Elvis and his Court'?"

"The Court is a group of people I trust enough to help me run Malibu Graceland."

I re-read the document and saw no problem.

I signed dramatically. "My John Hancock, fit for the King."

Elvis chuckled. He stood and pulled the handle of a gold-trimmed door between two of the eight marble columns. "Malibu Graceland awaits."

Bright sunshine illuminated an idyllic sight.

I stepped out onto a marble balcony, overlooking a courtyard full of people, palm trees, and river-like swimming pools. In the distance a sandy beach beckoned, and the ocean stretched forever.

"James, you're here. I've been waiting for you." Marilyn rushed to me from the balcony railing and grabbed my hand. "It's paradise, isn't it?"

I peered over the balcony. Two sweeping, ivory-colored marble staircases stretched out from each side of a balcony designed to resemble the wings of a giant swan. A magnificent pool was surrounded by people reclining on lounge chairs or sitting at outdoor bars. There were Jacuzzis, an ice cream kiosk, massage tables and a dance stage. Beyond the pool sat two thatch-roofed buildings, then another pool, and in the distance rows of bungalows extending to the ocean. I beheld fountains, sculptures, Tiki torches, bridges over the meandering pools, exotic birds on golden perches, and everywhere the sound of laughter.

"Don't look at things, silly, look at the people," Marilyn said.

I focused on the people below us. John F. Kennedy talking with Beyoncé and Angelina Jolie. Dumbfounded, I almost fell over the balcony. Then I saw Babe Ruth chatting with George Lucas, Jennifer Aniston and Charles Lindbergh.

"These people . . . they don't belong together." My mind was spinning.

"Look, Taylor Swift is waving to us." Marilyn waved her hand. "Hi, Taylor."

"Let's go down and have lunch," Elvis suggested.

We followed the King down the left arc of the swan staircase. I reached to hold Marilyn's hand, but after giving my hand a friendly squeeze, she pulled hers away. My heart sank. We weren't a couple. Amazing sex wasn't enough to warrant holding hands in public.

"This is the main courtyard," Elvis explained. "The two largest thatch-roofed buildings are restaurants, one serving Polynesian food and the other Mexican. There are also three smaller courtyards each with pools and restaurants, and there are over 200 rooms, including fifty-five ocean-side bungalows."

"People live here?" I asked.

"I'll explain over lunch." The King greeted dozens of people as we crossed the courtyard to Ho'oulu Lāhui restaurant.

To my astonishment, the hostess was a modern pop star. She did a hula movement with her hands, while her eyes bore into Elvis like she wanted to stab him with a knife.

"There will be three of us today," Elvis said.

Our pop star hostess seemed to summon every ounce of restraint. "Certainly, your table is ready."

"The punishment for breaking the Code of Conduct often includes working at Malibu Graceland," Elvis explained as we followed our hostess to a table on a veranda overlooking a pool. "Don't let our servers' demeanor impact our lunch."

Shortly after we sat, a teenage heartthrob whose face was often in the news brought Elvis a beverage and took orders from me and Marilyn. His jaw clenched, and he practically threw down the silverware. The entire time, he avoided looking at Elvis.

"They hate me now, but they'll forgive me when their punishment ends."

"Are those impostors? They can't be the real people," I said.

"Oh, they're real," Elvis assured.

"How do you get celebrities to agree to their punishments?" Marilyn asked.

Elvis grinned. "I've created heaven here. Malibu Graceland is the closest thing to nirvana anyone will find on earth. You can mingle in paradise with famous historic figures. There's no media and everything is free."

He sipped a strawberry daiquiri. "Modern celebrities don't know how historic people seem so authentic, but it creates a utopia. Also, anyone who disobeys me will be toxic in Hollywood and never work again."

I supposed controlling heaven gave someone a lot of power. I looked into the kitchen and saw two famous actors chopping vegetables. One had been in the news recently for punching a photographer, the other for yelling at the police after getting a DUI.

"Movie stars aren't bad people, just shielded from reality," Elvis said. "Their heroism is fictional, so they don't realize that a public display of toughness is just arrogance."

"So you discipline people?" Marilyn asked.

"Not often," Elvis said. "99.9% of Malibu Graceland is pure enjoyment."

Marilyn inhaled deeply as she admired the jasmine surrounding the veranda. Flowers outlined each pathway and building around the courtyard. "It smells divine. I love the vegetation."

I was tempted to reach for her hand, but I didn't want to be rejected again. During the week since our sex on the float, she'd been warm and flirtatious, but hadn't shown any signs of commitment. As Janie, she'd been strictly platonic toward Darrin.

Our popstar waiter brought Marilyn and me drinks, and took our food orders.

"What exactly is this place?" I asked.

"Malibu Graceland was my idea," Elvis said. "When Digital Impact finished its first movie using the transform-machines, the actors were desperate to spend more time as their characters. However, the studio was moving on to other projects. I saw an opportunity to improve society. If I could create a place special enough, I hoped it could compel celebrities to live up to higher standards."

"The entrance fee is being a good person," Marilyn said.

"Basically, yes. I searched Southern California for a suitable estate, found this place, made renovations, and named it Malibu Graceland. Now when actors finish a movie in which they used the transform-machines, they enter a sort of club. You can come here as often as you like."

Elvis sipped his daiquiri. "Thus, it began as a utopia of historic figures. Then I began inviting modern celebrities. They don't need to be transformed, of course, but they're bound by the Code of Conduct."

"It must have cost a fortune," I said.

Elvis grinned. "I was successful in my alternative identity." I wondered if he was a businessman or a musician.

We paused our discussion while our server delivered our food: a steak, a chicken and mango salad, and fish tacos, each of which looked exquisite.

"How do you keep this secret?" Marilyn asked. "Anyone could blackmail you."

"Look around you," Elvis invited. "Who wants to oppose heaven? Historic celebrities need this place to get transformed. Modern celebrities don't know how the historic icons are possible, but they relish the chance to interact with them."

"I think I read about this place online once. Then the entire story was rescinded," I said.

"A couple of historic figures here used to be modern journalists. I kept them from exposing us by offering them the opportunity to join us. Of course, I required them to memorize their character's background as thoroughly as you did."

I nodded. "So that's why we had to learn every detail of our identities."

"Exactly. It's far too extreme for a movie," Elvis said. "But here everyone is absolutely authentic. You can tell fascinating stories, share dynamic conversations, and react to situations in perfect character. You can be yourself in every way."

The immersion into our characters truly had been necessary. "Dutch and the other executives must know about this," I said.

"Of course. It solves their biggest post-production problem. After using the transform-machines, actors get hooked being their characters. Dutch didn't know how to satisfy them. He insists on strict secrecy and stops by sometimes to check."

"I know I'm addicted to being James Dean. But no one can perfectly imitate an Einstein or a Babe Ruth," I said. "Some people have unique skills."

"Everyone here is an expert in his or her field," Elvis explained. "You and Marilyn are actors. Einstein is a world-renowned physicist. Babe Ruth is a retired ballplayer. Einstein may not invent new theories, but he understands relativity. Babe Ruth isn't expected to hit the ball like he used to."

"How about being spotted by boats or planes?" Marilyn asked.

"The mansion has a security room, where people watch constantly for any situation. The palm trees and buildings are fitted with alarms and lights. White lights indicate you need to leave the beach; red lights mean to go inside. It happens occasionally."

"What about Teddy's murder?" I asked. "You claimed to know who did it."

"Yes. My Court is meeting this afternoon. I want you both to attend. You'll learn everything."

"Really?"

"Today at 5 p.m.," Elvis confirmed. "The top floor of the main building is my personal residence. Take the elevator. Now, I'm going to whisper a unique password to each of you. You'll need it for Court meetings."

Elvis leaned near Marilyn and cupped his hands around her ear. She nodded as Elvis whispered.

Then Elvis leaned toward my ear. He whispered, "Your password is 'Napoleon.' My response will be 'Galapagos.'"

"Wait—does this mean you're afraid there might be an impostor James Dean or Marilyn Monroe?"

"It's just a precaution." Elvis pointed to the activities center by the pool. "Enjoy your day. In the future, you can reserve a bungalow and stay the night if you plan ahead. For tonight, I reserved exit transformation times. 9:30 p.m. for you, Marilyn. 9:50 p.m. for you, James."

There was no bill to pay, so we simply walked down the stairs to the pool after eating. Elvis pointed to a glass elevator to the right of the double spiral staircase. "That's the elevator to take. Enjoy yourself until five."

The King of Rock left us, heading to the glass elevator.

"Who should we talk to?" Marilyn asked.

Before I could respond, Anne Hathaway and Cary Grant approached.

"We brought you some drinks," Anne said. "I hope you like margaritas."

By the time we'd accepted our drinks, Orville Wright, Jennifer Lopez, Tom Hanks, and Albert Einstein had joined us.

"I've been wondering when you two would finally show up," Albert said.

I felt liberated. No studio. No movie. Just time to be James Dean. This truly was Shangri-La.

Freed of any script, I was totally on fire, saying clever things and making friends quickly. Paradise was an understatement, as we interacted with iconic legends who weren't just authentic, but our colleagues.

Every Eden needs a snake, and soon Frank Sinatra joined our group. He turned to Marilyn and started to brag about a new song he was writing. No one else seemed to care how self-absorbed Frank was, but I could hardly stand it.

While Frank blabbed, I casually slipped my arm around Marilyn's waist.

She pierced me with a frosty look and stepped to the side. A shotgun blast to the gut would have felt nicer.

I turned my back to her and spoke with Einstein, pretending I didn't care. My hands trembled, and I tucked them into my pockets. How could she be so cold after our incredible night together?

Needing to get away, I left the group to explore the incredible estate on my own. Each path revealed new wonders: gardens, waterfalls, artwork, but especially famous icons from decades during which James Dean hadn't lived. I was befriending the most exceptional people. Yet, my exploration kept bringing me back to views of Marilyn, who was always surrounded by males and bubbling like champagne for their enjoyment. She flirted with everyone, making me realize I was just another man. She didn't have a care in the world; I was easily forgotten.

I resisted going near her until 4:55 p.m., and then went to the main courtyard and waited until she finally approached me.

"It's almost five, James," Marilyn said. "This has been the most amazing day ever. And now we get to see Elvis' Court." She beamed with excitement and warmth, unaware I'd been avoiding her.

As we walked toward the mansion, Marilyn chatted animatedly about the conversations she'd had. When we entered the elevator, she grabbed my hand. "Can you believe this place? It's so wonderful. And we can come back whenever we want."

I realized she'd be affectionate, as long as we weren't in public. I grabbed her butt, pulled her toward me and kissed her.

She pulled away and laughed. "It's a glass elevator, James. Why don't you just hold my hand?"

She was just being practical. It was so easy for her to turn on and off affection, since she didn't fear rejection. I held her hand and tried not to be upset. I had to accept things on her terms.

"You realize what this place means," she gushed. "We can stay as Marilyn and James forever, even after the movie ends. I've felt like we've been on death row, but now we've been pardoned."

"I feel the same way." Malibu Graceland offered countless new ways I could get Janie—as Marilyn—to fall in love with me.

The glass elevator carriage was transparent on three sides. As we ascended, I reveled in the quixotic view.

"We're finally going to get answers about everything," Marilyn said. "We'll find out what's scaring Elvis."

That reminded me of my top priority. Beyond seducing her, I needed to keep her safe.

The Sum of All Fears

The glass elevator opened on the top floor, revealing a warm, cheerful room furnished in a Southern style. Vintage 1950s furniture included cherry veneers and a jukebox, and the walls were covered with glass display cases containing Elvis' wilder costumes.

"Where is everyone?" Marilyn asked.

"Maybe we're the first here." I circled the room, admiring the stone fireplace, home theater system, and panoramic vistas.

"My goodness, James, what a view. You can see the entire courtyard and beach."

"Look—down that hallway. There are two men standing by a door."

We headed that way.

"It's John Wayne and Bruce Lee," Marilyn said.

Indeed, John and Bruce apparently served as bouncers for another room.

"Howdy, James. Marilyn," John said in his laconic drawl. "Elvis told us to expect you."

Bruce smiled. "So, you're big shots now. Come and join the other VIPs."

John opened the door for us. The room looked like an executive boardroom at a Fortune 500 company, with a long black walnut table surrounded by black chairs. I counted six seated people and seven empty chairs. Three people stood in line to talk to Elvis, who was whispering something to Lucille Ball.

Marilyn and I got in line behind Martin Luther King, Jr., Eleanor Roosevelt and Albert Einstein. Elvis whispered to each person for about thirty seconds. After Marilyn, Elvis motioned me forward.

"I hope you've enjoyed yourself so far," the King of Rock said.

"Absolutely. It was incredible. You've motivated modern celebrities so much. I heard about efforts to diminish AIDS, projects to alleviate poverty, and work with Oxfam and the Red Cross. Everyone said the Code of Conduct was their inspiration."

"That makes me truly happy," Elvis said. "Now, I need you to whisper your password."

I leaned close, shielded my mouth with my hand, and whispered, "Napoleon."

Elvis whispered back, "Galapagos." He took a deep breath, looking more relaxed. "There are no spies here today, unless someone was tortured and revealed their password."

Was that a real concern? I sat in the last empty chair between Bogie and Marilyn.

Clockwise, around the table, were Elvis, Eleanor Roosevelt, Martin Luther King, Jr., Lucille Ball, Nikola Tesla, Milton Friedman, Walt Disney, Jimmy Stewart, George Patton, Albert Einstein, Marilyn, me and Bogie.

Elvis sat at the head of the table, and everyone stopped talking.

"Aloha," Elvis said. "Let's take care of business."

The King looked at Marilyn and me. "Marilyn and James will be our guests today. I've gotten to know and trust them. They'll offer fresh thinking and creativity."

The other people at the table applauded. Marilyn blushed.

"Let's handle the boring crap first," Elvis continued. "Yesterday, Bob Marley got so stoned he fell off the dock. Muhammad Ali rescued him, or else Bob would've drowned and floated away, probably ending up on some public beach. I think thirty hours of groundskeeping will be sufficient punishment."

"Actually, Elvis, we have enough groundskeepers right now. We're short of dishwashers," Nikola Tesla said. The inventor winked at me. His mind seemed to be penetrating the cosmos with creativity, as if the world's problems were too easy.

"Fine. Bob can work in the kitchen," Elvis said. "Speaking of the kitchen . . ."

The Court discussed menu changes and opening earlier for breakfast. Next, the Court discussed pool cleaning and whether to allow small dogs at the estate. They did.

"Now for the important issue," Elvis said. "Joe Plain claimed responsibility for killing Teddy. It's the first murder he's committed at the studio."

There had been other murders. "Who's Joe Plain?" I asked.

Everyone turned toward me. "Fourteen months ago, a transform-machine was stolen from Digital Impact," Elvis said. "A man calling himself Joe Plain has been using it to kill our friends."

This statement was shocking in multiple ways.

"At Court meetings, it's okay to talk about the transform-machines and the fact that we have other identities," Elvis said.

Eleanor handed me a piece of paper. "Joe has killed all of these people."

MURDERED BY JOE PLAIN

Bette Davis	Whitney Houston	Thurgood Marshall
Henry Fonda	Rock Hudson	Paul Newman
J. Paul Getty	Lyndon B. Johnson	George C. Scott
Barry Goldwater	Gene Kelly	Frank Lloyd Wright
Rita Hayworth	Robert F. Kennedy	

"Holy crap!" A serial killer of American icons. My fists clenched. I'll kill him with my bare hands.

I looked at Marilyn. The danger to her now had a name. Joe Plain. I had to keep her safe.

"That's why Gene Kelly suddenly stopped filming," I said.

"Yes," Elvis said. "Gene was the latest actor killed. Now we need to add Teddy to the list."

"These are just the people we know about," General Patton, who wore his combat uniform, said. "The bastard also claims he has replaced people in the police, the FBI, and the government."

Fuck. How could we stop someone who could change identities?

"Who is he?"

"We don't know," Jimmy Stewart said. "As far as we can tell, Joe Plain started killing people over a year ago, just as our movie started and two months before modern celebrities were allowed into this estate."

"Is the studio going to cast new actors to replace those killed?" Marilyn asked.

"That's up to Orson. He hasn't yet, in respect to the actors who've died," Elvis said. "If their legacy scene is done, it's not necessary. Otherwise, Orson tries to change the script to work around them."

"Are we going to continue the legacy scenes with Teddy dead?" I asked.

"Yes. Rex can take over for him," Elvis said.

There was a knock on the door. No one seemed surprised besides Marilyn and me.

Elvis greeted a strikingly-handsome man I recognized from TV. It was Ernest Goldenhart—a modern politician whose wholesome smile immediately evoked honesty and virtue. I immediately hated him.

Mayor Goldenhart was undeniably more attractive than any man in the room. I observed Marilyn, checking to see if she would fall under the spell of his flashy grin and blond curls.

Marilyn was studying him warily. It was hard to read her impression. Although he was only the mayor of a medium-sized city, Santa Barbara, Ernest Goldenhart was a prominent national figure. Dutch had endorsed his presidential campaign, as had much of the media.

Mayor Goldenhart whispered something to Elvis, which I assumed was a password, and Elvis whispered something back.

"We're honored you're joining us, Ernest," Elvis announced. "I told the Court last week that you'd be observing our meeting today."

Elvis indicated to a spare chair, but the mayor ignored him and stood at the front of the room, as if he was a guest speaker, not an observer. He flashed his white teeth, and I imagined him looking for a baby to kiss.

"I was pleased when Dutch asked me to speak to the Court. Dutch and I have been best friends for years and discussed the merits of Malibu Grace when it was just a dream, especially how it could improve the behavior of famous people. The Code of Conduct is dear to my heart, because I've always believed integrity and morality are the bedrocks of my career and . . . ."

What the fuck . . . he's giving a campaign speech. The rest of the room seemed equally bored. I didn't really listen until he mentioned the murderer.

"Joe Plain can't be allowed to hinder the mission of Malibu Graceland," Ernest said. "I've faced evil before—and defeated it every time. As a mayor, I've fought injustice and crime. As a businessman, I opposed corruption and fraud. While in the Peace Corps, I dealt with dictators and dishonesty. I attack every challenge head on, which is why many people say I'd be a great president. The values my mom taught me . . . ."

I leaned over and whispered to Marilyn, "He makes everything about himself."

"Slick politicians are all the same," Marilyn whispered. "They're like dog poop covered with gold."

I felt happier knowing Marilyn's opinion. The verbose mayor didn't show any sign of stopping. Finally, he paused to drink water in the middle of a sentence.

Elvis immediately started clapping, and we rapidly joined him.

Mayor Goldenhart opened his mouth to resume, but Elvis quickly spoke. "Thank you, Ernest. We're so grateful that you've volunteered to help us defeat Joe Plain. Dutch said you're a great listener and problem solver."

"You're welcome. That reminds me of a story—"

I handed him the list. "All these people have been killed, Mr. Goldenhart," I said.

The mayor's toothy smile disappeared. "Oh, my." He settled into his chair. "I'm sorry I took so much time. This is far more important."

Marilyn raised her hand, as if it was a classroom. "What does Joe Plain look like?"

The Court members shook their heads. "No one's ever seen him and lived," Eleanor said.

"How does Joe normally kill people?" I asked.

"When Joe finds out someone's real identity, he goes to their home and poisons them," Bogie said. "Then he emails Dutch, bragging about it and repeating his demands."

"What demands?" I asked.

"Joe threatens to keep killing people until we stop filming and give him three more machines," Elvis said.

"Have you seen the emails?" I asked.

Elvis handed me a folder. It was full of printed emails. They were short and simple, demanding what Elvis had mentioned. After I read a few of them, I handed the folder to Marilyn.

Marilyn appeared to be in far more danger than I expected. I needed to assure her identity as Janie stayed secret. No one could be trusted—even the people at this table could be tortured and reveal their password. Unfortunately, Dutch, Rex and Jacqueline already knew Marilyn was Janie.

There was only one way to truly keep Janie safe—to help the people in this room stop Joe Plain.

"Dutch needs to agree to Joe Plain's demands," Lucy Ball said. "The movie isn't worth more people dying." The red-haired comedian was stunning in a classy way, although it felt like she might burst into giggles at any moment.

"No. You can't negotiate with evil. History has taught us that," Eleanor Roosevelt stated. There was nothing demure about the former First Lady. She was strong, smart and outspoken, and I could feel the respect everyone in the room had for her.

"Rex has volunteered to take over Teddy's responsibilities," Elvis said. "He strongly opposes stopping filming."

"Rex only cares about money," Milton Friedman said. "That should be our last priority."

The preeminent economist wasn't what I expected. He was as short as a hobbit, but had the calm, wise mannerism of an enlightened monk with purely humanitarian aims.

"What about going to the police?" I asked.

Everyone shook their heads. "Joe claims he's already killed and replaced the leaders of the CIA, FBI and police," Martin Luther King, Jr. said. When the reverend spoke, I felt a gravity of character, deep and discerning, which made me feel I should be focusing more on my own integrity.

"The emails can't be traced," Nikola added. "We've tried."

"And Joe Plain has threatened to kill Dutch, if we talk to any authorities or try to discover his identity," Walt Disney said. He had a boyish charm, and the twinkle in his eye of a man who intended to do the impossible.

"What if we warned the public about the transform-machines?" Mayor Goldenhart asked. "It's better than people dying."

"Imagine the panic. Any person could be a murderer," Albert Einstein said. "It wouldn't stop Joe Plain, it would make him stronger."

"Actually, we're afraid Joe will reveal himself publicly," Jimmy said.

"I don't see why Joe wants multiple machines," Bogie said. "What can you do with three you can't do with one?"

"It could be to synchronize a fucking revolt or a terrorist attack," General Patton snarled. "I don't see one damn scenario that doesn't involve mass casualties."

People reluctantly nodded.

Given his experiences, the general's vulgarities seemed to be overlooked. He had competed in the 1912 Olympics, fought in both World Wars, won many battles when severely outnumbered, liberated Nazi concentration camps, and was one of only a few Americans who had been knighted to the Order of the British Empire. I wasn't sure I was worthy to speak after him, but I did.

"Joe Plain might be the man I saw with a rifle at the Rodeo Drive set," I said.

The room quieted to consider this.

"It's possible," Elvis agreed. "Joe has been at the studio at least twice, to steal the machine and to plant the bomb."

Bogie frowned. "Too bad you failed to get a useful description of the alleged man, James. Saying he had an average face without any distinctive features doesn't help us."

"I think it's an astute observation," Albert said. The genius smiled at me. "James described a literally plain face. We can deduce that Joe Plain lives up to his name."

"Of course! Joe created the perfect face for a killer," Nikola added. "A face so ordinary he is never noticed. Except, James noticed him."

"Well, how about that!" Elvis beamed at me. "We've got our first solid clue about Joe Plain."

I hoped I hadn't misled them. It had been a quick glance from far away.

"We can extrapolate more," Albert said. "Joe Plain can't be any of the actors who were filming at the Rodeo Drive set that day. That eliminates a lot of people."

"We already know Joe isn't a modern celebrity. Joe started killing people before they knew about Malibu Graceland, and they've never even seen one of the machines," Nikola added.

"Dutch can't be Joe," I said. "He's far too fat." I received several disapproving looks. "Not that I'm judging or think he's capable of that."

"No, it's good. We need to consider every possible suspect," Elvis said.

Marilyn raised her hand again. "How does Joe find out people's real identities?"

"We fear he has a spy here at this estate," Walt Disney said.

"Malibu Graceland's security is state-of-the-art," General Patton boasted. "TSA-style metal detectors are installed on many of the damn doors, and we hired elite security professionals to ensure cars leaving the mansion aren't followed. However, in any war, spies are a son-of-a-bitch to stop."

"As I've said before, we need to spy on people when they leave the mansion," Bogie said.

"Damn right. We can hire hackers to investigate people and then interrogate suspicious bastards," General Patton growled.

"No." Jimmy hit the table. "That ... that ... that's not who we are," he stuttered. I remembered we had two generals in our Court.

Although a huge movie star by the 1940s, Jimmy had enlisted as a private in WWII and refused special treatment. He flew as a pilot in 20 combat missions, earned a Distinguished Service Medal, and finished his military career as a brigadier general.

"If we do nothing, Joe is going to keep killing our friends," Lucy said.

"I think Joe works for the CIA," Ernest Goldenhart said. "They'd have uses for multiple machines. They could be watching us by satellite."

"If the CIA or the FBI knew about the machines, they'd confiscate them all, not steal one and threaten us for more," Albert said. "Joe may control the CIA, but he doesn't work for them."

Marilyn raised her hand. "Why does Joe want the movie stopped?"

"Probably money," Milton said. "Each movie makes billions. Our current movie is expected to be the biggest."

"But why would Joe want to financially hurt the studio or Malibu Graceland?" Walt asked.

"Maybe it's not about money, but rather social values," MLK said. "Joe may oppose the Code of Conduct or something in the script."

"Have you looked for patterns in Joe's actions?" I asked.

"We study everything!" Albert affirmed. "Whenever there's a major crime in the news, we analyze it to see if the stolen machine was involved. Whenever a famous person acts strangely, we try to determine if he or she is an impostor."

"This isn't a social club, James. We read, ponder and scrutinize everything," Eleanor said. "We just haven't discovered anything yet."

"In summary, we don't know squat," Elvis said. "Joe could be planning terrorism, global domination or war."

For two hours, we discussed Joe's real identity and his goal. People were loud and passionate, and nothing useful was accomplished.

"That's enough for tonight," Elvis finally announced. "Let's hold our next meeting at 5 p.m. on Wednesday."

As I was leaving the room, Elvis pulled me aside. "I can't dine with y'all tonight. I've got too much work. But I'd like you to meet me back here at nine."

"Of course, Elvis."

Marilyn and I followed the others to the mansion's formal dining room, a venue elegant enough for royalty, with fancy crystal glasses, flowery antique china, and silver candlesticks. I felt like I was dining at Downton Abby, except the servers were a modern rapper and a reality TV star.

At 8:55, I said to Marilyn, "I've got to see Elvis."

She rolled her eyes. "You're his Chosen One. His best buddy."

"Whatever." I decided to dare a quick goodbye peck on her lips. I moved to kiss her, but she pulled away her face. Bogie snickered as I gave her an awkward kiss by her ear.

I pretended I'd intended just to whisper to her. "Drive safely, if I don't see you," I whispered.

"Goodnight, everyone." I tried to appear confident as I left the room.

One tiny goodbye kiss . . . she couldn't even give me that.

It was so frustrating. I couldn't have a meaningful talk about our relationship. As Marilyn, she wouldn't indicate she knew I was Darrin. As Janie, she wouldn't acknowledge our other identities at all. She flirted with everyone as Marilyn, and only wanted to be friends as Janie.

Well, Elvis had only asked to see me. Not the butthead Bogie. I headed to the elevator to see why.

The Right Stuff

I took the glass elevator to the top floor, strolling through the Southern-style room and down the hallway to the boardroom. There were no guards this time.

I found Elvis seated at the same spot as when we'd left, surrounded by stacks of paper and an empty plate. He looked exhausted.

He smiled when I entered. "Sorry I made you leave the others, James."

The King stood and led me back to the Southern-themed room.

"I call this my Memphis Room," he declared. "It's decorated like my home in Memphis."

"You could host great parties here."

"I haven't had time for parties. What I want to show you is underground."

The elevator door opened, but Elvis didn't step in. "First, I need your password."

"Napoleon."

"Galapagos."

We entered the elevator, and Elvis pressed G2. When the door opened, I was astounded to see a garage full of classic cars, many from the '50s, brightly colored with big engines, flashy taillights and decorated wheels.

"This is my favorite." Elvis pointed to a pink 1955 Cadillac Fleetwood.

"It's a beauty. Who are you, really?"

Elvis laughed. "I'm a successful musician. I was rich, but I wasn't improving the world. Then I found out about these machines." A spark of joy ignited in Elvis' eyes. "Imagine if all the world's role models were kind and unselfish. I truly believe that nothing could benefit humanity more."

I nodded. "People do imitate celebrities. It could eliminate violence and poverty."

Elvis' smile faded. "Instead, it's more likely Joe will use the stolen machine for something catastrophic."

"Why did you let Ernest Goldenhart come to the Court meeting? He's a politician, not a global icon." He reminded me of President Kennedy. The last thing I needed was more competition.

"Don't be jealous, James. You've got a great shot at Marilyn, if you control your emotions."

"I just don't trust politicians. Ernest would do anything to get ahead."

"Our historic friends weren't always angels as they climbed their way to fame and fortune, either."

"That's true," I admitted. However, they were different people.

"Dutch trusts Ernest and thinks he could be valuable to us. We need all the help we can get. Ernest may only be the Mayor of Santa Barbara right now, but his future looks limitless."

"As far as I can tell, there are only two people who could be Joe Plain: Ernest and Rex."

"I agree. Yet, what would be their motive?" Elvis asked.

"Easy. Ernest wants to be president. Rex wants to magnify his hedonist lifestyle."

"I searched online to see where Ernest was while we were filming. Ernest had a fundraiser in Santa Barbara. So, if Joe was the guy you saw, it wasn't Ernest."

"So, it's Rex."

"Joe is demanding that we stop filming. Why would Rex want that? Rex's assistants say he was in his office while we were at the Rodeo Drive set. Dutch has been Rex's friend since college, so we need some evidence before we accuse him."

I wish I knew Elvis' real identity. He was wise and magnanimous.

Elvis stopped. "Here we are. What do you think?"

I gawked at the car in front of us: a 1955 Porsche Spyder, bright silver, with "130" painted on the hood. The car that killed me.

My heart raced with intoxicating fear. The Porsche drew me to it with its streamlined grace and power. It had been my most treasured possession. I visualized my highway accident, and chills traveled down my body.

"Is this . . . the actual car?"

"Yes, and it's been perfectly restored." Elvis extended a set of keys toward me. "Racing this car was your favorite thing in the world. I want you to have it."

It was tempting fate. "I don't know . . . I mean, I can't accept something so . . ."

Elvis chuckled. "You can't drive it anywhere. It's a symbolic gift, a token of my appreciation for your friendship."

I took the keys and felt immediately empowered. It was illogical, but I felt pride in owning a car I couldn't drive. I sat in the driver's seat and gripped the steering wheel. I examined the clutch and dashboard, imagining the thrill of racing. I loved this car.

I hopped out of the Spyder and gave the King of Rock a hug. "It's the greatest present ever. Thank you."

"Friendship gives me hope. I'd give away a thousand cars for friends like you."

I felt honored and humbled by Elvis' praise. How had I earned this special degree of friendship?

Elvis pushed the button for the first floor. "It's time for you to go. I'll show you a shortcut to the ballroom."

We exited the elevator, and Elvis led me down a corridor. When we entered the ballroom, Martin Luther King, Jr. was waiting for us, reading Time magazine.

"The hottest place in hell is reserved for those who remain neutral in times of great moral conflict," Martin said.

"You misquoted yourself, Martin," I said.

"Impossible. I just said it."

Elvis grinned. "Martin likes to be my moral compass. He and Jimmy Stewart share responsibility for managing the transformation cabins."

"Can I return at any time?"

"Absolutely. In the future, you can stay overnight in a bungalow if you reserve one."

Martin directed me into one of the cabins and administered the anesthesia. Soon, I fell asleep . . . .

When I awoke, I was Darrin again. Yuck.

I said goodbye to Martin, walked to the parking lot and uncovered tarp #288 from my Taurus. Looking back at the estate's menacing exterior, it was hard to believe what existed inside.

Even buildings couldn't be judged by their appearance.

Psycho

⸻

Joe Plain had never felt fear like this before.

The beast charging toward him looked like a grizzly bear in camouflage fatigues.

"Don't move until he's fifteen yards away," Joe Plain instructed.

The man who stood beside Joe didn't respond. Perhaps he, too, was paralyzed by fright. Their target sprinted toward them with the ease of a gazelle, but could kill people faster than a lion.

For months, it had been Joe's mission to identify the toughest man in the world. He'd assigned several assistants to research candidates, and they'd concluded the fiercest man on the planet was Lieutenant Commander John Baily.

As a SEAL team squadron leader, Baily had killed Columbian drug lords with his bare hands. He'd shot Taliban leaders in caves, rescued hostages in Mogadishu, parachuted into ISIS strongholds, and survived three months of torture after being captured by Al-Qaeda. He'd led missions on four continents and had been awarded the Medal of Honor and two Navy Crosses. Each year, as a vacation, he summited Everest without supplemental oxygen.

And he was even more intimidating in person. Joe considered abandoning his plan.

They'd been waiting since predawn in the woods near Dam Neck, Virginia, ready to ambush Lieutenant Commander Baily. The SEAL did a ten-mile run each morning before lifting weights.

Now, Baily was sixty feet away running towards them on a path.

Joe saw Baily's eyes and wondered if this was a big mistake. Replacing Baily had modest strategic value. It was just a matter of pride, to prove that no one was beyond his reign of terror.

When Baily was fifteen yards away, Joe stepped from the woods onto the path, aiming a Glock 19 pistol. The replacement followed a step behind

Joe, holding a M4 Super 90 combat shotgun, also aimed at the real John Baily.

Baily raised his hands up and came to an abrupt stop. He glared at the man who looked identical to him. The SEAL commander's face showed surprise, but no fear.

"Who are you?" he demanded.

"I'm Joe Plain. This man is going to replace you."

"Many SEALs train here. If you shoot me, others will come investigate the sound."

Joe indicated toward the replacement. "That's fine. We'll just roll you into the woods, and the new version of you will claim he shot a rattlesnake."

Baily stepped toward them. "There are no rattlesnakes in the winter, moron."

"Stay back," Joe yelled. He imagined the SEAL moving with superhero speed. Baily had killed many dangerous men in urban warfare.

Baily kept walking forward. "You're going to have to kill me."

The replacement held his ground, keeping the shotgun aimed at Baily's gut. Joe had recruited him because, before becoming an actor, he'd been in the ROTC in college and he had a black belt in Muay Thai.

When the original Baily was ten feet away, Joe considered firing. It would be a failure in terms of Joe's terror experiment.

The replacement snarled. "Stop, or you're dead."

Baily slowed to a near stop. "What do you want?"

"We want to know the classified missions DEVGRU has done since you joined," Joe said.

"DEVGRU is the Naval Warfare Special Development Group," Baily said, taking another step towards his twin. "DEVGRU and its Army counterpart, Delta Force, are America's primary counterterrorism military force."

"We know that, asshole." Joe shot the SEAL in the neck with a Taser gun.

Baily tried to fight the electricity. He kept standing for a few seconds before falling to the ground. Once he collapsed, the replacement handcuffed Baily's hands.

"Let's start over," Joe said. "I asked about your classified missions."

Baily calmed his breathing. He stood, refusing to show any fear. "Just kill me. I know you're going to replace me, and you know I'm never going to tell you anything."

Joe was elated. They were in a conversation now. Joe could overcome Baily's macho bullshit.

"You don't fear pain or death," Joe said, "but there are worse things."

"I will never betray my country."

"I think you will," Joe said.

Original Baily said nothing.

"You—this new you," Joe said, pointing at the replacement, "is going to visit your family during the night and murder them. Then you're going to perform domestic terror—maybe a school shooting. Then I'm going to send you overseas to aid international terrorists."

"With Mr. Plain's help, it will all be easy," the replacement said.

Anger flared in the real Baily's eyes. Joe loved psychological experiments; this one was going well.

"I control the media, so I'll make sure the entire world knows who's doing this. I'll even provide photos."

"My SEAL team will stop your damn impostor."

"Oh, I'm going to kill and replace every member of your team," Joe said.

Baily's eyes scanned the area. The SEAL's handcuffed hands slowly moved toward the Taser darts embedded in his clothing.

Joe pulled the trigger and 50,000 volts sent Baily back to the ground. This time it took him longer to stand. The replacement kept the M4 aimed at his chest.

"Why are you doing this?" Baily grunted.

"You can prevent any violence," Joe said. "Just tell me the information I want, and I won't do any of those things. I'll change your replacement back to his old identity."

"Never." The conviction exuding from the SEAL's expression was almost palpable.

"Fine. We'll go with the plan where you kill your family and become a terrorist," Joe said. "I'll still get the information. The new version of you is going to have access to every secret you know."

Baily looked at his replacement for support. "You can't be as evil as him. We can compromise."

Replacement Baily took a step towards his mirror image. "Mr. Plain claimed you'd be terrified within the first five minutes we saw you. But you don't look scared. You look reasonable."

Original Baily focused his attention on his replacement. "I'm sure we can find common ground. I can give some information, if you promise not to kill anyone."

"We'll find out if you're lying," the replacement said. "That will make things worse."

"I understand. My information will be accurate."

"I'm glad you came to this conclusion," his replacement said. He offered the original Baily a water bottle.

Baily accepted the water as a token of trust, and took a drink, and then spit it out. "Hey, what is this?"

Joe laughed. "It's poison. You swallowed enough to kill you."

"Why would you poison me? I thought you wanted classified information."

"I've replaced generals. Do you think I need information from a fucking Lieutenant?"

"Then why . . . ?"

"For the fun of seeing you betray your country," Joe said. "I knew you'd compromise."

Baily grimaced and wobbled on his feet. "You bastard." He tried to grab Joe.

Joe easily side-stepped Baily. "You'll be remembered as the person who destroyed America."

Joe pointed excitedly at Baily's face. "There it is! Fear."

Replacement Baily checked his watch. "You were right, Mr. Plain. It was less than five minutes."

Original Baily collapsed to his hands and knees. He crawled toward Joe for a few feet until falling on his face. Joe checked his pulse.

"Dead," Joe said.

"Now I'm the toughest man in the world," new Baily said. An arrogant grin spread across his face.

"You're an actor," Joe scoffed. "You'd shit your pants before doing a tenth of what this guy did. I'm moving you to a desk job. I'll let you know what missions I want done, so you can file the paperwork."

The Unspeakable Lightness of Being

"I wish Joe Plain would kill them," I said, pointing at the three men below us.

Albert took a sip of black tea, listening thoughtfully.

Einstein and I were sitting under an umbrella on the rooftop patio of Tu Oso De Peluche, Malibu Graceland's Mexican restaurant. Below us, on the other side of the pool, Marilyn played shuffleboard with Bogie, Joe DiMaggio, and President Kennedy. JFK had his arm around Marilyn's waist, helping align her cue.

"One of those assholes holds Marilyn every time she takes a shot. I'd like to shove their shuffleboard sticks down their throats."

I gulped my Bloody Mary. Einstein sipped some cognac. He seldom drank alcohol, but I was consuming enough for two people. Even a sunny day in January couldn't warm my mood.

"She has a deep affection for you. I can see it in her eyes," Albert said.

"Well, today is my sixth visit to Malibu Graceland, and we never get any time alone. By the time I arrive, other men are already entertaining her."

"I saw you eat dinner together last week."

I finished my Bloody Mary. "Because I'd asked her a week in advance."

"Maybe she'd like you to ask her again."

"I did. She says her schedule is full."

A pretty waitress—a modern movie star with dimples—set a bowl of guacamole on our table. She smiled at me and offered me a martini, which I happily accepted.

Albert waved his arm to indicate the paradise around us. "Relatively speaking, I'd say we have it fairly nice."

"I know. I'm grateful, and I'm trying to be useful. I've been reading books on serial killers, dictators, and psychology, especially schizophrenia and dissociative identity disorder."

"I've appreciated your insight at Court meetings. You often make me think in new directions," Albert said.

Marilyn giggled often as her three handsome suitors entertained her. The joyful sound drifted up to the rooftop patio. "Sometimes I wonder if she'd be happier without me, Albert."

"I doubt it. Your emotion seems to pass the three-point love test."

"Love test?"

Albert patted my shoulder. "If love is unselfish, unconditional and enduring, then it's worth fighting for. I think yours is."

I stood to leave. "Thanks for being a good friend."

"Where are you going, James?"

"To the studio. I have to film today."

"Enjoy yourself. We don't know how long this movie is going to last," Albert said.

I left the Mexican restaurant and headed toward the mansion. People— modern celebrities and historic legends—lounged around the pool, socializing in this artificial heaven. But it was the opposite of heaven to me. I was consumed with frustration. I couldn't keep Marilyn safe from Joe Plain. I couldn't keep her from sleeping with other men. I couldn't get her to fall in love with James Dean. And, if I could win her heart as James, how would that help me in real life?

The situation was driving me crazy. Why should I have to beg for scraps of Marilyn's time, when Janie was my best friend?

I turned around and walked towards the shuffleboard court. Marilyn had claimed not to have any free evenings, so I had to aim lower. Bogie, DiMaggio and JFK watched me as I approached, and I wondered if Marilyn was having sex with any of them.

"Hello, James. I wondered if you were here," Marilyn said.

Bogie's hands were around her hips, and he shot me a look of disdain. DiMaggio and Kennedy completely ignored me.

"I've been with Albert. I'm helping him solve some quantum physics equations."

Marilyn laughed. "Then your brain needs a rest. Why don't you join us?"

"I can't. I have to go to the studio. However, I saw that neither of us will be filming tomorrow. The south courtyard has a place called Kula Chakula

I want to try. Would you'd like to have lunch tomorrow?"

"Sure. Sounds nice." Marilyn kissed me on the cheek.

I winked at Bogie and JFK as I headed towards the main building.

Several hours later, I was at the studio filming a scene with Elizabeth Taylor. I was wearing greasy mechanic overalls at a gas station, when the sultry, violet-eyed beauty pulled up in a convertible Corvette. I filled her tank and checked her engine while she flirted with me—a nifty little scene, but I wasn't sure how it would fit in the plot. After filming, I drove to the small house in North Hollywood which Janie and I, and our two roommates, rented. I made some pasta, talked to my uncle on the phone, and went to bed early. Janie never came home.

The next day, Martin Luther King, Jr. greeted me in the mansion's ballroom to conduct my transformation.

"Happy You Day," I said. "Elvis should give you the day off."

"The holiday is about an ideal, not an individual," Martin said.

MLK worked on the machine settings as I reclined in the chair. "I guess it's a major step down for you, transforming faces instead of minds and souls."

Reverend King smiled. "I don't think they're exclusive."

Soon I began to feel the effects of the anesthesia and drifted into unconsciousness . . . .

When I awakened, I quickly checked the mirror and saw a perfect James Dean.

I'd brought outfit #29—the beige sweater and tan denim pants from *East of Eden*—from the studio, and quickly changed clothes. I hurried to the octagon parlor, entering Malibu Graceland's wonderland once more.

From the top of the double staircase, I scanned the courtyard for Marilyn, gazing over thatch-roofed bars, sun umbrellas and Jacuzzis, until spotting her leaning against a palm tree entertaining Babe Ruth, Jesse Owens and Joe DiMaggio.

If I wasn't jealous, I'd be thrilled with the chance to talk with these sports heroes. I planned to fully appreciate Malibu Graceland once Marilyn and I were dating.

Her blue eyes sparkled when she saw me. I knew Marilyn liked me, I just had to cause her to fall in love with me.

"Hello, James. You know Joe. Have you met Babe and Jesse?" Marilyn asked.

"We haven't met, but I grew up hearing about you," I said. "Someday I'd love to talk with you both."

"Any time," Babe said.

Jesse nodded.

"Well, boys, James is taking me to lunch. I'll see you later," Marilyn said.

I led Marilyn onto a stone path that meandered southwest from the main courtyard to a smaller one. "I've heard this place is good. Elvis told me to try the mandazi."

"I'm not sure what that is, but I trust him," Marilyn said.

The path was lined with bird of paradise and diverged onto a Japanese footbridge over a koi pond. We stopped to watch exotic duck-like birds swimming below us. It was incredibly romantic, but I knew better than to try to kiss her in public.

Einstein rolled down the path toward us on a Segway. He paused by us at the top of the bridge.

"Colors require two miracles," Albert said. "Energy miraculously forms into precise frequencies and wavelengths. Humans miraculously translate these mathematical properties into brilliant hues."

Before we could reply, Albert rode off, shouting, "Got to go—I'm playing bocce with Cindy Crawford."

Marilyn put her arm around my waist. "You never know what you're going to get here."

Our path circled through gardens toward the southern courtyard. This part of the estate was less popular, and it contained a different crowd. More scientists, artists and writers.

We passed a sculpture garden where Ernest Goldenhart was sitting on a bench between John F. Kennedy and Ronald Reagan. "Maybe Ernest would be a good president, if he's seeking advice from the right people," I said.

Soon we were seated at Kula Chakula, drinking palm toddies. The African-themed bar had a thatch roof and outdoor seating on a deck beside an oval pool.

A few tables away, Chuck Yeager and Orville Wright were arguing about wing shapes, waving their arms around to demonstrate. Dick Van Dyke sat with Farrah Fawcett at a corner table.

"I wish I could take you somewhere special for Valentine's Day," I said. "But since we can't go anywhere but this estate, I'd like to make you dinner at one of the bungalows."

"Valentine's? That's a month away. I don't plan anything that far ahead."

"Well, I'm reserving the day. Don't plan anything with Bogie or Frank or Joe or Jack or Babe or—"

"I wish you'd enjoy yourself more, James, instead of always fretting about the future."

I sipped some of my palm toddy. "I love you the most. And I'm going to prove it."

Marilyn smiled and put her hand on mine. "How?"

I took another sip. "I'm not sure yet. But it will be decisive."

Marilyn stared into my eyes, and I wondered what she was thinking. Did she know I was Darrin? Either she didn't know, or she was the best actress ever.

"I could have beat Sputnik," grunted the stranger beside me.

"Excuse me?" I said.

The man indicated toward a TV monitor. CNN was interviewing a NASA spokesman about SpaceX's latest rocket launch.

"Were you an astronaut?"

The man shook his head sadly. "You don't recognize me?"

I tried to recollect the distinguished-looking man on the stool next to me. He wore a navy suit and red tie. "I'm sorry, I can't recall your face."

"I should be ranked among America's greatest heroes," the man lamented. "Instead the US government let the Russians beat me."

"Who are you?" Marilyn asked.

"Wernher Von Braun. I ran America's rocket programs in the '50s. My rockets were ready to orbit earth before the Soviet's Sputnik satellite, but President Eisenhower stopped me."

"Why? We were in a space race," Marilyn said.

"Our technology was far ahead. Ike knew that, if America launched the first satellite, the Soviets would declare it an act of aggression."

He took a drink, and looked like he was haunted by the past.

"The president devised a plan called 'Open Skies,' which basically meant holding me back. In 1956, more than a year before Sputnik, I launched a rocket that could have orbited the earth, but I was forced to fill the fourth stage with sand instead of rocket fuel."

"I remember how afraid Americans were when Sputnik flew over us," Marilyn said.

"The Russians called Sputnik a great triumph. They boasted and praised Communism. However, they also couldn't deny the right of other countries to go into orbit. Ike got his Open Skies. America got a space race it knew it would win. I lost my place in history."

For over an hour, Wernher told firsthand stories about space exploration. You weren't allowed to lie at Malibu Graceland, yet something sounded fishy. As soon as he left, I Googled him on my iPhone.

"Everything Wernher said is true," I told Marilyn. "But he omitted a lot. Wernher was the Nazi's leading scientist until he surrendered to American soldiers in 1945. He ran Hitler's rocket program, including the V-2 rockets that terrorized London."

Marilyn sighed. "The difference between a great man and an evil man is sometimes merely circumstance."

"No." I shook my head. "Only a coward can be made evil."

"I suppose you're right, James."

I shuddered, considering it. "It would be horrible to be transformed into a Nazi. I'm glad we were both cast as good people."

Marilyn clenched her jaw. I wasn't supposed to mention being transformed. She looked like she might slap me.

"I've been cast in many parts, James. Some were unchaste, but never evil."

At times like this, I worried her Janie-ness was slipping away. This jeopardized our connection.

Marilyn checked the time and stood. "Sorry, I've got to run. I'm getting a singing lesson from Frank. He reserved a bungalow, so we'd have privacy to practice."

Damn Sinatra and his magnificent voice. How was I going to compete with that? Marilyn had rejected all my attempts to get her alone in a bungalow.

I stood, too. "Why don't I come and watch? I'd like to hear you sing."

Marilyn rolled her eyes. "It's a private lesson. I'm lucky Frank will teach me."

"Whatever. Why don't I reserve a bungalow for tomorrow night, so we can practice?"

"Practice what? You don't need a bungalow to fix cars or ride motorcycles."

I put my hand on hers. "I'm good at other things . . . ."

She yanked her hand away. "Really? That's the best you can offer?"

"I'm going to capture Joe Plain," I said.

Marilyn twitched in surprised. "The entire Court has failed. You're going to do it by yourself?"

"Well, I have to keep you safe. And prove my love is better than singing or politicking or playing baseball."

"I'm not a competition."

"You're everything to me. I'm going to stop Joe Plain. My goal is to do it before Valentine's."

Marilyn gave me a peck on the lips. "I'll see you later, James." She smiled and trotted toward the beach bungalows.

I stayed at the bar, drinking, thinking, and watching people. Did Joe Plain have any weaknesses?

Joe wouldn't be patient or humble. He'd be a control freak. Maybe, he was overconfident. Perhaps, he overlooked details. I doubted he had any real friends, but controlled people by fear.

Did Joe have any loyal supporters? I doubted Joe would sacrifice anything for anyone. Malibu Graceland was full of people who cared deeply about each other.

Leaving the bar, I wandered haphazardly, trying to think up a plan. Instead, all I could think about was Marilyn alone with Frank Sinatra. My mind filled with felicitous scenarios which would embarrass Frank, Bogie, and JFK. Then, delightedly, I realized that one of them would also hurt Joe Plain.

I searched for Elvis, until I spotted him leaving the Polynesian restaurant. I hurried to him. "I've got a plan, Elvis, that will reveal Joe Plain's identity."

Pretty Woman

"Love looks through a telescope;
envy, through a microscope."
—Josh Billings

Stars twinkled above the stage Elvis had built beside Malibu Graceland's largest pool. Moonlight reflected in ripples on the curvaceous pool, around which twenty round tables had been decorated for al fresco dining. A light, balmy breeze swayed palm trees, and there were numerous heat lamps, but the atmosphere at our table was cold and nasty.

"Bitches!" Marilyn coughed into her napkin.

Her face was red, her mascara moist, a vein on her neck pulsing. She bit her lip, fuming. The three other women at our table smiled at Marilyn's reaction.

"I've never seen such a lovely necklace, Jackie," Lauren Bacall said.

"You make everything look classy, Jackie," Ava Gardner added.

"Thank you," Jackie said. She grabbed President Kennedy's hand and gave it a kiss. "The necklace has sentimental value from a very romantic anniversary."

Marilyn wore an almost identical necklace, although none of the women mentioned it.

Jackie turned to Ava. "Your skin looks stunning in that red dress."

"Absolutely. It's such a pretty color, Ava, and you wear it so well," Lauren said.

Marilyn's dress was an equally vibrant red. Ava, Jackie and Lauren had been complimenting each other all evening, while slinging not-so-subtle insults at Marilyn.

"You're ten times more beautiful than any of them," I whispered to Marilyn.

The three other men at our table—Bogie, Frank Sinatra, and JFK—had laughed all evening during their own conversation, ignoring me and the women as their wives harassed Marilyn.

The King of Rock, on stage since our arrival, entertained us as emcee. Elvis had enthusiastically implemented my plan, especially his role. Every actor and actress ever to use a transform-machine—except those who'd been murdered—was here, eating under the stars and awaiting the special surprise Elvis had promised.

Main courses covered buffet tables illuminated by Tiki torches, and drones soared through the air, serving hors d'oeuvres and refilling drinks. It was the first purely social gathering of the iconic historical figures, and the exhilaration was enhanced by Elvis' declaration that there would be an important announcement.

Elvis and his Court believed Joe Plain had spies at Malibu Graceland, which meant he would know about tonight's event. The killer would demand to know immediately about Elvis' surprise announcement. The purpose of the drones wasn't really to serve guests. Nikola Tesla had programmed the drones to fly behind people who were using their phones, zoom onto the screen, and record the message.

If anyone sent a text about the evening, we would know. There was also the possibility that Joe himself was seated among us. He could replace or become anyone. The drones might even catch Joe sending orders to his underlings.

"I still can't believe Teddy was murdered. There must be another explanation," Ava Gardner said.

Only people who'd attended Court meetings knew about Joe Plain.

"There might be murder at that table." Jackie pointed to where Liz Taylor flirted with Eddie Fisher. Richard Burton, moving down the buffet line, hadn't noticed yet.

"That could get ugly," Marilyn agreed.

Lauren flashed a venomous look at Marilyn. "Liz doesn't bother me. She's a great actress. I hate it when a bimbo with no talent gets to the top."

Marilyn dropped her knife and fork with a clang. "Bimbo is what women call someone prettier than they are."

"No, a bimbo is someone who sleeps with other women's husbands," Jackie said.

The fangs and claws were out. Marilyn looked furious enough to gouge out someone's eyes, and I didn't think she was acting.

Our emotions were real, even if our hatred was of fake identities, and our jealousy involved fake spouses.

Janie was as defensive about Marilyn's past as I was proud of James Dean's. Everyone here tonight had completely transferred her or his identity. We were fully living lies.

No. One thing is real: my love for Janie. In the midst of overwhelming deceit, I hoped my love would prevail.

Bogie clinked his glass with his fork. "Elvis is about to say something important."

Elvis stood on the stage beside the pool, waiting for quiet.

"Thank you for all being here. I have something special to announce," Elvis said. "Tonight, we're having a surprise talent show."

"That's it?" JFK moaned. There were other groans of disappointment and some joyful cheers. I also saw several people texting on their phones as drones circled behind them to record. Nikola was confident he could determine the recipient of any texts, and Einstein felt he could decode any messages.

"I'm going to randomly pull a name from a hat," Elvis said. "I will perform first, and whoever I pick will perform second. Before each act, I'll pick another name. This way everyone can prepare, during the performance before theirs."

There was mumbling. Some people were clearly eager to perform, while others would rather not.

Elvis reached into a black top hat and pulled out a piece of paper. "Albert Einstein," he read.

A spotlight searched the crowd, until stopping on Albert, who looked quite shocked.

"You've got three minutes, Albert. That's the length of my song," Elvis said. The King strummed his guitar and began to sing "It's Now or Never."

Einstein ran towards the beach bungalows, where people could spend the night if they didn't have to film the next morning. The audience smiled as Elvis performed, realizing this was going to be a pleasurable evening.

When Elvis finished singing, Albert hadn't returned. The King of Rock reached into the top hat, pulled a name, and read "Lucy Ball." As the spotlight found Lucy's face, Einstein rushed onto the stage, huffing and puffing, carrying a violin he must have retrieved from a bungalow.

The physicist placed the instrument on his chin. "I will play Mozart's 'Sonata in B-flat Major'." He smiled and suddenly the bow was flying with vigor across the strings.

Einstein was superb, as the original Einstein had been. The studio had only cast people ideal for their characters.

Bogie, Frank and JFK held their spouses' hands. Marilyn's hands were in her lap, showing no inclination to hold mine. I looked around the courtyard and saw Joe DiMaggio sitting calmly. He gave me a little wave.

The baseball star was different than my other rivals. Most men had used Marilyn and then abandoned her. Joe DiMaggio had adored Marilyn. Yet, he'd treated her so jealously that Marilyn had divorced him on grounds of "mental cruelty."

It was an important lesson. I needed to find a perfect balance between devotion and possessiveness.

Elvis had let me decide the evening's seating, so I'd placed DiMaggio at a table with seven gorgeous young ladies. Hopefully, he'd find a girlfriend. However, this could backfire—Marilyn was hardly immune to envy.

Yet, Janie wasn't a jealous person. Would Marilyn act more like Marilyn or Janie?

Another strategic question: would she like me more or less if I flirted with other women? Also, would Marilyn let my history as Darrin affect her love for James Dean?

I was mentally exhausted. I'd spent my life trying to be perfect for Janie. Now I had to shape myself to please three people: Janie, Janie acting as Marilyn, and Marilyn. They were all very different.

The audience of about 200 people howled with laughter as Lucy performed a comedic routine. Most seemed clueless that a ruthless murderer was hunting them.

Keeping Janie safe is the priority. I had to stay focused. Hopefully, the drones would discover Joe Plain's identity. Then, we'd see how invincible he was.

158

Braveheart

"For it was not into my ear you whispered, but into my heart.
It was not my lips you kissed, but my soul."
—Judy Garland

"Darrin."

Janie was whispering my name. Was I dreaming? I was incredibly warm and cozy.

Where am I?

I opened my eyes, but it was too dark to see anything. A soft pillow was in my arms. I was too tired to move, and shut my eyes again.

A warm body snuggled next to mine. I felt a smooth leg, a hip, a shoulder. Janie's wonderful curves. Janie's jasmine scent beguiled. I kept my eyes shut and enjoyed the dream. It had to be a dream, as Janie would never be this intimate.

After the talent show last week, Marilyn and I had taken a walk in a garden, our lips had found each other near a statue of Venus, and we had made love in the grass under a willow tree. Since then, we'd lunched together twice at Malibu Graceland, and held hands under the table. However, Janie still never showed any affection to me as Darrin.

A few hours earlier, I'd left Malibu Graceland to drive home to the North Hollywood house we rented. I had to be at the studio by 6 a.m., so I needed to sleep in my unattractive face tonight. Janie was also filming in the morning, so I'd been surprised not to see her car in the driveway. Our other two other roommates, young aspiring musicians, never came home on weekends, so I had decided to wait for Janie on the living room couch.

The last thing I remembered was pulling a blanket over me as I stretched out on the couch.

"Darrin," Janie whispered sweetly.

Best dream ever.

Only in my imagination had I ever held Janie this tenderly. I caressed the soft skin of her thigh and listened to her breathing. My arm traced her torso and cupped her breast.

Wait, I'm not dreaming.

My eyes opened wide, adjusting to the darkness. I could see Janie's profile. She'd arrived while I slept and crawled under a blanket with me.

I felt my own face. *Yes, I am Darrin.* I checked her profile. It really was Janie. She was intimately embracing me as Janie.

"Is this okay, Darrin?" she whispered.

"Yes," I gasped. I'd longed for this my entire life.

She was being affectionate as Janie! Would my dreams come true... would I get to kiss her as Janie?

"I'm sorry," Janie said. "I've been a fool for being loyal to a stupid contract rather than the man I love."

Love. She said love. "What made you change your mind?"

Janie gently kissed my hand. "Marilyn did. She's been teaching me for months, but I'm a slow learner."

Her fingers stroked my hair, and she seemed attracted to me, even as Darrin. "Tonight, I realized I was making the same two mistakes Marilyn did. She let studios control her. And she gave herself to rich, powerful men who didn't offer her a future. All Marilyn really longed for was to be loved and to have a family, yet she never had a stable marriage and was forced to have several abortions she didn't want.

"I love being Marilyn, but I can learn from her mistakes." She kissed my forehead. "I'm going to love you—all of you. James and Darrin."

It was everything I'd ever wished for. "I've loved all of you forever, Janie. I've never cared about the movie or Malibu Graceland or anything else."

"I know," Janie said. "I feel that way now, too. I'm sorry it took me so long to get here."

I grabbed her face and kissed her hard on the lips. Our first intimate kiss as Janie and Darrin. It was different, more genuine, no longer a role-playing game. Janie kissed differently, with greater urgency, than she did as Marilyn.

It was the kiss of soul mates—who knew they'd never kiss anyone else again. I couldn't imagine ever being unhappy again.

"You must think I'm stupid. The machines show that everything but love is superficial, and you're the man who always loved me." Janie wrapped her body around mine, and I wished the rest of the universe would disappear. I didn't know if we were headed toward sex or sharing feelings, but I couldn't help getting an erection.

We kissed for a long time, each moment more incredible than the last. "I love you. You're also the only person I trust," Janie said. "We spend our days with people who could be spies or Joe Plain."

It felt great to talk openly. Janie knew I was James—I'd never been sure before.

"We can't trust anyone involved with the studio," I said. "Joe is either connected to the movie or Malibu Graceland."

The drones at the talent show had recorded texts from several people. However, all of them seemed unrelated to Joe Plain. If they were encoded, it was too complex even for Einstein.

"From now on, we need to be a team," Janie said. "The studio's secrecy helps Joe Plain. People don't confide in each other because of their contracts."

"Yet, maybe the reason we're alive is that people don't know our real identity."

Janie leaned away from me. For the first time I noticed a little bump on her belly. Her hands rested on the bump, almost instinctively.

Was it possible . . . that Janie was Janie pregnant?

If so, did it happen during our December date in Rex's car? Is this why she was committing to me?

"Is there anything you want to tell me, Janie?"

"I am telling you! I love you!"

I kissed her on the lips. "You can tell me anything."

"I'm scared, Darrin. Do you think anyone can stop Joe Plain?"

"Of course.

"Dutch knows everyone's identities," Janie said. "So do Rex and Jacqueline and other executives. Do you think they could capture Joe?"

"No. I think the Court has the best chance. We just don't know where to start looking."

"Is there anyone you think could be Joe?"

"I've tried, using every acting technique I know, to place myself into Joe's mind, as if I'm preparing for my most important role ever … like this …." I shut my eyes and concentrated.

"I call myself Joe Plain and have a generic face I created myself. I had access to the studio, learned about machines which change appearances, and stole one. Now I use the machine to murder and replace powerful people. I'm probably not an actor, for they are controlled too tightly, and I was at the Rodeo Drive at the same time as the cast.

"Could I be Ernest Goldenhart? Did I go from a squeaky-clean life in business and the Peace Corp to a serial killer? Possibly. If I want to be president, would it be helpful to control the media? Yes. Do I want to control the police or the FBI? Possibly. Do I demand Dutch stop filming? Probably not. Did I fake an entire fundraiser to have an alibi? Probably not.

"Could I be Rex Shackleford? Am I a rich playboy entertainment executive who wants more thrills? Maybe. Does my life of glitz, glamour and girls make me feel invincible and egocentric? Probably. Do I want to control the media, the police, etc.? Maybe. Do I demand that Dutch stop filming? Probably not."

I opened my eyes. "I've done this exercise several times. This is as far as I get."

"The entire movie industry hates Impact Studio. Maybe someone is paying Joe Plain to hurt Dutch and the studio," Janie suggested.

"I don't think Joe could be paid to do anything. He could get infinitely rich by replacing rich people with substitutes."

Janie sighed. "I wonder if Dutch and Rex will agree to Joe's demands."

"Well, Elvis is afraid they will. He thinks they'll stop filming, at least for a few months. And give Joe some more machines."

For an hour, Janie and I talked about Malibu Graceland, the Court, and the movie. The partition between Janie and Marilyn was gone, and we had all the conversations I'd imagined in my mind. Mostly, though, I thought about Janie's belly. Her hands kept drifting toward the bump on her stomach, but she pulled them away whenever she saw me looking.

"How do you think Elvis picks members of the Court?"

"He wants diverse skills from people he trusts who can help run the estate."

I mentally ran through the responsibilities of permanent Court members. Milton managed finances. Patton handled security. Albert was in charge of IT. Eleanor handled the staffing. Nikola was responsible for maintenance. Lucille Ball oversaw entertainment. Walt procured the estate's supplies. MLK and Jimmy Stewart oversaw transformations. Bogie was second in command.

"Do you think Orson could finish the movie using legacy scenes, if we stopped filming?" Janie asked.

"Maybe, but many people haven't filmed them yet. It wouldn't be the movie they're hoping for."

"However, it could stop Joe from killing people." Janie rested her head against my shoulder, and I reached toward her little belly bump. She yanked my hand away.

"I've gained a little weight." She looked shy and embarrassed.

"You look perfect to me."

Janie gripped my hands. Her posture softened, as if an internal conflict had melted. "You really love me, don't you?"

"Entirely. Nothing will ever change that."

"Tell me more."

Janie seemed so vulnerable. I admitted to moving to LA simply for the chance to be near her. I revealed that I'd only become an actor to support her dream. "You're my foremost thought no matter what else I'm thinking."

She stared at her tummy and burst into tears. "I've been afraid, but no longer."

"Do you have something to tell me?"

She looked so fragile. "Maybe tonight is enough. Even one night. Maybe your love is enough."

My gut felt like cement. "But you love me, too, right?"

Janie stared at me with excruciating pain in her eyes. "I'd love you forever if I could."

"What's wrong?"

Janie sobbed. "I'm not the real Janie." She lifted her blouse and revealed a foamy pad. She pulled away the pad, exposing wires and electric components.

"Get away," Janie cried frantically. "They know."

A stoic, but peaceful expression swept over her face. She rolled off the sofa, hit the floor and curled into a ball.

I heard a bang, a dreadful sound like the popping of gunpowder. A blast of light flashed around her; then smoke rose near her stomach.

"Janie!" I switched on a light and rushed to her side. Her eyes blazed in terror. In the light I could tell they weren't the eyes of the real Janie.

I rolled her onto her back and saw blood gushing from her stomach. The device must have been both a microphone and a bomb.

She smiled. "See, I did love you."

"I'll call an ambulance."

"Too late. Just hold me."

I grasped her tightly. Watching her die nearly broke me. She looked identical to Janie except the pattern of her blue eyes.

"I'm sorry." She wept. "Joe Plain made me do it. He listened to everything you said tonight about Elvis, the Court, and Dutch."

Suddenly I panicked. Joe wouldn't make an imposter without killing the original.

"The real Janie—where is she?"

"I don't know. Honestly, I don't." She looked miserable, as if betraying me was worse than death.

I believed her. She'd sacrificed her life to show me the truth.

"Who are you?"

Fake Janie coughed up blood. "Nobody. Just an unemployed actress. Joe paid me to study you and Janie for months."

She was gasping for each breath. "Joe is ruthless. I tried to quit. The more I learned about your love for Janie, the more I hated what I was doing."

"Tell me about Joe."

"He's probably on his way here. You need to run. He'll kill you."

It felt like the real Janie was dying in my arms. "I won't leave you."

She smiled weakly. "I don't mind dying. For the first time, I know how love feels. Now run away."

My heart was breaking. "I won't leave you."

She shut her eyes. "Then pretend . . . pretend I'm really . . ."

She died in my arms.

I shook her in panic. She wasn't breathing. *Fuck. Fuck. Fuck.*

I grabbed my cell phone. No service. Out the window, I saw movement. Armed men in black ski masks were running toward our house. Across the road sat two unmarked white vans and a black delivery truck.

I heard the back door being smashed open. Three huge men in ski masks entered the family room and aimed their guns at my chest. More men bolted into the house and began to search the other rooms. I thought of everything I'd told fake Janie.

I've revealed all of Elvis' secrets.

And I'd be dead before I could warn him.

Would they replace me?

A plain-looking man entered the room with a face so generic, it hardly registered as humans. The face didn't exude any humanity at all. He walked past the armed men and smiled with a nondescript appearance.

"You're Joe Plain."

"I am. Thank you for all the information tonight."

"What did you do to Janie?"

"The real Janie is dead, just like the fake one."

My soul felt like it popped, leaving just a shell of a body. I couldn't breathe.

Joe laughed. "We tortured her until we got her password. Then I killed her, just as I'm going to kill you."

I charged at Joe. I only took two steps before one of the masked men grabbed my arm and easily tossed me across the room. I crashed into the wall and slid to my knees.

"What's your password?" Joe demanded.

I gazed around the room for a weapon as two masked men came toward me. I tried to run, but they grabbed my wrists and pulled them behind my back and lifted my arms until I was helpless. They forced me to face-to-face with Joe.

Joe smiled calmly. "If you're curious, Marilyn's password is 'gingerbread.' Elvis' response is 'firefly.' Janie gave us a few false passwords before we got the real ones."

Behind Joe, two masked men spread a black tarp on the floor. They picked up fake Janie's body and dropped it roughly on the tarp. Without the slightest sympathy, they rolled the tarp over her and carried her away.

Joe turned to one of his minions, a man smaller than the rest. "Go to the van and get my equipment."

The man left, and Joe faced me. "You only have one more decision to make before you die. How long will you be tortured before you tell me your password?"

"Fuck you, you freakish-faced maniac."

The man returned with a suitcase of torture instruments. I tried to hide my terror as Joe calmly arranged items on my coffee table: razors, needles, a propane torch, an electric sander.

"If there's an afterlife, you'll see Janie soon," Joe said. "I'm curious how long you'll decide to suffer first."

Die Another Day

"My password isn't a word, it's a hand symbol. I'll show you," I said.

One of the men loosened his grip, allowing my hand to move. I gave my middle finger to Joe Plain.

Joe slapped me. I used that momentum to kick the coffee table, sending the torture instruments scattering. I reached for a razor—

My head felt like it had exploded as a fist hit my jaw. The punch lifted me up and knocked me backwards. I tumbled across the room and hit the wall. My jaw seared in pain, while my legs quivered and I collapsed to the floor.

I tried to stand on wobbly legs, and almost was balanced when I heard a diesel engine.

The house rumbled and my attackers jumped back as the living room wall crashed forward. A delivery truck drove into the room, breaking the couch into two pieces and separating me from my assailants.

A man in a cowboy hat and sunglasses with a bandana around his face was gripping the steering wheel.

I opened the passenger door and jumped inside. The cowboy shifted into reverse; dust and plaster tumbled off the truck as it revved backwards. Joe and his men were right in front of us, scrambling onto their feet.

"Stay down," my rescuer yelled as he spun onto the grass. Bullets sprayed through the truck as we turned onto the street. Beyond the window, an irate Joe screamed commands and his men ran to their vans.

Everything seemed to unfold slowly in the distance. Janie was dead. Did anything else matter? People were shooting at us? Who cared? All bullets would do was kill me.

Janie is dead. What was the use of being rescued?

Janie is dead. Nothing mattered now.

Janie is dead. How could I live without her?

"You're in shock, James. Look at me," the cowboy shouted.

Bullets made metallic pings as they blasted holes in our truck. The cowboy drove recklessly as two white vans pursued us.

Revenge. That was my purpose.

"I need you to drive, Darrin, so I can shoot back," the cowboy said.

Kill Joe Plain. Happiness would never exist again. But I would avenge Janie's death.

"Snap out of it. I need your help." The voice sounded familiar.

The cowboy pulled down his bandana. Elvis.

"Marilyn is alive. Now grab the wheel."

Alive! Janie is alive? Elvis wouldn't lie. Relief flooded me. I grabbed the steering wheel as he slid off the seat. I moved onto the driver's seat, alert to everything and pumped with adrenaline.

I hit the brakes and started a U-turn.

Elvis yanked the wheel and turned us straight again. We almost hit a tree. "What the hell are you doing?"

"I'm going to run over Joe."

Elvis kept the truck straight. "Holy crap, James, you'd only get us killed. There's at least six of them guns. And if Joe controls the police like he claims, they will be here soon."

"I have to kill him."

"We will. But not by being reckless. Drive away from them."

Elvis went to the back of the truck. We were on a tree-lined residential street in the middle of the night. The two white vans attempted to pull in beside our truck to shoot us, so I swerved back and forth, trying to force them behind us. Elvis reappeared, carrying a short, chubby weapon. The barrel was too fat to be a shotgun.

"It's from the studio. Turn right at the next street," Elvis instructed as he leaned out the window.

I skidded into a right turn, and Elvis fired the weapon. A loud noise followed, and in the rear-view mirror I saw a projectile hit the ground and create a thick cloud of gray smoke. The vans swerved, trying to avoid the hazard; one made it through the smoke, and the other crashed into a wooden fence.

"Another right turn!" Elvis shouted.

I turned. Elvis fired again. Once again, the projectile created a massive amount of smoke. The remaining van skidded toward the curb, out of control. I saw Joe's angry face just before they hit a telephone poll.

"Take that, you plain-faced fucker!" Elvis pumped his fists and high-fived me.

"Go west, James."

"West? It's faster to Malibu on the 134."

"We'll never get to Malibu in this truck."

I heard police sirens approaching us. I turned west, and the sirens passed. Yet there were more behind them.

"If Joe Plain controls the police, there will be helicopters soon," Elvis said. "Head toward the studio. Let's see how far we can get."

I drove down Burbank side streets, avoiding sirens until the mechanical roar of a helicopter blitzed our ears.

A searchlight appeared behind us, illuminating the street and heading towards us.

"Ditch the car under that tree," Elvis said.

I parked where he pointed as the searchlight passed over us, assaulting us with a harsh light and then moving on. Sirens blared from nearby streets.

"Now we walk." Elvis left the smoke shooter in the truck. We set off at a fast pace down a residential street. It was 3:25 a.m., and the middle-class homes were dark and tranquil. The studio was about eight to ten blocks away.

Elvis knew my real identity. "Where's the actress playing Marilyn?" I asked.

"She's still Marilyn, and she's at the mansion. I saw her late last night, and was surprised she hadn't gone home, since we're filming in the morning. When I asked her, she said you'd told her not to transform. That seemed strange. When neither of us could reach you by phone, I put on this hasty disguise and drove the delivery truck from the mansion. Dutch told me your identity. I only intended to check on you, not drive through a wall."

"You saved my life."

"They removed a body, and it looked like they were going to kill you, so I drove into the house. Who did they kill?"

"An imposter of Marilyn's other identity." Joe knew Janie's identity, so it was better if Elvis did, too. "Her name is Janie."

"You love her," Elvis said. Definitely not a question. "You love her in both identities."

"I'd love her under any circumstance. I wish we'd never gotten involved with the movie."

Two police cars turned down our street, and we hid behind a thorny shrub until they passed.

"At least now we know for sure that Joe controls the police," Elvis said.

"Can I use your phone to call Marilyn?"

"No. Joe is probably tracing calls. I never use my phone if I can avoid it."

As I walked beside the King of Rock, I felt many emotions—anger, relief, gratitude, fear—but the primary one was guilt.

I forced myself to look him in his eyes. "Elvis, I screwed up. I told Joe everything."

"No, Darrin. I screwed up. I put you in danger. I didn't protect your identity well enough."

"I revealed everything I know. Everything the Court has discussed."

"I need a word-by-word replay of exactly what Joe heard. But first, Galapagos."

"Napoleon."

Then I repeated, as close as I could recall, the conversation between me and fake Janie. I was only half done when Elvis stopped me. We were a block from the studio, and about to leave the safety of residential streets.

Elvis pulled out a set of keys and pressed a button. In the nearest driveway, the lights of a gray F-150 pickup came on.

"The studio owns this property," Elvis said. "Dutch bought it as a safe house for emergencies."

An inconspicuous two-story yellow house occupied the corner lot. Three cars sat in the driveway, including the pickup.

"Joe probably spies on the entrances of the studio," Elvis said. "But I doubt Joe knows about this."

Thirty minutes later, me driving the pickup and Elvis reclining out of sight, we cruised through Malibu a few miles from Malibu Graceland. By then I'd shared my entire conversation with the imposter Janie.

"So, how tall was Joe Plain?" Elvis asked.

"About 5'9", far shorter than Dutch or Orson."

"Joe can't be Ernest either. He's campaigning in Iowa."

"We've eliminated everyone but Rex," I said.

Elvis didn't respond. He was convinced Rex wasn't Joe.

I intended to drive straight to Malibu Graceland, but Elvis directed me to turn onto an unfamiliar street. "We can't drive straight to the estate, especially tonight. Joe's men are always watching. They'd kill us before we reached the gate," Elvis said.

Elvis guided me to a spectacular mostly-glass, modern house. Three stories of vertical glass panels blended with cascading redwood beams that crisscrossed to form balconies. Janie would love the simple grace of the architecture.

The King entered a code at the gate. It opened, and we drove past dense arboreal landscaping before parking in a circular driveway between two jacaranda trees.

High vaulted ceilings greeted us as we entered the house. The living room had floor-to-ceiling windows on three sides and overlooked a pool illuminated by turquoise underwater lights. Elvis led me outside to the guest house behind the coruscating pool. His face showed more excitement than he'd ever displayed, even when we performed stunts.

"Prepare to see the coolest thing ever," the King of Rock said. "You'll have to wear tights."

Up

Elvis opened the guesthouse closet, revealing two unusual outfits hanging on the wall. They were black with tanks on the back, something that astronauts or scuba divers might wear in a James Bond film.

"They're jetpacks," Elvis said. "They have an 8.5 thrust-to-weight ratio and a range of 2000 feet. See if these tights fit."

He tossed me a black outfit that covered everything besides the hands and face. I tried it on and it was a little large, but I made it work.

"They watch the roads and the beach, but not the air," Elvis said as we carried the jetpacks outside. We helped place them on each other's backs.

The backyard was surrounded by Italian cypress trees, but if I looked through gaps between the trees, I could see lights to the north. "That's the beach at Malibu Graceland," Elvis said.

He pressed a button attached to his keychain, and all the outdoor lights turned off. "I've designed a path that keeps us hidden when we approach."

"It's so dark. How can we fly?"

"Your eyes adjust. Just squeeze the throttle for power and lean to turn. Follow me."

He squeezed his throttle and slowly lifted off the ground. Elvis ascended about twenty feet and hovered. Peering into the darkness, I could only see his outline.

I held my breath and gently squeezed the throttle. My feet began to feel light. Then gravity disappeared. I was drifting to the left, so I leaned right. I went too far and wobbled like a bobblehead.

Each sideways motion multiplied, and adding throttle made it worse. Yet slowly I lifted upward . . . 3 . . . 10 . . . 15 feet off the ground. Each slight tilt brought panic that I'd flip over and crash headfirst into the ground.

"Keep going," Elvis encouraged.

I kept squeezing and ascended almost as high as Elvis, but before I reached his side, he leaned forward and soared over the cypress trees.

Cautiously, I tilted my body forward and followed Elvis into the darkness.

There seemed to be something between me and Elvis. Too late, I realized it was a palm tree. I hit the fronds and lost stability. I zipped and zagged trying to stay upright. When I regained my balance, Elvis was gone.

What now? It was so dark, I couldn't tell if I was over land or water. I was afraid I'd lose stability again if I tried to turn.

Suddenly, from behind me, Elvis appeared. He deftly hovered beside me. "Keep your elbows by your side and your legs straight. Only lean with your shoulders."

He leaned back and forth to demonstrate, and then zoomed forward. I was scared to get left alone in the darkness, and leaned forward to follow.

It proved smoother than I'd imagined. With slight adjustments, I successfully kept him in sight.

Bright stars shone about us, which made me feel part of an infinite galaxy. In the starlight, I could see the white of crashing waves, which revealed we were headed out to sea, flying about fifteen feet above the ocean. It felt magical, and too beautiful for words. I sped forward until I was by Elvis' side.

Elvis made a slight adjustment right, and I matched him. I was soaring over the sea, side-by-side with the King of Rock 'n' Roll.

For fun, I did a figure eight, reveling in controlled flight.

"Stop messing around. You'll run out of fuel," Elvis said.

Run out of fuel? Crap. I'd drown with all this weight on my back.

I stayed close to Elvis as we approached shore. We flew over the gardens on the southern edge of the estate. There were no lights on the beach, but some of the bungalows had a glimmer of light and the mansion glowed brightly.

Elvis hovered over a small maintenance shed. "Land slowly. Keep your legs wide and your knees slightly bent."

We lowered, Elvis smoothly, me shakily, until our feet hit the ground. I stumbled forward, but didn't fall.

"Not bad for the first time," Elvis said as he helped me out of my jetpack. We stowed our flying machines and black outfits in the shed. Hurrying to the main building, we headed straight to the elevator.

When the elevator door opened in the Memphis Room, the entire Court was waiting for us. My gaze went directly to Marilyn.

My heart was deluged in joy. A part of me had never been convinced she was okay. I dashed to Marilyn and felt her face. "It's really you." I checked her eyes. "You're alive!"

I kissed her, overwhelmed with gratitude, and held her tight. I vowed silently to devote my life to keeping her safe.

As we hugged, I sensed something was very wrong. I felt a strange, awkward sensation. Was she upset I'd kissed her in public? It seemed more severe than that. My gut told me I'd done something terrible.

Suddenly I realized I was Darrin. Uncouth, ugly Darrin. It was worse than being naked—I had the wrong face.

How could Darrin have kissed Marilyn Monroe? I pulled out of our embrace and stared at Marilyn with contrition.

Elvis seemed to read my thoughts. "Never be ashamed of who you are."

"Appearances don't matter, we've all learned that," Jimmy Stewart said. Now the Court knew both my identities.

I grabbed Marilyn's hand. "Joe Plain knows your other identity. Your life's in danger."

Bogie sized me up, sneering like I was cow shit. "So, you're the kid who plays James Dean . . . ."

I ignored him, only concerned about Marilyn. "Why didn't you come home? You were supposed to transform and come home."

"I got a message from you when I was about to transform. You said your uncle was sick and you intended to spend the night in Bakersfield. You suggested I stay here tonight and meet you at our house in the morning."

"That was Joe," I said. "Joe left you the message. He intended to find out my secrets and kill me. He probably planned to kill you when you showed up in the morning."

"We can't let this happen again," Elvis said. "We can't trust anyone unless we see them face-to-face. No phone calls, messages, or texts. And I'm going to have to add you both to the list of people who can't safely leave the estate."

"What? Some people can never leave?" I asked.

"Not easily. My other identity, and those of Bogie and Orson."

"How will we film?" Marilyn asked.

"I'll arrange for secret transportation."

I wanted to protest, but I also wanted to keep Janie alive. I looked around the room. Three Court members were missing. "Where are Albert, Lucy, and Martin?"

"They didn't stay at the estate tonight," Marilyn said. "Bogie and I assembled every Court member here."

"Well, what the hell happened?" General Patton barked. "Did you see Joe Plain?"

The King of Rock put his hand on my shoulder. "Let's all sit down, and you can tell everything from beginning to end. I'd like to hear it again, anyway."

Everyone selected seats and gazed at me from sofas and chairs. I remained standing in the middle of the Memphis Room.

Their safety was more important than my embarrassment, and Joe Plain knew everything about me and Janie. So, I repeated my conversation with the imposter Janie word-for-word.

I explained the story of being awakened by a fake Janie, who turned out to have been bugged. I repeated my observations and opinions about the Court, and even my private declarations of love to fake Janie. I felt stupid for revealing so much, but I only kept one part of the night secret.

Marilyn gazed at me tenderly when I asserted my undying devotion for Janie. When I described kissing the imposter, Marilyn blushed.

The only thing I didn't mention was wondering if fake Janie was pregnant.

As I depicted Janie dying in my arms, Marilyn began to cry. Tears rolled down her cheeks. Finally, I related how I was nearly tortured and killed.

Everything I shared added to our collective gloom and discouragement. Before I finished, I wanted to think of something optimistic. "On the good side, Joe hasn't had time to transform his face yet," I said. "That's more proof we can trust everyone in this room. No one here can be Joe."

When all the questions were over, Elvis stood beside me. "It appears that Joe Plain controls at least some of the police and can manipulate phones. He may control every organization he claims he does, up to the highest levels in the government. We will need to double our safety measures."

The Court debated briskly for about ten minutes. The consensus: Rex was the only viable suspect, but he had no motive to want the movie stopped. I had trouble concentrating, as my gut was thrashing with rage, grief and fear. Joe had killed a fake Janie and planned to kill the real one.

"It's late. We'll talk more at tomorrow's Court meeting," Elvis said. "Now, it's time for everyone to return to your bungalows."

Everyone left, except Elvis, Marilyn and me. "Living here full-time won't be bad. I'll assign you permanent bungalows and arrange your transportation to and from the studio," Elvis said.

My mind wouldn't stop replaying the vision of fake Janie dying in my arms. "I don't want to hide, Elvis. I want to kill the bastard."

Elvis sighed. His weariness showed. "I need you alive. We all want to stop Joe, but we must be smart. We're still clueless about who he is. You can stay in one of my guest rooms tonight, since you have the wrong face to walk around outside."

Elvis led Marilyn and me through the north-wing corridor. "I'll contact Orson and have him move your filming to later. Meet me in the Memphis Room at noon, and I'll make sure you get to the studio."

As we passed Elvis' bedroom, a woman in a bathrobe stepped into the hallway. "Oops." she exclaimed. She twirled around and dashed back through the same door, so all I saw was a slim figure and brunette hair.

"You surprised her," Elvis chuckled.

"Who was that?" Marilyn asked.

Elvis ignored her and led us to a door farther down the hall. "Here's your room."

The King of Rock never questioned whether we'd share a bedroom, even though I was Darrin. I almost protested. Marilyn and I entered a large guest room grandly decorated with Louis XIV furniture. There were tapestries and paintings, a chandelier, and a canopy over the bed.

I was exhausted, but as soon as Marilyn and I were alone, all I could think of was whether I'd see her naked. However, everything felt awkward with this face. I longed to see her, but I didn't want her to see me.

As she examined the fancy decor and furniture, I wondered how intimate she'd be. There was a large sofa, but I assumed she would let me share the bed. She'd probably sleep in her clothes and turn her back to me.

Elvis had given us a toiletry kit and, as I brushed my teeth, I planned my strategy. While Marilyn used the bathroom, I turned off every light and shut the drapes. If it was dark enough, maybe she'd forget my face. Maybe it was superficial to dislike myself because of my unappealing appearance, but I couldn't help it.

I stripped to my boxers, and was under the covers when Marilyn came out of the bathroom. She turned off the light, and I heard her undressing; unfortunately, in the utter darkness, I couldn't see anything. As she disrobed, I imagined her naked. When she snuggled next to me, I was thrilled she wasn't repelled by my Darrin-ness.

Yes, she was naked. She gently kissed my shoulders and neck.

"Fake Janie was a better Janie than I am. She learned from Marilyn, without even being Marilyn."

I didn't respond. I just enjoyed her kisses.

"Fake Janie was more romantic, too," Marilyn added. "And she got to hear all those wonderful things you said."

"They were meant for you."

"They were the sweetest things I've ever heard, but I only got to hear the rehash." She kissed me tenderly on my lips and rubbed her hips against mine, enticing blood to rush to my groin.

"But I can learn from her, too. From now on, I'm not going to take your love for granted." She grabbed my boxers and started to coax them downward.

"Let's get these off you," she said. I lifted my hips, and she pulled off my underwear. She kissed my neck, then my chest, lingered with her lips caressing my belly, and then teased her mouth downward until she was an inch away from sending me to ecstasy.

I cupped the back of her head to stop her.

"What are you doing?" she asked.

"Just wait." I felt around in the dark until I found my phone and turned on the flashlight app. I shined it on her surprised face.

"Are you making a video?"

I studied her eyes. "No. I just had to check you're not an imposter."

She laughed and stroked my hardness. "Neither are you."

I kept the flashlight on as she teased my shaft with delicate nibbles. Had she forgotten I was Darrin? Or was it possible she no longer cared. I caressed the top of her head with my hands as my pleasure soared. She made my body tremble in rapture for several minutes and then moved upward again, kissing my belly, chest, lips, and finally shifting her body to straddle me.

"Oh, Darrin," she moaned as I slid inside of her.

She didn't care! It didn't matter to her I was Darrin. We held hands as she gently gyrated on top of me. It was the tenderest love making we'd ever shared.

"I've wanted to make love with you for so long."

"You mean since I've been James Dean."

"No, silly. I've been thinking about you since our first play together as kids. You've always been the best thing in my life. I wouldn't have moved to California with anyone but you."

"But you said you just wanted to be friends."

"You didn't give me a choice. We couldn't have dated casually. And I wasn't sure you were the man I wanted to spend my entire life with."

Ouch. I thought it was because I was unattractive, but really I was just a wimp.

"How long have you known I was James Dean?"

"Since we first changed faces and filmed in the diner. I was happy for both of us. We needed jobs. You needed to learn to love yourself. I realized it might give our relationship a chance."

"Why didn't you say anything? I've given you lots of opportunities."

"I couldn't say anything, or it would've broken the illusion. I felt . . . well, you were becoming the strong, confident man I knew you could be, I didn't want to interfere."

Marilyn leaned forward, still riding me, and kissed me.

"I never wanted to hurt you. I know no one will ever love me as much as you."

"When you were flirting with all those other men, were you really considering dating them?"

"I was being Marilyn, and having fun. And letting you have a chance to be James Dean. When we started this movie, I decided to follow my heart and wherever it led me, but I was hoping it would lead to you. I've adored you since we were kids."

"I wish I'd known that."

"You always thought I was the one not ready for a relationship. But really it was you, Darrin. When all you did was try to please me, there was nothing for me to hold on to."

I'd been my own worst enemy, more toxic to my goal than any rival. "I love myself now, but I'll never think anyone is worthy of you."

"You've always put me on a pedestal," Marilyn said. "For this to work, you have to climb up there and stand with me."

I turned off the flashlight, and we made love in the dark. Her pleasurable moans could have been from either Janie or Marilyn, and I could pretend she had any face I wished. My imagination switched back and forth between Janie and Marilyn. I couldn't pick one. When I climaxed, it was Janie's face I imagined.

She collapsed on top of me and I held her in a state of profound bliss. Did this mean she was ready for a public relationship?

When would I finally get to make love to her while she had Janie's face?

The Grapes of Wrath

"You should feel lucky. Normally, I kill people without giving them any options."

Samantha Jordan was too terrified to speak. This couldn't be happening. In five minutes, she was scheduled to present a TED Talk, the culmination of two decades of fervid corporate philanthropy.

They were in a small room in Memorial Auditorium at Stanford University, and she was about to go on stage. The world was watching.

"Let me explain again," the intruder said. "My name is Joe Plain. This is your replacement, the new Samantha Jordan. She is going to give your TED Talk. You have to pick one of these needles and inject yourself."

Samantha looked at the three syringes in front of her. They were each labeled.

Option #1: Fast, painless death.

Option #2: Paralysis followed by slow, painful death.

Option #3: Paralysis only. Strangled to death by your replacement after the talk.

"If you pick needle two or three, you'll get to watch your TED Talk live on the Internet. But you won't like what you say, so I suggest needle number one."

Joe Plain held another syringe, which was labeled:

Option #4: A special type of hell.

"If you don't pick a syringe soon, I'll inject you with this one," Joe said. "Believe me, it's the worst. I'm a fearologist, and one of my areas of expertise is pain."

"Why are you doing this?" Samantha pleaded.

Joe frowned and wrote in his notepad. "I'm giving you a 6.5 on my fear scale. I need better."

There was a knock on the door. "You're on in two minutes, Ms. Jordan," a man said.

Samantha tried to scream, but her identical replacement placed a hand over her mouth. When she tried to wiggle free, the vacuous-faced psychopath punched her in the stomach.

"Thank you. I'll be out in a minute," her replacement said.

A few feet away, seated in the auditorium, were the CEOs of Google, Apple, Facebook, and other leaders of technology. Plus, professors, students, engineers, and the media.

"You have twenty seconds to decide." Joe held the option #4 needle to her neck.

"Wait. Please, I have three children," Samantha begged. "I'm a single mother."

"Okay. That's about 7.3," Joe said, writing it down. "Don't worry, your replacement will take care of Grace, Margo and little Ben. Considering the type of world I'm creating, your children will be better off without you."

The imposter Samantha smiled at her. "I'll raise them to be just like me."

Samantha felt her chest tighten with fright. She decided on a different option: to kill her replacement. She looked at syringe #1. She just had to pick it up, pretend she was going to inject herself, and then quickly stab her twin in the leg.

It would be hard to stab the plain-faced monster behind her. Killing the imposter was her best option. Then Joe Plain could kill her, but he couldn't replace her.

She reached slowly for syringe #1, so terrified she could barely move. It felt like a nightmare where her brain gave instructions, but her body resisted. She was surprised her arm obeyed her thoughts; finally, she picked it up.

"Good choice," Joe said. "It will all be over soon."

This morning, when Samantha arrived in Silicon Valley, she had felt like the luckiest woman alive, validated for decades of conscientious capitalism. She'd inherited a bituminous coal mine at a young age, and was the richest person in Alabama. Her heroes since childhood had been the high-tech leaders shaping society; today was her chance to be admired as their colleague—someone the forward-thinking innovators in the audience would consider as a visionary.

Samantha had dedicated her company to having a carbon-negative footprint, by investing profits in the Amazon rainforest. She'd devised a self-sustainable system which benefited indigenous farmers while reducing pollution. Yet, the media always portrayed her as a good-hearted hillbilly. She'd never been shown respect, because of where she was born.

This was supposed to change today. Her TED Talk, "Fuel and Lungs," was a blueprint treating carbon as a resource instead of a villain—after all, carbon was what plants used to create more oxygen—to heal the planet. Samantha had even been offered a teaching job at Harvard Business School.

She held syringe #1 tightly and swung her arm towards her identical replica's leg. The needle stuck deep in her would-be replacement's leg.

"Ouch," the imposter said.

Joe laughed. "That's just water. The three options I gave you are fake. Only this needle is real." Joe injected the option #4 syringe back to her neck.

"Don't worry, I was going to kill you with this needle no matter what you did," Joe said. "My plan requires understanding how people react to fear, so I wanted to watch you struggle between hopeless choices."

Samantha's face etched in panic. She swung her arms feebly for a few seconds, trying to hit him.

"That's good," Joe said, writing in his notepad. "I'm marking that as an 8.8 fear level."

Samantha groaned in despair and collapsed. Despite the syringe's label, it was fast. Joe loved creating fear, but he hated wasting time.

"Hurry. Go give your talk," Joe instructed.

New Samantha left the room, and two of Joe's bodyguards arrived to take away the original Samantha.

Joe sighed as he left the building. He was bored with these replacements. He'd only had a few seconds of enjoyment, while Samantha experienced bona fide terror.

Sure, he'd made a few billion dollars. And he controlled more of America's energy supply. Plus, the TED Talk would be unlike any others, planting hints of the future he was creating. Yet, Joe yearned to proceed beyond these quick little stints of terror and finally make the entire world tremble.

A Beautiful Mind

*"*W*ho's this dork?"*

Marilyn laughed. Lucy Ball and Bogie did too. What else could anyone do? The guy was ridiculous.

Elvis was holding Court, and people were lined up to exchange their passwords. Meanwhile, a nerdy white guy with light-brown hair stood awkwardly at the front of the boardroom.

"Those glasses are the ugliest thing I've ever seen," Marilyn whispered.

Truly, the man's glasses looked like a vaudeville gag. The frames were black and wide, holding square lenses that seemed to be an inch thick. The man also wore an oddball necklace, which looked like a crystal golf ball.

The dorky guy stood stiffly, obviously nervous as people exchanged passwords with Elvis. A non-famous person had never visited the Court before. His smile was friendly, and he wore a nice suit, yet it was hard to see anything except his absurd glasses.

"Why would Elvis cover the windows?" I asked Marilyn. Black sheets had been hung over all the windows in the boardroom.

She shrugged. "I guess he doesn't want us to look outside."

Marilyn and I were official members of the Court now, and we were publicly dating. It was Valentine's Day. Tonight, we had dinner plans at Hoʻoulu Lāhui, the Polynesian restaurant. For half a month we'd been living full-time at Malibu Graceland, shuttled back and forth secretly to the studio without any reason to change identities.

So, I'd gone two blissful weeks without being Darrin—I didn't miss him at all. Elvis had assigned Marilyn and me adjacent bungalows with a connecting door, which was the greatest gift I'd ever received. Without Darrin in the way, our relationship was flourishing; Marilyn was sleeping over every night.

It would be heaven, if not for Joe Plain. Our trips to and from the studio were especially filled with fear. Joe had killed two more people, Bob Hope and Richard Pryor, since Fake Janie had died in my arms. We never knew who would be murdered next. I couldn't prove that Rex was Joe Plain, and everyone else seemed certain he wasn't. All we could agree upon was that Joe's plan was probably escalating towards a terrible goal.

Elvis listened to the final person's password and then stood beside the oddball with the preposterous glasses. The man whispered something to Elvis, which must have been clever. The King smiled as if he'd received a special gift.

"It's my honor to introduce Chris Finnigan," Elvis said. "Besides Einstein, Chris is the smartest man I've ever met. I owe him my life, and most of you do, too."

We looked at each other in confusion.

"Chris invented the transform-machines," Elvis explained.

"I thought Teddy Millner invented the machines," Milton Friedman said.

"No, Teddy was V.P. of Technology and adapted the machines to movie-making," Elvis said. "Chris is the CEO of a biomedical company called BioSynthetic."

"I built the machines for Dutch, but we agreed it was best if I kept my involvement secret. Better for the studio, and now it's safer for me," Chris said. "However, in light of recent events, it seems prudent that this Court should be made fully aware of everything concerning the machines, the studio and Malibu Graceland."

"Chris owns 33% of Digital Impact—an equal share as Dutch and Rex. He also owns a third of Malibu Graceland. I paid for this estate, but I couldn't put it in my name," Elvis said.

"I've wanted to attend a Court meeting for a long time," Chris said. "Elvis gives me weekly status reports, but I thought my attendance would be a distraction without any benefit. I have come to Malibu Graceland with Dutch a few times just to walk around."

I whispered to Marilyn, "He's about the same height as Joe Plain. Now, we have another suspect."

"Tell them your connection with Dutch," Elvis said.

"Dutch and I met in college, at Caltech, where he introduced me to Rex. I was sort of a nerd, and they were my only friends. A few years ago, Dutch recruited me to build a face-changing machine. It was Dutch's idea to keep it a secret and pretend we'd invented a new type of animation software—an idea that made billions of dollars. I've used my share of the money to found BioSynthetic and dedicate my life to biomedical research."

He paused to drink some water.

"Unfortunately, Joe Plain has twisted our efforts into tragedy," Chris said. "Dutch has been struggling over whether or not to give into Joe's demands. And, yesterday, Joe Plain raised the stakes."

What did Joe do? We all turned our gaze to Elvis.

"Joe has added to his demands," Elvis said. "Dutch notified me this morning. Joe still vows to keep killing people if we don't stop filming, and now he also demands that we close this estate."

No! Absolutely not! I needed Malibu Graceland to be James Dean.

It was unbearable to imagine not being James anymore. Inconceivable. Would Janie date me if I was only Darrin? Could I keep her safe if Malibu Graceland closed?

Closing Malibu Graceland was not an option. I had to prevent this by any method possible.

The desperate faces and cursing around the table revealed everyone shared my conviction.

"You can't close the estate," Eleanor Roosevelt declared. "This Court is our only chance to stop Joe Plain."

"We're the goddamn resistance," General Patton growled. "Imagine a world controlled by a son-of-a-bitch like Joe Plain."

"I can't imagine that," Chris said. "However, maybe we can stop Joe from killing your colleagues."

"What about helping society? Closing the estate will make the Code of Conduct futile," MLK noted.

"Maybe Joe's goal is to stop this Court. You can't let him," Walt Disney insisted.

"The fact Joe Plain wants the estate closed is sufficient reason to keep it open," Lucy added.

"And the legacy scenes are becoming more important as people die. You should keep the estate open so we can film them here," Nikola Tesla said.

"Maybe Joe is trying to bankrupt the studio, which will destroy the resistance," Milton said.

"Joe undoubtedly wants to weaken—or kill—everyone who knows about the machines," Albert Einstein added. "We are his only threat. That makes us the world's only hope."

"Those are all good points," Chris said. "However, the most important thing to me is keeping each of you alive. I know Dutch agrees."

"Does Dutch have any other close friends or coworkers we don't know about?" I asked.

"No, just me," Chris said. "You can add me to your list of suspects."

"Are all the machines, aside from the one Joe stole, either here or at the studio?" Bogie asked.

"Yes. They are all accounted for. No one else could build a machine without my knowledge. Even Teddy couldn't have done that."

"And I had Chris encode a safety feature after Joe stole one of them," Elvis said.

"I programmed accelerometers in each machine. If it is moved more than 200 feet, it is disabled," Chris said.

"Could you make more machines if you wanted?" Albert asked.

"Yes. Although it would take about six months."

"Then we can eliminate you as a suspect," Albert said.

"Do you think Rex Shackleford could be Joe Plain?" I asked.

Chris grinned. "I've known Rex a long time. He is not technically inclined. I can't see him figuring out how to do the things with the machines that Joe Plain has. Also, violence is not in Rex's nature."

The room fell contemplatively silent.

"We are low on suspects," Elvis remarked.

"I'm stymied, too. I've also given this a lot of thought," Chris said.

"I'm curious, why are the windows blocked?" Marilyn asked.

Elvis stood and started removing the sheets. "Sorry. It was for something else. It's no longer needed."

"I've distracted you enough," Chris said. "Just hold your meeting as normal. I'm meeting Dutch and Rex later so we can decide whether to give into Joe's demands."

Chris sat in the back of the room, observing while we discussed ideas to stop Joe Plain. The room was full of frantic faces. Our chance to keep our identities might be lost unless we could think of something.

The grand revelation I hoped for never came. Two hours later, as Elvis ended the meeting, we remained just as clueless.

As Court members headed to the fancy dining room for our post-Court dinner, I walked toward a bathroom. As soon as I was out of sight, I waited in a stairwell to spy on Chris.

Chris, Elvis and Bogie were the last people out of the boardroom, and moved together toward the glass elevator. Chris was probably leaving through the foyer, so I sprinted down the stairs, ran to the foyer, and hid in the coatroom.

Soon I heard voices and cracked the door open. Chris, Elvis and Bogie were talking near the mansion's entrance. Chris had taken off his absurd glasses and necklace, and looked like a normal businessman. I strained to listen.

"I'm hopeful for the first time in months," Elvis said. "This changes everything."

"We're no longer helpless," Bogie added excitedly. "We can defeat Joe now."

Why were Elvis and Bogie hopeful? What weren't they sharing?

"We need a good strategy to take advantage of this," Chris said. He opened the mansion door, and was about to leave.

I jumped out of the coatroom. "A strategy for what?"

The three of them turned around startled. "You spied on us!" Elvis declared.

I walked to Chris and yanked the glasses out of his hand. "What do these do?"

"That's not your business," Bogie said. "When Dutch hears you were spying on us, you'll be fired."

"It's okay, Bogie. We can trust him," Elvis said.

Chris looked wary, but Elvis reassured him. "James is clever and can keep a secret."

"Well," Chris said, "then we might as well go in the closet."

Chris, Elvis and Bogie walked into the coatroom. Confused, I followed.

Chris took the round crystal-like necklace out of his pocket. "Put on the glasses," he said.

I held them. "Why are they so heavy?"

"They're one of a kind. Try them."

I put the glasses on. Two faces glowed with a purplish fluorescent hue. Chris looked normal. "Your face, Elvis—it's purple. So is yours, Bogie."

"Chris invented them," Elvis said delightedly. "They reveal faces that have been transformed."

"The transformation process adds chemicals to the skin, which can be made to reflect infrared radiation," Chris explained. "The necklace sends pulses of radiation that identify the frequency, and the glasses amplify it."

"Amazing." My mind swirled with possibilities. This was a great weapon against Joe Plain.

"I've been working on them for months," Chris said. "Teddy Millner helped. I finally got them working this week."

Hearing Teddy's name made me sad and angry. "If Joe transformed people to infiltrate this estate with spies, these glasses can identify and interrogate them."

"We're trying to devise a strategy to do that," Chris said.

"Why wait? Let's walk around the courtyard right now. One of Joe's spies could be here."

"The glasses don't work in sunlight. The sun emits too much radiation over the entire infrared spectrum," Chris said.

"Then we can walk around the estate at night," I suggested.

Bogie flipped off the light. The closet became dark, and the purple on his and Elvis' faces disappeared.

"In the darkness, there isn't enough radiation to amplify," Bogie said.

Bogie flipped the light back on and blazingly-bright light scorched my eyes.

"Aahh!" I yelled, yanking off the glasses. It was like staring at a hundred welding torches. I was blinded.

"See, the glasses are very sensitive," Bogie said.

"Bogie! That was mean," Chris scolded.

"James deserved it. He spied on us," Bogie said.

I punched where I thought Bogie's face was, but only hit air. I was helplessly blind.

"Your sight will return in a minute or so, James," Chris assured.

"Then I'm going to kick your ass, Bogie."

"In the darkness, the lenses were at full power, trying to amplify any radiation they could find," Chris said. "When Bogie turned on the light, they were still at full power. It takes a moment for them to adjust."

We stepped out of the closet, Elvis leading me by the hand. "The point is, the glasses require light, but not sunlight," Elvis said. "That's why the windows were covered in the boardroom, today. I asked a few modern celebrities to come to the boardroom and talk with me. None of them showed purple through the glasses, so they can't be imposters."

My eyes still hurt, and I couldn't open them.

"We could check everyone in small groups like that," I said.

"The problem is, once Joe learns about the glasses, they'll become useless," Chris said. "Makeup can cover the radiation."

"So, each time we use the glasses might be the last time they are useful," Elvis said. "The glasses and necklace will be noticed by any spies."

"We can assume Joe has scientists working for him. Hopefully, we are ahead of him," Chris said.

"Do the glasses work if you transform back to your original face?"

"Yes, the chemicals remain in your skin."

"So, we need a big room without windows, full of people where at least one person will be an imposter," I said.

"Ideally, if one exists," Elvis said.

My eyes were adjusting back to normal. I resisted the urge to punch Bogie, because there was a bigger issue. "That's easy. I know how we can guarantee to find an imposter."

Chris laughed. "You've already solved the problem, James?"

"The Oscars are in two weeks. I'll go and wear the glasses."

They paused. Chris grinned. "That's very clever. There is a good chance Joe has replaced at least one celebrity who'll attend the Academy Awards."

"But, what if Joe hasn't?" Bogie argued. "It could waste this opportunity.

We can't be sure he's replaced a modern celebrity."

"It gives us our best idea," Elvis said, beaming proudly at me.

"It's genius . . . better than any option I've thought of," Chris said. "We'll send someone to the Oscars with the glasses."

"Me. I want to do it," I said. "You can give me an anonymous face."

"No. Definitely not," Bogie asserted. "The studio has invested too much in making him James Dean. No way does he get a third identity."

Elvis frowned. "Sorry, James, Bogie's right. A third identity won't be possible."

"But . . . why?" I protested.

Chris turned to me. "We've found that one alter identity is all the human brain can handle safely. With two identities, you can flip back and forth like two sides of a coin. More identities cause the brain exponentially more stress."

"Fuck that," I said. "I'm an actor. I'll still be James Dean. I'll just play the role of an actor at the Oscars."

Elvis laughed. "There you have it."

Chris studied me as if he'd noticed something profound. What had he seen in me?

Was it my perspective? It never occurred to me that I'd be Darrin acting as someone else. My default ego was James Dean.

"I'll check with Dutch and Rex," Chris said. "If they approve, we will let you act as someone else. That should eliminate any psychological issues."

"I need to be a presenter," I said. "The Oscars are huge. I won't be able to see everyone's face from the audience. If I'm on stage to open an Oscar envelope, every face in the theater will be staring straight at me."

"Impossible," Bogie said.

"Fine. I'll have Dutch arrange it," Chris said. "Assuming, they let you have a third identity."

Elvis slapped me on the back. "A live performance with another face. We've never done this before. And on the biggest stage."

"I'm used to stressful situations, and I'm an actor. I should be the person to do this," Bogie said.

"No, I think James has the perfect temperament for this job," Chris said.

Bogie glowered at me.

Elvis carefully studied me and scratched his chin. "Hmmm . . . what modern actor is about your height?"

I balked. I saw the problem in the plan. "Won't this put the real actor in danger?"

"No, it will put you in danger. When Joe Plain figures this out, he'll know it was an imposter," Elvis said.

"Joe knows the studio doesn't tell modern actors anything. He will try to kill whoever was wearing the glasses on stage," Chris said. "Luckily, he's already trying to kill you."

The Killing Fields

As the FBI's Chief Information Officer, Drew Oyama equipped his home with futuristic gadgets most people never imagined. He used his ranch-style house to test security devices before they were installed in the White House or at American embassies.

Located in Cleveland Park, a bucolic suburb of Washington, D.C., his house was impenetrable, both physically and digitally.

Drew was on his command chair in the family room, using audio commands to compose email on his 240-inch all-purpose screen, when a computerized female voice announced, "Stevie has gone outside. I am raising Jacuzzi fence and activating lifeguards."

"Show Stevie," Drew said. The screen immediately displayed a four-year-old boy carrying a plastic shark toward the pool.

The computer system forecasted Stevie's movement, and followed him with spotlights.

Robotic lifeguard drones hovered over Stevie, ready to drop floatation devices as the boy placed his plastic shark in the water.

"A car has stopped at gate. You have visitors," the computer voice said. "The license plate cannot be identified. Facial recognition indicates the passenger is Nora Madison."

The screen displayed a white SUV waiting at the gate carrying two people Drew was not expecting. Joe Plain was driving; Nora Madison, the Director of the NSA, sat in the passenger seat.

"Open gate," Drew instructed. The entry's steel sliding doors parted, and the SUV parked in the driveway.

Two people could not look more opposite, Drew thought, as they walked to his front door. Joe Plain's white face was completely dull and nondescript; he could pass 100 times on the subway without anyone noticing. Nora's black face was stunning and unforgettable; she'd won several beauty pageants before putting her sharp intellect into the service of her country.

"Nora Madison and another person are at the front door," the electronic voice declared.

Joe Plain was startled when a little boy holding a toy shark answered the door.

Stevie pointed at Joe. "You're funny-looking."

Joe Plain scowled at the boy. Drew rushed to intercede. "Go downstairs, Stevie. Tell the TV what you want to watch."

As Stevie ran away. Joe's minatory glare told Drew he was dangerously close to being replaced.

"Explain."

"I'm babysitting my four-year-old nephew tonight, while my brother and his wife celebrate their anniversary."

"No more babysitting." Joe strutted past Drew and into the house. Nora followed him.

Drew shook the woman's hand. "You must be becoming Nora."

"Obviously. You know what to do," Joe said.

Drew recalled how easily Joe had inserted him into his identity thirteen months earlier. The high-tech house had simply let him and Joe inside. Joe had enjoyed tormenting and replacing the original Drew. Since then, Joe sporadically came to his house to replace powerful people.

Drew called the real Nora and told her that he had critical information he needed to show her in person. She agreed to come straight to his house.

"A car has stopped at the gate," the computerized voice announced fifteen minutes later. "The license plate indicates it is Nora Madison's vehicle. She is the driver."

Drew invited Nora into the living room and offered her a beverage. As soon as she took a sip, Joe and the new Nora walked into the room.

"You . . . you . . . you're me!" original Nora gasped.

"I'm you from the future," her replacement said. "I came to warn you not to drink the poison. Sorry, I'm too late."

"Huh?"

Joe frowned. "Don't be funny, Nora. You're not a funny person."

New Nora quivered in fright. "I'm sorry. I'll never do it again."

"Watch her die. The same thing will happen to you, if you ever displeased me."

Joe used his phone to record the original Nora's terror as she glared at her facsimile and collapsed to the floor. He sent the video to Dutch and Chris, imagining the dismay this would cause, especially when the Court saw it. Joe needed to intensify the fear he inspired, until his demands couldn't be resisted, and the next stage of the plan could begin.

Ten minutes after the original NSA Director arrived, the new one drove away in her car.

"A genius would realize that I'm not replacing people," Joe said to Drew. "I'm recreating people."

"Yes, sir." Drew felt awkward whenever Joe Plain became philosophical.

"Makeovers are so fashionable these days, and I'm providing a complete makeover," Joe said. "And being open-minded to new ideas is even more highly esteemed."

"That's true, sir."

"When people go to school or travel, they gain new beliefs and values," Joe explained. "Yet, they're still the same person. They still have the same history and appearance. The same reputation, career, and possessions. Only their thoughts have changed."

"Absolutely, sir."

"Real identity consists of only two things: external form and internal thoughts. Think about it logically—nothing can uniquely define you that isn't in your appearance or your past experiences."

"You're very wise, Mr. Plain."

"Appearance and past are everything. And I control both. You've only seen me replicate people. But I can invent new ones. I can take people with any background and give them any appearance, position and identity I desire. I can recreate their background and scare them into doing what I want." Joe's eyes glowed maniacally. "So, I can fill the world with the exact humans I specify."

"Yes, sir." Joe Plain was even scarier as a philosopher than as a murderer. Drew didn't want to imagine what his ultimate plan entailed.

Mission: Impossible

As I awoke from anesthesia in a transformation cabin, a wave of disappointment hit me. Being Darrin again felt like a prison sentence.

It had been a long time since I'd changed faces. I wished I could be James Dean forever.

I took a deep breath and prepared myself to see Darrin's ugly face in the mirror.

Tom Croft stared back at me. *I'm an identity thief.* I had stolen a movie star's face.

My thoughts blurred as my brain tried to comprehend. I recalled my mission. Dutch had selected me to become Tom Croft, because the popular modern actor was my height and body type. I felt the handsome face I was wearing, and became dizzy. I looked like Tom, but it felt wrong. A third identity truly was a heavy mental overload.

"You're James Dean, just playing a new role."

I turned and saw Elvis sitting nearby. "My head feels like silly putty being pulled in all directions."

"We warned you. Remember, you're only acting like Tom Croft," Elvis said.

I closed my eyes and tried to convince my brain my identity hadn't changed, just my face. When I opened my eyes, the nausea had lessened.

"I fit the wig on your head while you were sleeping," Elvis said.

"It's strange to be someone who is still alive."

"Stop speaking in James Dean's voice."

"Oops. Sorry," I said in the Tom Croft voice I'd been practicing.

Elvis handed me a tuxedo. "I'll leave you to change."

I put on the tuxedo, examined myself in the mirror, and imagined standing on the Oscar stage. How could I be so arrogant? Did I really think I could trick the entire world?

When I stepped outside the cabin into the ballroom, Elvis carefully inspected me. "You look great, Tom."

"Thanks."

"You're welcome, but all I did was press some buttons. Tom's face was already in the machine's database."

Elvis put on the nerdy glasses and associated necklace, which had been in his pocket. "They're working. You're glowing as purple as a neon sign."

He handed me the glasses and necklace, and I used them to see purple radiating from Elvis. I put them in my pocket.

"Can we walk through the courtyard a little? I need to adjust before going to the Oscars."

"Sure."

We walked to the octagon parlor and stepped onto the balcony above Malibu Graceland's courtyard. I expected people to point and declare me a fraud. I waited, but no one gave me a second thought.

Elvis seemed to read my mind. "You're uncomfortable, not others. That's how deception works."

We walked around the pool, and I looked for Marilyn. I spotted her playing volleyball with Matthew McConaughey, Brad Pitt and Audrey Hepburn. She waved to Elvis, but ignored me. She didn't know Tom.

Dutch had made us vow not to tell anyone. Only five people knew the glasses existed: Dutch, Chris, Elvis, Bogie and me. Marilyn knew I was doing a project for Elvis tonight, but she hadn't pressed me for details. "Just promise not to do anything dangerous," Marilyn had said.

Elvis waited with me a minute as I watched Marilyn, and then we walked around the southern courtyard and headed back to the mansion.

"No one knows the identity beneath my face," I said to the King.

"They never do."

We went around a fishpond, down a path lined with birds of paradise, and entered the mansion. When we turned the corner by the library, Ernest Goldenhart stood in the hallway, talking with a modern actress.

"What's Mayor Goldenhart doing here?"

"Ernest's also going to the Oscars. He came here to pick up his date," Elvis said.

My hand unconsciously went to my pocket. There was no natural light in the hallway.

"Go ahead. I know you want to," Elvis said.

I put the necklace on. Ernest hadn't spotted us. I quickly put the glasses on, glanced at him, and put them back in my pocket. There was no glow on his face or the actress's, but there was on Elvis.

"No purple at all," I told Elvis.

"It was worth checking. But I think Dutch could tell if one of his best friends was an imposter," Elvis said.

"I just hope there's an imposter at the Oscars." I was also looking forward to checking Rex tonight.

Elvis and I walked past the formal dining room and the library. When we arrived in the foyer, Chris, Bogie and the real Tom Croft were waiting.

Tom jumped up from a sofa to shake my hand. "Nice to meet me."

"Nice to be you."

I felt uncomfortable as Tom stared into my eyes. I bet he felt worse. I imagined seeing another James Dean, which was horrific to contemplate.

"You're going to have to spend the evening alone in a bungalow, Tom, so you aren't seen at two places at once," Elvis said.

Tom inhaled deeply, trying to stay calm. "I really hate you right now, Elvis."

"Don't hate anyone unless you've walked in their shoes."

Tom rolled his eyes and turned to me. "Make me look good, Tom." He strutted out of the room.

I took a sanitary wipe and rubbed it over Chris' face.

"Hey . . . be gentle!" Chris cried.

"What the fuck, James!" Elvis said.

"I need you to get in the coat room with me," I said.

Chris took a deep breath. "Okay. Fine." He was handling this better than I expected.

Elvis accompanied us to the coatroom. I checked him. No purple.

"Sorry."

We stepped back into the foyer. "The necklace is only strong enough to work at close range," Chris said. "However, we put a large infrared light in the chandelier that will fill the auditorium, so you won't need the necklace at the Oscars."

"I'll have the Court assembled when you return," Elvis said. "Whether or not you spot an imposter, there's no reason to keep the glasses a secret from the Court any longer."

"The glasses will be quite conspicuous. I bet it takes Joe Plain less than twenty-four hours to figure out what they do," Chris said.

Above us on the balcony, a woman appeared. Jacqueline Dumont, the attractive studio executive with whom I'd auditioned, smiled at us from the top of the stairs. She looked stunning in a shimmering fuchsia dress that covered strategic areas in front, but gratuitously displayed her back.

Chris took a step back and glanced toward the exit as if he wanted to escape. Beads of perspiration formed his forehead. What was he afraid of?

Jacqueline descended the staircase as if entering a ball. Elvis, Chris and I each stood a little straighter. Chris clasped his hands behind his back and appeared anxious.

Jacqueline shook my hand. "I'll be your date tonight, Tom. I'm not sure who you really are, but we'll make this work."

"You look beautiful," I said.

"Heads are going to turn," Elvis said.

"Thank you both."

Jacqueline smiled at Chris. "Nice to see you, Chris."

Chris stuttered. "As well nice also you to see."

I laughed. The brilliant man's tongue seemed to fill his throat.

Ha! She's the kryptonite of his superbrain.

Chris blushed and looked down at his shoes. Elvis frowned at me.

Shit, I'm a terrible person. I made a distressed man feel worse.

Elvis grabbed my arm with a serious expression. "Everything depends on you today. You need to be extremely cautious. Even if there isn't an imposter in the audience, don't assume you're safe. Joe could be hiding. And he monitors phones. Don't contact anyone unless it's an emergency."

Jacqueline and I entered a limo, and I was suddenly headed for the world's most illustrious red carpet.

I made casual conversation with Jacqueline, but it felt awkward as Tom

Croft. She knew I was fake, but not my real identity. I was relieved when we arrived at Hollywood and Highland, site of the annual celebrity pilgrimage to the mecca of glamour.

I hadn't prepared for stepping out of the limo . . . .

Camera flashes burst my face, threatening to blind me. Screams assaulted me from every direction.

"Tom! Tom! Tom!"

The shrieks and squeals were deafening. I helped Jacqueline out of the limo, and together we headed toward the Awards Walk, our every move televised globally, participants in the world's ultimate fashion show.

Behind the blockades, fervid fans pressed together in a sea of undulating bodies. They looked desperate, as if struggling to escape a burning building, merely to catch a glimpse of me.

"It's so silly, especially since I'm fake," I whispered to Jacqueline.

Jacqueline shrugged. "It's just a face. They'd see the same thing if you were real."

It hit me how blind I'd been. The triumph of the machines wasn't creating identities. It was exposing what wasn't identity. Appearances could be altered and new backgrounds could be memorized.

There is no real identity in appearance or past.

Then what was identity?

Before I could contemplate this, the media onslaught hit.

Interviews with BET, E!, Fox News, The Hollywood Reporter, MSNBC, Variety—I confronted each with as much humor as I could summon. I answered vaguely about Tom Croft's current projects, hopefully not embarrassing the real Tom as he watched on television. Finally, we escaped the media and reached the red mosaic staircase leading to the Dolby Theater, home of the Academy Awards and its apex of glitz.

Dolby Theater's five-level lobby and fabled staircase were gilded with cherry wood balustrades, garnished with shimmering photograph panels, and topped with a silvery dome. Every celebrity seemed anxious to greet me, while my only goal was to reach my seat without incident.

The 3,400-seat theater was intended to be the world's most glamorous room. A gigantic silver-leafed "tiara" held an immense grid of lights on the ceiling to spotlight the 120-foot-wide stage. I spotted a large white object hidden within these lights, which must be the infrared device to make the glasses work. Jacqueline and I finally reached our plum-colored seats, which were in the front row.

As the ceremony began, and winning actors read thank you lists, I imagined an inverted Oscars which honored real people, rather than actors . . .

In my mind, a firefighter walked on stage, accepted an Oscar statuette, and gave an awards speech:

"I'd like to thank Bradley Cooper for portraying a fireman in this movie and Scarlett Johansson for playing his wife. I'd like to thank the screenwriters for summarizing the kind of work we do into two hours. Finally, I'd like to thank the talented director for his entertaining vision of what he thinks our lives are like . . . ."

For science fiction, maybe a robot could accept the award.

Halfway through the program, my enjoyment of the show had to end. As unobtrusively as possible, I stood and stepped out a side door.

Jennifer Arnaz was already in our backstage waiting room. I opened the door, then jumped back, embarrassed to catch the pretty actress in the middle of changing outfits.

"Sorry."

"It's okay. I'm not changing clothes, this is what I'm wearing."

"I see." The petite brunette star was clad in a risqué genie costume at the border of sexy and indecent. The actress's bare coverings were comprised of sheer transparent pants, a violet thong bottom, a string bikini top and sheer sleeves. For accessories, she wore sandals and shell bracelets.

"Elvis told me to wear an outfit that took attention from you and included this thing." Jennifer set a turban-like headdress on her head that was as big as a volleyball.

"What is that?"

Jennifer shrugged. "No, idea. But it's designed to look like a giant pearl."

"Yeah . . . I can see that . . . it looks great. You'll be the biggest Oscar story this year."

A makeup artist entered the changing room and snickered when she saw Jennifer's outfit. She shook her head disapprovingly, while she prepared us for the stage lights.

"Did I go too far?" Jennifer asked after the woman left.

"You're bold and gorgeous. Whatever reasons Elvis has, he'll be grateful to you." It looked like the pearl was a backup infrared light for my glasses.

Jennifer smiled and looked pleased. Elvis had assured every face in the audience was aimed at us.

There was a knock on the door, and a young man entered. He leered at Jennifer. "You're on soon. You both need to be in position in two minutes."

The man's head swiveled to gawk as he walked away.

Jennifer checked the mirror one more time before we exited the changing room. It took all of her concentration to balance her humongous pearl turban.

An Academy Awards official met us at the edge of the stage and handed me an envelope.

"We're in commercial. You've got twenty seconds." He glanced at the pearl. "I hope Horton the Elephant doesn't hatch during the show."

Jennifer and I forced an uneasy laugh.

"Don't worry, it's simple," he assured. "You've been to rehearsal, so you know what to do."

Actually, Elvis had sent the real Tom Croft to rehearsal. He'd decided that sending me would have been an unnecessary risk. My heart pounded, unsure what to expect.

"Three . . . two . . . one. Go."

I stepped onto the colossal stage. Hundreds of millions of people were watching, but my job was just to find one imposter.

Apocalypse Now

"He who has a thousand friends has not a friend to spare,
while he who has one enemy shall meet him everywhere."
—Ralph Waldo Emerson

The stage seemed endless, and I thought I'd never reach the front. Finally, I stood center stage, staring into thousands of faces and omnipresent cameras.

Shit. Where's the teleprompter?

I was supposed to say the first line. Jennifer waited for me, nodding anxiously. I felt the weight of millions of impatient eyes. Dutch said the teleprompter would be easy to spot . . . .

It seemed an hour before I found it.

"I know you'll do anything to show your navel, Jennifer. But, honestly, why are you wearing . . . that?"

Luckily, I'd remembered to speak with Tom Croft's voice. This was fortunate. People in 225 countries were watching.

"I forgot tonight was the Oscars. I was cleaning my house and didn't have time to change."

Crap. The special glasses. I'd been so anxious I'd forgotten to put on the nerdy glasses before walking onto the stage.

"Well, if you're a genie, grant me three wishes."

"Sorry, Tom. Three wishes aren't enough to win you an Oscar."

"I wasn't going to wish myself to win," I said, still reading the teleprompter. "All of the nominated actresses are so incredibly talented, my wish is that they could each win an Oscar."

I decided to improvise, and stopped reading the teleprompter. "In fact, the talent of the nominees is so bright that I need protection." I reached into my pocket and pulled out the thick, aberrant sunglasses.

Perhaps it was my imagination, but putting on the glasses seemed to cause the loudest laugh of the night. I felt my face warm as I blushed.

Jennifer glared at me, but stayed with the teleprompter. "The nominations for Best Actress have supplied performances so magical that each of them could be a genie . . . ."

Purple. Everywhere.

Purple faces glowed all over the audience.

I turned sideways with Jennifer toward the immense video screen, where short clips were being shown of performances by the nominated actresses. However, instead of the screen, I looked at the audience.

Not one, or two—but dozens of purple faces. All staring back at me. I was stupefied.

In the front row, three of Hollywood's highest-paid actors—people I'd met many times at Malibu Graceland—smiled at me with purple-glowing faces. I felt betrayed. Behind them, the face of an actress Marilyn and I had dined with two nights before glowed, as well as most of the people near her. This was just a sliver of a largely-purple audience. Perhaps 100 purple faces, maybe more.

I was shocked. How could so many people be imposters? Why had Joe Plain focused so much on Hollywood? I thought he wanted to control the government.

Joe wants to control everything. Why?

Befuddled, my mind spinning, I went through some actions, opening an envelope and reading something . . . jolted as I peered at an audience of deceitful purple-faced imposters.

How would I keep Janie safe from an army of imposters? I tried to make a mental list of the purple faces, but there were too many.

People were cheering louder than normal. What did I miss? The teleprompter was blank, while Jennifer and another woman walked off the stage. I hurried to catch up with them.

My mind raced as I left the stage, sweat running down my back.

"Why are you so pale?" Jennifer asked. "Are you okay?"

"My attention wandered. I don't remember what I said. Did I screw up?"

"Yes. You put on those stupid glasses," Jennifer said. "Otherwise, it was okay. Now, I'm going to change out of this outfit."

Jennifer left, and I returned to my seat in the audience.

"Why did you put on those glasses?" Jacqueline whispered.

"They allow me to identify imposters Joe has created."

She raised her eyebrows. "Really? Did you see one?"

"Yes . . . . actually many. Maybe a hundred."

Jacqueline's jaw dropped. "In this audience?"

I whispered names, as many as I could remember, but only a small fraction of the total. She wrote them down.

When the awards ceremony ended, I put the glasses on as we mixed with the departing crowd. Using the high-tech necklace, I identified additional imposters and asked Jacqueline to add them to our list.

Finally, Jacqueline and I made it to our limo.

"To the Beverly Chateau," I instructed our driver. The luxurious hotel, a magnet for Hollywood elite, was the site of Vanity Fair's post-Oscars Party.

I raised the limo partition. "How many names do we have so far?"

"Forty-one," Jacqueline said. "Do you think Joe was in the audience? Maybe we should skip the post-Oscar parties and head straight back to the estate."

"No, this is our best chance to identify imposters. By tomorrow Joe may have figured out what the glasses do."

The Beverly Chateau had human-size Oscar statues in the lobby and 15-foot-high inflatable Oscar statues floating in the pool. Reporters stampeded to ask me questions, but I managed to escape into an elevator with Jacqueline.

"Dutch was right. It would be hard for you to mingle," Jacqueline said as we rode to the fifth floor.

The hotel was designed around an atrium with rectangular balconies circling each floor. As we navigated the walkway to my suite, I looked down at the après-Oscars gala and the people crowded around the sapphire pool. The music and talking was loud until we entered the suite and I shut the door.

"Hello, Tom. Hi, Jacqueline."

Rex Shackleford was sitting on a sofa between two stunning women—he never seemed to date one woman or the same woman twice. The blinds were already shut.

"Excuse me, ladies. I need to talk with Tom," Rex said. "Wait outside by the balcony, please." His companions frowned, but left us alone in the room.

His face wasn't purple. Could he have been warned? He was the only suspect left.

"What happened?" Rex asked. "Dutch said you were looking for an imposter and I could help."

"Stand up, please," I said.

Rex stood, looking confused as I patted him down for weapons. He was unarmed, without any bodyguards.

"I'm not really Tom Croft. I'm James Dean."

Jacqueline looked almost as surprised as Rex. I explained quickly, and Jacqueline showed Rex our list.

"Shit. Shit. Triple Shit," Rex gasped, reading the names. "Every imposter you saw meant Joe murdered the original." He was at the verge of tears. "Those were my friends. That sick fucker has to die."

I let them both test the glasses and see my purple glow.

"Here's the plan tonight," I said. "You need to meet as many celebrities as possible and send them to my suite. Tell them Tom Croft wants to discuss a potential movie. Skip the imposters we've already identified."

Rex nodded. "Okay. I'll do my best." He left the room and headed toward his dates with bravado, but I saw both sadness and fear beneath his smile.

"Good luck," Jacqueline told me. "Let's meet back here in two hours."

She left, and I closed the blinds and poured myself a drink. I reclined on a sofa and put on the special glasses. In just a few minutes celebrities began visiting me.

Famous people streamed in and out, and I noted which ones had purple faces. I casually chatted with everyone. Maybe I could redeem myself to Elvis, especially after revealing so much information the night Fake Janie was killed.

After about 90 minutes, there was a lull in the visitors. I was counting the number of imposters we'd uncovered when the door burst open. Four men rushed into the room, bulging with muscles like professional bodybuilders. I had just enough time to check their faces weren't purple before they assaulted me.

Two men grabbed my arms, and another put a hand over my mouth. I fought futilely, squirming and kicking, as helpless as a wimpy kid on a playground.

The man not restraining me aimed a Glock with a silencer at my chest. "Don't yell or resist," he said.

I nodded in submission. I felt emasculated, but resistance wasn't helping.

The men roughly searched me, checking I was unarmed. Satisfied, all four men pointed guns with silencers at me. "It's clear," one of them yelled.

Joe Plain sauntered into the room and I shivered at his unnatural face. It glowed bright purple.

He smiled, which made his generic face more terrifying. "Hello, Tom. I'm Joe Plain."

Joe snatched the glasses off my face and put them on.

"Interesting. Your face is purple, Tom." He looked around the room and then at a mirror. "Are you really Tom Croft? I'm guessing this shows your face has been transformed."

Joe took off the glasses and examined them. "Ingenious. Definitely designed by Chris Finnigan."

He poked at my cheeks and twisted my nose. "You're not Tom Croft, you're someone Chris trusts. And you've identified some of my replacements." He pressed his finger into the tip of my nose. "It won't matter. Once I get some information from you, you'll be eliminated."

He turned to one of his burly men. "Stand outside, and don't let anyone in—unless it's someone you think I'd enjoy killing. Play heavy metal to cover up the screaming."

The man stepped outside, and Joe indicated toward his three other minions. "If these men prove themselves worthy, I'm going to have them replace brawny movie stars along the lines of The Rock and Chris Hemsworth."

They smiled, anticipating their future.

"Were you always depraved? Or did wearing that empty-fucking face expunge all your humanity?" I asked.

Joe pressed his pistol between my eyes. "Who is Elvis' real identity?"

"Screw you."

"You're one of Elvis' dimwitted Court members, aren't you?" Joe said. "Elvis replaced Tom Croft with you."

"Fuck you."

"There's a more fun way to do this," Joe sneered. He opened a small bag and removed two devices. The first looked like a cattle prod with electrodes protruding at one end. The other device was a Dremel rotary tool with a circular blade.

"This is my torture travel kit. With just these two devices, I can cause infinite pain."

"It can't be as painful as looking at your ugly face."

Joe turned to his jumbo-sized men. "Hold him down."

Six vice-like hands gripped my arms and torso. I tried to scream, but a hand clamped over my mouth. The men seemed to be showing off for Joe.

"I know everyone's real identity except Elvis'. You're going to give me his." Joe turned to one of his goons. "Squeeze his throat."

A steel-like hand crushed my throat. I couldn't breathe at all. I shook and writhed in desperation. The pain was intolerable.

"Keep squeezing. We'll start with simple oxygen deprivation," Joe said mercilessly.

I struggled with all my might, ready to do anything for air. As the agony grew, so did Joe's smile.

"If I give you some air, will you tell me who Elvis is?" Joe asked.

I nodded. Anything for air.

Joe indicated to the man choking me and his hand released. Air! I gasped air. Nothing had ever felt so good.

"Who is Elvis?" Joe asked. "Don't lie or the pain will get much worse."

I gulped more oxygen.

"WHO IS ELVIS?" Joe demanded.

"Elvis is a famous musician," I said. "People call him the King of Rock and Roll."

Joe grinned. "I was hoping you'd be stubborn. This means more pleasure for me."

He took the electric prod and set a dial to one. Then he prodded me in the chest.

My body went taunt. Every cell felt on fire. Too excruciating to survive. I thought my heart would stop.

Joe pulled the device off me, and my body quivered in recoil. I gasped for breath.

A smile spread over Joe's face. "That's the lowest setting. The shocks go from one to ten . . . that was a one." Joe switched the dial to two.

I couldn't imagine a higher setting. Just thinking about it made me wish for death.

"Maybe we can compromise," I said. "Why did you replace so many celebrities?"

"Celebrities are a tiny part," Joe boasted. "I control the FBI, CIA, the military and the government. In a week, I'll control every important person in the LAPD. In a month, I'll control every significant businessman. There won't be any aspect of society I don't own."

"What's your relationship with the studio?"

Joe poked me in the forehead. "Why should I answer your questions?"

"I have information you need, or you wouldn't be torturing me."

"Wrong. I'm torturing you for fun."

Joe set down the electric prod and picked up the Dremel tool. "I can learn anything you know in other ways. I have spies everywhere, and I use NSA satellites to track vehicles leaving the estate. Nothing is hidden from me."

He turned on the rotary tool, and moved the blade until it was spinning near my eyes. "My favorite thing is seeing how much pain a person will endure out of ego."

Joe took the rotary blade away from my face and held it near my fingers. "I'm going to slice off little pieces of you until I get answers. As we do this, it's important to keep in mind that I'm invincible, so your suffering isn't helping anyone. It's just for your own pride."

Slowly, Joe moved the saw toward my pinky. "Let's start with a simple question. Who knows about these glasses?"

How many slices could I endure before telling him? The blade moved within a millimeter of my finger. Would Marilyn love me if I was deformed? Even if I resisted all the cutting, I couldn't resist the shocks. There was no reason to lose body parts.

"Last chance, who knows about these glasses?" Joe asked.

"Fuck you, ass-face!" I shouted.

Joe snarled in anger. "For that, I'm taking off your thumb."

He moved the spinning blade toward my thumb, but the door opened. Rex stepped inside.

Rex's eyes bulged. "Let go of him." He ran at Joe, his fists clenched.

Joe's three bodyguards reached for their guns. They fired almost simultaneously. Rex's chest and forehead exploded in blood. The grips on me loosened, and I grabbed the electric prod.

Joe's eye's bulged as he saw me turn the dial to ten. Before he could react, I shoved the prod into the front of his pants.

His plain face turned white, and he screeched like a demented parrot. His arms flapped uncontrollably and his hips jerked in all directions. Joe's bodyguards worked to pull the prod out of his pants, while his body continued to writhe in torment.

While his minions helped their boss, I grabbed the glasses and dashed for the door. The moment they yanked out the prod, a gasping Joe pointed at me.

As his goons reached for their guns, I glanced both ways on the walkway which circled the hotel atrium. No chance to run. I hurled myself over the railing as guns fired at me.

Time seemed in slow motion while my tuxedo jacket fluttered like a cape. I didn't feel any pain, so the bullets seemed to have missed. The partygoers five floors below looked upward and watched in astonishment. I'd aimed my jump at one of the inflatable Oscars in the pool and stretched my arms toward it, wondering if I'd reach it. The pool looked shallow and deadly from this height.

The floating statue popped when I slammed into it. Air escaped the inflatable Oscar with a sound like a giant fart. It felt like I'd been hit by a tsunami as I splashed into the water. I struggled desperately with the golden plastic entangling me as I sank underwater. I held my breath, my limbs trapped by a slippery, bubbling substance. I rolled around in plastic, gulping air when I could. Finally, I wriggled free and floundered toward the edge of the pool, where Jacqueline stood with several actors. They stared in shock at the spectacle they'd seen.

I climbed out of the pool under the gaze of hundreds of partygoers and at least two TV news cameras.

"Sorry to interrupt, but it's time for us to leave." I straightened my soaked tux and, dripping like a fountain, took Jacqueline by the hand.

Without looking back, we sauntered through the hotel lobby to our waiting limo.

Raging Bull

Elvis was waiting at the mansion's entrance, anxiety wringing his face.

The King hugged Jacqueline first and then pulled me into a bear hug. "You've been all over TV. Why did you jump into the pool?"

"Rex is dead," I said. "Joe killed him."

Elvis' face dropped. "Are you sure?"

"There were dozens of purple faces at the Oscars. Joe tortured me at the after-party. When Rex tried to help me, he was shot by Joe's men."

Elvis groaned. "It just keeps getting worse! Come upstairs. There's something terrible you have to see."

He acted like his news was as bad as mine. What could possibly compare?

"Should I change faces?" I asked.

The King shook his head. "It's not worth the delay. Joe is already trying to kill you. It doesn't matter if he finds out it was you imitating Tom Croft."

Elvis, Jacqueline and I took the elevator upstairs and walked to the boardroom. The lights were dimmed and Court members sat facing a screen, their faces gnarled in terror, as if they were watching a horror film. They were so engrossed by whatever they were viewing, they barely glanced at us.

"He's a sadistic monster . . . a complete psychopath!" Bogie exclaimed.

"It's a game to him, a sick, morbid game!" Lucy Ball cried.

I turned toward the screen. Joe Plain was at the Getty Center wearing a tuxedo at what seemed to be a fancy Christmas gala. He was poisoning famous people, one after another, as other celebrities cheered him on. It was a highlight compilation of murders and substitutions, complete with a peppy pop rock soundtrack.

"Joe Plain emailed this video to Dutch and Chris about an hour ago," Elvis explained to Jacqueline and me. "He also vowed to kill one person Dutch knows every day until we stop filming and close Malibu Graceland."

"He must have had the video ready since Christmas, and sent it as soon as I discovered the purple-faced imposters," I said.

"Joe is boasting to us," Elvis said. "I bet he was itching to send it."

I surveyed the room, and noted that the entire Court was present, as well as Chris and Ernest. This was the first time I'd seen them together.

Chris isn't Ernest. That answered one issue I had pondered. Chris had invented the special glasses, so he could have replaced Ernest and used makeup to keep from glowing purple.

"They've watched the video several times. It's enough," Elvis said.

The King stopped the video, and brightened the lights. It was an hour before sunrise, yet everyone was alert. Chris stood and offered his chair to Jacqueline, his infatuation evident. Marilyn was observing me carefully. I wondered if she knew who I was.

I stood beside Elvis, as everyone sat at the long walnut table. "You've all seen Tom Croft on TV tonight," Elvis said. "However, it wasn't really Tom, it was James Dean."

Marilyn frowned at me with an I'm-angry-you-risked-your-life-but-I'm-glad-you're-alive expression.

Elvis explained the glasses, and Chris answered some technical questions. Then I described the events I'd experienced. The purple-faced imposters didn't shock people as much as they would have if they hadn't just watched Joe's murderous video. When I recounted being tortured by Joe, the room filled with traumatized looks. For the second time, Marilyn had to listen to me describe being assaulted by Joe. There were gasps of dismay when they learned Rex had been murdered.

When I finished, everyone looked grieved, but Chris seemed in the worst condition. Utter despair lined his face. He had been friends with Rex for years.

Court members passed around the glasses, observing that every face had a purple glow except Chris's, Ernest's, and Jacqueline's. I sat down between Marilyn and Bogie.

"I'll call Dutch after the meeting. This will crush him," Chris said. "Rex, Dutch and I have been friends since college."

I could tell Chris was trying hard not to cry, especially in front of

Jacqueline. I needed to take attention away from him.

"I was wrong about Rex," I said. "He died trying to help me."

"Tom . . . or rather, James . . . did you have any problems getting back safely?" Jimmy Stewart asked.

"We took a roundabout way, and we switched vehicles from the limo to an armored truck," I said.

"That was pre-arranged," Elvis explained. "There's no reason for us to be subtle anymore. However, even armored trucks aren't invincible. Hopefully Joe won't increase the firepower of the men he has watching the estate's entrance."

"It makes sense that Joe Plain knows everyone's alter-identities. That's why it's so easy to kill people in our movie," Eleanor said.

"If Joe knew everyone's real identities, he would've killed me," Bogie said.

"But what about all these modern celebrities?" Lucy asked, misery rattling her voice. "Why is he murdering and replacing them? I thought his wrath was aimed against the studio."

"It's obvious," General Patton barked. "It's to spread propaganda."

He had all our attention.

"Hitler and Stalin controlled every goddamn aspect of their governments," the general continued. "Yet, they couldn't have committed so many bloody atrocities without concealing them with false information, especially from their own nations."

"He's right," MLK said. "By controlling celebrities, Joe Plain can spread any message, and perpetrate any barbarity."

"So, we're decided now . . . his plan is to be a ruthless world dictator," Eleanor said.

"No, power is only part of it," Walt said. "He's setting up to do something bigger."

Bigger than a world dictator. The room paused, considering this. But we knew Walt was right.

I was distraught by the gloom assailing my iconic friends. I loved each of them. In many ways, I was sure they appreciated their identities more than the originals had. They were filled with nostalgia and awe, deepened by a historic perspective of their importance.

"We can't allow Rex's death to be in vain," Bogie said. "We finally know the identity of some of the imposters. We must interrogate them."

"How?" Elvis said.

"By going to their homes, capturing them, and prying out information about Joe Plain," Bogie said.

"By any means necessary," General Patton added.

"No . . . we won't endorse torture . . . right?" Jimmy said.

There was uncomfortable silence around the room. People avoided looking at Jimmy.

"It's drastic," Eleanor said. "However, now that we know Joe Plain is willing to kill hundreds, perhaps even thousands, of innocent people, it's up to us to stop him."

Chris' phone made a high-pitch ding.

"It's Dutch," Chris said, reading his phone. He looked about the room with an apologetic expression. "He thinks we need to give in to Joe's demands. He wants to know if I agree. He wants Elvis' opinion, too."

An awful silence ensued. No filming, combined with closing Malibu Graceland, meant no transforming into our identities. This was as dreadful as death to us.

"No. No. No. We can't give in! Every monster can be stopped," MLK said.

"Let's stay calm and logical," Albert said. "We have more information than before. Maybe we can identify Joe, and stop him before giving into his demands."

"That's right. We know Joe must have intimate knowledge of the studio and the estate," Nikola added. "And now we know that no one who was at Dutch's Christmas party can be Joe, nor can anyone who was at the Oscars, nor anyone whose face has never been transformed."

"Chris, Ernest, and everyone in this Court have all been checked with the glasses," I affirmed.

People counted on their fingers, or jotted on notepads, revising their lists of people who could possibly be Joe Plain. I'd already reviewed my mental list several times.

"We don't have a single suspect," I said.

"Joe is someone. Let's list our assumptions," Albert said. "We are assuming Joe is associated with the movie or Malibu Graceland, is within three inches of 5'9", has undergone the transformation process, and can't be in two places at once."

"Obviously, one of our assumptions must be wrong," Nikola added.

I realized I was responsible for the Court making many of these assumptions.

"The question remains. Will you give into Joe's demands?" Marilyn asked.

Chris took a deep breath. "What's the use of Malibu Graceland, if Joe kills everyone?"

"With Rex dead, you own more of the studio now, don't you?" Bogie asked. It sounded like an accusation.

Chris nodded. "Dutch and I now each own half the studio and Malibu Graceland. Are you suggesting that's a motive?"

"Nothing worth billions of dollars is a motive. Joe Plain can easily make trillions," Milton said. "And you can build the machines."

"Chris doesn't glow purple, and Joe talked about Chris as his enemy," I reminded the Court.

It seemed impossible that Chris was Joe, yet I could conceive of one possible motive. Could he, in some convoluted way, be doing this for Jaqueline? Love made people do things otherwise unimaginable.

"What about you, Elvis? Do you think Malibu Graceland should close?" Bogie asked.

Ever since Chris had received the text from Dutch, Elvis had been pacing back and forth, his eye's flaring like a caged tiger. Like us, his identity-addiction needed a place to transform.

"I'll never give up on Malibu Graceland and its mission," Elvis said. "However, temporarily . . . until we know how to stop Joe . . . I don't see any option other than to close it. And the movie will have to halt."

The room fell silent as we all comprehended the consequences of such an action. We'd lose our identities, which felt worse than a normal murder.

My ears were ringing, from fear, rage, or maybe slamming into the water from my five-story fall. I saw flashbacks of Teddy's massacred body, fake Janie dying, Joe with his torture devices, Rex being shot, and celebrities getting poisoned.

"If we interrogate an imposter, we can learn Joe's identity!" Bogie exclaimed.

"They won't talk," MLK said. "They'll be more afraid of Joe than us."

"Martin is right. The replacements know Joe kills without remorse," Milton said.

"We can do something worse than kill them," I said.

All eyes turned to me. "What?" asked Elvis.

"We can interrogate them by duplicates of themselves."

People shivered, imagining the horror.

"I'd rather be tortured than see a damn replica of myself," General Patton growled.

"Joe's imposters aren't historic figures, but they are all famous and powerful. I bet they're pretty attached to their new identities," Walt said.

"That would work, if we had time," Albert said. "However, our friends—perhaps, people in this room—will die before we learn Joe's identity. We all know he will carry out his threat."

"Joe Plain knows my other identity and wants to kill me. Marilyn, too. I feel safer with the estate open," I said.

For the next forty minutes, a vociferous discussion erupted about whether the risk of people getting murdered was worth the chance to learn Joe's identity.

As the Court debated, my brain refused to function properly. The world seemed cloudy and surreal with a quagmire of emotions, including my bitter hatred for Joe Plain, my anxiety about keeping Janie safe, my grief for so many people dead, and my fear that I'd never be James Dean again.

"Okay!" Elvis shouted, hitting the table. "I think it's clear what we need to do. We need to close the estate, but continue to resist in secret."

"Agreed," Chris said.

My brain fired a surge of neurons. Nothing less than Joe's death would keep Janie and me alive. Joe's boasts while torturing me kept poking at my conscience. I googled the LAPD on my phone.

I whispered to Marilyn, "Joe claims he controls the FBI, military, and federal government. Why would he brag to me about controlling the police?"

She shrugged. "I don't know."

"Local law enforcement must be important to Joe's goal."

"Why are we whispering?" Marilyn whispered.

"Because I don't want anyone to try to stop me."

Marilyn's eyes got big. "Whatever you're thinking . . . no."

I put my hand on hers. "I know where Joe Plain will be on Friday. I'm going to use the studio's special effects to kill him."

Of Mice and Men

━━━⌇∿⌇━━━

"Dream as if you'll live forever.
Live as if you'll die today."
—James Dean

"Work as if you were to live a hundred years.
Pray as if you were to die tomorrow."
—Benjamin Franklin

According to my insignia, I held the rank of Sergeant. My cap almost hid the boyish homeliness of my Darrin-face, while my pockets contained devices provided by Elvis.

An Uber dropped me off in front of the Los Angeles Convention Center, a behemoth of crisscrossed steel and towering glass panels. I stepped out of the sedan, wearing an LAPD navy dress uniform and police cap, and headed toward the main concourse.

A suicide mission? I hoped not. Only Marilyn, Elvis and Dutch knew what I was doing, and each had tried to convince me not to undertake this task. However, after being tortured by Joe and watching him murder a friend, I was far too angry to be dissuaded.

Janie wouldn't be safe until Joe was dead.

Hordes of similarly dressed police officers headed to the green and white building, accompanied by spouses and dates, the women in a variety of colorful dresses. Couples laughed and held hands, traversing into the colossal complex with the eagerness of people who seldom attended elegant events.

I converged with other people entering the concourse foyer. The bright modern space was crowded and cheerful, with open bars, roulette wheels and blackjack tables. Live bands could be heard from various exhibit halls. I assumed the crowd was full of concealed weapons, but I didn't know how many of the officers worked for Joe.

Once they realized they couldn't stop me, Dutch had provided special effects and Elvis had helped me to leave Malibu Graceland. I hoped Marilyn would forgive me if I never returned. Joe Plain had bragged that he would control every important police officer by the end of the week. This was the first time in its history that the LAPD had held a department-wide ball, so I was sure it was Joe's doing.

Joe would be here; I would kill him.

The main concourse lobby was as loud and active as the Brazilian Carnival. I pressed through the crowd and entered the South Exhibit Hall, which brimmed with people two-stepping to live country music. No sign of Joe Plain, just off-duty law enforcement enjoying a well-deserved night of harmless amusement.

Next, I explored the West Exhibit Hall, where the band was classic rock. Lots of drunk cops. No plain-faced maniac.

But I knew Joe would be here somewhere. I recalled Elvis' warning: "You're going to make Marilyn a widow before you even marry her." Elvis implied Marilyn would someday want to marry me. Yet, he assumed I could keep her alive—and that she'd want to marry Darrin as Janie.

Palm trees and flowers decorated the concourses, and every time I saw vegetation, I dropped an audio device inside the planters. I thought about Bogie and General Patton, who had a plan to capture one of Joe's imposters tonight. If I succeeded in killing Joe, their efforts would be unnecessary.

As I ambled through the Galaxy Food Court, I spotted a man carrying a red envelope. I had studied police insignias, and knew the three stars embedded on his uniform meant he was First Assistant Chief of Police. Previously, I'd seen other high-ranking officers carrying similar red envelopes.

I tailed the First Assistant Chief, staying about thirty feet behind, feeling James Bond-ish as I slipped through the crowd. I spied two captains with red envelopes moving in the same direction.

The First Assistant Chief entered Petree Hall, one of the major exhibit rooms. I stood in the hallway, watching other officers with red envelopes also enter, ranging in rank from Detective III to Commander

My phone signaled a text from Dutch:

I'm with Chris now. If you see JP he is not Chris. Be careful!

I responded with a thumbs up emoji. Dutch had arranged a meeting with Chris tonight to satisfy me that Joe wasn't Chris. Dutch had pleaded, if I saw Joe, that I wouldn't approach him unless I had a good chance to survive.

Not everyone wandering into Petree Hall held a red envelope, and I headed toward the entrance. An on-duty sergeant stationed at the door glanced briefly at me. I doubted anyone would recognize my Darrin face, besides Joe himself. I smiled and entered.

The conference room was carpeted with colorful geometric patterns. A DJ played pop songs and two open bars attracted long lines of people on each side of the room. An empty podium stood next to a divider wall, which separated the exhibit hall in half. The other half of the exhibit hall didn't seem in use for the police ball.

The officers with red envelopes seemed unsure why they were here, and glanced around the festive room awkwardly. My gut told me something was going to happen.

After about ten minutes, the music suddenly stopped. A door in the divider wall opened, and Chief of Police Bernardo stepped into this half of the exhibit hall, accompanied by a very large man. Conversations halted.

Chief Bernardo went straight to the small podium. I recognized the goon swaggering behind him as the largest of Joe Plain's four minions when he'd killed Rex. Now the giant was in uniform and seemed to be Chief Bernardo's bodyguard.

The police chief glanced around the room. "Good evening, I hope everyone is having a good time."

People applauded respectfully, albeit with an air of uncertainty about why their leader was giving a speech.

"Some of you have a red envelope. I'd like everyone else to leave," Bernardo said.

Most people headed towards the door. Before I followed them, I lingered beside the DJ table. Dutch had given me a camera disguised like a water bottle, and I placed it next to the DJ mixer.

I exited the room, and stood along the concourse wall near the door, looking at my iPhone which showed the water bottle camera's view of Petree Hall. The police chief was speaking, and I listened with air pods.

"Tonight, I'm introducing a new task force. You're going to receive a new weapon and more freedom to do your job," Chief Bernardo said. "I'd like you to form a row by rank, starting with First Assistant Chief Jefferson on my far right. I'm going to ask you to relinquish your weapons, so I can replace it with a better weapon."

The officers looked confused as they arranged themselves side-by-side according to rank. Chief Bernardo passed by them, collecting their weapons and placing them into a container carried by his supersized bodyguard.

Once the officers were unarmed, the partition door opened. Joe Plain entered! My pulse quickened, my chest tightened. Today, you die! For Teddy, Rex and Fake Janie. Especially for threatening real Janie.

My jaw clenched as Joe stood beside Chief Bernardo. This was it. My assassination plan was no longer theoretical. The concourse's bustling activity seemed distant as my mind jumbled. Could I really kill someone? Was I ready to die, if necessary?

"This is Joe Plain," Chief Bernardo said. "He is highly qualified and will be running the new task force. This is a special occasion and he has prepared a toast."

Joe Plain and Chief Bernardo moved down the row of police officers, pouring each of them a flute of Champagne. Joe smiled at each man and woman, and shook their hand.

He's going to poison them.

My breathing accelerated as hate turned into panic. I needed to hurry. Unless I stopped him immediately, Joe would kill these brave men and women. His vapid face showed a dearth of humanity, but I read in his expression a perverse jollity about the upcoming mass murder.

While watching Joe and the Police Chief return to the podium, I moved toward the door of Petree Hall. The same sergeant still guarded the door.

"I need to get in."

"Sorry, no one is allowed," he said.

A 9mm Smith & Wesson was in my ankle holster, but this would be my first time to use a handgun. My odds of surviving the evening had always been slim; now they seemed almost nonexistent.

During my last conversation with Elvis, he'd said "Promise me you won't risk your life unless you're certain you can stop Joe Plain." The King of Rock had forced me to shake his hand and promise.

I had to break this vow. Otherwise, all the officers in the room would be poisoned. I lowered to a knee and pretended to tie my shoe. Instead I grabbed my pistol. The concourse and Petree Hall were full of armed police officers, so I tried to hold the gun so only the sergeant guarding the door could see it.

"Step aside," I said. My plan was simple: enter the room and run toward Joe Plain while firing at him until I was stopped.

My hand shook. If I failed to kill Joe, countless more would die, starting in Petree Hall and then the other victims of Joe's plan.

The sergeant looked at me, saw the pistol and determination in my eyes, and took a step backward. I put my hand on the door. *No matter how many bullets hit me . . . keep firing until Joe is dead.* My 9mm magazine held 17 rounds.

I touched a button on my collar to turn on the voice-recognition sensor which controlled the special effects. One effect would cause the water-bottle device on the DJ table to make a loud noise to serve as a distraction.

"Activate effect seven. Full volume," I said softly.

Nothing happened.

Crap. There should have been an almost deafening noise inside Petree Hall.

"Activate effect seven. Full volume," I repeated more loudly.

Nothing. The signal didn't seem to be transmitting through the wall.

"He's got a gun!" a woman yelled.

I started to open the door, but the sergeant rushed at me. I aimed the gun at him, my finger on the trigger, but I didn't shoot. He grabbed my arm and his body crashed into me. Then another man jumped on top of us. My face planted into the floor.

"Grab his gun!" a man yelled.

There was more weight on me, crushing my ribs. The pistol was yanked out of my hand. A choke hold contused my neck. Muscular men were enthusiastically hurting me.

My arm seared in pain as a man twisted my left wrist behind my back. Another man did the same to my right arm. Hands grasped me under my armpits, and I was lifted. The goal felt like it was to pull my arms off.

My legs were off the ground, flailing in the air, and my shoulders were contorted back like chicken wings being torn off an unfortunate bird. I could only breathe in gulps.

The merciless men led me into Petree Hall and held me in front of Chief Bernardo. Joe Plain was standing at the Chief's right side.

"This man had a gun. He was trying to force his way into the room," one of them said.

The officers with red envelopes still stood in a row, holding their Champagne glasses. Thank God. They hadn't drunk to Joe's toast yet. I could still save them.

Resisting the piercing pain, I gulped a breath and yelled: "He's going to poi—"

Chief Bernardo put a meaty hand over my mouth. "Shut up."

"I know this man," Joe Plain said. A smile diffused across his degenerate face. "He's dangerous and crazy. Hold him over there until I have a chance to question him."

Joe nodded to Chief Bernardo's immense bodyguard, who moved the men holding my left arm out of the way and put his massive arm in a choke hold around my neck. The man holding my right arm let go, seeing he was superfluous. The searing pains in my shoulders ceased, but now I felt like I was slowly being decapitated. The goon's massive bicep garroted my larynx without mercy. Crushed neck cartilage was agony I hadn't experienced before.

One of my arms was trapped behind me, but with my free arm I struck my elbow into my new tormentor's gut. He responded by squeezing my throat until I started to pass out.

Helpless, I was dragged toward a wall. I stopped resisting, and he let me inhale some air.

The Police Chief asked the men who had entered during the commotion to leave. Once they were gone, he relinquished the podium to Joe Plain. I had to gasp hard to get air, but I was able to watch from the back of the room.

Joe raised his Champagne. "To each of you—who will change the future in ways you've never imagined."

I tried to shout, but couldn't even make a peep. I used my heel to kick the shin of the Goliath holding me. He simply laughed and lifted me higher. The searing pain incapacitated me; my shoulder may have dislocated. The giant turned me toward the row of officers, and forced me to watch.

The officers drank, about thirty of them. I was horrified, assuming it was poison. However, they didn't seem in any pain.

"I'm giving you the greatest gift: freedom," Joe said. "You'll no longer be constrained by laws and social norms. You're going to do unimaginable things. Well, not exactly you . . . ."

The partition door opened, and dozens of police officers marched through the door. They looked around the room and approached the men and women in the rows.

"Oh, fuck!"

"Oh, my God!"

The officers holding the red envelopes gasped in shock. Each of them was met by a person identical to them. The officers who had just entered the room stood beside the person they replicated.

"What's going on?" First Assistant Chief Jefferson demanded. As he spoke, he lurched to one side, legs quivering.

"You've all been poisoned," Joe Plain announced. He seemed giddy with exhilaration. "These are your replacements. You'll be dead soon, but the new you will be unstoppable."

Horror filled the room. The original officers teetered on their feet, staring at those who would take their spots in the world. One-by-one, the originals collapsed to the floor.

When only the replacements remained standing, Joe said, "Put the body of your original in a body bag and report to Bernardo. He'll give you instructions."

As the replacements carried out his command, Joe approached me, his inhuman smile broader than ever.

"Hello, Darrin. You've made a pleasant day even more enjoyable. I'll get to torture you until I coerce your password. I already have a replacement being prepared."

"Fuff uw." The bicep pinched tight around my neck, slurring my words.

"Fuff me?" Joe laughed. "Fuff you. Everyone in the movie you're making is going to be killed and replaced, including that woman you love—the actress playing Marilyn Monroe. I forgot her real name, but I'll think of you when I kill her."

I kicked at Joe, and felt the torturous hold on my neck tightened. Joe chuckled as my shoe missed him by a foot. "You'll already be dead when I kill her. Neither you, nor she, nor any of your pathetic friends will ever see the new version of the world I create."

Joe instructed the man choking me, "Take him into the other room and tie him up. You can hurt him, but don't kill him."

The man forced me towards the partition door into the other half of Petree Hall. I tried again to kick his shins, but I lacked leverage. He was stronger than an ox.

We passed new officers as they stuffed the dead versions of themselves into body bags. A young, blond officer was zipping up a bag, and I pointed in a frenzy at the face in the bag.

"What, did you know him?" my brutish escort asked indifferently, not relaxing his grip.

I moved my hand and fingers about rapidly, like a one-handed sign language interpreter desperate to convey a message.

"Let him speak," Joe Plain said. "Maybe he knows something."

The hulk holding me released my throat slightly.

I spoke into my collar: "Activate effects seven and ten."

Gunfire, at least the sound of it, erupted from the DJ table and echoed around the room. At the same time, red splotches burst onto the chest of my uniform. I went limp, as if I was dead.

The man restraining me looked about, trying to see who'd shot me. Every officer in the room had brandished his or her gun, heads turning in all directions, searching for the source of gunfire. The huge man dropped me and also pulled his gun.

"Activate effects—all," I said as I landed on the floor.

From the concourse, I heard more gunfire and explosions. I knew there was smoke, too, from the devices I had placed in the planters. Officers rushed toward the door and ran into the concourse. In the confusion, I got up and followed. No one besides Joe Plain noticed as I exited Petree Hall. Joe and I momentarily locked eyes Then I disappeared from his sight, rushing in the general direction of the stampeding crowd.

I ran through the West Lobby, just one uniformed man among hundreds, and exited the Conference Center. I took off my cap and held it to my chest, covering the red splotches. West 12th Street was closed to traffic, but crowded with pedestrians. I sprinted south towards the Figueroa Street entrance to Staples Pavilion about three hundred feet away. As I ran, I checked no one followed.

The security guard at the arena entrance stepped aside when I showed my badge.

A Lakers game was in progress, and Staples teemed with fans. No one walking through the corridors or working at the concession stands paid attention as I entered a public bathroom. I entered a stall and removed my police uniform, exposing the Lakers jersey and baggy basketball shorts I'd worn beneath. I also had a fake mustache in my pocket.

My hands shook uncontrollably as I tried to affix the mustache. My breathing was rapid and frenzied, yet I couldn't seem to get enough air. I had almost shot the sergeant guarding the door, a man probably innocent. When had I become so debased? Yet, if I'd shot him, all those other officers might be alive. Joe might be dead; I probably would, too.

It took about five minutes to regain self-control. I implemented my disguise and emerged from the men's room, hardly recognizing the man I'd become. I bought a LA Dodgers cap and some popcorn, climbed the stairs to one of the top sections of the arena, and found an empty seat in the highest row.

A Few Good Men

Marilyn's hand flopped onto my bare chest. She made a gentle purring sound and continued to sleep. We were naked, entangled in silk sheets in the serenity of my bungalow. Moonlight streamed through the skylight and illuminated her curves.

There was no way I could sleep. I stared at her form while listening to her breathe. I'd escaped Joe, but I knew for certain that killing her remained high on his priority list.

When the Lakers' game ended, I'd ridden a public bus to Santa Monica and then an Uber to Elvis' ancillary house in Malibu. All by myself, I'd flown a jetpack to the estate. Elvis expected me, so he made sure the lights were off along the beach. I was pleased with how deftly I flew, considering it was only my second time.

As I hovered over the beach, slowly descending onto the sand, Elvis greeted me with a grim expression.

"Joe Plain killed two more people tonight," Elvis said. "I was worried he'd killed you, too."

"Who?"

The King took a sad deep breath. "Bing Crosby and Arthur Ashe."

My chest tightened. A familiar anguish surged. Two more dear friends dead. Two humble, thoughtful, compassionate people. At least they acted that way, which seemed the same.

"Joe sent a video of them dying to Dutch and Chris."

"But we've agreed to Joe's demands . . . ."

There was only one reason Joe would kill more people. Retaliation. "Joe murdered them because I went to the police ball, didn't he?"

Elvis ignored the question. "What happened tonight?"

I told Elvis about my failed assassination attempt and subsequent escape.

"Bogie and George captured and interrogated two imposters," Elvis said. He described the interrogations, which had implemented my method.

"Bogie said the imposters were terrified to the point of answering any questions, when they were confronted with identical imposters. They were aspiring actors Joe recruited and forced to memorize an identity. Unfortunately, they didn't know Joe's plan or his identity," Elvis said. "On the good side, they seemed too scared to tell Joe we questioned them."

I wondered if six months ago as Darrin, I could have been convinced by Joe to become an imposter. I hoped not.

"So what's our next plan to stop Joe?" I asked.

"Nothing. Joe gave us until 5 p.m. Monday to stop filming and close the estate."

Elvis and I had walked in silence from the beach to the ballroom, and he'd conducted the transformation to return me to James Dean. I hadn't slept since.

Now it was the middle of the night. It felt peremptorily nostalgic to stare at Marilyn in the moonlight. Soon we'd no longer be James and Marilyn. I traced the curve of her cheeks with my fingertips. For hours, I pondered ways to keep Janie safe.

"Why aren't you sleeping?" Marilyn mumbled as she squinted into the darkness.

I kissed her. "My mind won't stop replaying all the innocent police officers dying while their replacements watched."

I didn't mention the deep ache in my shoulders. I was trying to deemphasize how close I'd come to being killed.

Marilyn had been furious when I told her what I'd done. "If you loved me, you wouldn't run toward danger!" She had paced the room, cried, and then we'd made love twice.

Marilyn rolled onto her side to face me. "If Joe controls everything, why doesn't he just send the police or FBI into the estate? Or launch missiles and kill us all? He can easily cover it up."

"He doesn't seem to want the estate destroyed. He wants it closed. I'm not sure why."

"Well, Joe got his way," Marilyn lamented. "Soon, our identities will just be a dream."

She snuggled into my arms, and I relished the warmth of her soft skin and the citronella scent of her Rose Geranium perfume. It was nice that she could be Marilyn. Yet, frankly, I didn't give a damn, I just needed to keep her alive.

"At least we know Chris can't be Joe," I said. "Dutch met with him last night while I was with Joe."

"No one can be Joe," Marilyn mumbled. "We've eliminated every candidate in multiple ways . . . ."

Marilyn fell back asleep. I closed my eyes and pretended I was Joe Plain, just as if I was preparing to play him in a movie.

. . . I control everything. What else do I desire? What threatens me?

What kind of world am I creating? Why do I hate Dutch so much? Why do I want to close Malibu Graceland?

If I desire panic and chaos, I should tell the public about the transform-machines. If I want my power to be a secret, I should kill everyone who knows about the machines . . . .

As morning rays glinted through the bungalow windows, Joe's perspective on the world finally came into clear focus.

Joe had a weakness!

For one brief period Joe would be vulnerable, and he was desperate to eliminate it.

I quietly slipped out of bed. I needed to tell Elvis immediately.

As I dressed, I stared at Marilyn's sleeping figure, studying the colors and contours of her back and buttocks. The sex last night had been spectacular—it always was, no matter how tired or afraid we were. Without Joe Plain, my life would be perfect. Now, though, I knew his weakness.

The courtyard was gloomy, the antipode of joyous effervescence it normally radiated. People trudged the immaculate pathways with fearful frowns. I saw Bogie and hurried toward him.

"Holy crap, Bogie. It's like doomsday out here."

"Everyone knows a ruthless murderer is planning to kill us, and that we're losing our identities."

"Do they know about Arthur and Bing?"

Bogie sighed. "Yes. Some people envy them. No one wants to return to their old identity."

"Stay positive, Bogie. I'm heading to see Elvis."

"Don't bother, kid. It's hopeless. You know Elvis doesn't like to be interrupted during the day."

"Hang in there, Bogie," I said, heading toward the mansion.

I passed a gazebo full of disconsolate historical icons as they comforted each other. Modern celebrities had been absent at Malibu Graceland since the Oscars. I continued to the glass elevator and rode to the top floor. The Memphis Room was unoccupied, as was Elvis' office, so I knocked on his bedroom door. There was no sign of him anywhere.

Elvis wouldn't want me to call or text anyone, so I went down to the ground floor, and entered the ballroom, where I found Martin Luther King, Jr. reading.

"Hi, James. I didn't expect to do any transforming today. Everyone's afraid to leave sooner than they have to."

"It's an emergency."

The reverend didn't question me, which made him rise even higher in my esteem. Two hours later, I had my Darrin face. I couldn't fly a jetpack during the day, so I put on a hat and sunglasses and made my way to a delivery truck. Normally, I hid in the back, but these were desperate times. I drove myself out the entrance.

No one stopped me as I drove from Malibu to Burbank, but I imagined a satellite tracking me and Joe Plain deciding where to murder me. When I reached Digital Impact, I parked and walked briskly across the lot, hurrying past the water tower I'd once climbed, heading straight to the executive building.

Dutch Hollander's executive assistant Devon, the attractive blonde woman who'd ignored me at the holiday party, frowned as I marched into her office.

"Hello, Devon, I need to speak with Dutch immediately."

Devon examined me, pretending not to remember me. She'd probably come to Hollywood with aspirations to become an actress.

"I'm sorry, sir. Mr. Hollander is very busy. Do you have an appointment?"

"Just tell Dutch that Darrin Clark is here."

"Today won't fit on his schedule," Devon replied dismissively. "Let's see . . . I can fit you in at 2:45 p.m. next Tuesday."

"No. Tell him right now that I am here."

Devon smiled venomously. "You'll regret this." She pushed an intercom button: "Dutch, I'm so sorry to bother you, but a Darrin Clark is in the office and asked to see you. Should I arrange a future appointment?"

There was a pause. Then Dutch's voice over the intercom: "Please send Darrin in."

Devon scowled. "You can—."

"Thank you." I proceeded through the huge walnut doors behind Devon's desk.

Dutch's office was enormous and opulent. I glanced at the sofa where I'd sat during my first audition, when I'd been so nervous that Jacqueline had made me take deep breaths before we started. The corpulent studio president sat behind an obnoxiously large desk in the middle of the room. Behind him was a trophy case full of Oscars. Autographed photographs covered his walls: James Cagney, Ingrid Bergman, Ronald Reagan, Henry Fonda, Betty Davis, and numerous others.

Dutch snuffed out a cigar as I entered. He wore his usual pinstriped suit, with suspenders stretched over his bulging belly.

"You were very brave at the Oscars, and I'm in your debt." Dutch stood, shook my hand, and then plopped his enormous bulk back into his chair. "But you need to be smarter. Why would you risk your life to come here?"

"It's the legacy scenes. That's what threatens Joe. That's why he wants the movie stopped and Malibu Graceland closed."

Dutch waved me into a chair. "Halting the legacy scenes is only incidental to Joe's demands."

"Because Joe is trying to hide his weakness. Joe killed Teddy and Rex, the two key people for the legacy scenes. His first demand was to stop filming at the studio. When we considered moving the legacy scenes to the estate, he added another demand: to close the estate."

Dutch glanced nervously around his office. "That's interesting, but it's too late now. We're stopping everything, so no one else has to die."

"But we must—"

Dutch interrupted loudly, "Read this press release I'm working on." He put his fingers to his lips, leaned toward me, and whispered: "I sweep my office for bugs every day, but we can't be too careful. Last year, I found a bug. Joe would do anything to hear what happens in here."

I imagined being paranoid, even in my own office. "While filming the legacy scenes, people spend part of the time hypnotized. They're vulnerable," I whispered.

Dutch's eyebrows shot up. "That's true . . . we could ask them anything and get an honest answer."

"Even if they are spies for Joe. Or Joe himself," I whispered.

"True . . . we've always known Joe had an inside connection."

"If Joe is scared of the legacy scenes, there is a reason. So we need to film them secretly. Orson can film them."

Dutch nodded contemplatively. "I've been looking for a way to resist," Dutch whispered. "It broke my heart to halt production of our movie today. But I did it for the actors. To keep them alive."

Dutch stood, lifting his rotund girth with effort, and walked to his trophy case. He reached to the top shelf and picked up an Oscar, handling it like a doting parent. "Our film was going to be the greatest ever. I know how important the estate is, but if we defy Joe, a lot more people may die . . ."

I stayed silent as Dutch ruminated. He caressed the Oscar until he finally walked toward me and whispered. "We need to find a place to secretly film the legacy scenes and sneak people in one at a time."

"Exactly. We won't give actors any advanced warning. While they're hypnotized, we'll ask if they are Joe or work for him."

"I know everyone's real identities. They'll be happy to transform," Dutch whispered. "If they refuse, we'll know they're a spy . . . or Joe."

"If we sneak people into the mansion, we can film them there," I suggested. "We already have the equipment and machines."

Dutch set the Oscar on his desk and pointed towards a side door. "That's my storage room." He leaned against his desk and smiled conspiratorially. "I've been stocking up on special effects devices and other technologies that no one knows I have. I'm hoping for a chance to use them against Joe."

Dutch pushed himself off the desk and picked up the Oscar again. As he held the golden statuette, I noticed his fingers. They were worn on the tips.

"Let me see your left hand."

Dutch recoiled. "Excuse me?"

"I want to see your hand." I reached for him, but he shoved his enormous belly in the way.

"What are you doing?" Dutch demanded, unduly angry.

I jumped at him, pulled his arm down and grabbed his hand.

"Are you mad?"

"You have calluses on your left hand."

"So what? I do lots of paperwork," Dutch said.

"Oh, my God. Those are guitar calluses. You're Elvis!"

Dutch jolted in shock. "That's crazy. It's from paperwork."

I stared at his fingertips. "You're Elvis."

Dutch burst out laughing. "That's preposterous. I weigh twice as much as Elvis."

"I should have figured it out earlier. Your fat suit tricked me."

Dutch stopped laughing. "Fat suit? There's no fat suit."

I poked the studio president hard in the chest. It felt more like rubbery padding than flesh.

When I looked up at Dutch, he glared like a cornered feral cat. He rotated his shoulder away from me and raised his arm upward. I flinched as I saw the shiny Oscar statue pause over my head. I waited for the impact of the golden trophy on my skull.

I would be the first actor killed by an Oscar.

However, Dutch wasn't attacking. He was deliberating. As he reached up to the top of the trophy case, I realized it wasn't anger in his eyes, but fear. He returned the statuette to its home on the highest shelf, then looked me straight in the eyes.

He put a finger to his lips and indicated for me to take a seat. He plopped his rotund body down in his own chair.

"What's your password?" he whispered.

Clever. He'd reflected the pressure on me. Was I certain enough to expose our password?

"Napoleon," I revealed.

"Whisper," Dutch urged, taking a deep breath. "If Joe finds out I'm Elvis, he'll kill me immediately. Galapagos." Dutch exhaled. "Oh, Darrin. I'm sorry I kept this secret from you. I've wanted so badly to tell you. Even Bogie doesn't know I'm Elvis."

I wasn't expecting an apology. I thought Dutch would be irate or maintain his denial.

"Who else knows?"

"Just Chris." Dutch loosened his tie and unfastened the top three buttons on his shirt. "Feel this—I've had to wear this for years, just to keep my identity secret."

It was strange to feel the padding. The rubbery foam-like outfit exposed under Dutch's shirt felt personal, like I'd entered Dutch's secret world.

"Now you carry an extra burden," Dutch whispered as he rebuttoned his shirt.

I thought about the occasions Joe had nearly tortured me. "It's lucky I didn't know your identity earlier."

"Whisper," Dutch implored. "Our enemies would do anything to learn Elvis' identity."

He had a good reason to be cautious, I realized.

"To make Malibu Graceland a reality, I had to be both Dutch and Elvis. I had to coordinate between the estate and the studio. It's been difficult, but I've succeeded so far."

"So, everything revolves around you. That's why Joe is focused on you."

"I can't be captured or killed, or everything is lost," Dutch said. "That's why I use passwords, and use a jetpack to get to Malibu Graceland."

"How long have you been planning this?"

"Since college," Dutch whispered. "You know Chris, Rex and I were best friends at Caltech. Chris was so smart, we knew he could invent anything. We wanted a plan that could benefit humanity, and I conceived of an estate that improved the behavior of celebrities."

"I thought you, Chris and Rex started Digital Impact first, and then devised the estate after he invented the machines."

"Chris never cared about movies, his interest is biomedical engineering.

But he saw the unrivaled humanitarian benefits of our plan. The estate was always his priority. He left Digital Impact as soon as he could. Everything was succeeding perfectly until Joe Plain stole the transform-machine." Dutch clenched his fists. "Joe ruined our plan to improve the world. Instead, he's terrorizing it. I wish I'd seen you put the electric prod in his pants."

"Are you sure Chris is trustworthy? I know he isn't Joe, but he could be working with him."

"Chris is our only hope to defeat Joe. There's no one as loyal or brilliant."

"Anyone can be blackmailed or bribed."

"How can Chris be bribed? He could've made billions from his inventions. Instead, he's put all his wealth into causes he thinks can help mankind."

"I don't trust anyone anymore, until I know them very well."

"Chris would think that's wise." Dutch smiled. "And you are right about the legacy scenes."

"What?"

"Chris and I are using the legacy scenes to try to identify Joe—just as you suggested. The hypnotism really does improve the acting, but while people are unconscious, we ask them if they know Joe Plain's identity. It was our secret scheme."

"Yet, Joe seems to have guessed it."

"I'm afraid so. However, Chris and I are committed to keep filming them. It's our best weapon."

"It sucks that you and Elvis are the same person. There were few people I trusted, and now there's one less."

"That's not logical. I'll be doing the same things as before. You can still think of Elvis and Dutch as different people, if you want."

"Can I look in your storage room?" I hoped he had some potent technology that Joe Plain wouldn't expect.

"Of course."

I walked to the door and opened it, revealing a large, crowded space resembling the prop department of a studio.

"These aren't just props, they're priceless relics. Look around all you want. The special effects I've collected are at the back."

I ventured into the crammed room. Three aisles of wooden shelving formed narrow corridors stuffed with nostalgic memorabilia. I recognized props from some of my favorite movies.

There was a huge sign promoting "Rick's Café Americain"—Humphrey Bogart's bar in *Casablanca*. I plugged it in, and the room illuminated in a neon glow. I examined the golden idol from *Raiders of the Lost Ark*, and when I saw Harry Potter's Hogwarts robe, I couldn't resist trying it on and waving his wand.

It felt great to release some tension. Christopher Reeve's blue Superman suit was on a hanger, and I put Superman's red cape over Harry's robes, picked up Gandolf's staff from *The Lord of the Rings* and started whacking Grego Clegane's armor from *Game of Thrones*.

"I'm going to kill you, Joe Plain," I said as I brutally attacked the armor.

After numerous strikes, I looked beyond the armor and saw Elvis' Ebony Dove guitar. I held my breath in admiration. It looked almost sacred on its stand.

I knew about this guitar from pictures Elvis had shown me. It was his favorite instrument. I rubbed my fingertips along the guitar neck. It seemed to have been recently strung.

Imagining hordes of concertgoers, I swiveled my hips and played some chords. "You ain't nothing but—"

Boom.

A thunderous explosion concussed the room.

I was thrown into the air as light bulbs shattered. The room went pitch-black. My back crashed into wooden shelving, and I crumpled helplessly into a fetal position. I tried to protect my head as movie props rained down on me. Within seconds, I was covered with rubble.

Abruptly, the noise subsided. An earthquake? A bomb?

Dazed and disoriented, I tried to stand, pushing upward through the wreckage. Each movement created shattering noises as I broke irreplaceable props. In the quagmire I struggled to gain my balance.

Eerie orange emergency lights came on, revealing dust and destruction. I hollered to Dutch and tried to locate the door.

No answer. Smoke came from one direction and I waded through rubble until I saw a door.

Oh shit. The door was caved inward with gray smoke coming from beneath it. There must have been a huge explosion in Dutch's office. I yanked the handle, but the door was hopelessly jammed.

Smoke quickly filled the room. I began to panic, banging and shouting. There were no windows or ventilation.

I found a woman's dress of lacy material, and tried to stuff it beneath the door to stop the smoke. It immediately caught fire.

As I stomped at the flames, I began to cough. Thick, acidic smoke burned my eyes and lungs. I thought of my uncle and his agonizing, disfiguring burns. I grabbed the door handle again and yelped in pain. Too hot to hold. I could only imagine the devastation in Dutch's office.

My lungs felt on fire. Was the gas toxic? My chest ached so fiercely, the pain nearly incapacitated me.

Somewhere around here were the special effects. Maybe I could use them to knock down the door. In the dense smoke, I had no idea which direction to go. I took a step backwards and tripped, falling to a knee. My coughing increased to labored gasps for air. Whatever I was breathing wasn't oxygen. As if in slow motion, I collapsed towards the floor.

I am going to die. Dutch must be dead already . . . so . . . Elvis is dead.

Lying on the floor, I writhed in the rubble, desperate for air. In the debris, I felt a gun. Clint Eastwood's *Dirty Harry* .44 Magnum. With my last bit of strength, I forced myself to my knees and aimed the giant Smith & Wesson at the door. I pulled the trigger.

Nothing. No bullets. A prop.

I fell to the floor, suffocating.

My best friend, Elvis, was dead. Now, I would join him.

I imagined Janie's face, then lost consciousness.

An Extraordinary League of Gentlemen

Men shouting. Air in my lungs. Alive.

I opened my eyes.

My face bounced against a yellow firefighter's coat.

Arms were holding me. The rugged face of a fireman smiled at me . . . I lost consciousness again . . . .

I awoke, lying on a stretcher. "You're going to be fine," a paramedic informed me.

It was sunny. We were outdoors in the studio lot. Sitting up cautiously, I saw a crowd of people staring at me.

"What happened to Dutch?"

The paramedics glanced at me, and looked away. None of them answered. I climbed off the stretcher, discovering I was unhurt besides scrapes and bruises.

Exposed steel beams and smoking wreckage remained where Dutch's office used to be. Devon stood by an ambulance, sobbing. A group of police officers noticed I was conscious and headed toward me; I walked to meet them.

"Where's Dutch? Why aren't you searching for him?" I demanded.

"We found him." A policewoman shook her head. "I'm sorry."

I was speechless, dizzy with sadness and confusion. Dutch was dead. Did these officers work for Joe Plain?

"Was Dutch Hollander holding something big and rubbery?" a detective asked. "His body was covered in a melted gooey substance."

The fat suit. Dutch had spent years keeping his identity hidden, and I'd given it away by confronting him in his office. I wondered if his office was bugged, or if Joe had tracked me to the studio.

"There was a large rubber prop by his desk," I lied. "It was a replica of the Pillsbury Doughboy."

The detective nodded. "He must have fallen on it."

Joe Plain must have rigged Dutch's office with explosives. Did Joe include explosives wherever he planted bugs? Or was Dutch a specific target, and Joe was waiting for the right time to kill him? Did Joe detonate it because I gave away Elvis' identity?

Either way, it was my fault that Dutch—Elvis—was dead.

Detectives and FBI agents took turns interviewing me, and they seemed genuine, but who could tell? At some level Joe controlled their bosses. As I answered questions, my mind asked its own. Had Joe detonated the bomb himself, or had someone who worked for him? Had he heard us discussing the legacy scenes? Was the bomb intended to kill me or just Dutch? Did Joe wait to murder Dutch until I entered the closet?

Either Joe had intentionally kept me alive, because he intended to use me somehow, or he'd attempted to kill me and would try again when he learned he'd failed.

A burst of relief buoyed me when I saw Chris and Jacqueline approaching. Grief etched their faces, but their presence comforted me. They waited nearby until I was finished being questioned.

Finally, the detectives and FBI agents gave me their cards and walked away. Jacqueline hugged me. Surprisingly, Chris did, too. He looked utterly distraught. I'd catalogued him as a logic-driven brainiac, but he was reeling in emotions now.

"Come, we've got a limo," Jacqueline said.

Chris didn't say a word. He was always awkward around Jacqueline, but now anguish seemed to render him mute.

I followed them, entering the back of a black SUV stretch limo. Marilyn, Bogie and Orson sat inside. Marilyn jumped into my arms, kissing me.

"Your photo has been all over the news, right next to Dutch's," she said. "I didn't know if you were dead."

Marilyn's affection always surprised me when I wasn't James Dean. I felt inadequate as Darrin. Unconditional love seemed too good to be real.

"I can't reach Elvis," Bogie fretted. Sweat beaded on his forehead and a cigarette passed rapidly between his fingers. "Dutch's death will compromise everything. Elvis should have contacted me by now."

Bogie noticed me glance at Chris, who was staring blankly at the limo floorboard. "Chris has barely spoken since we left the mansion," Bogie said. "He's gone comatose."

"Dutch was his best friend," Jacqueline said.

Bogie held Chris's arm. "We're all heartbroken, but we need your help. Do you know where Elvis is?"

Chris sighed listlessly. "Yes. Darrin does, too."

Chris went back to staring at his shoes. He had known Elvis' identity, which was another reason he couldn't be Joe.

Bogie, Jacqueline, Marilyn and Orson turned to me. "Well, where is he?" Bogie demanded.

The car felt unbearably dismal. I wanted to get out and scream.

"Elvis is dead," I said. "His real identity was Dutch Hollander."

"That's crazy," Bogie snorted. "Dutch was enormous."

"Dutch wore a fat suit."

"Fat suit?" Bogie exhorted.

"Yes. I felt it on him."

"It's true," Chris muttered.

It took a while for them to comprehend this. We were all at the edge of despair.

"What happened before the explosion?" Marilyn asked.

I told them about my conversation with Dutch. Bogie looked so fragile, a touch would shatter him. Elvis had been his foundation.

"Do you think Joe overheard you talking about the legacy scenes?" Chris asked, lifting his head to look at me.

"I don't know."

"It was a brilliant plan and you ruined it," Bogie said. His eyes were fierce and contemptuous. Clearly, he blamed me for Elvis' death.

"Now, we can't film them!" Bogie added.

"We have to film them." I turned to Chris for validation. "Let me film them. I'll do it myself. It's our best chance."

Bogie scowled at me. "It's far too dangerous, especially if Joe overheard you talking with Dutch."

"It was Dutch's dying instruction," I pleaded.

"I'm sorry, Darrin. Besides the danger, filming the legacy scenes is very technical. Most of the people qualified are dead," Chris said. "I'll try to figure out if there is any possible way to do it."

"With Dutch and Rex both dead, do you own the estate and the studio?" Marilyn asked.

"Yes," Chris said. "The safety of the actors is solely my responsibility. I'm going to offer everyone a choice, either to go into hiding or to resume their original lives. Either way, I'll help them. As long as we yield to his demands, I don't think he'll want to kill anyone but you, Darrin."

"How is Darrin a threat?" Marilyn asked.

"He's not. Joe just hates him."

"He put an electric prod in Joe's pants!" Orson chuckled.

"Who inherits the estate if you die, Chris?" Bogie asked.

"Ernest. Then your alter-identity, if Ernest is killed. Then Jacqueline. Finally, Orson, and members of the Court's alter-identities."

Crap. Did Chris really think it could go that far?

"Why is Ernest first? He's not exactly one of us," Marilyn asked.

"Dutch and I decided this together," Chris said. "Ernest has been our friend for decades, and he's committed to the estate's purpose. And since he's a presidential candidate, he has 24-hour Secret Service protection."

I didn't know Ernest well, but he'd been in Iowa the first time I met Joe, and I'd seen him with the glasses, so I knew Ernest wasn't an imposter.

"If the estate ever opens again, will Bogie run it?" Marilyn asked.

"No. James Dean will run the Court," Jacqueline said, smiling at me.

"Elvis made it clear he wanted James to run the Court if he died," Chris confirmed.

Marilyn and I looked at each other. "What?"

"If there's ever another Court, you'll run it," Chris said.

"Why not Bogie?" I asked.

"My alter-identity makes that impossible," Bogie said.

"Who's your other identity, Bogie? You know ours."

"Hell if I'm telling you. Look what happened when you revealed Elvis' identity."

That hurt. Maybe I deserved it.

"If Joe knew my real identity, he'd kill me," Bogie added.

I turned to Chris. "Well, if not Bogie, why not another Court member?"

"Dutch and I were impressed that you wanted to use the machines to help burn victims," Chris said. "You're passionate and fearless without any selfish agenda. After considering everyone's alter-identities, we selected you."

"I'm assuming we are still shutting down the movie," Jacqueline said. She was sitting next to Chris, and seemed to want his approval.

I realized Chris would select the next studio president. With Teddy, Rex, and Dutch all dead, Jacqueline was suddenly in line to become president. I couldn't imagine Chris ever saying no to her about anything.

"Yes, filming will still have to stop," Chris said. "And I'll need to announce an interim studio president."

Jacqueline gave Chris a modest smile.

"I'll film the legacy scenes," Orson said. We all turned to him in surprise. I felt so proud, I wanted to hug him.

"Are you sure?" Chris asked. "Joe will kill whoever—"

"I'm Elvis' friend. And I'm qualified," Orson interrupted. "This is my chance to make a difference."

"It's impossible. All the transform-machines are at the studio or Malibu Graceland. Joe will probably come and check on the machines," Bogie said.

"You can build another machine, Chris," I suggested.

"I could... in six months if I work hard..." Chris seemed overwhelmed by so much responsibility and no chance to consult with Dutch.

"That will be too late. Joe may have destroyed the world by then," Bogie said.

"Joe may visit the machines, but he won't come into the library," Orson said. "We'll close down all of Malibu Graceland except the library. I'll live and work there in secret."

It struck me how similar Orson was to the original Orson Welles. He was bold and daring, even convincing the entire nation in 1939 that earth was being invaded by Martians.

"We can sneak people in every few days, with maintenance or landscaping trucks," I suggested.

"It's going to be terribly dangerous, Orson," Chris said.

"I was born for this," Orson said.

Jacqueline set her hand on Chris's. "There will be risks. We can't stop people from being brave."

"I'll get people's real identities from Jacqueline," Orson said. "I'll call them on the same day I film them. People will be eager to transform, even for a short period. If they refuse, we'll know it's Joe or one of his spies."

Jacqueline squeezed Chris' hand. "It's our best shot."

Chris seemed stunned, not the least of which by so much attention from Jacqueline. "Fine. Let's do this," he agreed.

"I'm going to D.C. to see who else Joe has replaced," Bogie announced. His lust to avenge Elvis was palpable. Maybe he wanted to do it before Orson was killed. "I'll bring the special glasses. My alter-identity will keep me safe."

"You're assuming Joe hasn't had his imposters cover their faces with makeup," I said.

"Joe won't imagine we'd dare resist him as far away as the East Coast," Bogie said.

"Are you sure? That doesn't seem safe," Marilyn said.

"My other identity will keep me safe."

"I really think we deserve to know your alter-identity," I said.

Bogie surveyed the limo cabin. "Fine. As soon as Joe is dead, I promise to announce it to the entire Court."

"How will you stay safe, Chris?" I asked. "We need you more than ever."

"As long as Joe thinks we've surrendered, I should be safe," Chris said. "Besides, I practically live in my office at my company, BioSynthetic. There's an advanced security system."

Bogie looked at me. I saw concern in his eyes, and I felt forgiven. "That leaves you, Darrin. You're the person Joe wants to suffer."

I looked at Marilyn. "That means you're his target. You and I can't go anywhere near the Malibu Graceland until Joe is dead, not even for legacy scenes."

"What's your plan, Darrin?" Chris asked.

Joe had to be killed. I couldn't count on anyone else doing it. I couldn't even be sure this limo wasn't bugged. However, I had figured out a scheme to kill him.

"Marilyn and I need anonymous faces. Then we need to leave. We can't return until Joe is captured or dead."

Chris nodded. "Don't even tell us where you're hiding."

We wouldn't be hiding. We'd be hunting. However, I didn't tell him that.

Marilyn kissed me. She noticed something in my eyes the others missed. "Whatever your plan, Darrin, we'll do it together."

War of the Worlds

Time Warner Center in midtown Manhattan is one of New York's elite skyscrapers with 750-foot-high dual diagonal towers, which contained deluxe offices, luxury stores, and several restaurants, including Masa, considered the world's most expensive place to eat.

Joe Plain gazed upward at the mighty structure, feeling kinship with its strength and invulnerability. He flashed his visitor pass to the security guards, and took the elevator to the fifty-fourth floor.

Joe scheduled a weekly meeting in a conference room overlooking Central Park. He came in person as often as possible, and ran other meetings virtually. The attendees varied each week as Joe deemed expedient.

Upon entering the room, Joe saw eight people laughing like best friends. On the left side of a mahogany table sat an MSNBC news anchor, a liberal filmmaker, a famous left-wing activist, and a popular daytime television talk show host; on the right side sat a prominent conservative radio host, a Fox News host, a right-wing social media guru, and a Republican politician-turned-public speaker.

They ceased speaking the moment Joe entered the room.

Joe turned to the left side of the table. "What are you doing for me this week?"

"I'm going to burn an American flag in front of the NRA headquarters."

"I will praise college students for beating up Republicans on campus."

"I'm going to—"

"Fine. Fine," Joe interrupted. He turned to the right side of the table. "What about you?"

"I will use the n-word when I discuss a Black Lives Matter protest."

"I'm going to propose that we don't allow gay immigrants into the country."

"I plan to—"

"That's all good," Joe interrupted. "I know you've mastered the art of creating hate. The key is to coordinate together to maximize the impact."

"I assure you, Mr. Plain, we are doing that," the radio host said. "We've carefully scheduled the entire week. I'll start on Monday by proposing the FBI assign a permanent drone to each Muslim American that follows them constantly."

"All eight of us are working on jokes together in response," the MSNBC host said.

"I'll attack him as an islamophobe and misogynist."

"I'll respond with an offensive comment that mentions Jews."

"Then, I'll claim white males have been racist for so long, it's in their genetic code."

"The news cycles and talk shows are planned for the whole day."

"On Tuesday, we'll start by interviewing a redneck radical who will . . ."

Joe listened as the eight people shared their plan to polarize the news for the next week.

"Race and religion will be the bedrock of our rage, but we need to branch out," Joe said. "People must be divided by wealth and lifestyle, too. Better yet, you should create new categories to ignite more hate."

"Yes, sir," everyone promised.

Joe Plain reveled in the brilliance of forming this secret media alliance he called the Collusion of Conflict. Throughout its history, the media had gained power by creating contention. The more divided a nation, the more hungrily the masses turned to the news to feed their fury. If news professionals didn't facilitate belligerence, they were merely rehashers of events.

Joe had taken this to its natural conclusion, and arranged a synergy between outspoken conservatives and liberals—a partnership in splitting the nation to extremes. The eight people present were only a small piece of this perpetual hate-machine. He invited different people to the meeting each week.

The coalition was a win-win situation for the media and both political parties. However, dividing the nation was only half his objective. Joe was also forging a figure who would rise gloriously out of the chaos and unite the nation.

"What are you doing this week to promote Ernest Goldenhart?" Joe asked.

Their responses were enthusiastic as they tried to please him.

"I am publishing a book called Fearless Integrity. It shows how Mayor Goldenhart brilliantly combines the best of conservative and liberal qualities."

"I'm hosting a weekly talk show called Earnest Women Discuss Ernest's Ideas."

"I've arranged for Mayor Goldenhart to be the keynote speaker at the NAACP Annual Convention—a rare honor for a Caucasian."

"I'm filming a documentary about Mayor Goldenhart's work in the Peace Corps. He is portrayed like an American saint—selfless and incorruptible."

"Fine," Joe said. "The book and the movie will have an unlimited marketing budget."

After they each shared their methods to promote Ernest, Joe finally smiled. With immense pride, he looked around the table, remembering the eight replacements he'd done to give these men and women their identities. His satisfaction was grand—the fondness of a creator toward his creations.

"This is a good start, but we must think bigger," Joe said. "Mayor Goldenhart must be a household hero, moderate on all issues, an icon of virtue. Meanwhile, the reputation of every other politician must be thrust to the extreme left or right."

"Yes, sir," they all asserted.

Joe left Time Warner Center gorged with confidence. The world was a chess board, and his replacements were the pieces he maneuvered with God-like control and sacrificed as he wished. Moreover, his pieces were all queens, while the rest of the world was comprised of pawns.

As a child, Joe had loved playing chess against inferior opponents. He relished the warm, gleeful feeling when his adversary realized it was hopeless. Joe never ended a game quickly, whether it was a board game or the game of life. He savored his opponent's anguish as, one-by-one, he eliminated each of his opponent's pieces.

The outcome of Joe's plan was irreversible, he was in such a dominant position. The purely fun part would soon start.

Real Genius

"Will it fly?" Janie asked. Behind her, staggeringly-high, snow-covered mountains soared into a cloudless blue sky.

I twisted a telescopic lens and attached it to a device which looked like a bald eagle, but was actually a cleverly disguised drone covered with real eagle feathers.

"Yes. His name is Sam. He's been used in a few movies. I borrowed him from the prop department."

I stared at Janie, who looked cute in a face I was falling in love with. It was a stranger's face—a redheaded girl with a button nose—which Janie created by merging photos she'd found on the Internet. She'd also designed a fake face for me. I tended to forget this and then be surprised when I glanced in a mirror. I'd taught Janie the trick of considering herself as an actress playing the part of a woman with an anonymous face. This way, we learned to reduce the mental strain of having a third identity.

We'd traveled in an RV for almost the entire month of March, roaming through grandiose national parks and avoiding people as much as possible. We'd been anxiously waiting for today—the day we would kill Joe Plain.

Janie looked longingly at the skiers swishing down the mountain on the other side of the snow-covered valley. Fluffy tassels on her red wool hat flopped around as she imitated skiing. "I wish we were normal people like them," she said with a sigh.

I laughed. "They're hardly normal. Those are some of the world's richest people."

We had parked our RV on a rugged dirt road overlooking the über-luxurious Yellowstone Club, the world's only private ski and golf resort. It was located in Montana, northwest of Yellowstone National Park, among some of the most picturesque mountains on the planet.

"Hold this," I said, handing Janie the remote control.

I lifted Sam and tossed him into the air. Sam automatically adjusted his wings and soared. The rotors were nearly invisible, and he looked like a majestic bald eagle. I'd tested Sam once at the studio, but the full effect of his splendor hadn't been apparent.

Janie handed back the remote, and I guided Sam west toward highway US-191. Sam quickly flew out of sight, but we could track him on an iPad, viewing everything he saw through his camera eyes.

"Are you sure Joe will come?" Janie asked.

"He bragged about replacing every powerful businessman by the end of March. It has to be here. All the world's top CEOs will be here for their annual summit."

"Joe also bragged about replacing the LAPD, and when you figured that out you nearly got yourself killed."

"My plan is better this time. Joe will be dead before he even knows we're here."

Sam reached the highway. I aimed his telescopic lens at the cars on the road. The drone's technology was so astounding, I could see faces clearly through the windows of each vehicle.

"Joe will be traveling with a transform-machine and a lot of replacements," I said. "So we need to look for a large vehicle."

Janie slipped her arms around my waist as I maneuvered the mechanical eagle. At first, she hadn't been very affectionate after we acquired our anonymous faces—she wouldn't kiss me for a week, and we only had sex in the dark. It seemed unfair that she took so long to adjust to my new face, since she'd selected it. Finally, after two weeks, she'd fully embraced it.

I'd had sex with her as Marilyn and with an anonymous face, but I hadn't even kissed her as Janie. I daydreamed about her as Janie, longing for the first time we'd be intimate while she had her real face. As soon as Joe Plain was defeated, my dream would come true. She preferred Marilyn, but she'd have to be Janie some of the time.

My phone rang, and I handed Sam's controls to her.

"Hello."

"Hi, kid." It was Bogie. "I spotted six more imposters this week. That makes forty-nine total. Twenty-one senators. Seven Supreme Court justices. A bunch of congressmen. And leaders of the FBI and the CIA."

Bogie was in Washington D.C., looking for imposters. We were talking on disposable phones, having agreed not to say phrases like "special glasses" or "purple faces."

"But not the president," I said.

"I haven't had an opportunity to check, yet. However, Joe doesn't bother with having his imposters cover their faces with makeup or look for the large glasses. He seems overconfident."

"Any clues about Joe's identity?" I asked.

"No. His imposters either don't know Joe's objective, or are too frightened to reveal it, even when I threaten to kill them."

Bogie's interrogation tactics were limited, since he didn't have a transform-machine. I imagined him holding purple-faced imposters at gunpoint, questioning them, and then releasing them.

"Have you heard from Chris and Orson?" I asked.

"Yes, they're fine. Orson says you haven't come in to do your legacy scenes."

"We're not going back until Joe is dead."

"It's safe to come back for a day. Joe doesn't know we're filming."

"Or, Joe knows about it. He's likely just waiting for Marilyn and me to show up. We're the people he wants to kill."

"I'm afraid Joe has bigger plans than to worry about you two," Bogie said.

"Maybe, but he'll be dead soon, and then he won't be a threat to anyone."

"You really think that, wherever you and Marilyn are, Joe is going to show up?"

"Yes. Today."

"I don't like you facing Joe by yourself. If you see him, you should wait until I can help you kill him."

"Don't worry, we're not taking any chances. Next time we talk, Joe will be dead." I ended the call.

I then smashed the phone with a rock. We never used one twice.

"Bogie is starting to treat you with the respect he showed Elvis," Janie said after I shared the details of our conversation. "If we really do kill Joe, you'll be running the Court and the estate."

Sam's surveillance technology worked well, letting us check the faces of people in each vehicle traveling from the airport.

"Every aspect of society is now controlled by imposters Joe has put in power. What do you think they will do, after we kill Joe?" I asked.

"I don't know, James. What if they already have instructions to do something terrible? How would they even know he died." We called each other by James and Marilyn, because we preferred those identities.

"At some point, Joe intends to return to his real identity. That means his plan must be designed to run without him," I said.

Janie frowned. "I imagine Joe, as his other identity, sitting behind the scenes and controlling everything like a murderous Wizard of Oz."

Janie and I had spent the past four weeks dissecting Joe Plain's identity. It was a jigsaw puzzle with only one piece left, but the last piece didn't fit. Every candidate had been eliminated, most in many ways.

"We know Joe well . . . I feel it in my gut," I said. "He's someone we've worked with, who had a personal connection to Dutch. He knew about the machines from the beginning, and he must have a connection to either the estate or Digital Impact."

"But every historic icon was at the Rodeo Drive set when you saw Joe. And Joe can't be Chris or Ernest. Modern celebrities didn't even know about the machines until Joe had killed numerous people."

Janie stared far away at the mammoth, snow-capped peaks. "We should focus on who Joe is, instead of who Joe isn't," Janie said.

"What kind of person enjoys torture, wants to control the government, celebrities and business, and has a goal bigger than politics, fame or wealth?" I asked.

"Someone who wants to dominate every single person, in some personal and fundamental way," Janie surmised.

Sam was providing us close-up views of drivers and passengers. It was a diverse group, of all ages, races and social status. There were billionaires going to their fancy club, farmers hauling crops, mothers transporting kids. The only thing they had in common was that they all sat in cars. They all wore clothes. They all looked out windows.

And thinking.

A realization jolted me. "Joe wants to control what people think."

"Yes, like propaganda."

"No, bigger. We've been looking at this backwards. We've been thinking of Joe Plain as wanting to be the next Hitler or Stalin. But he doesn't want to be Hitler or Stalin in the 20th century. He wants to be a world dictator in the digital age."

"What's the difference?"

"Hitler and Stalin had to hide the atrocities they committed—even from their own people. Political scientists say that technology has made the world safe from similar horrors. The Internet, smart phones and satellites make information unstoppable."

"Good. So Joe Plain can't ever become an unlimited dictator," Janie said.

"Wrong. Joe doesn't need to stop the truth. He just needs to control what people watch."

Janie grinned as a lightbulb turned on in her head. "People have access to everything now. You just have to control what people believe."

"Exactly. Joe wants to rewrite history. That's how you shape civilization."

"Can that really be done?"

"It's always been done. From cavemen until a hundred years ago, whoever won wars rewrote history. But technology has altered this. Now history is decided by whoever controls Hollywood and the media."

"That's why Joe replaced celebrities and media personalities," Janie said. "They propagate society's beliefs, not kings and generals."

"Yet, no one has solidified complete control before. Joe wants absolute power over writing history . . . and therefore complete control over the beliefs that decide the future."

Janie's eyes flashed in epiphany. "Joe isn't afraid of us filming the legacy scene to make a movie . . ."

I finished her sentence. "He is afraid of us using them to influence how people think."

"The legacy scenes could spread any message. If Joe has every modern celebrity saying triangles are the best shape, we could create a movie showing Einstein in his Princeton laboratory proving circles are the best shape. That's just an example."

"Exactly, Janie. Joe's plan is vulnerable to the legacy scenes and the transform-machines. Conceivably, we could also make a database of modern celebrities."

"Then why didn't Joe destroy the studio and Malibu Graceland, instead of just forcing them to shut down."

My brain was spinning. "He must intend to use them himself." Joe had an historic-sized agenda. What beliefs did he want to promote?

"I feel like Joe is Ernest Goldenhart," Janie said. "The media glorifies Ernest in every way. But Ernest's face wasn't purple, and he was sometimes in different locations than Joe."

"Ernest is Joe," I said excitedly as the final jigsaw piece fell into place.

Janie beamed. "I knew it! . . . How?"

"Joe is Teddy Millner."

"What? Teddy is dead. We saw his mangled body."

"Teddy killed himself. Rather, he created an imposter of himself, and killed the imposter."

Janie looked at me like I was crazy. "Who would replace and murder himself?"

"His ego isn't in himself. He's willing to give up that life. He must have a greater cause. I'd create an imposter of Darrin, but I'd never create an imposter of James Dean."

"How do you know it was Teddy?"

"Teddy was VP of technology. He worked with Chris on the machines and probably on the special glasses. He would know that makeup could prevent the purple glow, and he had access to the machines from the beginning. It was easy for him to create Joe's identity and start killing and replacing people. At some point, he made a replacement of himself. It would have been easy to put a bomb in the podium and kill his replica."

"Heavens to Betsy, it fits," Janie said. "At some point, Teddy killed the real Ernest and became Ernest."

"Exactly."

"You're a genius, James. However, couldn't anyone kill themselves? Like Rex or Dutch? Or maybe Chris is an imposter, and he hasn't killed himself yet."

"Dutch is far too tall. Besides, Joe is destroying everything Dutch built.

"And, Rex couldn't have replaced Ernest," I continued, "because he didn't know about the glasses before the Oscars. Also, if Rex was an imposter controlled by Joe, why would he attack Joe at the post-Oscar party? Besides, Rex enjoyed his lifestyle and multiple girlfriends too much to give up his life to an imposter."

Janie nodded. "Chris doesn't want his real identity to disappear. He would've had to maintain three identities or replace himself forever."

"Precisely," I affirmed. "And Chris could have stopped the filming and created more machines without making demands. Also, Chris already knew Dutch was Elvis."

"Joe is Teddy . . . that maniac is the best actor of us all!" Janie declared.

"The only thing we don't know for sure is whether Teddy has already replaced Ernest," I said.

"So, the real Ernest may still be alive?" Janie asked.

"There's one way to find out."

I typed on the iPad, and opened the website of Ernest Goldenhart's presidential campaign.

"Ernest is giving a campaign speech right now in Denver. His next event is tomorrow morning in Seattle. His schedule is perfectly designed to come to the Yellowstone Club for their meeting this afternoon."

"If you're right, the real Ernest is dead," Janie said. "And Teddy will replace the CEOs today as Joe."

"I've got to tell Bogie." I activated another disposable phone.

Bogie picked up on the first ring. "Hey, kid."

"We figured out Joe's identity." I explained our revelation.

"That's crazy!" Bogie sounded upset. "You're totally wrong. I knew Teddy for years. He only wanted to use the machines for good, and he was murdered because of it."

"It was an act. He fooled everyone."

"Teddy wasn't evil, and definitely not Ernest. He was a complete nerd. Teddy was totally incapable of imitating a glitzy politician."

"Ernest is flying over Montana today, while the world's top CEOs are here at their annual summit. It can't be a coincidence."

"All I know is Teddy isn't Joe and he isn't Ernest."

"You're wrong, and we are going to prove it soon."

"Don't be reckless, James. Joe is a highly-skilled killer. And he's always been one step ahead. If he does show up, don't confront him with just you and Marilyn."

"I'll call you tonight when Joe is dead." I disconnected.

I was brimming with surplus energy. I felt like a new person. I hadn't realized what a giant burden I'd been carrying. Now that I knew Joe's identity, I wanted to leap and run and celebrate. My friends would get their revenge.

Sam was circling above us now, and I lowered him to the ground. I felt invincible, ready to do something more dangerous than confronting Joe Plain.

I put on a backpack and grabbed Janie's hand. "Let's go. There's something I want to show you."

"But you said Joe is coming today."

"We know his schedule now. Joe has to transform, fly to Bozeman, and then drive here. Even if he has a machine on the plane, he can't get here in less than three hours."

Janie looked around at the magnificent mountains. "Why not?" she shrugged. "By this evening, either Joe will be dead, or both of us will be dead."

I took Janie's hand and led her toward a trail that serpentined up the mountain. Rich pine scents rewarded our climb and a herd of buffalos grazed below us in the valley. Pine, spruce, and Douglas-fir trees crowded the rocky trail. In the distance, snow-crested rocky peaks held up a seemingly endless azure sky.

We hiked until we reached the top of a butte overlooking a regal vista. I stopped. "I have a surprise for you."

"What?" Her eyes widened. Behind the anonymous face I saw Janie's enthusiasm.

"I've written a script. I know for certain it's the best script ever written."

Janie laughed. "I didn't know you were interested in screenwriting."

"You inspired me. There's a perfect part for you."

She looked doubtful. "For me as Marilyn or Janie?"

"Whichever you want. I have it in my backpack. Will you look at it now?"

Janie smiled. "I guess I can read a couple of pages."

"All right. I'm eager to hear you read your part aloud."

I reached into my backpack and took out the script. If Janie expected a thick manuscript, instead I handed her a thin, rolled document bound with a red ribbon.

Janie unfastened the ribbon and unrolled what she discovered was a single sheet of paper. There was only one word: Yes.

Confused, Janie turned to me. I was kneeling with a diamond ring in my fingers. "I love you as Janie, Marilyn, or anyone else. Will you marry me?"

"YES!" Janie exhaled. "Yes. Oh, yes. I want this part forever."

I slipped the diamond on her finger. Her face, the anonymous face created by the machine, beamed. I stood and kissed her, my chest bursting with joy. No one had ever felt happier than I. The rest of my life would be spent with my soul mate.

"Did you propose now, because you're afraid we'll die?"

"No. For the first time I'm not scared." I dipped her in my arms. "I've been afraid I'd never be worthy of you. I'm done with that. You deserve whoever will love you most, and that's me."

Janie grinned at me. "What brought about this revelation?"

"I thought you needed a man with a perfect face and career. But you need someone who thinks you're perfect as you are."

"Does this mean you'll stop trying to change into who you think I want, and let me see who you are?"

"Yes."

Janie laughed. "I always wondered what you'd be like, if you stopped trying to impress me."

"We'll find out. I hope we like me."

She jumped into my arms, and we kissed. And then kissed some more. My chest almost burst, I loved her so much. My love was no longer the flimsy, scared emotion I'd experienced in the past. It was a solid, unchanging force.

"Poets are wrong about love," Janie said as if she could read my thoughts. "It's not a delicate rose petal or a fragile glass figurine. Real love is more indestructible than these mountains and meant to be handled vigorously."

Between kisses she gleefully proposed ideas for our wedding. Once Joe was dead, we could do anything we wanted.

"Let's have two weddings!" Janie exalted. "One at Malibu Graceland as Marilyn and James with our historic friends as guests. Another wedding as Janie and Darrin with everyone in their original identities."

"Albert will be my best man at one. Uncle Stanley at the other."

"Your uncle will be as happy as we are," Janie said. "And I want to meet this Anna, who's so smitten with him."

It was heaven. I wished we could stay longer. However, we had a mastermind villain to kill. I broke off our conviviality. "Joe is coming. We'd better head back."

We hiked down to our RV. Life seemed magnified. The sky bluer, the clouds whiter, the sun brighter, the buffalo grander. Every few moments Janie gazed at her ring and smiled.

When I sent Sam flying, I felt euphoric. I assumed Ernest had come immediately from his campaign stop to Montana, transforming his face on the flight.

"I bet we see Joe in the next hour," I said.

I wasn't nervous. Kneeling in front of Janie to hear her answer had been terrifying. Now, I felt unstoppable.

Through Sam's camera, I examined each vehicle on the highway, confident I'd see Joe soon. Eighteen minutes later, all my assumptions were validated.

"There he is!" I exclaimed. "Driving a U-Haul." I zoomed onto Joe's generic face.

"The machine must be in the U-Haul," Janie said.

"A luxury tour bus is following them. The passengers must be the actors Joe intends to transform into replacement CEOs."

As I peered at Joe's face, I felt a pang in my chest. I was going to kill a human being. His face was appallingly vacuous. He was a mass murderer. Yet, I didn't feel the satisfaction I'd expected.

It needed to be done. I turned Sam around and headed him back to us. Sam would reach us quickly, while Joe would drive several miles before passing our location.

"Hurry," Janie said as the eagle came into sight.

Janie watched the road with binoculars as I rapidly disconnected Sam's head with a screwdriver. I removed the heavy zoom lens and reattached the head.

"I see the U-Haul." Janie sounded horrified. "Joe will be here in a minute."

I'd acquired two bars of casted H6 explosives from the studio's special effects department, each with enough power to explode an armored tank. I attached one bar onto each of Sam's talons and threw him off the cliff.

Sam nosedived under the extra weight. He plunged toward the ground as I manipulated his wings, trying to get air under them. About thirty feet before crashing, he swooped into level flight and ascended upward. Joe was about half a mile away, and I soared the eagle toward him.

I aimed directly at the vehicle's front window. The U-Haul was an enormous target, and I couldn't miss.

Lethal Weapon

Sam responded perfectly to the controls, gliding straight at the front of the U-Haul.

I thought of Teddy Millner's smile. He always seemed sympathetic and humble. He had a gentle, self-deprecating laugh. Could I really kill him?

My hands started to shake. Sam began to wobble in the air.

Janie put her hand on my shoulder. "Teddy already killed the good side of himself. You're stopping a madman from killing more people."

I recalled how many people Joe had killed. I imagined the Janie look-alike dying in my arms. Twice, Joe had tried to torture me.

My hands steadied. Sam soared toward Joe Plain's vehicle.

The U-Haul suddenly stopped at the side of the highway. I adjusted Sam's trajectory accordingly. This made it an even easier target. I could see Joe's plain face clearly as he opened the U-Haul door and stepped outside.

Shit. Joe was holding a real large weapon.

Joe placed the weapon on his shoulder, aimed at Sam. *Oh, crap!* A missile launcher. A meteoric streak flashed in the sky. Sam exploded in a brilliant blaze.

Joe scanned the area on both sides of the highway. When he looked upward, he saw our RV on the cliff. He grabbed some binoculars, and so did I. We locked eyes.

"Get in the RV," I yelled.

I floored the RV before Janie could shut the door behind her. In the rear-view mirror, I saw Joe reload the missile launcher. He pointed the weapon at us. A fiery light flashed from the launch tube. Almost instantaneously, the RV windshield illuminated in a white flash as the road exploded in front of us.

A smoking hole opened before us, and I swerved right to avoid it. The RV wasn't nimble. It tipped so far right, our left wheels lifted off the road. Janie screamed as we leaned precariously over the cliff. I adjusted left and we balanced on two wheels for a while. Slowly the left wheels returned to the ground. Joe had already begun to follow us by turning onto our dirt road. I floored the pedal again.

We had a quarter-mile lead, but the U-Haul had a smaller turn radius than the RV. Every turn on the cliff was a traumatic ordeal in the RV. The road climbing up the mountain was full of switchbacks. It wouldn't take long for Joe to catch up.

Curve left—I risked the fastest speed I didn't think would be fatal; Janie screamed as we skidded. I floored the RV again. Curve right—another scream and my side of the vehicle scrapped the rock wall. Every turn was a struggle not to skid over the precipice or to hit the rock wall.

"Joe has caught up," Janie said, "and he's holding a gun out the window!"

Metallic pings reverberated as bullets made holes in the back of the RV. How could I possibly keep Janie alive?

The road branched. I swerved left onto a road ascending steeply up the mountain. There was snow on the ground, but there didn't seem to be any ice. "Let's see how he handles these curves."

Janie clasped her seat in terror. This road was narrower, and had been carved out of the wall of the mountain. My side of the vehicle was next to the vertical rock wall, while Janie looked down a 200-foot fall without a guardrail.

"You're a better driver, Darrin," Janie encouraged. "Make Joe drive off the cliff."

She hadn't called me Darrin for two months. And she believed in me.

A hairpin turn loomed ahead. Janie shrieked. I turned left hard. I hit the brakes and the RV tires skidded on the grit.

Another switchback ahead. I couldn't maintain any speed.

Damn, the RV turns so wide. How could I put any distance between us?

Joe was on the switchback below us, but dense pine trees prevented him from firing at us. Also, he probably wanted both hands on his steering wheel at the moment.

Every turn was a hairpin, and the RV skidded to the edge of the cliff each time. Joe kept gaining on us in his smaller vehicle.

"We're headed above the treeline," I said. "He'll have a clear shot."

I wasn't sure where this road went. I feared it would be a dead end.

"Joe stopped!" Janie exclaimed.

Using the rear-view mirror, I watched Joe exit the U-Haul on the previous switchback. He faced us carrying the shoulder-fired missile launcher. How could I maneuver an RV to avoid a missile?

Joe aimed carefully; we were too big to miss. Our options were awful.

"Jump," I cried.

Janie held open her door, but hesitated. I slowed but we were still moving. I released the steering wheel, put my arm around Janie and heaved us both out of the RV. Simultaneously, a missile slammed into our vehicle, which burst into flames.

The RV flew at least ten feet in the air, flipped over and hit the rock wall before it bounced down the cliff.

I was bruised but unhurt from rolling on the snow and dirt. Janie seemed fine, too. We ran up the road away from Joe. A cliff menaced to our left, and a rock wall towered over us to our right.

A missile flashed next to us and exploded into the mountain above us.

"Look out." I grabbed Janie's arm as an avalanche of rocks and snow crashed in front of us. I yanked Janie back before any large objects hit her.

Our path was blocked.

"We're trapped," Janie cried, turning to look at Joe's merciless face.

Joe walked up the road toward us, smiling, with a rocket launcher on his shoulder. I held Janie's arm as we looked over the cliff. It was straight down. "We need to go up," I said.

We scurried onto the detritus from the avalanche, scrambling upward into the pile of rocks and snow. It was steep and loose, and we slid down with each step. After 30 seconds, we'd only gone a few feet. Behind us, I heard Joe laugh.

A missile shot over us, and the mountain erupted above our heads. I fell backwards, and slid on my butt toward the road. Dirt, rocks and snow tumbled past me, covering me to my waist. The air was so thick with dust and debris, I couldn't see anything.

"Janie? Where are you?"

I stood, extricating myself from rocks and snow.

"Over here."

The dust granules were thicker than fog. I followed Janie's voice until she appeared. Her cheeks were streaked with black grime, and she was grimacing in pain. I couldn't see Joe.

"Play dead. It's our only chance," I said. "Lie down. I'm going to bury you."

Janie reclined on her back, and I frantically covered her with snow and dirt. The dust mist was settling, but I hadn't seen Joe yet. Where had he gone? I needed time to hide her. Then I'd distract Joe by running toward him.

Janie was two-thirds covered when the outline of the U-Haul appeared about fifty feet away. Joe parked and stalked calmly toward us, his figure framed in the haze. A dastardly grin spread across his insipid face.

I hurled a rock at Joe as he placed the missile launcher on his shoulder. The rock fell harmlessly at his feet. I frantically searched for any escape. It was hopeless.

"Good riddance," Joe said.

I looked at Janie and our eyes said goodbye.

Joe pulled the trigger. At the same time a red splat appeared on his chest. The missile fired high, soaring over us into the sky. Joe took a wobbly step. Then a second red spot formed on his chest. This time, I heard the echo of the gunshot. Joe dropped his weapon, his face contorted.

Joe looked at his chest and then glared at me with loathing. "It's too late, anyway," Joe sneered. "You're doomed."

He fell flat on his face.

Out of the haze, a limousine drove into sight. The sunroof was open, and Ernest Goldenhart stood in the opening gripping a black revolver.

Janie sat up, shaking debris off her. "Joe isn't Ernest."

I helped extract her from the snow and rubble. "I was wrong . . . again," I said.

The limo stopped by the U-Haul and Ernest rushed toward us. A muscular man followed behind him with a first aid kit.

"Are you okay?" Ernest asked.

"Yes," we both said.

"This is Carlos, my driver." Ernest examined us quickly. "We need to hurry. I'll bandage your cuts in the limo."

"Why are you here?" I asked.

"Carlos, go check that guy is dead," Ernest said. The large man walked towards Joe's body.

"Bogie called," Ernest said. "He asked for my help. You're James and Marilyn, right? Bogie said you were going after Joe Plain, and he was worried you'd get yourselves killed. Luckily, my campaign plane was in the area, so I made a detour to check on you."

Police sirens could be heard in the distance, getting closer.

"Let's go," Ernest said.

We headed toward the limo.

"He's very dead," Carlos said as we passed Joe's body near the U-haul.

Ernest looked at the large weapon beside the corpse. "There's probably more missiles. Try to find one."

Carlos looked in the U-haul and extracted a missile. "I know how to load it," he said.

"First, put the body in the U-haul," Ernest instructed.

Carlos picked up Joe's corpse and carried it to the back of the U-haul, while Janie, Ernest and I climbed into the back of the limo. The sirens grew even louder.

I stood in the open sunroof, watching as Carlos loaded the missile launcher and returned to the limo.

"Hold this," Carlos said, handing the heavy weapon to me. "Don't fire unless Mr. Goldenhart says to. Watch the recoil."

Carlos got into the driver's seat, backed up about forty feet away from the U-Haul and stopped.

"Shoot it. Besides Joe's body, there's a transform-machine inside," Ernest said.

I tried to balance, standing in the opening of the sunroof with the missile launcher on my shoulder. I braced my back against the roof, aimed and pulled the trigger. The recoil was like a baseball bat hitting my shoulder, yet the adrenaline rush erased any pain as the U-Haul erupted in flames and flew over the cliff.

"That's for Elvis!" I shouted, watching the burning vehicle containing Joe's body crash down the mountain.

Carlos backed up a little further to a spot where the road was wide enough to turn around. Then he accelerated down the mountain. Half a minute later, two police cars sped past us.

"I need to get back to the airport. My campaign staff doesn't know where I am," Ernest said.

"Look," Janie said, pointing out the window. "There's the luxury bus with the people Joe was going to turn into CEOs."

Ernest laughed. "How long do you think they'll wait until they realize Joe isn't returning?"

"You'll never get your faces changed," Janie yelled at the bus passengers as we zipped past, although they couldn't hear her.

I glanced back at the bus as we drove away. "I wish we could question some of them. We still don't know Joe's plan."

"They're just actors who've memorized the lives of rich businesspeople," Janie said. "They don't know anything."

"Even in death, Joe has tricked us," Ernest said. "We still don't know his identity."

"We'll find out who he is, when that person doesn't reappear," Janie said.

Unless Joe was Teddy, and he had killed his own replica, but hadn't taken a different identity yet. Then nobody would show up missing. However, it was improbable anyone could spend months with no identity besides Joe Plain.

Joe's identity was still perplexing, and the mystery worried me.

"The danger is still high," I said. "The people Joe replaced may already have their instructions."

Janie smiled, caressing her engagement ring. "Stop fretting. Joe is dead. They won't carry out any plan once they learn Joe is dead."

I hoped she was right, but feared she wasn't.

Ernest patted my shoulder. "You'll be running the Malibu Graceland now."

"Wow . . . you're right. I'd forgotten." That still seemed impossible. I'd be taking Elvis' position, responsible for everyone. We would also learn Bogie's alter-identity.

Janie put her hand on my leg. "And we'll be planning a wedding."

They both seemed carefree. Yet, I couldn't stop hearing Joe's last words: It's too late, anyway. You're doomed.

Life Is Beautiful

Janie dashed across the room and jumped into Chris' arms. The stoic businessman jerked in surprise, before relaxing. Next, Janie hugged Bogie and Orson, gushing like a little girl returning home from summer camp.

"Guess what? We're engaged!" Janie exclaimed, proudly showing off her ring.

I embraced them, too. Our reunion took place in the Memphis Room at Malibu Graceland. With Joe dead, I felt like we'd returned to Eden after the expulsion of the serpent.

"Ah, so these are the faces you've been wearing," Chris said.

"Yep. We're dying to get back to Marilyn and James," Janie said.

I turned to Bogie. "You saved our lives by sending Ernest. Thank you."

"I'm just happy we avenged Elvis' death. I wish I could have been there."

"We're going to have two weddings," Janie extolled. "One here, with all our historic friends. And one in the real world as Janie and Darrin. Everyone is going to be invited to both."

As Janie told the details of our engagement and wedding plans, my gaze shifted beyond the window, to the courtyards and the people. My legendary friends were gallivanting merrily, and I craved to join them. I yearned to be James, to have his face and voice and mannerisms.

Yet... for the first time, I didn't despise Darrin. I didn't dread becoming him again. I'd met Janie as Darrin. I'd fallen in love with her as Darrin. And it would only be as Darrin that I'd be able to live and travel with Janie outside the estate.

I was the luckiest man ever. James Dean gave me the love of a goddess in a utopian paradise; Darrin allowed a real-world romance with my soul mate.

"I see a lot of modern celebrities have already returned," I said.

"We notified them yesterday the estate was reopening," Orson said. "From now on, those are the kind of decisions you and the Court will make. You'll be running Malibu Graceland now."

"We drove back from Montana in a rental car," Janie said. "Sixteen hours, and James spent all of it worrying about his responsibilities."

"Well, there's still danger," I said. "Someone warned Joe Plain, so he had a missile launcher."

"I'm the only person who knew you had the eagle drone," Chris said. "I swept the prop department for bugs, and didn't find any. There are security cameras at the entrance, but not inside."

"Is anyone missing?" I asked.

"No, no one at all," Chris said.

"Every actor is accounted for, and everyone else who'd worked on the movie or had been to Malibu Graceland," Bogie confirmed.

"Whoever Joe originally was, it's hard to believe Joe wasn't also using another identity," I said.

"Unless he liked having a generic face which made him practically invisible in a crowd," Orson said.

"I wish Elvis was here. I'll never be able to run things as well as he did."

"You'll do fine. We'll all assist you," Bogie encouraged. Chris and Orson nodded.

I turned to Chris. "We need a method to guarantee the transform-machines are never used for crime again. But I want to use them to help burn victims. Will you help?"

"Absolutely," Chris said.

"When are you holding our first Court meeting?" Bogie asked.

"Tomorrow. Orson promised to film Marilyn and my legacy scenes today."

"I'll finish you both by 5 p.m.," Orson promised.

"We're driving to see Darrin's uncle tomorrow morning to tell him we're engaged. He'll be over the moon," Marilyn said. "We'll be back in time for Court."

"At the Court meeting, I'll reveal my alter-identity," Bogie said. "Then you'll understand why I can't run it. And you'll see that we have some powerful resources at our disposal."

I smiled at everyone, my mood improving. "It's good to be back together."

"Now, tell us about killing Joe. The mountain chase sounds horrifying," Orson said.

I let Janie answer, holding her hand as she portrayed, in dramatic detail, each hairpin turn and missile explosion. My mind tried to grasp two miraculous things at once, each too big to comprehend. I would marry Janie, my previously unattainable dream. And I would run Malibu Graceland— responsible for paradise.

"We should dedicate the movie to Dutch," Janie said when she finished describing Joe's death.

"Yes. I've thought the same thing," Chris said. "I've hired a new studio president to replace him."

"Is it Jacqueline?" I asked.

Chris grinned. "No." There was clearly more to this story, but Chris didn't seem to want to talk about it.

"Are you doing your legacy scenes today to set an example?" Bogie asked.

"Partly. Everyone needs to do their legacy scenes. However, I don't want to be hypnotized once I'm managing the estate. I need to be ready for anything."

Janie squeezed my hand. "These scenes are a lot of pressure. What if I screw up? It will define Marilyn's legacy for eternity."

"It's easy. I had a blast doing mine," Bogie said.

Orson chuckled. "If a prima donna like Bogie can do it, anyone can."

"Could I hurt Marilyn's legacy?"

"You can't," Chris said. "The computers remove any imperfections. Remember, they combine three sets of data: your physical body, you imitating the original Marilyn, and you hypnotized as Marilyn."

"What if I do something embarrassing while I'm hypnotized?" Janie asked.

"I'll be in control. I'll make sure you don't," Orson said.

Janie turned to me. "I'm so nervous. Will you watch me film and hold my hand while I'm hypnotized?"

"Of course." I wondered how Janie would behave while hypnotized. I also wanted to observe the process before it happened to me.

"He can't stay with you the whole time, if he has his James Dean face," Orson said.

"Why not?" Janie asked.

"The hypnosis is fragile. You'll wake up thinking James Dean is dead. Unless we had a chance to explain the situation, you'd break out of the hypnosis in shock."

"I don't mind keeping this face a little longer," I said. Changing faces was becoming as insignificant as changing clothes.

Janie looked at Bogie and Chris. "Will you stay, too? I'd like my best friends to watch."

"Sure," Bogie said.

Chris hesitated. I figured he was incredibly busy with a company to run. "Okay."

"You're going to have fun," Orson said. "After dinner, we'll look at the raw footage and play with the results. We can put you together in any love scene you want."

"I want to see James Dean as James Bond," I said.

Janie poked me in the chest. "No way. James Bond has too many women. I was thinking of Marilyn in *Kill Bill*."

"We can decide tonight," Orson said.

Orson escorted Janie and I to the ballroom. We entered a transformation cabin, and Janie sat down. I watched him start the machine on Janie, and I held her hand until she fell asleep from the anesthesia.

"I'll see you soon," Orson said as he left.

I kissed Janie's forehead and looked at her cute anonymous face for the last time. I pulled up a folding chair and sat beside her.

If Joe Plain had set a plan in motion to harm Janie or me, he'd do it while we were most vulnerable. And there were two times we'd be helpless, while getting transformed and while hypnotized.

Lost in Translation

"The power of imagination makes us infinite."
—John Muir

"**T**hanks for waiting with me," Marilyn said as she awoke.

She stood and kissed me—the world's sex symbol kissing an anonymous face. Her face brightened into a delighted smile as she gazed into the mirror. First, she made a demure pose. Then, she puckered her lips and blew herself a kiss. "I'm back!"

We held hands as we walked to the mansion's spacious library, which had been prepared to film legacy scenes. The room flaunted thirty-foot-high ceilings with ancient Greek décor. The walls were stacked with books, but a huge, bright green screen had been placed before one wall.

Bogie, Chris and Orson waited, all three complimenting Marilyn on her appearance.

"Thanks for staying," Marilyn said to Bogie and Chris.

"Take a seat. I'll explain what we're doing today," Orson said.

Marilyn, Bogie, Chris and I sat in director-style chairs in a semicircle. Orson faced us, glowing with excitement.

"There are two parts, a Be-Yourself part and a Copy-Yourself part. The Be-Yourself portion is pure movement, a variety of actions, like walking, running, jumping, twisting, throwing, while I direct you in front of a green screen. Walt will run the cameras . . . ."

Orson waved to Walt Disney, who was positioning equipment.

"Then we'll show some scenes from Marilyn's movies on that screen . . ." Orson pointed to a large monitor. "You'll imitate Marilyn in front of the green screen."

"The process has been designed to create every permutation of motion that muscles can make," Orson continued. "After about two hours, you're going to get hypnotized, and repeat the actions again. Then we'll add James Dean, so you can do scenes together that have two people interacting, like fighting and dancing—"

"And kissing?" Marilyn interrupted.

"Kissing, too," Orson continued. "When we're done, computers will analyze the motions and facial expressions, correlate them with the original Marilyn and compute the 3-D digital essence so it can be recreated under every situation."

"Is it acting if I'm hypnotized?" Marilyn asked.

Bogie nodded. "Absolutely. It's as far into character as you can get."

Orson seemed less certain. "It depends how you define acting. When you actually believe you're the person, you stop acting and just perform. You know your character so well, the result will be phenomenal. Your emotions and body will perfectly align. You'll see tonight when we create scenes with the database."

"When we finish, we'll be obsolete," I said.

"Then directors would be obsolete, too," Orson said. "Making movies is an art form. Photography didn't end painting. Audio recording didn't end concerts. In most situations, real people are preferred. You have instincts and creativity the database lacks."

"Yet, movies don't stop if we die. Actors become expendable," Marilyn said.

"True," Orson said. "But it actually increases safety. Dangerous scenes can be made digitally. And the database can't be used without the actor's permission."

"What if I do something I regret while I'm hypnotized? I could run around naked or get a tattoo."

Orson laughed. "The real Marilyn never got a tattoo, and you won't either."

"You better all behave." Marilyn pointed at each of us playfully. "Now, let's get started."

Two minutes later, Marilyn stood before the green screen, moving in myriad ways as directed by Orson. She walked at different speeds and angles, her hands in different positions. Soon, she progressed to running, jumping, carrying objects and climbing stairs, always being filmed by multiple cameras.

It pleased me to see her so delighted. Occasionally she'd wave to me as Bogie, Chris and I watched from the back of the room.

"She's no longer nervous. She loves the attention," Bogie said.

"She's incredible. There's almost no hint of Janie," I said. I was an expert at Janie's subtlest gestures and postures.

"It's going to get even better," Chris said.

Once she'd performed a vast variety of movements, Orson turned on the projector and displayed clips of movies made by the original Marilyn. She imitated the icon with impeccable accuracy. The head, shoulders, hips, lips—the timing wasn't always in sync, but the essence of the actress was vibrantly expressed.

"It's ironic," I said. "We call it 'filming,' and we produce a 'film.' Yet there's no film involved, just data stored on computers."

Chris raised an eyebrow. "That's true. Modern movies are all digital."

"Digital means it's a number, right?" I asked.

"Exactly. The legacy scenes are capturing a person's entire essence as a large number."

I wasn't sure I liked being reduced to a number.

"Nothing is real," I noted. "We create fiction. It's stored virtually. Now we're removing the need for an actor. Neither the plot, emotions, setting, acting, or storage has any real substance."

"It's real," Chris said. "It's just an idea. Nothing is more eternal than a number."

"I need new friends," Bogie scoffed. "You two are so lame, you make movies sound like science."

Marilyn was so dazzling, I lost track of time and was surprised when Orson told her to stop.

"Well done, Marilyn. The next part is even more amazing," Orson said.

"I'm ready." Marilyn was effervescent as she walked to me and gave me a kiss.

The five of us traversed the hallway to the glass elevator, ascending to the Memphis Room. Orson led us down the north-wing corridor. Sadness gripped me as we walked past the Louis XIV-style rooms which had been

Elvis' residence. The King had been the truest friend I could ever wish for.

Near the end of the corridor, we entered a room in which all four walls were painted shades of red. The furniture was Victorian, and there was a feminine aura. I was surprised to see Jacqueline Dumont waiting for us.

Chris straightened his posture, smiled gawkily, and clutched his hands together behind his back.

"Hello, Marilyn. It's a pleasure to see you again," greeted Jacqueline. "I've heard great things about your acting."

She looked at me. "And that's you, Darrin?"

"Yep, it's me."

The swank movie executive grinned at me. Her maroon suit complimented her classy features and sleek dark hair.

"Why are you here, Jacqueline?" Marilyn asked.

"I'm sorry, I haven't been honest with you until now," Jacqueline apologized.

"Jacqueline isn't really a studio executive," Chris explained, eager to please. He seemed as nervous as ever around her. "Jacqueline is a highly-respected MD and a leading expert in mental therapy."

"You're a doctor?" Marilyn asked.

Jacqueline sat serenely, her legs crossed and her hands in her lap. "Sorry for the deception. When you auditioned at the studio, I was examining your mental stability and emotional fitness, attributes that are crucial for your roles and the legacy scenes."

"Jacqueline's background is exemplary," Chris said. "She grew up in London, attended Harvard Medical School and did a post-doctorate at John Hopkins University in neurophysiology. She is broadly recognized as the world's finest hypnotherapist."

"Thank you, Chris." Jacqueline indicated toward a posh reclining leather chair. "This will be your seat, Marilyn."

"Ohh . . . it's very comfy," Marilyn said, sinking into the luxurious chair.

"Pull up a chair and observe carefully, Darrin. I'll be hypnotizing you soon. Chris and Orson can stay the entire time, but Bogie will have to leave before we finish."

Jacqueline faced Marilyn. I sat next to her, holding her hand. Bogie,

Chris and Orson took chairs nearby. The peculiar room was a hybrid between an office and an elegant Victorian sitting room. The décor was entirely shades of red, including walls, furniture and carpet. In the corner of the room was a transform-machine. It was covered by a scarlet cloth, but I recognized its shape.

"Hypnotism is a time-tested practice that has existed for over 4000 years," Jacqueline explained. "The word 'hypnos' comes from the Greek word for sleep, and hypnosis and sleep both alter consciousness, but they have important differences.

"Sleep changes the physiological state. It alters metabolism, blood pressure, eye-movement, glucose level, respiratory rate and blood flow in cerebral vessels. Hypnosis is the same physically as being awake, just with a different state of consciousness."

"Hypnosis is a dream while being awake," Marilyn said.

"Yes," Jacqueline confirmed, "but a dream controlled by someone else." She paused to sip some water. "A hypnotist can't force anyone to get hypnotized if they resist. However, once a subject relinquishes her consciousness, hypnotherapy can relieve chronic pain, alleviate stress, erase harmful memories, increase endurance, eliminate fears, destroy bad habits, and even improve the performance of athletes.

"Chris was generous to call me the world's best hypnotherapist," Jacqueline continued. "I don't take credit for what occurs. It's the human mind that's amazing in its ability to imagine, dream and form unlimited states of consciousness. I've made one significant advancement in my field, which is developing a robust type of paraldehyde drug. It increases the stability of hypnosis. If a subject doesn't encounter any conflicting evidence, she can keep her altered consciousness for eight to ten hours."

"When Marilyn is hypnotized, will she actually believe that she's the one and only Marilyn Monroe?" I asked.

"Certainly, until a person or memory wakes her from this false belief or the drug wears off," Jacqueline said. "While Marilyn is hypnotized, we must be careful not to remind her of any other identity. Anything inconsistent to the beliefs we suggest will incite her back to her normal consciousness."

"Are there any side effects?" Marilyn asked.

"You'll feel increased alertness for about twenty-four hours after you wake up. That's all."

Marilyn and I asked questions for five minutes. Jacqueline was clearly competent, although there was something deep and mysterious about her.

"Well, I think we should get started. Are you ready, Marilyn?" asked Jacqueline.

"Yes. I'm more excited than nervous."

"Very good. Bogie, please bring Marilyn the pills from the cabinet and a glass of water."

Bogie retrieved some water and an orange container of pills. "Just take one," Jacqueline said.

Marilyn looked at me and swallowed a white pill.

"You'll need to remove your engagement ring," Jacqueline said. "Reminders of your real life will wake you. I'll return the ring this afternoon."

Reluctantly, Marilyn took off the ring. She held it tenderly, and handed it to Jacqueline.

"Recline and close your eyes."

Marilyn pushed a button and her chair reclined; she shut her eyes.

"Cover her with a blanket, Darrin," Jacqueline said.

I noticed a pile of blankets folded on a table and tenderly placed one over Marilyn. Then I held her hand again.

"Are you comfortable?" Jacqueline had changed from her sturdy, pithy voice to a soft, soothing, melodic tone.

"Very," Marilyn said.

"Good . . . relax from your head to your toes," Jacqueline invited. Her smooth velvety voice made me sleepy, even as an observer.

"Pretend your chair is on an escalator going downward," Jacqueline coaxed. "Your cozy chair is on a gentle escalator, and every inch the escalator descends, you forget a little about your past as Janie. Take deep breaths and let your mind empty . . . ," Jacqueline's somniferous voice enticed Marilyn so gently, I nearly fell asleep. ". . . you don't remember where you live . . . you don't remember anything before moving to Los Angeles . . . it feels so good to release your identity . . ."

I forced myself to keep my eyes open. Soon, Marilyn seemed completely mesmerized. Jacqueline continued erasing memories, then she switched to asking questions.

"Did Joe Plain ever approach you to spy for him? Nod or shake your head."

Marilyn shook her head.

"Do you know Joe Plain's identity?"

Marilyn shook her head.

"Have you ever supported Joe Plain in any way?"

Marilyn shook her head.

Jacqueline looked at us, smiled, and continued the hypnosis. "The escalator is still descending . . . your memories keep washing off you . . . you don't remember coming to LA or what you did there . . ." Jacqueline mesmerized. "You don't remember your name or face . . . you have no memory of the past years . . . they never really occurred to you . . . ."

It required every bit of my willpower to stay awake. The soporific voice droned removal of every memory.

"Gently the escalator reaches the bottom near some water," Jacqueline lulled. "You see a little submarine waiting for you . . . a small, cozy, yellow submarine. You climb inside, and the pilot closes the hatch. You submerge smoothly underwater. Your memories are gone, and as the submarine descends you also forget your physical identity . . ." Tenderly, the voice encouraged every recollection of bodily sensation to float away. Marilyn's face displayed extreme peacefulness.

"Now you've reached the bottom of the ocean. Your submarine descends into a beautiful marine tunnel. As you submerge, you release your desires. You're free of fears, guilt, and aspirations . . ." I listened as Jacqueline brought Marilyn to the ultimate depth of emotional liberation. "Nod your head when you feel completely free of ego."

Marilyn wore an angelic smile; I thought she might be asleep. However, at these words, she vigorously nodded her head.

"Good," Jacqueline soothed. "You have no memories, body or emotions."

Jacqueline winked at me, and I remembered to stay awake.

"Now the submarine begins to ascend through the underwater tunnel. As it climbs, some memories return. You remember your name, Marilyn Monroe." Jacqueline reviewed a document in her hand. "You were born in Los Angeles on June 1, 1926 and given the name Norma Jeane Mortenson . . . as a baby your name was changed to Norma Jeane Baker. Your father abandoned your family . . . when your mother was institutionalized, you were raised in foster homes and orphanages . . ."

I listened to Jacqueline depict the facts of Marilyn Monroe's life while the proverbial submarine ascended.

"The submarine has reached the end of the underwater tunnel and is emerging into open water. As it ascends through the ocean depths, you remember the body of Marilyn Monroe. You've been in countless movies and recall the way your body feels while you act . . . every physical sensation is crisp and sharp in your mind . . . all the pleasures and pains . . ."

Chris whispered to me, "Beware, James, you won't recognize her when she awakes."

"The submarine has reached the surface, Marilyn. In front of you is a leather chair attached to an escalator. You get out of the submarine and move onto the chair and—"

Marilyn raised her hands and body, as if trying to open a submarine hatch. Jacqueline pushed her back down, asserting, "You're comfortably seated in the escalator chair now."

Marilyn settled snugly into the leather chair. "The escalator is ascending gently and you remember your ambitions and fears and disappointments . . ." I listened as Jacqueline described Marilyn's relationships with three husbands and several boyfriends. Marilyn's face became less peaceful as Jacqueline mentioned darker periods. " . . . you remember why you distrust relationships and expect to be hurt . . . the betrayal of powerful men . . . the grief of being childless . . . the tragedy of multiple abortions forced upon you by studio contracts and deceitful lovers . . . the despair of never truly being part of a family . . ."

I almost cried as I heard these things, for I knew they were true. In her short, 36-year life, Marilyn Monroe had faced a nearly unbearable amount of disappointment.

"All this has created an unrelenting desire to prove that you're worthy of being loved . . ." Jacqueline continued.

Chris whispered to Bogie: "You'd better hide now."

Bogie nodded and stepped out of the room.

"You're near the end of the escalator," Jacqueline soothed. "When it reaches the top, you'll open your eyes, but not remember anything about this room. Your last memory is August 5, 1962. On that evening, you were relaxing in your Brentwood home, when two men broke into your room and forcibly drugged you. You fought them and lost consciousness . . ."

Chris whispered to me, "We can't be sure this is how Marilyn died, but we don't want to install any suicidal tendencies."

"When you open your eyes, you'll feel joyful to be alive," Jacqueline said. "Now breathe deeply, Marilyn. The escalator has reached the top . . . open your eyes."

The room was perfectly silent for a moment.

Marilyn opened her eyes. She glared at me, saw we were holding hands, and ripped her hand away.

"Where the hell am I?"

A Star Is Born

"Miss Monroe. You're alive!" Chris Finnigan exclaimed.

"Marilyn! You're okay," Orson declared euphorically.

Marilyn apprehensively stared at her surroundings, seeming to recognize nothing. She finally focused on Orson. "Orson? It's so good to see a friend. Where are we? What's going on?"

She was a different person. Whiny. Breathy. Demanding. I didn't recognize her.

Chris stepped forward. "Let me explain, Miss Monroe. You're going to find this shocking, so—"

"Who are you?" Marilyn demanded. She wasn't familiar at all. Janie would never be so rude or assertive. Marilyn was like a timid girl trying to portray a false sense of confidence.

"My name is Chris Finnigan, and I'm the head of a large company called BioSynthetic. You were proclaimed clinically dead in 1962 and injected with preservative drugs and kept cryogenically unchanged so—"

"Is this a joke? You're not funny," Marilyn interrupted.

I clasped her hand. "I assure you—"

"Don't touch me!" Marilyn hissed.

"Please, Miss Monroe, we're all here to help you," Chris said. "My company spent years developing a technology to revive people in your state. The technology is relatively new, but it's worked successfully on many people." Chris pulled the cloth partly off the transform-machine. "This is the machine that awoke you after years of unconsciousness."

"YEARS?" Marilyn bellowed. "I'm not a moron."

"Miss Monroe, my name's Jacqueline Dumont. I'm a doctor," Jacqueline said. "You're going to be fine. However, you were dormant over five decades."

"Five decades!" Marilyn screeched. "You think I'm that gullible. This isn't funny. Is Frank Sinatra behind this?"

Who was this woman? Her Janie-ness was all gone. Without killing her, they'd removed Janie's existence.

"It's true, Marilyn," Orson said.

Marilyn practically spat, "I don't like this joke, Orson."

"I know it's shocking," Orson said gently. "I assure you it's real."

"I don't believe any of you." Now, Marilyn was nearly crying.

"The best proof may be to meet someone who's been similarly revived," Chris suggested.

Chris sent a text, and Bogie entered the room. Marilyn gasped and her eyes bulged.

"Humphrey Bogart?" Marilyn exhorted. "You're dead! You died more than five years ago."

"No, I died six decades ago," Bogie said. "I was cryogenically preserved, like you."

Marilyn held her head in her hands as her eyes darted around the room.

"Please, whatever you're doing, I don't like it," Marilyn pleaded. "Bogie. Orson. You're my friends . . . tell me what's happening."

I couldn't endure Marilyn's sadness, but I resisted reaching for her hand. "My name is Darrin Clark. I know it's hard to compre—."

She sneered at me. "If this is real . . . where's Joe?"

"Joe DiMaggio?" I asked. "Don't worry, he was preserved and is alive again too." Hopefully, the lie would calm her.

"I want to see him," Marilyn said.

"Later," Chris said. "This is a critical time. It's important to test your muscles and get them used to moving. We're going to film you doing a series of activities for doctors to evaluate."

Marilyn's head snapped back. "Wait. Six decades? Where's my mom?"

Chris smiled sympathetically. "Your mother lived a long, happy life. Not everyone could be preserved."

Marilyn looked furious. "Why not?"

"The government secretly began preserving people in the 1940s," Chris said. "Nobody knew if it would work. They selected famous and powerful people."

Marilyn did something I didn't expect. She collapsed forwards, put her arms around me and cried uncontrollably. I held her for about two minutes as she wept. Finally, she pulled herself away and wiped her eyes. "I'm sorry, I shouldn't have done that to a stranger."

"There's a lot to get used to," Chris said. "Darrin is a modern actor, who volunteered to help you transition to the 21st century. We're going to leave you with Darrin for a while, and he can answer your questions. Try to relax. When you're ready, Jacqueline will do a brief medical examination, and we'll film you doing some activities to test your muscular mobility."

"Uh . . . okay," muttered Marilyn.

Jacqueline nodded to me, and then she, Bogie, Chris and Orson exited the room.

I found myself alone with Marilyn. I definitely wasn't with Janie. She didn't even know about Janie.

I offered the 50s sex icon a glass of water, which she gulped down. "So, I guess the Russians didn't blow up the earth."

"No, but a lot of things have happened."

"Tell me." Marilyn crossed her legs in a seductive manner. Her flirtatious behavior seemed involuntary. I jumped right into the past five decades.

Everything astounded Marilyn: the landing on the moon, the civil rights movement, JFK and RFK being shot. Her mood alternated between sentimental and amazed.

By the time I summarized the Cold War, the Vietnam War and the collapse of the Soviet Union, Marilyn seemed quite comfortable with me. While I told her about DNA mapping and the Internet, she stood and poured herself another glass of water.

"You're really smart, Darrin." Marilyn switched seats and sat beside me on the sofa. Our legs were touching. "I'm sorry if I was rude to you earlier." Was she flirting? It seemed like her natural state.

She sighed sympathetically when I described AIDS, terrorism, coronavirus, and environmental problems. She stared into my eyes intently as I outlined modern movies, literature and music—topics that stirred her interest. I knew she needed to adjust before they filmed her, but it seemed like they were leaving us alone a long time.

Everything Chris did was calculated. However, I knew he was a romantic. It was for my sake, I expected, that Chris had assigned this task to me and allowed us extra time together.

Marilyn's seductiveness seemed innate and unquenchable. There was nothing particularly attractive about my current face, yet she treated me like a sexy potential lover. It took great restraint not to kiss her. To answer Marilyn's questions, I had to lie. I told her Chris had bought the mansion we were in to provide a sanctuary for people who'd been preserved and revived back to life.

Informing Marilyn Monroe on modern society was immensely gratifying. I'd been afraid that Joe had prearranged some type of attack on us today. Instead, I was having a wonderful day as I helped the original Marilyn with her legacy. The lies were for her benefit, as well as Janie. Their differences seemed less evident than ever.

After a while, Jacqueline came to the room to do the medical examination. "You need to wait outside, Darrin. Marilyn is going to have to strip."

"He can stay." She turned to me. "Darrin, face the wall. Don't peek."

Jacqueline shrugged. Marilyn giggled as she discarded clothing by my feet. Of course, I stole a few glances before the examination was over.

"Did Orson also die?" Marilyn asked while I escorted her to the library.

"Yes, he died after you, but he was also brought back to life," I ad libbed. "He designed this examination to be fun, while documenting that your body can still do every action properly."

Soon, Marilyn stood in front of the green screen, performing the exact same activities she'd done earlier. Bogie, Chris and I sat near the back of the library, observing Orson as he directed her.

"She's a completely new person," I said.

"No matter how many of these I watch, it's always amazing," Bogie agreed. "A different consciousness creates a different person."

"Look at this," Chris said, typing on a laptop. "It's a program we developed to test how the legacy scenes are going."

An image appeared on the laptop. Marilyn was walking through the center aisle of the U.S. Capital in front of a joint session of Congress. It looked like a live broadcast on CNN.

Marilyn climbed onto the podium and raised her arms. "The earth is flat. Science proves it," Marilyn proclaimed. Members of congress stood and roared their approval.

"Pretty scary, huh?" Chris said. "It's a powerful tool."

"She's still not even done yet. The computers are still gathering more data to optimize," Bogie added.

"It's only scary because we're keeping it secret," I said. "If the public knew that celebrities can be made to say anything, people would have to think for themselves."

Bogie shook his head. "Man, are you naive."

After a while, Orson stopped filming and approached me. "She's doing great. Now you need to get transformed."

I was so eager to become James Dean, I practically leapt out of the room. Marilyn—this version of her—wouldn't miss me at all. Chris followed me to one of the transformation cabins inside the ballroom.

"I've been personally conducting a lot of transformations recently," Chris said. "Albert and Jimmy are outside enjoying themselves with everyone else in the courtyard."

Chris looked like a maestro as he typed at the machine's keyboard. If he hadn't invented the machines, I'd never have been able to be James Dean. It would have been like part of me never had been born.

I felt jittery with eagerness. Finally, I was going to be James Dean again. I never felt free and whole except as James. I imagined someone who had been in a full body cast for weeks, and the doctors suddenly announced it could be removed. That's how I felt.

"Do you think it's completely safe here at the estate, Chris?"

"I think so. However, until we figure out who Joe Plain was, it's hard to guess what his replacements will do."

"Do you think someone could stay in the ballroom and watch my cabin while I'm unconscious?" I asked.

"Definitely. I'll do it myself or ask Bogie."

Chris applied the anesthesia, and I thought about our earlier conversation. "You're wrong, Chris. Love is more eternal than a number. People forget numbers."

I drifted asleep, imagining kissing Janie while she had her original face, my greatest dream and the only one that hadn't come true.

Total Recall

James Dean stared back at me in the mirror. My heart soared. Hallelujah! I caressed my face and indulged myself with several smiles. I looked perfect. I couldn't wait to mingle with our famous friends around the estate.

Outfit #31, the black suit I wore in *Rebel Without a Cause*, was hanging for me in the transformation cabin. Since Joe had died, I'd taken precautions to prepare for any danger, including writing two minuscule notes which I'd folded smaller than a penny. I took the notes and a roll of fashion tape from the pockets of my original pants, and taped the notes into my new outfit, making sure they were well hidden. In an emergency, such as being locked up or forced to do something while I was hypnotized, they would remind me I was Darrin.

I dressed, checked to see that I looked flawless, and stepped out of the transformation cabin and into the ballroom. Chris was waiting for me, typing on a laptop computer.

"Bogie was busy, so I kept watch myself," Chris said, standing.

"Thank you," I said. "I'm going to propose a system in which someone is always watching the ballroom while anyone is getting a face-change."

"Dutch would have approved," Chris said. "Jacqueline said she'll meet us in the Memphis Room."

We headed toward the elevator.

"My uncle is going to be my best man in my original-identities wedding. Do you think he could use a transform-machine on his burns before that?"

Chris pondered. "I'd love to do that. I'll get working on it."

The one perk I wanted from my new position was ensuring Uncle Stanley had an opportunity to benefit from the machines.

We entered the elevator, and Chris pressed the button for the top floor. As we ascended, he clutched his hands behind his back—his nervous habit around Jacqueline.

"I was surprised Jacqueline is a doctor," I said.

"Yes, she's an extremely talented woman."

"You shouldn't be intimidated, Chris. You're brilliant, hardworking, and idealistic. I bet Jacqueline would be pleased if you asked her out."

Chris looked down at the floor. "Oh, I'm far too busy for that."

"Marilyn and I were just friends once, too. I was just as scared of her as you are of Jacqueline."

"Yes . . . well . . . I'm far too busy to date anyone."

The elevator door opened, and we saw Jacqueline sitting on a sofa in the Memphis Room.

"Hello, James. Hi Chris," Jacqueline said, standing. She looked at me. "Thanks for doing the hypnotized part of your scenes first, James. The order doesn't matter, and it frees up my afternoon."

I wondered if Jacqueline ever used the machines herself. I'd never seen her enjoying Malibu Graceland.

Chris walked a step behind us as we headed together to the Red Room.

"It's so romantic how you and Janie love each other with any faces," Jacqueline said. "I heard you proposed while you both were anonymous."

"Yes, I couldn't wait any longer."

"I hope someday I'll find a love so pure," Jacqueline said.

I glanced at Chris, who looked tempted to say something.

When we reached the Red Room, I reclined on the same leather chair as Marilyn had, which sank like a pillow. Chris handed me a pill and Jacqueline smiled reassuringly as I swallowed the hypnosis-bolstering drug.

"Close your eyes and enjoy yourself," Jacqueline soothed. "You'll have the same experience as Marilyn."

My fear was the opposite of Marilyn's. I was afraid the hypnotism would fail, and I'd disappoint Jacqueline, Orson and everyone else. I hoped to get hypnotized, but doubted the process would succeed. I wasn't the type of person that mental tricks worked on. My mind was naturally alert and self-aware.

Jacqueline tried to hypnotize me, but it wasn't working. I took deep breaths and strained to get mesmerized by her melodic voice. However, my mind stayed sharp. Everything was clear. I could envision Bogie's smug smile when he found out I'd failed.

How could I be a good example to everyone if I couldn't do my legacy scene?

In fact, I was even more alert than normal. I was noticing things I'd been too busy to see before. For example, I'd been so focused on Marilyn when she got hypnotized, I hadn't looked carefully at the leather chair. The chair really did have a cool mechanism attached to the bottom. Some clever engineer had figured out how to put the chair on an escalator. Through an opening in the floor, the escalator moved down toward the lower floors of the mansion.

Even though I couldn't be hypnotized or complete my legacy scene, I could tell the Court about the cool escalator. Who wouldn't want to have such a pleasant experience?

As my chair declined, I realized the contraption wasn't really that clever—just a chair on an escalator. We made things complicated in our mind when they were actually simple. This was a great lesson about life. We created our own anxiety by attaching our ego to things. When I read a book or watched a movie, I enjoyed a new experience, but I didn't let it define me. Why couldn't I surrender my own memories as easily? I decided to free myself and let go of the past. Even my name didn't matter. Why should a word define me?

Look at that. The escalator was stopping beside some water and a cute little submarine was floating nearby. I was curious to look inside, so I climbed aboard. I went to the back and sat beside a porthole without the pilot noticing. As we submerged, the turquoise water reflected light like a prism, constantly forming brilliant patterns. Everything was new and inviting. My existence should be like that. Past feelings were illogical, because the past was already gone. I could be a blank slate. A fresh, novel feeling washed over me like warm water, and I dismissed my physical baggage and set myself free.

The submarine dove into a marine cavern. I'd never imagined a place so serene. With no need to impress anyone, there was no object I needed to obtain. My desires had no connection with a body, so they were obsolete.

When the submarine reached the bottom of the underwater tunnel, the water was very clear and so was my life. Of course, I knew my name; no one forgets his own name. I was James Byron Dean, a Hollywood star and the heartthrob of women across the country. I joyfully recalled details of my acting career, my hobbies, my love of automobile racing.

A pleasant voice told me that I'd feel a prick in my arm, but not to worry, it was merely a shot of anesthesia. I felt a slight prick, and my thoughts floated away . . .

"If you hear me, nod your head . . ." a familiar voice instructed.

I nodded. The submarine was now ascending through the open ocean. Colorful fish scattered as we entered brighter waters. I must be the luckiest person alive with a life that included one grand sensation after another: acting, riding motorcycles, racing cars. I was remarkably quick and coordinated.

The submarine surfaced, and I opened the hatch. A leather chair was in front of me, and it was fitted onto an escalator. It looked like a fun ride, so I reclined on the chair and the escalator began its ascent. If I was lucky in my career, I was even luckier in romance. My most recent girlfriend, Ursula Andress, was gorgeous. I was committed to her, although I was still fond of Liz Sheridan and Pier Angeli . . .

My life was so good, I really should get rid of my bad habits. My temper always got me in trouble. I was far too reckless. Some humility was needed. I vowed to be more thoughtful and empathetic.

The escalator reached the top, and I was delighted to see my prized race car parked nearby. How lucky could one guy be? I climbed into my silver Spyder Porsche and headed north on Highway 466. It was September 30, 1955 and I was near Cholame, California. My mechanic Rolf was in the passenger seat, and we laughed as we discussed how well I'd raced this weekend in Salinas, California.

I drove fast, exhilarated by the power and speed of my Porsche. I could hardly wait until my next race.

Suddenly, a Ford Tudor pulled out in front of me—

Damn!

Screech!

I tried to swerve.

Oh, golly. It is too late. I'm going to crash.

A flash of pain. Darkness.

Silence. Lots of silence.

Am I dead?

I'll never do all the things I planned . . .

Everything was quiet, yet I sensed the presence of people nearby. I was afraid of what I'd see if I opened my eyes.

Despite my fright, I opened my eyes.

"Mr. Dean! You're alive." An ecstatic stranger in a business suit stared at me.

"You survived, Mr. Dean. You're conscious!" another man said.

The first thing I noticed was my reflection in a mirror. A flood of relief overcame me: I wasn't disfigured by the accident.

I was in a strange red room. Was this a hospital? Two men and a woman were in the room with me, all strangers wearing peculiar clothing.

A man with light-brown hair leaned forward and shook my hand. He wore a type of suit I'd never seen before. "How do you feel, Mr. Dean?"

"I'm okay. Are you a doctor?"

The man smiled. "No, I'm a businessman. My name is Chris Finnigan. It's a great privilege to meet you."

The woman, an attractive brunette, offered her hand. "Hello, Mr. Dean. I'm Jacqueline Dumont. I'm a medical doctor."

Crazy. The woman thought she was a doctor. And she was wearing pants.

The final person in the room had thick wavy hair, a genial face, and a broad smile. I felt an immediate fondness for him.

"I'm honored to meet you, Mr. Dean," the man said. "My name is Elvis Presley."

Twister

"Remember you are just an extra
in everyone else's play."
—Franklin D. Roosevelt

Elvis. What an odd name, I thought. What mother would name her kid Elvis?

I looked at the faces in this peculiar red room. I'd never heard of a female doctor. What did the businessman want? Why did Elvis act so chummy, as if we were friends?

"Is this a hospital?"

"No, you're in Elvis' mansion," the businessman replied. "We felt you'd be more comfortable here."

I turned to Elvis. "Who are you?"

"I'm a musician."

"If you'd lived one year longer, you'd recognize Elvis," the businessman said. "1956 is the year his fame skyrockets."

"What? I'm going to die before 1956? Do I have internal injuries?"

"No, no, that's not what Chris meant. You're perfectly healthy," the woman who claimed to be a doctor said.

I sat up in my chair. These people were nutty. How could they predict Elvis would be famous next year?

"How is Rolf, my mechanic?" I asked. "He was in the passenger seat."

"Rolf Weutherich survived your accident," the businessman, Chris, answered. "But he died in another accident in 1981."

I laughed so hard, I started to cough. They'd put me in the loony bin.

By mistake, I'd been placed in an insane asylum. The woman thought she was a doctor. The businessman thought he could predict the future. Elvis had illusions of grandeur.

"Is there someone in charge I can talk to?" I asked.

Chris stepped forward. "I'm in charge. I know this sounds crazy, but after a tragic accident in 1955, you were proclaimed clinically dead. However, as part of an experimental governmental program, you were injected with preservative drugs and cryogenically maintained. I'm the head of a company named BioSynthetic, which developed a technology to revive people."

It was a practical joke; I felt relieved. Rolf was a jokester. Two other friends had been following in another vehicle. I was knocked unconscious during the accident, and they were taking advantage of the situation. They wouldn't do this if anyone was hurt.

Okay. I could play along. "What year is this?"

The woman held my hand as if to provide comfort. "You've been unconscious for over six decades."

"Fat city! Let's drive flying cars and take a rocket to the moon!"

"Um, it's not quite like that," Chris said.

I pointed at the mirror. "I'm jazzed at how well I look for being over 80."

The three people seemed flustered. "We're trying to explain that you were preserved," the woman said.

"I dig it. You're saying this leather chair is a cryogenic machine."

"No. That machine woke you." Chris pointed at a weird contraption in the corner.

"Nifty . . . where are my friends hiding?"

"Actually, you do have friends who want to see you," Chris said. "Maybe they can convince you of the truth."

I rolled my eyes. They'd get a nice laugh at my expense. "Swell—send them in."

The businessman nodded to Elvis.

Elvis smiled as he opened the door. Three people entered the room.

I gasped in shock. First, Marilyn Monroe entered the room. Then, Humphrey Bogart. Next, a dignified man with a brazen face walked into the room with a slight limp.

"President Roosevelt!"

Impossible. President Roosevelt died when I was a boy, before the war ended. Yet, there was no doubting the familiar figure. It was undeniably Mr. Roosevelt, the leader who'd inspired us through the Second World War.

FDR patted me on the shoulder. "Young man, I know it's hard to fathom, but somehow they did it. Future technology has done marvels. They kept us alive. And fixed my legs."

"But . . . but . . . you died when I was a boy," I muttered.

"I know. I was preserved like you."

I turned to Miss Monroe, relieved to have a friend in the room. "Marilyn, what's happening? I don't know what to believe."

Marilyn's eyes glistened when she smiled at me. How could anyone be so gorgeous? She looked slightly older than the last time I saw her, but more beautiful than ever.

"James, I died in 1962, seven years after you. They preserved me, too. I was revived today also."

I gaped. Why was she lying? Nothing made sense. However, all I could think of was how lovely Marilyn was. Why hadn't I pursued her romantically in the past?

"I remember the day you died, James," Marilyn said. "I cried. Everyone in America cried."

"I died two years after you," Bogie said.

I glared at him and FDR. Then I stared at Marilyn. It was clear where I was: I was in heaven. Ministers never told you that the angels played pranks on people when they arrived in heaven.

Unfortunately, I'd died. I knew that accident couldn't be survived. But—wow—I'd made it to heaven, despite all my flaws and sins.

Also, it was cool that angels had a sense of humor. It made sense. Heaven wouldn't be much fun if no one teased or played jokes.

I wondered what the rest of heaven was like. How was the food? Did they race cars? I'd get to see my mom . . . .

"Where's my mother?"

"I'm sorry. She wasn't preserved," Chris said.

"Cut the horse manure!" I snapped. "Is this heaven or what?"

They looked at me, surprised. "We're trying to help," Marilyn said.

"There's no need to get angry."

Oh, fudge. Was this a test? Maybe they were still deciding if I'd go to heaven or hell? I'd died, and they were judging my behavior. I'd already botched it.

Yet . . . why would Marilyn Monroe be involved in deciding if I went to heaven? And why would she be here if I died first?

"Not everyone survives. That's why we're so excited for you," Elvis said. "Do you mind if I call you James? We use first names here."

"Um . . . that's fine."

I felt like I was in a sci-fi movie, one of the outlandish flicks shown at drive-in theaters. No one seemed to be lying or joking. FDR was alive.

Could this really be the future?

Six decades? Then the people I loved were old. Too old.

"My aunt and uncle? What happened to them? And my dad? I'd just reconnected with him."

Chris shook his head, his expression filled with compassion. "They lived long, happy lives, James. I'm sorry, they're no longer here."

"But if you revived me, you can revive them, too."

"No. They weren't preserved."

"I don't understand." My fists clenched. "If you have the technology— if you're being honest—how could you let them die?"

"It was a secret government program. No one knew it would work," Chris said. "Only public figures were preserved."

I was speechless. I didn't want a future where everyone was dead. The grief and confusion were too much. Chris seemed to understand.

"We're going to leave you with Marilyn for a while. I know you're friends," Chris said. "She can help you get accustomed."

My heart jolted excitedly. Wherever and whenever we were, Marilyn looked unbelievably lovely. I longed for any reason to be alone with her. "Okay."

"After she answers your questions, Marilyn will take you downstairs where you'll be filmed," Chris said.

"Your muscles were regularly stimulated with electric impulses to keep them healthy," the female doctor, Jacqueline, informed. "However, we need to check your coordination doing a variety of movements, and document your condition."

FDR and Bogie gave me a comforting nod, as if this was ordinary. Then everyone left but Marilyn. She went to a small refrigerator and returned with a clear bottle that looked like glass but had soft, flexible sides.

"You twist off the top and drink the water inside."

Aquafina, the label said. I could squeeze it and see the water inside move. I twisted off the strange cap and took a drink directly from the bottle.

"I was just revived this morning. I know how confusing it is," Marilyn said.

"It feels like a dream."

"They're going to film you in front of a big screen. It's easy. After I finished, I had about twenty minutes to explore outside before coming to see you." Marilyn's eyes gaped wide. "It's cloud 9, James. There's a courtyard full of famous people. Some from the future. You'll see."

I believed her. Somehow, I felt sure I could trust her. "Has everyone been revived like us?"

"Most of them. But there are some 21ˢᵗ century people, too. Oh, James, it's the most fabulous mix of people anyone has ever dreamed of!"

"Why am I in these threads? I wore this suit in *East of Eden*."

Marilyn shrugged, indicating the white dress she wore. "I think they put us in outfits to make us feel comfortable. Although I dig the modern clothes I've seen."

"What's the future like?"

Marilyn nodded enthusiastically. "A gentleman named Darrin Clark told me what's happened since 1962. I'll explain what I know . . ."

I listened, enthralled as Marilyn told me the future. America sent men to the moon, but no one went to Mars. People had computers in their homes, but not robots. Aliens never landed. Ladies wore jeans and pantsuits. Cars didn't fly.

Marilyn was still revealing the future when Jacqueline the doctor entered the room. "I'm sorry to interrupt, but I need to give you a quick examination. Then you can start filming."

"There's much more to talk about," Marilyn said, smiling at me.

"Perhaps we can have dinner together this evening?"

My heart soared. "Ring-a-ding-dong. You couldn't stop me." We'd only been casual friends before, but now I was completely enamored.

Marilyn seemed hesitant to leave. Jacqueline gave her a stern look, and she reluctantly stepped into the hallway. Then Jacqueline turned to me.

"Please strip to your undergarments, Mr. Dean."

Seriously? She expected me to strip in front of her?

What the heck, maybe this is normal in the future. I took off my clothes. I glanced at my torso in surprise. "Hey, why do I have these scars?"

"Those are from your car accident. They've healed fine," Jacqueline said. "Do you feel any pain anywhere?"

"No."

"There is one side effect," Jacqueline explained. "You'll have some memory loss. Don't be surprised if your memory is fuzzy at times."

Jacqueline gave me a perfect health diagnosis, then Marilyn escorted me through the mansion to the library. That cat Elvis had a lot of bread if he owned this pad.

Orson Welles greeted me when we entered the library. Nothing shocked me anymore. I knew this truly was the 21st century when I examined the electronic technology Orson was using. Flip my lid! It looked like sci-fi movie props from the 1950s, yet the equipment really functioned. My doubts fled. I was in the future.

Orson placed me in front of a huge green screen and had me do a myriad of activities. Marilyn watched. Whenever she smiled at me, it set my heart ablaze.

What were the futuristic protocols of courtship? When I looked at Marilyn, I knew my 21st century would be devoted to her.

"Let's film some activities with you and Marilyn together," Orson said.

Orson directed us to do activities that included hugging, dancing and lifting her in my arms. It took my breath away to be near her.

The future was far better than heaven could have been. Marilyn was one classy chassis, and I intended to make her mine.

On the far side of the library, Chris sat alone and watched. His pulse quickened when Jacqueline entered the room. Like always, her proximity turned his brain into Silly Putty. The tingle of excitement surged when she sat next to him.

"Finally, we have Marilyn and James," Jacqueline said softly so she wouldn't be overheard.

"James was fanatical about safeguards against staying hypnotized," Chris said. "He even left tiny messages in his clothing reminding him that he was really Darrin."

"Are you certain you found every reminder?" Jacqueline asked.

"Positive," Chris assured. "I double checked when we added the scars. I destroyed the notes with Darrin's personal items. None of his former possessions exist."

"It wouldn't matter anyhow," Jacqueline said. "Even if James found all the notes, he wouldn't believe them."

Chris nodded. James Dean's brain synapses had been permanently changed by the hypnosis pills.

Jacqueline had been experimenting with memory enhancement drugs when Chris met her, studying how neurons retained and expunged connections. With his help, she'd been able to perfect the chemistry of a drug which could completely erase all past memories.

They watched Marilyn pretend to faint. James caught her in his arms.

"Sometimes, I envy them," Jacqueline said. "Imagine taking a pill and waking up believing you were fabulously famous."

Chris paused and considered this. "Well, your work is nearly finished. Almost everyone has been hypnotized."

"As I was walking through the courtyard today, I felt a huge urge to grab one of the historic figures and shake him or her, and try to convince the person of their other identity. You know, show photographs and remind them of their most traumatic moments."

"He or she would merely think you were crazy," Chris said. "Those neuron connections are gone. There's no way to bring them back."

Marilyn giggled as James put his arm around her waist, and whispered something into her ear.

"It's just hard to believe … they will be James Dean and Marilyn Monroe forever."

"Yes. Forever."

The World Is Not Enough

"Do you think we've gone too far?" Ernest asked.

"Absolutely," Jacqueline replied, "but it's too late to stop . . . just look at him."

They stared through the one-way window of the foreman's office onto the warehouse floor below, where future imposters were held captive until being inserted into new identities. Joe Plain was strutting past rows of cots, petrifying miserable souls like a snake slithering past mice in a cage.

"I guess things went smoothly in Montana."

"I missed the fun part," Ernest grumbled. "I didn't get to see the mountain chase or enjoy the terror on James' and Marilyn's faces."

"At least you got to pretend to shoot Joe," Jacqueline said.

"Yeah, that was cool. The special effects worked perfectly. After Joe pretended to die, Carlos carried him behind a rock near the U-Haul. We let James blow up the U-Haul. Police we control arrived as we left and drove Joe to the bus containing the imposters. The CEOs were replaced that evening."

They peered down through the window, watching Joe torment people. Only a few captives remained, since most had already been inserted into new lives as replacements.

"There's no purpose for Joe to be here today. He's just here for pleasure," Jacqueline said.

"He loves that identity. It's going to be hard to say goodbye."

They watched Joe stalk across the floor and exit through a side door. They heard him climb the stairs. The door to the foreman's office opened and Joe entered with a grin on his indistinct face.

"Two men pissed in their pants just looking at me," Joe gloated. "It's incredible how easy it is to get anyone to do anything."

"It wasn't easy to get James Dean to do his legacy scenes," Jacqueline said.

"Mother-fucker James Dean!" Joe spat. "What a pain in the ass. He refused to return to Malibu Graceland until he thought he'd killed me."

"What did you expect? We've spent months instilling his rebellious spirit. We're the ones who made him stubborn and reckless," Jacqueline said.

Ernest frowned. "It would have been easier to kill him."

"You know we couldn't," Joe snapped. "He and Marilyn are critical to our plan."

"I can't imagine what people discussed at those Court meetings . . . not one of them came close to figuring out your identity. It should have been obvious," Jacqueline said.

Joe shook his head in derision. "James thought I was Teddy . . . as if Teddy could master fearology?"

"No one could do that but you," Ernest agreed.

Joe put his arm around Jacqueline's waist. "We're unstoppable. Our entire plan is almost ready. There are still a few foreign governments we don't control, but we will soon."

Ernest beamed at Joe with admiration. "You've created a whole new world."

"Don't forget Chris," Jacqueline said. "He made it all possible."

Joe laughed condescendingly. "What a moron. Chris invented these machines, and thought we'd just create one happy little paradise. His little experiment is really stupid, for a such smart man."

"Poor Chris," Jacqueline said. "He's too naïf to imagine what we're doing. I'm worried about when he finds out."

"You worry too much, sweetheart. Chris is so in love with you, he can't see anything but what we tell him. We've done the opposite of everything he wanted. We own every major government and business, we've made fear into a science, and now we control almost 200 historic icons who are convinced they are real. The thrilling part is just starting."

"My role sucks. You get to do all the cool things," Ernest whined. "All I get to do is be president."

"Waah, waah, waah. All I get to do is be president," Joe mocked. "Do you even understand the genius of our plan?"

"Of course. We're the first people to conquer the entire world."

"Wrong!" Joe said. "Conquering the world was easy. Our brilliance is understanding why it's worth conquering. History will never be the same."

"Plus, our way is far more fun." Jacqueline turned to Ernest. "What do you do when you play a boardgame, like a Monopoly or Risk, and someone gets far ahead?"

"You stop playing, because it's no fun," Ernest said.

"Exactly. Dictators think the world is a board game. Our world will be more like a reality show," Jacqueline said.

Ernest's face brightened. "And the more you manipulate people, the more exciting it is."

"Don't get sidetracked," Joe said. "That is just a side effect of our plan."

"Nevertheless," Jacqueline said, eyes gleaming with anticipation, "our plan will reform cultures, beliefs, morality . . . even romance."

"Speaking of romance, did you hypnotize James Dean and Marilyn Monroe to love each other?" Joe asked.

"No. Of course not. They were perfectly hypnotized to match their identities, just like everyone else."

"Curious . . ." Joe said. "They're acting as happy as newlyweds back at Malibu Graceland."

Ernest shook his head. "It makes me sick. Can we ruin their love? Can we make James and Marilyn hate each other?"

Joe shrugged. "Sure. If you want. That won't interfere with the rest of our plan. The world hasn't seen anything, yet."

End of Book One

**Read on for a sneak peek at
Book 2 of the American Fairytale Series,
Mad 'n' Fast Destiny.**

MAD 'N' FAST DESTINY

#2 IN THE AMERICAN FAIRYTALE SERIES

J. C. FARMER

It's a Wonderful Life

"There are only two ways to live your life.
One is as though nothing is a miracle.
The other is as though everything is a miracle."
—Albert Einstein

"You're really good at being naked."

"Thanks." Marilyn stood completely nude in front of a full-length mirror, brushing her hair. "Life is so wonderful here, it makes me get up early . . . don't laugh, for me 10 a.m. is early."

As I watched her preen, my heart marveled at the splendor of our new lives. Each day brought incredibly novel experiences, but the grandest part was being loved by Marilyn. I reluctantly climbed out of bed and opened my bungalow's blinds, deluging the room in sunlight and exposing the cobalt ocean outside.

"Another bee-you-tee-ful day," Marilyn chirped. "Our friends are already at the pool, James. Let's join them."

As I slipped on clothes, I looked around the bungalow Elvis had given me. It was full of mind-blowing technology. A handheld remote device controlled a color television with hundreds of channels. A rectangular appliance heated food with electromagnetic radiation. I even had my own miniature computer—smaller than a coffee table book—which contained more information than a million libraries.

"Have you noticed that music has funny names in the future?" Marilyn asked. "Hip-hop. Reggae. Heavy metal. Rap."

"It's wacky. I wonder if future people are just as kookie. I can't wait to leave this place and meet some."

"I'm dying to meet them, too," Marilyn said. Witnessing her joy was the pinnacle of this paradise in which we lived.

We'd been revived for two weeks—fourteen unbelievably blissful days of living in the 21st century.

Everything still felt miraculous. Elvis, a musician who managed this estate, had given Marilyn a bungalow adjacent to mine. She and I had spent every moment together until she officially became my girlfriend. When we weren't making love, we were socializing with our fabulously interesting friends.

The aroma of sausage and eggs enticed us as we entered the courtyard. The estate was a paradisiacal mix of a castle and a 5-star resort. It was on a pristine beach in Malibu, California protected on each side by high stone walls. Elvis lived on the top floor of the main mansion, and everyone else resided in ocean-front bungalows on the beach. There were two restaurants, and each morning they served a joint buffet breakfast by the largest pool.

Marilyn and I filled plates from the lavish buffet and looked for a place to sit.

"James. Marilyn. We've saved chairs for you," Natalie Wood called. She was part of the clique we'd formed.

Marilyn and I walked to Natalie, who was tanning on a lounge chair in a magenta bathing suit; beside her were Judy Garland and John Lennon.

I pulled a patio table next to our chairs, so Marilyn and I could eat while our friends sunbathed.

At forty-three, Natalie was the second oldest in our group. Her eyes sparked as brightly as when we'd starred together in *Rebel Without a Cause*. Lounging next to her was Judy Garland, age forty-seven, wearing white shorts and a lime tank top. Beside her, John Lennon, age forty, sported a plaid, knee-length swimsuit and sunglasses.

Each of us were the age we'd been at death, due to a modern cryogenic revival process. Despite some slight memory loss, we were in perfect health. Some revived people had even been healed of chronic physical ailments they'd suffered in their original lives.

"There's a rumor that Harry Truman will be revived today," Judy said. "I heard they've finished reconstructing his neurons."

"I've heard that, too," John said. "Supposedly, Chris Finnigan is here at the mansion right now performing the awakening."

"I hope it's true," I said. "President Truman was one of my childhood heroes."

The estate already had over 100 formerly-dead people, and new men and women were added daily as a scientist named Chris Finnigan used a technology he'd invented to revive them. Chris, a magnanimous genius who worked tirelessly to bring us all back to life, owned this luxurious estate and allowed us to enjoy it until we reentered the world.

Chris had briefly explained how restoration worked: every human brain contained about a hundred billion neurons, and he'd invented a biomedical technology called nanocloning to reconstruct them. Chris said the brain was the only challenging part of restoring people who had been preserved. Nanocloning could repair the rest of the body with cloned tissue and organ transplants. No matter what age people died, everyone was restored in a physically fit state.

Marilyn and I ate our brunch while reclining on lounge chairs beside our friends. It was a sunny April day with a few puffs of clouds and a slight sea breeze.

"Does anyone have a smoke?" I asked.

"Cigarettes cause cancer—I read about it on my computer," Natalie said.

I frowned dubiously at her.

"It's true, James. Cigarettes aren't cool anymore," John affirmed.

Two weeks ago, I hadn't heard of John Lennon. Now we were great pals. John told exaggerated stories about a band he'd been in with a stupid insect name—something like The Bugs or The Bees.

"Lighting something on fire and putting it in your mouth always seemed stupid to me," Marilyn commented.

"Fine," I sighed. "I've gone two weeks without a smoke, I can go another day."

"Actually, it's been seven decades," John corrected.

"Hey, there's Ike Eisenhower with Jonas Salk," Judy said.

"Who's Jonas Salk?" I asked.

"The man who cured polio," Marilyn explained.

"Polio was cured?"

"You're an idiot, James," John said.

"Hey, I died young."

"By the Jacuzzi, John Kennedy is talking to Charles Lindbergh," Natalie said.

The handsome man next to Lindbergh looked familiar. "Was John Kennedy a movie star? I bet women were keen on him."

Marilyn blushed.

Bejabbers! I remembered now... Kennedy had been a president and he'd had an affair with Marilyn. This estate was full of men who'd had relationships with her.

"Forget Kennedy. Take a peep over there... what a beauty!" John gushed.

I looked across the pool, where a pretty woman with short blonde hair was dipping her feet in the water.

"That's a modern actress," Judy informed. "I've met her, but forgotten her name."

"Why are modern celebrities allowed at our estate?" John asked. "I thought this place was for people from the past who were revived."

"The mansion's purpose is greater than that," Judy said. "Chris Finnigan has a vision of a celebrity society where famous people from every era can come, as long as they live up to a certain standard."

"Modern celebrities had to sign a 'Code of Conduct'," Natalie said. "Chris said we will too before leaving the mansion."

"An honest attempt at utopia," John remarked. "Americans have such an untiring sense of idealism."

I turned to John. "Speaking of that—why is a British chap here? I thought only American celebrities were cryogenically preserved. Chris said it had started as a secret government program in the '40s."

"I was living in New York when I died," John explained. "The US government preserved my body and faked my cremation. There are other foreigners, too. Bob Marley is Jamaican but died in Miami. T.S. Eliot was born in America but had British citizenship."

"Your dream girl is a nutcase, John," Natalie said, pointing at the modern woman with her feet in the pool. "She's arguing with herself."

Sure enough, the attractive actress was talking into the air, waving her hands animatedly.

"I thought only revived people had memory problems. That poor girl clearly has mental issues, too," Marilyn sympathized.

"She's holding one of those gadgets that modern celebrities type messages on," I said. "Maybe it works for talking, too."

"Groovy . . . like a phone without a cord," John said. "If we could get some, we could stay in contact after we leave this estate."

About 2 p.m., my companions and I vacated our pool lounges and went to Ho'oulu Lāhui, the estate's Polynesian-themed restaurant. Our platinum-haired waitress claimed to be a modern singer.

On the way to our table, we passed the dance floor. Two couples were trying to outperform each other while cutting the rug to a future song called "Livin' La Vida Loca." Ginger Rogers and Fred Astaire had adapted adroitly to the catchy rhythm, but Rita Hayworth and Gene Kelly matched them in quickness and spirit.

Our booth was near a big, clear TV tuned to a channel called CNN, which reported news all day long. Watching live video of the world outside the estate was an alluring tease, as the future seemed so vibrant and exciting.

"I can't take this much longer," John Lennon declared. "The future is just beyond the estate's walls. I have to experience it."

"I know. It's driving me ape," I said.

"Everyone feels this way," Marilyn added. "I'm afraid there will be a revolt soon if we're not set free."

"We just need patience. Elvis guaranteed we'll see the future soon," Natalie said. "Chris Finnigan is going to reveal his revival technology to the world, and then we'll be free to leave."

"He'd better do it quickly," John said. "I've made a long list of things to do."

"Chris promised it will be within two or three weeks . . . it's so close I can taste it,' Marilyn said.

A gleam of delight flashed in all our eyes, as we imagined exploring the future.

"The 21st century . . . can you believe it?" John said whimsically.

The TV screen changed to the wreckage of an explosion at a movie studio. The screen filled with pictures of two men: a fat man about 50, and a thin man about 25.

A news anchor reported: "Authorities have determined the cause of the explosion at Digital Impact studios which killed studio chief Dutch Hollander and buried an actor named Darrin Clark under rubble. It was caused by a gas leak beneath the building . . . ."

"What a coincidence," Marilyn said, examining the younger man carefully. "After I was revived, a nice man named Darrin Clark told me about the future. His eyes look like yours, James."

Marilyn was infatuated by modern actors. I examined the man, Darrin Clark, on TV, to see if I should be jealous. He wasn't even a little bit handsome.

Soon, CNN moved on to another story. We were tantalized by everything happening in the world. It seemed like fantasy but was real.

"I'm going bonkers. Truly. I can't wait longer," John said. "We need to escape."

"Don't be silly," Judy said. "We live in paradise."

John turned to me. "If I escape, will you come with me, James?"

Marilyn grabbed my hand. "No, he won't."

"I've found my true love after seven decades of dormancy. I can wait a couple weeks."

"Besides, Chris is right. It would be a disaster if we entered society before the world was prepared," Natalie said.

The three women nodded, as if this was decided. John pouted but didn't respond. I knew the estate was full of impetuous people contemplating escape.

"Do you want to share a banana split, James?" Marilyn asked.

"Sure." The restaurants' superb menus changed daily, but always offered classics from the 1950s.

Marilyn kissed me on the cheek. "James and I are going to travel the world together, as soon as we're free. We're using the Internet thing to make plans."

"I read something called Wikipedia to learn about myself today," Natalie said. "My memory was foggy about a few things, and it cleared it up."

"You can Google anything," John said, a dreamy look in his eyes.

"Imagine a world without ignorance. Where everyone understands everyone's perspective. I bet there's no hate or bigotry or intolerance."

"I'm not sure the Internet does that," Judy said.

"We'll, it's wonderful for romance," Marilyn exulted. "James and I have researched everything about each other. We've only been dating a few days, yet I feel so close to him."

"I suppose all courtships are built on honesty now . . . what a beautiful thought," Natalie said.

Marilyn leaned against me and nestled into my shoulder. "Before I died, my relationships were full of secrets and jealousy. It's glorious just to focus on love. There are no mysteries or surprises between James and I."

"That's true." I kissed her on her lips. "Everything is exactly as it seems."

Acknowledgements

My family has a saying that "A Farmer needs to be out standing in his field." I was inspired by many Farmer family members who are outstanding in their fields.

My parents, Carolyn and Jerome, gave me unconditional love and then taught me to be curious and brave. They didn't direct my path, but encouraged me to be tenacious in whatever path I chose.

I'm blessed to have an incredible brother Scott who is hardworking and skilled at everything he does. Scott's amazing wife Heidi and my insuppressibly-spirited nephews Sloan and Boden add immeasurably to my life. I cherish the memory of many years with my wise and supportive grandparents. And I'm grateful for the great joy of having adding the Messners, Felts, and Trujillos to our family.

So many people have touched my life—more than you may realize—and all of you have affected the ideas, themes and characters in my writing.

A hearty thanks is due my friends and teachers from Lawton, Slauson, and Pioneer. You can't fully realize how special your youth was until it's over. We had it great!

A profound thank you to my Pinckney friends. I've learned that nothing is greater than the generous hearts of people in small-town America.

A shoutout to my Ann Arbor friends: there's no place in the world more vibrant than a college town. If you have special people to share one with, then you are blessed indeed.

To all my mentors, teammates and coaches: I feel like I've been carried on the shoulders of champions. Thank you for going beyond teaching techniques to imparting principles. I am going to condense the list to head coaches: Rusty Fuller, William Brewster, Don Sleeman, Bill (& Betsy) and Craig Petoskey, Chuck Lori, Chris Horpel, Jim Keen, and Cliff Keen,

A very special thanks to my lifelong friends who mean the world to me: Jimmy, Caroline, Tommy and the entire Keen family; the Grahmas, Dioknos, Wagstaffs, Eastons, Frys, Rileys, Forces, Reindels, Browns, Teoreys, Jacksons, Dunbars, Daltons, Templetons, Reeves, Michoses; Mohns, Hendersons, Metzgers, Brehauts, Workmans, Kays,

Wandells, and Spillsons; and Tony Nam and Steve Pierce (who are more like brothers than friends).

To my Stanford friends, who continue to inspire me: Tommy Vardell, Jill Clark Hawley, Sarah Fiarman, Wendy Neely, Jen & Jon Steele, Matt Hicks, Adam Muchnik, Ricky Davis, Loren Vigil, Ron & Julie Perry, Ken, Chris, Scrappy, Dave & Phil, Samer, Vince & Anita, every Theta Delt, org. member, study group member and lab partner...it's a treasure to be surrounded by curious people who have a passion for learning.

As for my friends from Princeton, especially the 11/12ers—thank you for including me on some of your magnificent adventures.

I'm in awe of my ingenious engineering friends, in Silicon Valley and the places I've consulted—the future is in good hands with people as talented and conscientious as each of you.

I'd like to thank all the women I've dated. Sometimes I felt like the Jack Bauer of romance, but it made me stronger.

A special note of gratitude to all the people I've met travelling—you have proven the amount of inspiration you gain from someone isn't dependent on the length of time together.

Thank you to my Boise friends: our discussions and companionship are precious to me.

I treasure my Bay Area friends—the Foersters, the Eddingtons, Genelle Austin-Lett, Pete and Liz Williams, Peyton Farrand, Michael Wang, Gwen and Jeff Watt, Lattice coworkers—each of you touched my heart deeply. I feel lucky to have lived in the Bay Area at such an exciting time.

I've been boosted by the loving support of my girlfriend Adriana Rossarolla, who filled me with creativity, inspiration and humor during much of the writing process.

My friends and business associates in Southern California have given me a million laughs and stories to tell, plus taught me a lot. This infamous list includes Rob Miller, the entire Jones family, Jena and all the Troutmans, Felicia and all the Kennedys, the notorious Asher House gang; Rick, Gabe and Lindsay McManus, BK and Dawn-joy Thornton, Adam Davis, Scott McDonald, and Eric Oyama; Joe Nebolon, Cory McCluskey, and everyone at Expertise; Tressie Armstrong, Marsha Pecaut and Bill Bloc; the dedicated workers at

Sunland; Ritesh, Priya and their friends and families; the Chittles; Abhishek Sharna; everyone from Anderson; Ricard Garcia— I miss surfing, camping and rock climbing with you; Angie Popek; all my rock climbing buddies; Joey York, Brian William, Steve Fujimoto and my martial arts instructors and training partners; my sailing friends at the Fairwind Yacht Club.

I'm grateful for everything I learned at The Walt Disney Company and Sony Pictures Studios, which helped inspire the idea for this novel many years ago and provided insight on the workings of a studio.

Thank you to everyone who helped me negotiate a better contract. It meant a great deal!

My life was raised higher by Stacey Pollard, Todd Smith and everyone at the AGSM in Sydney, Australia; Annabel Hossel, Kevin Kozin, Deepika and Ned Carr and everyone at TMC in Boston; Nate Talbot, a true pillar of wisdom and integrity and Margie Talbot, who keeps Nate running; and Craig Lafferty, who literally taught me to fly.

To my spectacular publishers at Acorn Publishing: it lifts my heart that you share the dream of this novel. Thank you, not just for your amazing expertise, but also for adding a personal side to this writing process. I can't give enough gratitude to Holly Kammier and Jessica Therrien. A tremendous thank you for the support of Laura Taylor, whose fabulous writing skills and support raised my game. A deep thanks to many profoundly talented authors including Chantelle Osman, Jean Jenkins, Debbie Kennedy, Danielle Harrington, Hanna Spraul, Lara Henerson, Shawn Butler, Rose De Guzman and so many others. Some of you already a successful writing career and the rest of you have a brilliant future ahead; I'm honored to know each of you.

If you've read this far and hoped to be acknowledged, don't worry—you are unforgettable. I'll remember you as soon as this goes to press.

For everything great and small, I need to acknowledge God, the Divine power, who I consider as infinite Love. You make all things possible; thank You for making this book possible.

About the Author

Jerome Connelly Farmer has had a successful career as an engineer, inventor and technology consultant. He has three engineering degrees from Stanford and an MBA from the Anderson School. He has several patents and spent many years managing engineering teams and consulting for high-tech firms, movie studios, and Fortune 500 companies.

J.C. was born and raised in Ann Arbor, MI. He is an airplane pilot, sailor, scuba diver and avid traveler; he has explored Tibet, camped in the Australian outback, canoed through the Amazon River, and retraced segments of Ernest Shackleton's famous rescue in Antarctic. J. C.'s passion for wildlife photography has taken him to all seven continents, including searching for Komodo Dragons in Indonesia, wild macaws in the Peruvian jungle, endangered species in the Galapagos Islands, Duck-billed Platypus in Australia, and White Rhinoceros in Botswana.

J.C. is the author of the children's book *Santa's Dashboard*. Writing combines his love for adventure, invention and exploration.

When he is not traveling, J.C. lives in Solana Beach, CA.